Falling Star

THE HENRY TIBBETT MYSTERIES
BY PATRICIA MOYES

Night Ferry to Death
A Six-Letter Word for Death
Angel Death
Who Is Simon Warwick?
The Coconut Killings
Black Widower
The Curious Affair of the Third Dog
Season of Snows and Sins
Many Deadly Returns
Death and the Dutch Uncle
Murder Fantastical
Johnny Under Ground
Murder by 3's (including *Down Among the Dead Men,
Dead Men Don't Ski,* and *Falling Star*)
Falling Star
Murder à la Mode
Death on the Agenda
Down Among the Dead Men
Dead Men Don't Ski

Falling Star

by Patricia Moyes

An Owl Book

HENRY HOLT AND COMPANY
New York

Published by Henry Holt and Company, Inc.,
521 Fifth Avenue, New York, New York 10175.

Library of Congress Cataloging in Publication Data
Moyes, Patricia.
Falling star.
"An Owl book."
I. Title.
PR6063.O9F34   1982   823′.914   81-7030
ISBN 0-8050-0755-5 (pbk.)   AACR2

First published in hardcover by
Holt, Rinehart and Winston in 1964.
First Owl Book Edition—1982
Printed in the United States of America
5 7 9 10 8 6

ISBN 0-8050-0755-5

Falling Star

1

"Have another coffee, Pudge," said Keith Pardoe. "It can hardly make you any fatter."

We were having lunch in a small Italian restaurant in Soho —Keith and Biddy and myself. As he spoke, Keith tipped his chair back and stretched his legs in the loose-limbed, graceful way that comes easily to a man who is six foot two and as thin as a piece of string.

I tried to suppress my annoyance. "No, thank you," I said quietly. "We haven't time. If you remember, the call is for two o'clock at the location."

As soon as I started to speak, I knew that I sounded pompous, which had not been my intention. I often think that there is no way for a young man as stout as I am to avoid appearing pompous, especially if he has the added disadvantages of a pink-and-white complexion and very fine fair hair with such a tendency to recession that he is half-bald at twenty-eight. The only alternative to pomposity seems to be to turn oneself into a buffoon, and that I am not prepared to do. On some days I feel that there must be a middle course; on others I admit that there is not. This was one of the other days. I was in a bad temper, I agree, and I was not put into a better humor by seeing Keith and Biddy exchange the briefest of amused glances.

"Oh, come now, Pudge," said Biddy. "You're too conscientious. It'll be hours before Sam's ready to shoot. *I'm* going to have more coffee."

"Anyhow," added Keith, putting the finishing touches to his insult, "there's nothing useful you can do down there. Not at this stage," he added, rather hastily. He must have noticed the expression on my face. I was aware myself of a mounting flush of irritation, which I was powerless to check.

"I would like to know at what stage you consider I might be useful," I said, "if not now. After all, I am responsible for the budget of this film."

"And a very fine budget it is, too," said Sam Potman's voice in my left ear.

I turned round, surprised and not overpleased. I had hoped to be free of Sam at least during the lunch break, for he had announced that he had business to do and would take a snack at a coffee bar; but there he was, lounging up against the wall behind my chair, smoking one of his nasty little cheap cigars.

"Carry on, Pudge," he said, waving one stubby hand in the air. I could not help noticing that his fingernails were black. "We're all lost in admiration. I could sit and look at that budget of yours for hours. In fact, I frequently do."

"I don't suppose it ever occurs to you to try to keep your expenditure within it," I said. This time the flickering glance was three-pronged. I felt sure that they were up to something. "I try very hard to be reasonable," I went on, trying very hard to be reasonable. "I know that you three are artists, while I'm just the fellow who pays the bills. As artists, you are traditionally allowed a certain licence . . ."

"Oh, balls," said Biddy. I do not mind admitting that Biddy's language still shocks me, even after three months of close collaboration with her. It is not just the fact that she is such a slip of a girl, and only twenty-five. She is what my father still has the courage to call "a lady"; not what you would call pretty, but finely bred and fragile and practically quivering with sensitivity and intelligence. This is hardly surprising, considering that she took a first-class degree in English literature at one of our finest universities and is now a successful writer of fiction. What I am driving at is that I could never get over the incongruity of hearing her come out with language that would have shamed a bargee. It was as though my father, in his ermine and scarlet and his gray-powdered wig, were to break into a tap dance on the Bench

of the High Court of Justice. I am not, I hope, a prig, and I have nothing against swearing, any more than I have against tap dancing; it is just that one does not associate either with a certain type of person or occasion.

I often wondered whether Biddy's foul-mouthedness upset Keith. He could be as insulting as the devil, but I never heard him swear. If it did worry him, however, he never showed it; he obviously had the sense to realize that the fact of being married to Biddy Brennan gave him no right to dictate to her. In fact, it never seemed much of a marriage to me. For instance, she had steadfastly refused to take his name, and had been furious when the authorities had insisted on issuing her passport in the name of Mrs. Pardoe—as though there were something shameful about the state of matrimony. But then, Biddy was like that, and you had to take her or leave her.

Now she grinned at me in her most disarmingly *gamine* manner. "For Christ's sake, get that chip off your shoulder, Pudge," she said. "We've each got a job to do on this picture. The fact that Keith designed the sets and I wrote the script gives us no more right to throw fits of temperament than the bloody props man." She stubbed out her cigarette in the saucer of her coffee cup. "If anyone's entitled to be a bit edgy it's poor old Sam. After all, the director has to take the final responsibility."

"I would dispute that," I said. I was suspicious of Biddy's sweet reasonableness and her Celtic charm. More than ever, I was convinced that the three of them had planned some spendthrift lunacy behind my back, and it made me very angry. It was not as if they were unaware of our perilous financial situation. "The final responsibility lies, and will always lie, with the man in control of the money. Hard economic facts and figures are a more potent . . ."

"If anyone's temperamental in this set-up, it's Pudge," said Sam. He pronounced it "set-oop," stressing the slight North Country tinge in his voice, which he knew irritated me. "Proper little prima donna, he is. 'How much did that carpet cost?'—'Why do you need ten extras for the ballroom scene?' —'Couldn't you have made do with one bicycle?'—I tell you, Bob Meakin fair blew his top the other day, when we were shooting the British Museum interiors. Old Pudge came up and started fingering the coat he was wearing, asking how much it cost and who had authorized the fur lining. Just so happens it was Bob's own coat that he'd put on because he felt chilly. Took me half an hour to get him calmed down enough for the next take."

"If you'd rather I didn't come on to the set at all, Sam," I said, "you only have to say so. But in that case . . ."

"Oh, come off it, Pudge," said Sam, in his unvarying tone of placid amiability. "Can't you take a joke?"

"With you people it's sometimes a little difficult to distinguish between a joke and . . ."

"Shut up, both of you," said Keith, more sharply than usual. "Things are bad enough, without us fighting amongst ourselves." He was right, of course, and I am glad to say that Sam had the grace to look somewhat abashed. "How *is* the Meakin menace?" Keith added. "What news from the battle front?"

I looked up, interested and far from pleased. Nobody knew better than I the various hazards and headaches which were currently plaguing the existence of Northburn Films, Ltd., but it was the first I had heard of any sort of trouble between the company and its star. In fact, I personally had been pleasantly surprised at how easy and reasonable Robert Meakin had proved in his dealings with us. He had the reputation of being a difficult and temperamental character, and I knew that several large companies refused to employ him, in spite of his undoubted acting talent and his great box-office appeal. Trouble with Meakin would mean trouble for us all.

"What's that about Meakin?" I asked. There was a silence. Once again, I had the sensation of conspiracy, and it was not pleasant. "Well?" I said.

"It's nothing, Pudge," said Biddy. I noticed that she had gone rather pink, which was not like her at all. "Just a silly . . ."

"If you must know," said Sam easily, "Bob Meakin has taken a shine to our resident genius, young Bridget here. You can imagine the effect that it's having in some quarters."

"You mean, La Fettini?"

"That's exactly what I mean. But don't worry, it'll blow over. Biddy's not encouraging the gentleman, are you, love?"

"I should hope not," said Keith. He sounded really angry.

Biddy studied the toes of her shoes and said nothing. Keith pushed back his chair and stood up. "Well," he said, "I'm off. It's ten to two."

"I'll come with you," said Sam. "There are a few points I'd like to discuss with you about the Masterman house interiors. We can walk through Covent Garden. Why don't you stay here with Pudge for a bit, Biddy?"

"If you don't mind very much," I said, "I intend to be at the location at two o'clock. I have received a call, just as you have." I was damned if I was going to be shouldered out in that casual way.

"Of course, old man," said Sam, "but it'll be a good hour before . . ."

"Correct me if I am wrong, but my call sheet says two o'clock."

"I know it does, but . . ."

"The lighting is set up, and you rehearsed before lunch. You only need a final run through on moves with Meakin . . ."

"Are you trying to tell me how to do my job, Pudge?" Suddenly Sam sounded quite dangerous, in spite of the fact that he's only a little mouse of a man. He didn't raise his voice, but there was a hardness in it that I had not heard more than two or three times before.

"I'm sorry, Sam," I said. It went against the grain to apologize at that moment, but I could not risk having Sam upset. "I certainly never meant to imply . . ."

"Oh, stuff it," said Biddy. "I'd like to watch that scene anyway. Let's all go together."

So we all went.

It occurs to me that this is the point to tell you a little more about us, in case you haven't heard of Northburn Films. There's been quite a lot about us in the papers recently, what with one thing and another, but at the time I am speaking of we were a new venture and virtually unknown.

The idea of Northburn Films was born in a smoky club off Shaftesbury Avenue in the small hours of a November morning. I was not there myself, of course. The Can is not the sort of place I frequent. It is a club which caters almost exclusively to minor people on the technical side of films—writers, directors, cameramen, set designers, and so forth. Most of the members are either bright young people on the way up or sad middle-aged ones on the way down. The people at the top don't go to The Can, and I must say that I do not blame them. It has always seemed to me a seedy, depressing place, and I consider its name most unfortunate, in spite of the fact that I am assured that it refers to the tin canister in which exposed film is sealed on its way to the laboratories for processing—hence the expression "to get a shot in the can."

Be that as it may, two of the bright young members were Keith Pardoe, who had just finished his first big job as Art Director for Superba Films, and Sam Potman, the boy from Bradford whose film *Melting Point*—made in an iron foundry with an amateur cast—had carried off a prize at Cannes under the noses of the French and Italians. Both Keith and Sam were at crucial stages in their careers. Both had received offers from Hollywood, and neither wanted to go. Each wanted to do the sort of work he enjoyed—intellectual, experimental stuff, the sort of thing a man could only do if he were free to work as he wished. Neither of them could remember, afterward, who first suggested forming a company of their own, but once the idea had been formulated, there was no holding them.

Keith was engaged to Biddy Brennan at the time—which is a euphemism for saying that they were living together in Keith's flat in Earl's Court—and she had just hit the headlines with her first novel, *The Butterknife*. I must confess it was rather above my head—full of symbolism and literary allusions and psychology and so forth—although the story boiled down to quite a simple tale of a girl who was fascinated by an older man because he reminded her of her father. I rather think he turned out to *be* her father in the end, although I can't be sure, because I never actually managed to finish the book. Anyhow, it sold twenty-five thousand copies, and Keith found it quite easy to convince Sam that a writer like Biddy was just the person they needed to complete their board of directors.

The snag, of course, was money. All three of them were doing well, but none of them could lay hands on anything like the sum that it takes to embark on even the most modest film. (*Melting Point* had been sponsored by some federation of trade unions.) Keith and Sam found the City discouraging.

Too many financiers had lost too much money on films in the past, and even the big, established companies were not finding it easy to raise funds. Three virtually unknown young people, even if their talents were promising, had no hope at all. And that was where, if you will forgive the pun, I came into the picture.

My name is Anthony Croombe-Peters, although I am generally known as Pudge, for reasons which you will have gathered. The important thing about me, however, is that my father is Lord Northburn, who, as you probably know, is not only an eminent judge but the head of one of the richest families in the land. Being a prudent man, he had recently made over the bulk of his fortune to me in order to escape Death Duties; and while, naturally, he retained a firm grip on the family's financial affairs, I nevertheless found myself able to dispose of considerable sums in whatever way I chose.

Keith Pardoe and I had done our military service together and had struck up one of those unlikely friendships that form in unpropitious circumstances. If I am to be honest, we never really liked each other, but we settled reluctantly for each other's company in the absence of more congenial society. I suppose the only thing we had in common was a Public School education; and even this tended to cause more friction than harmony between us, for I was proud of the honorable traditions in which I was fortunate enough to be born and reared, while Keith seemed positively ashamed of his middle-class background, and cultivated what appeared to me to be a thoroughly self-conscious and bogus pose of bohemianism. Even granted that he was an artist, it always struck me as quite unnecessary to grow his hair down to his collar—which was perpetually sprinkled with dandruff as a consequence—and to omit to wash his neck. However, as I said, a friendship of a sort sprang up between us, but as soon as we were demobilized we went our separate ways with relief, and I had not seen or heard from him for more than five years when he suddenly telephoned and invited me out to lunch. My instinct was to refuse, but I was intrigued by two things. Firstly, he suggested an extremely snobbish and expensive restaurant, the last place with which I would have associated him; and secondly, he told me that he was bringing his fiancée, Bridget Brennan. I had not even attempted to get through *The Butterknife* at that time, but I was aware of the stir it had caused, and was curious to meet the author. So I accepted.

Keith also told me that he would be bringing a friend by the name of Sam Potman. It was just as well that I had never met Sam at that time, or I would certainly have refused the invitation and Northburn Films might never have been born. I do not mind admitting that I was appalled when I got to the door of the restaurant and saw Keith sitting there at the bar, talking to this small, scruffy individual in a tight blue suit, with oiled-down black hair and grubby fingernails. If I could have slipped quietly out again without being seen, I would have gone straight home and telephoned to say that I was ill. However, Keith spotted me right away, and there was no escape.

In fairness to both of us, I must add that Sam impressed me from the beginning, in spite of his unprepossessing appearance and blunt manners. While he seldom raised his voice, and always maintained an easy, amused tone, as though he took nothing seriously, I soon realized that he was a man who knew exactly what he wanted and how he intended to achieve it. There was no need for him to be aggressive or dogmatic, because he *knew*, quietly and without hesitation, what he was going to do and how. He had authority, and that is a quality which I recognize and respect. Of course, it took me a little while to grasp all this about Sam, but in the first minutes of our acquaintance he made a gesture which I couldn't help admiring.

This particular restaurant—the Orangery it's called—employs one of the most famous barmen in London. His name is Mario, and everybody I know respects him and his judgment. In fact, quite a few of my younger friends are frankly scared of him. Keith had introduced Sam and myself and asked us what we wanted to drink, and Sam had ordered a Bacardi. Keith and I were both having straightforward whisky, which was at our elbows in a second; but Mario made quite a performance over the Bacardi, tossing in the ingredients with a fine flourish and making great play with the shaker. Sam, who had resumed a technical conversation about sound tracks with Keith, appeared not to notice what was going on behind the bar. It was only when he had taken a sip from the ice-misted glass that he looked up and said amiably to Mario, "Hey, chum. This isn't a Bacardi."

Mario's face was a study. I don't think anyone had ever accused him of mixing a drink wrongly before, and he went white with anger. "I beg your pardon, sir," he said, in a voice that might have come frosted out of his own Martini jug. "That is a Bacardi."

"It's not, you know," said Sam, with a lazy smile. "You used bottled lime juice."

"But, sir," Mario made a big, Italianate gesture, "fresh limes are unobtainable in London in December . . ."

"Then you should've told me you couldn't make a Bacardi, shouldn't you?" said Sam reasonably, "and I'd have 'ad something else."

That was the first time that I heard him deliberately playing on his North Country accent, and it wasn't lost on Mario. What made the whole thing so beautiful was that Sam was completely and utterly in the right. I saw Mario taking a split-second decision, and then he swallowed his pride and decided to accept defeat gracefully.

"Ah, sir, it is not often we have the privilege of serving a real expert," he purred, beaming furiously at Sam. "Of course I will remove the drink at once. What may I offer you in its place, sir?"

"I'll 'ave a whisky," said Sam, shortly, and turned back to Keith to discuss dubbing.

That may sound like a very small incident, but it summed up Sam's character as I later got to know it, and I must say I took off my hat to him. Soon after that Biddy arrived, and put an end to any doubts I might still have had about enjoying the lunch party. I had never before met anybody with such a blazing personality. Not that she was flamboyant; far from it. She was small and neat, and her suit was plain and black and beautifully tailored. With it, she wore thick black woolen stockings and shiny Wellington boots—an eminently sensible choice for the coldest day of the winter. The effect was to make all the other women in the place look silly.

Once again, the Wellington boots were a sure indication of character. No rules of etiquette or conventional way of life could ever have contained Biddy, for she was one of those rare people who make the rules instead of following them. Because she took nothing for granted, everything became fresh and fascinating when seen through her eyes. When I felt shocked at her bad language, I realized that the fault was mine and not hers, although it was against all my principles to admit such a thing. When she drew attention to the qualities of her Wellington boots—"Aren't they *elegant*? So beautifully made. Look at that seam in the middle. And only nine and eleven in the Edgware Road"—I felt that they were indeed remarkable objects. I wondered how I could have been so crass as to have lived for twenty-eight years without ever appreciating the merits of Wellington boots. That was the kind of effect that Biddy had on people. I don't think I have mentioned that she had dark red hair.

I enjoyed that first lunch. I may not be very bright, but it was obvious even to me that the others wanted me to join the company for no other reason except my capacity to put up the necessary cash; and, curiously enough, this did not worry me. I barely bothered to listen to Keith's stumbling protestations about how valuable my business experience would be—I had fooled around for a year or so in an insurance office at one time. I noticed that neither of the other two deigned to support this bare-faced flattery. They both said, fair and square, that what was needed was money, and left it at that. Still less was I impressed by Keith's even more feeble efforts to sway my decision by promising me champagne parties with glamorous starlets. Over coffee and brandy I told the others that I would think the matter over and let them know. This was a mere matter of form, because I had already made up my mind.

My decision to join the company was prompted by two reasons, which, I suppose, boiled down to the same thing in the end. Quite frankly, I was bored and dissatisfied with life. Not only was I bored with doing nothing, but also by the way in which my equally boring friends seemed to take it for granted that I was incapable of doing anything useful or constructive. So there were my two reasons. I wanted to work, and I wanted to work with people like Biddy Brennan and Sam Potman. I telephoned Pardoe the next day and told him that I would finance the venture on one condition: that I should be an active member of the board, responsible for all budgeting and finance. In fact, although I did not know enough about the film business to realize it, I was demanding the job of Executive Producer.

I was irritated but not surprised by Keith Pardoe's obvious dismay at my proposal. He said he must put it to the others, and we had another lunch together, which was rather less agreeable than the first one. Keith blustered and Biddy tried some Irish blarney and Sam said nothing at all until we were on the point of leaving. Then he said, with his usual slow grin, "Well, Mr. Peters, it is usual for an Executive Producer to have some knowledge of the business, but since you're paying the piper, you're entitled to call the tune. We'll get you a good, experienced Production Manager and hope that all goes well."

Sam's idea of a good, experienced Production Manager was a female dragon by the name of Louise Cohen. I suppose he hoped that she would be able to bully me into leaving everything to her. We had a couple of monumental fights, after which Louise retired into her own office and wrote furious memos to Keith and Sam accusing me of making it impossible for her to do her job. I can't say I cared. There was nothing they could do about it, because they dared not lose me. The board of Northburn Films—the name was a graceful compliment to my father, of course—may have hoped to acquire a nonentity with a checkbook, but I was determined to show them that I could produce a film as efficiently as the next man, and what is more I enjoyed myself thoroughly, for the first time in years.

I have to admit, however, that enjoyment soon gave way to anxiety. At the time when this story opens, we were in the middle of our first production, and things were not going well. In fact, not to put too fine a point on it, we were on the brink of disaster, and through no fault of our own.

The film was called *Street Scene,* and Biddy had written the script from an idea of Sam's. The story concerned a provincial university professor visiting London, who met a girl from the East End and fell in love with her, not realizing that she was a prostitute and a thief. At least, that was my interpretation of the thing, and it seemed a pretty good yarn to me, even if a bit sordid. When it appeared, if you remember, the critics wrote columns about its symbolism and hidden meanings and so forth, and for all I know they may have been right. Biddy, Sam, and Keith never discussed that aspect of the film with me, and I hardly liked to bring the subject up. They all had this quiet assurance of *knowing*. In any case, the artistic side was none of my business.

Robert Meakin, the actor whom I've mentioned already, was playing Masterman, the professor. He was a big name, and we were lucky to get him, but during the casting sessions Sam had developed a most unexpected streak of sheer commercialism and declared that we must have a second star, a big female name. What we had to do, he said, was to beat the commercial boys at their own game. So Biddy took the script back, changed the girl's name from Rosie to Rosa, making her an East End Italian, and we signed up Fiametta Fettini.

From the beginning I was against using Fiametta. She cost us a fortune, and I considered that she was wrong for the part, and a bad actress. However, I was overridden by Keith and Sam, who kept pointing out that they were professional film men and I was not. Of course, I could not dispute that La Fettini was the current sex symbol on both sides of the Atlantic, but I maintained from the start that she would be more trouble than she was worth. I didn't know then how right I was.

Fiametta Fettini arrived in London in the middle of May, in a blue mink coat and a blaze of publicity, accompanied by her husband, a crushed little man called Giulio Palladio who figured on our salary sheet as her manager, two maids, a chauffeur, her personal hairdresser, and a pet monkey called Peppi. We were reckoning on getting her part of the film "in the can" by the end of June.

One of Sam's ideas for *Street Scene,* which he did take the trouble to expound to me, was that London herself was to be, in some mysterious way, the central character in the film. This involved trundling our camera round the docks, up King's Road Chelsea, into the British Museum, through City streets, and into Undergrounds, buses, and taxis. Consequently, the amount of studio work was cut to a minimum, which was also designed to be an economy.

Fiametta Fettini's interior scenes went well and smoothly, and in early June we moved out onto location in the City of

London. I had budgeted to cover every contingency except that one eternal imponderable—the English weather. While we had been shooting in the studio there had been a heat wave. The day we moved outside it began to rain. We were now in the middle of August, with half the location scenes still to shoot. Since the end of June we had been paying Fiametta Fettini a thousand pounds a week over and above her agreed salary as a penalty for overrunning our schedule. Admittedly, the weather was not her fault, but it hurt just the same.

The other disaster, however, was her fault, and was, in my view, utterly inexcusable. To put it as briefly as I can, the miserable woman had to go and fall hopelessly in love with her co-star, Bob Meakin. Now Bob, off the screen, was very much like the character he played in the film: gruff, unromantic, inarticulate, and stubborn—the last person for La Fettini to vent her southern passion on. The thing soon assumed the proportions of a major scandal. Poor little Giulio Palladio was sent down to the country with the pet monkey, and Fiametta's pursuit of Bob Meakin around the London scene became the favorite topic of every gossip columnist in the country.

I found the whole thing degrading, and it irritated me beyond measure when Keith and Sam insisted on regarding it all as good publicity. Even they, however, had to admit that things had gone too far when La Fettini was found by one of her maids in a state of collapse, having swallowed a number of barbiturate pills; not a fatal dose, I need hardly say, but enough to give everybody a severe fright and to keep her off the set for a week. The day she was taken to the London Clinic was the first day of sunshine we had seen for a fortnight. Her illness held us up for a further ten days, and, of course, our insurance company very properly refused to compensate us for what was clearly a self-inflicted injury. There was no question of accident, for the drug she had taken was available on prescription only, and her doctor denied strenuously ever having prescribed it. We never found out where she got the pills, but Fiametta was still, basically, a cunning little guttersnipe from Naples and could have got hold of a bottle of cyanide if she'd set her mind to it. I got some small satisfaction from withholding a week's salary from her, but that was a drop in the bucket.

I don't want to give the impression that I was the sole financial support of Northburn Films. I provided the major part of the money, but there was a limit beyond which I could not go, and that limit was getting dangerously close. Biddy had contributed everything which the income tax authorities had left her from the sales of her first book, and she was busy writing another. Sam and Keith had thrown what personal funds they had into the kitty. All four of us were deeply involved, but in slightly different ways. Biddy, Keith, and Sam faced, quite simply, bankruptcy—if we ran out of funds before the picture was completed. I had a secure income, but I was bedeviled by the thought that the money which I might lose was not really mine but my father's. I did not relish the prospect of having to tell him that it had gone and nothing to show for it.

The others, being the type of people they were, took the whole thing rather more lightheartedly than I did. They were also, as I have hinted, continually spending more than I had authorized and then trying to hush it up. It was on my insistence that we stopped lunching at the Orangery and now frequented the cheaper Soho restaurants. I think I may be forgiven for being somewhat on edge at that time. According to my calculations, there was just enough money to finish the film. There was not enough to weather another catastrophe; and there seemed to be one waiting around every corner.

2

Such, then, was the situation on the August afternoon when Biddy, Keith, Sam, and I left the restaurant in Soho to walk across Covent Garden to the unused Underground station which was our location for the afternoon. Since we were shooting below ground, I need hardly say that the weather, for once, was perfect. London was looking her best, basking in warm sunshine under a deep blue sky, but we were all too preoccupied to notice it.

Sam and Keith were involved in a discussion about the set for a studio retake scheduled for the following week. Biddy, in the inconsequential way she has, was reciting "Albert and the Lion" aloud to herself, and swearing when she couldn't remember the words. When I asked her why she did this, she replied that it helped her to think. I pass the information on for what it is worth. It certainly did not help me to think. I was trying to calculate in my head the exact cost of the day's shooting, allowing for twelve extras and the hire of the station, train, and driver from London Transport. I had nearly reached the answer when Biddy waltzed up to me chanting, "He lay in a som-no-lent post-u-are, Pudge, with the side of his face in the . . . damn . . . in the . . . to the bars! With the side of his face to the bars!"

"I wish you'd be quiet," I said. "Now I've forgotten where I was."

"O Pudgekin," said Biddy. "What does it matter? It's only money."

And before I could remonstrate against this absurd statement, she had danced away again, singing something about Albert having heard about lions, how they were ferocious and wild. I was glad when we reached our destination.

This was, as I have indicated, a derelict tube station on a small branch line which had not been in use for several years. We had arranged to hire it for the scene in which Professor Masterman is pursuing Rosa through London in a vain attempt to find out where she goes in the afternoons—the answer, of course, is a brothel. Since readers of this book are going to have to learn quite a lot about film-making before they are through, perhaps the best thing I can do is to reproduce the relevant passages from Biddy's shooting script, in order to describe the little sequence we were hoping to shoot that day.

DISSOLVE TO:

LONG SHOT, Underground Station
Platform (Location.) Several
travelers are waiting for a

train, among them ROSA. She
looks at her watch.

CUT TO:

Stock shot. Underground train   Noise of train
approaching from tunnel.

CUT TO:

MEDIUM SHOT, Platform. The train   Background station noise
pulls in. ROSA boards it, along   (Stock)
with a few other passengers.

CUT TO:

LONG SHOT, Escalator. MASTERMAN is
running frenziedly down it, jostling
other passengers.

CUT TO:

Platform. CLOSE SHOT, GUARD.
                          GUARD: Mind the gap!

GUARD blows his whistle.   Sound of whistle.

CUT TO:

LONG SHOT, Platform. The train doors
close and the train begins to move out.   Train noise.

CUT TO:

MEDIUM SHOT, MASTERMAN running pell-
mell down the stairway leading to the
platform.

CUT TO:

MEDIUM SHOT, Platform. MASTERMAN   Train noise.
arrives at a run, simultaneously with
another train. Passengers alight and
board it. MASTERMAN scans them
desperately. ROSA is not among them.

Now, if you read that carefully you will see that there are
only four shots in which the Underground train actually appears, and one of them we could get from a library of stock
shots. Since the train was extremely expensive to hire, we had
decided to do the other three shots as soon as possible, without

any reference to the continuity of the action. That's the way it is with films—the sequence of shots gets completely mixed up. For instance, we'd needed Meakin—that is, Masterman—for other shots the previous day, before we moved down to the tube station; so the very first shot we had taken was the last one of the sequence—where he arrived on the platform. During the morning, we had shot the train moving out, and later on, Rosa boarding it. That should have disposed of the train, but we had kept it standing by until we heard from the laboratories that all was well with the previous day's takes. Just before lunch Sam had rehearsed Meakin in the shot where he was to run down the staircase, and this was what we were about to shoot.

I was not overpleased by the amount of work the unit had done during the morning. Two simple shots and a third rehearsed did not seem good enough to me. It was only after questioning Keith and Biddy pretty rigorously that I discovered there had been a hold-up due to Fiametta Fettini making some sort of fuss about her costume, to which she had taken a dislike. This was typical of La Fettini. She must have known perfectly well that there was no hope of changing her costume, because some weeks ago, in the studio, we had shot the scenes which would immediately precede today's on the screen—a sequence of Rosa and Masterman lunching at a large popular café. The details of exactly what Rosa had worn then were meticulously recorded on the Continuity Girl's record sheets, and what Rosa wore today had to tally exactly. This sort of logical argument, however, counted for nothing with Fiametta Fettini, who had contrived to delay shooting for nearly an hour. Clearly it had simply been a display of childish bad temper—she was always impossible to work with when Bob Meakin was not on the set, and he had not been called until the afternoon. I mention these small frustrations and annoyances merely to explain why I was inclined to be short-tempered myself, and why I was determined to be on the spot in person, in order to nip any further hold-ups in the bud.

The Underground Station was buzzing with activity when we arrived. Big arc lamps had been set up around the spot where the staircase debouched onto the platform, and Fred

Harborough, the cameraman, was strolling around with a smoked monocle held to one eye, shouting instructions like "kill that baby!" and "put a jelly in number three!" to his gang of electricians. In the brightly lit area at the head of the stairs stood a man who vaguely resembled Robert Meakin, being of the same height and coloring. This was the stand-in, whose humble function was to act as guinea pig for Fred and his electricians, only to step out of his place in the limelight when the camera started turning.

The dozen or so extras, looking remarkably ordinary, wandered up and down the platform or smoked and chatted in small groups. Only their conversation, which was exclusively devoted to film "shop," distinguished them from a typical crowd of travelers in a London tube station. Self-consciously apart from the extras, the Guard sat on a bench reading *Stage Whispers.* He was an elderly and reliable actor called George Temple, who had moved from repertory to films, and who made himself a modest but steady living by playing tiny character parts. His close-up, with one line, set him firmly in a different category from the extras. He was an artiste, and he did not intend to let anyone forget it. He carefully refrained from looking up as an attractive, dark girl in a blue cotton dress walked past.

"Hello, George," she said. "What's new?"

"Hello, dear. How *are* you?" said George distantly.

The girl was La Fettini's stand-in. As such, her status was somewhere between the positions of George and the extras. He did not answer her question, but continued to read his paper in a marked manner. The nuances of social distinction in the lower grades never fails to amuse me. And *we* are the ones who are accused of being snobs. . . .

I had barely time, however, to pay attention to such details, because I was instantly aware of trouble brewing at the far end of the platform. One develops an instinct for such things, and although nobody had raised a voice in anger, I took one look at the little knot of men and I knew that something was up, something connected with the union. I walked quickly up the platform trying not to appear agitated.

It was at once obvious what the trouble was. Propped up against the wall was an imitation London Transport station name board, which bore the legend "Cambridge Square" and which would be featured in the coming shot. The question was whether it should be the carpenter or the property man who inserted the screw which would fix it to the wall. Apparently deadlock had been reached, and the Shop Steward called in to give a ruling.

The discussion was progressing perfectly amiably and in a leisurely manner. The protagonists reminded me of golf players engaged in a friendly match, consulting the rule book on a tricky point of procedure. The carpenter and the props man were leaning up against the wall, smoking and talking about football pools. The Shop Steward, who was a plasterer by trade, and therefore had nothing to do that day except draw his extra lunch money for coming on location, was at present holding the floor, haranguing Gervase Mountjoy, the First Assistant Director, who represented the management.

"It's in the agreement," he was saying. "You can't get away from the agreement, Mr. Mountjoy. The carpenter shall enjoy the sole and unique right to insert screws, nails, thumbtacks, self-screwing hooks, staples . . ."

"My dear fellow, of course, . . ." murmured Gervase with a tired smile.

Not for the first time, I raged inwardly that we should be cursed with such an inefficient First Assistant. I should perhaps explain that the First Assistant Director is the executive —as opposed to the artistic—boss of all that happens on a film set. With his two subordinates, the Second and Third Assistant Directors, he organizes, controls, and disciplines the technicians and the actors. It is he who is responsible for making sure that people and equipment are in the right place at the right time; who chivvies slothful actors and smooths down temperamental ones; who insures that the Director's smallest whim is accomplished quickly and accurately; and who blows his whistle, symbol of his profession, and shouts the magic words, "Red light on! Quiet everybody please! We're turning!"

Most First Assistants aspire to be Directors themselves one day, and some of the best men in the business have come up by that arduous route. However, I could not imagine Gervase Mountjoy being anything but a disaster if let loose to direct a film. He was a slender, effete young man with pale blue eyes and lank fair hair, and it was widely acknowledged that he would never have held down the job if his father had not been Edward Mountjoy, the financier. I disliked Gervase cordially, but I always went out of my way to be polite to him. I knew very well what people said behind our backs: that Gervase and I had both more or less bought our positions in the unit, myself by direct financial contribution and Gervase by providing a comforting sort of assurance that his father would surely not allow the film to die for the sake of a few thousands. It was hardly for me to point out that one of us also contributed a full working day and a great deal of energy to the film, while the other put his feet up behind the set and read detective stories.

Now Gervase was draped spinelessly over the back of Sam Potman's canvas chair, allowing the Shop Steward to drone on unchecked about his agreement and making no effort whatsoever to settle a situation which might hold up shooting by an hour or more. It made my blood boil.

"Well, Mountjoy," I said sharply, "what's the matter here?"

"Just a small matter of union procedure, Pudge, old boy," said Gervase insolently. And to the Shop Steward, "Do go on, old man. It's frightfully interesting."

I could cheerfully have hit the man. For a start, he knew that I did not consider it right for him to use my nickname. I did not expect to be called "sir," but I thought that it would have been only civil on his part to have called me Mr. Croombe-Peters. After all, he was not of the top echelon, so to speak. Of course, Sam and Keith had already undermined the position for all of us by allowing everyone, down to the clapper boy, to use their Christian names—but then neither of them was known as Pudge.

The Shop Steward took a deep breath and started off again about the rights of carpenters over any object made of or constructed from wood, hardboard, or ply, but I cut him short.

"I don't give a row of beans," I said, "who screws that notice to the wall. You will see to it that it is in position not more than two minutes from now or there will be trouble."

"You take that attitude, chum, and there *will* be trouble and no mistake," said the Shop Steward nastily.

Gervase smirked. "Don't pay any attention to old Pudge,"

he said. "He got out of bed on the wrong side this morning."

That was too much, and I am afraid I rounded on him and let him have it, squarely and from the shoulder. "The discipline of this unit, Mountjoy," I said, "has been steadily undermined by your utter lack of control over the men. This is the most absurd waste of time I have ever come across, and if you're not prepared to put your foot down, I am."

"Any more of that," said the Shop Steward, "and I'll have the lot out on strike."

"You see?" said Gervase, shrugging his shoulders.

"Here was I," said the Shop Steward, "having a quiet and friendly talk with Mr. Mountjoy, what would have settled this matter in no time, and what happens? You come butting in and insulting my members. I've got a good mind to hold an extraordinary branch meeting here and now and take a vote on strike action."

"You'll do that if you want your cards on Friday," I retorted. "You *and* your gang of Communist troublemakers."

"If you're threatening me with victimization . . ."

It was at that moment that Sam strolled up. His face wore its usual, humorous expression, but I thought I could detect signs of strain underneath, and I was not surprised. Frankly, I was beginning to regret that I had ever got embroiled in this business with the union. A strike was all we needed to finish us at that moment, but I had been maneuvered into a position where I could not climb down without loss of face. The fault, of course, lay with Gervase Mountjoy. If he had been firm at the outset all would have been well.

I must say I had to take my hat off to Sam. Of course, he was in rather a special position. Although undisputedly the lord and master of the set, he seemed to the workmen to be one of them, with his North Country accent and his scruffy clothes. As I have already indicated, I considered that he was too friendly with them, but the result was that they idolized him and would do just about anything for him. In any case, he handled this situation extraordinarily well. In no time at all, the Shop Steward was laughing, some sort of decision had been agreed upon, and the notice was on the wall.

I felt it was only fair to give honor where it was due, and I was just about to swallow my pride and congratulate Sam, when he turned to me and said, "For God's sake never do that again or I *will* ban you from the set."

"Never do what again?"

"Upset a Shop Steward. Don't you know a strike would ruin us?"

"I have no quarrel with the Shop Steward," I said. "It was Gervase . . ."

"Gervase knows how to handle these things. Just leave him alone to get on with his job, and mind your own business in future."

"I consider that this is my business. Every minute wasted on this set represents, in terms of hard cash . . ."

"Pudge," said Sam quietly, "shut up."

Not a trace of a smile. Not even trying to be agreeable. Before I could recover myself enough to reply, he had turned on his heel and gone off to talk to Margery Phipps, the Continuity Girl. Really, sometimes I couldn't help feeling that I was carrying the whole weight of that film on my shoulders. The others were not only being unrealistic; now that things were serious, they had begun to go to pieces. Automatically, I looked around for an ally whom I could enlist on my side. Keith was nowhere to be seen—he afterward told me that he had gone out to buy some cigarettes—but Biddy was sitting on the bench chatting to George Temple. Naturally, I would not have discussed top-level matters in front of a small-part actor, but I decided to try to prise Biddy away from George. For all her fecklessness, Biddy had a certain basic sense of justice, and I did not think that she would approve the way in which my authority was being undermined.

Before I could reach her, however, a diversion occurred which effectually drove all other matters into second place. This was the arrival of Fiametta Fettini and Bob Meakin. They had been lunching together, and it was obvious long before they appeared on the staircase that they were quarreling. At least, La Fettini was quarreling. She was shouting hysterically at the top of her voice, in a mixture of Italian and English. "*Cattivo!* Brute! Swine!" she shrieked. At that point she must have given her unfortunate co-star a considerable shove, because he came stumbling down the steps and fell onto the platform at Sam's feet. One of the electricians started to laugh, but Sam silenced him with a sharp look. There was a thick, awkward silence as Bob picked himself up and dusted the knees of his trousers.

"Now, now, children," said Sam, "what's oop, then?"

"Up? Well may you ask what is up! Ask him! Go on, ask him! I dare him to tell you!"

Fiametta Fettini had made her entrance, and she had certainly done it well. She was standing plumb in the middle of the lowest step of stairs, striking the sort of exaggerated attitude that only she could get away with, her head thrown back and an accusing finger pointing at poor Bob. Her long, dark hair was tousled, her magnificent black eyes were flashing fire, and anger had heightened the color in her honey-brown cheeks. She looked superb and extremely dangerous, and remembering previous tantrums, I moved quietly out of range. It was hard to see what she would find to throw, but I was sure that there would be something, and I was not wrong.

"Fiametta, darling," said Sam, "don't you think . . . ?"

He got no further. With a quick, graceful gesture, La Fettini bent down and slipped off her spike-heeled shoes; Bob and Sam got one each, full in the face. Bob was lucky. He was hit on the cheek by the sole of the shoe, which did no damage. Sam, on the other hand, received the business end of the stiletto heel just under his left eye, where it ripped a deep cut in his face. He did not move.

"That," said Bob Meakin, "is the end. Will you get her out of here, or do I have to call the police?"

"I shall go to my room to change," said Fiametta, like Bernhardt playing Medea.

"Either she leaves this set or I do," said Meakin. He was shaking with anger. "I've warned you . . ."

"I am an actress," announced Fiametta unnecessarily. "I do not walk out on films. My work comes first." She stepped down onto the platform and turned, with another ridiculous gesture. "Mario! Hilda! Giulietta! Come!" And, surrounded by her little court of hairdressers, wardrobe women, and make-up experts, she swept down the platform and out by the far exit, where a couple of pre-fabricated dressing rooms made out of canvas and hardboard had been rigged up for her and for Meakin.

Sam let her go and concentrated on Bob. I had seen our leading man angry before, but never quite to this pitch of cold fury. For the first time—and, let us be honest, with provocation—we were experiencing one of the famous Meakin temperaments. I suspected that what had upset him most was stumbling so inelegantly onto the platform. Fiametta had set out to make him look ridiculous, and she had succeeded. Very few men will stomach that, least of all aging actors who are intent on preserving their public image as juvenile leads. On the screen or across the footlights, Robert Meakin seemed ageless. The vague, boyish air, the ruffled hair, the infectious smile could surely, one felt, never grow old. It had caused me a severe pang of disillusionment, the first time I met him face to face, to realize that the hair was not only dyed but augmented at the forehead by a most discreet toupée, and that the face bore the slightly taut appearance and the tiny, telltale scars that betray what is known as cosmetic surgery. I also had grave doubts about more than one of his teeth. However, none of it showed on the screen, and that was all we cared about.

Now, he was embarking on the gambit of ice-cold, deadly reasonableness. "I don't think I have complained very much in the past," he was saying, standing very straight and apparently oblivious to the fact that Murray, his wizened little dresser, was trotting around him in circles, brushing his suit carefully with a wire clothesbrush. "I have been prepared to put the film first, and to endure considerable discomfort and indignity, to say nothing of extremely bad publicity, without as much as a murmur. But work is work, and requires concentration and an atmosphere which, if not happy, is at least tolerable. I cannot and will not even attempt to work on a set where today's episode is likely to be repeated at any moment. If you feel I am being unreasonable, please say so."

"What a bloody splendid speech," said Biddy. I had not noticed that she had come up and was standing on the other side of Bob. Her slightly husky voice was full of genuine laughter. "Forgive me if I don't take it too seriously, Bob darling. I just can't stop laughing at what an almighty fool La Fettini made of herself. If the Sunday gossip boys got hold of it, she'd never be able to show her face again."

"Well, I take it seriously," said Sam quickly. It was like watching a smooth double-act slip into gear. "Bob is quite right to be upset and angry. I don't think it's funny."

"Please don't think I've no sense of humor," said Bob, and I knew that the battle had been won. "It's just that it gets a bit ragged around the edges under the impact of well-aimed winkle-pickers."

"You're telling me," said Sam ruefully, putting a hand to his face.

"My dear fellow, . . ." Meakin seemed glad of an excuse to abandon his previous attitude. "I hadn't seen—here, take my handkerchief—Murray, get some sticking plaster for Mr. Potman."

"Please don't bother," said Sam. "I shall survive."

"What was it all about, anyway?" asked Biddy, and I felt my stomach turn over in alarm. First she saves the situation, I thought, and then she goes and puts her foot right slap in it. But, surprisingly, her very directness and honesty pulled her through once again. Bob Meakin actually laughed, in the youthful, embarrassed way that his fans loved.

"I really have no idea," he said. "The whole thing is so embarrassing. She doesn't seem to realize . . ."

"Look, Bob," said Sam, "you're Robert Meakin and she's a little upstart from a Naples slum. She's completely dazzled by you, and she doesn't know how to behave. It's easy to laugh at her, as Biddy does, and it's easy to get angry, as I was. But I'm not sure that in the end we shouldn't feel sorry for her. She's just a little nobody, trying to play at being a big star. You *are* a big star."

This barefaced piece of insincere flattery really took me aback. It was, of course, utterly untrue. Meakin, although admittedly a big name, was virtually unknown outside England, where his appeal was largely to middle-aged audiences. Fettini, whatever one might think of her, was an international star, and invariably crammed the cinemas with her own generation—the teenagers. There was no comparing their relative box-office value, and I could not believe that Meakin would take Sam seriously. But I had underestimated the capacity of an actor for absorbing flattery. Meakin lit a cigarette, beamed at Biddy, and told Sam that he was perfectly right.

As the atmosphere relaxed, Keith came down the stairs, and Biddy slipped off and spoke to him quietly. The next I saw of him, he was making his way down the platform toward Fiametta's dressing room, and I gathered that he had been deputed to apply a dose of calming flattery in that quarter. A few minutes later Sam, too, excused himself.

"Wish me luck," he said, laughing. "If I'm not back within the hour, send a search party."

"Poor Sam," said Biddy to Meakin. "He hates having to tick people off."

I knew very well, of course, that there was not the faintest possibility of Sam giving a ticking off to La Fettini. The same sort of softsoaping would go on in her dressing room that we had just heard applied to Bob on the platform. Bob must surely have known this, but apparently it soothed him to think that the fiction of La Fettini being treated like a naughty child was being maintained. He smiled warmly at Biddy, and the two of them walked off down the platform to his dressing room, apparently in high good humor. As I have often remarked, show me an actor and I will show you a child.

Sam emerged from Fiametta's booth a few minutes later, wiping a smear of lipstick off his cheek. The reconciliation had evidently been effected, although Sam had prudently left Keith *in situ*, to make sure that, once calmed, Fiametta stayed that way.

Gervase, who had been called away to the telephone, hurried up to Sam and said something quietly. I heard Sam say, "Goddamn it"; and then the two of them began to pace the platform, deep in talk. After a minute they were joined by Fred Harborough, the cameraman, and then by Biddy, who had just come out of Bob's dressing room. It was obvious that there had been a hitch of some sort, and a worrying one, and the exclusion of myself from the executive group was most marked. I went up to the others.

"What's the matter?" I said.

Sam was obviously not pleased to see me, but he made no attempt to get rid of me. He said, "The labs have just telephoned. Yesterday's train shot has been spoilt. We'll have to retake it."

"What happened?" I demanded.

Sam looked inquiringly at Gervase. "Light got into the film," said Gervase.

"Where? At our end or at the labs?"

"I don't know."

"Well, you ought to know. If it happened our end, find who is responsible and take disciplinary action. Who seals the film in the cans?"

"Steve, the clapper boy."

"Well then, get hold of him and . . ."

"It may have been the labs' fault," said Gervase. "It happens sometimes. They can't be infallible."

"Then they bloody well should be, over things as important as this. What do they think we . . . ?"

For the second time, Sam said, "Pudge. Shut up." Then I think he must have realized he had pushed me too far, because he put his hand on my arm in a friendly way, and said, "We'll have all the post mortems you want afterward, but at the moment the important thing is to get the retake in the can. You do see that, don't you?"

"Of course," I said. I am perfectly prepared to be reasonable if people will be reasonable with me.

"So," said Sam, "how long will it take you to set up, Fred?"

"Only a few minutes," said Fred cheerfully. He is an incurably optimistic character, for which, I suppose, we should be thankful. Although, mind you, he has plenty to be cheerful about: a big fat salary every week and no responsibility.

"A good thing you insisted on the train and driver standing by," said Sam to Gervase. "That was nice work. I appreciate it."

"Thanks, Sam," said Gervase. He forbore to mention that I had issued a specific instruction that the train should be kept at readiness during the afternoon. This was the sort of thing I found so irritating.

"You'd better tell Bob," said Sam to Gervase, and the latter sloped off to the canvas booth to break the bad news to our star. He was back a few moments later, and I decided that it might be prudent for me to go and have a word with Meakin, to complete Biddy's good work. I didn't like the thought of him alone in his dressing room, brooding. However, I wasn't halfway along the platform before Bob appeared from the corridor, just as George Temple came ambling past.

"Hello, General. How *are* you?" cried George warmly. He always called Bob "General"—a reference to some film in which they had both appeared years ago. I think George felt that the use of a nickname gave him an unanswerable right to speak to the star on equal terms.

"How are you?" echoed Bob, turning slightly away. I had noticed that this particular question was one which no actor ever answered.

"Care for a dekko at *Stage Whispers,* General?" asked George, undaunted, waving his magazine in Bob's face.

"No, thanks, dear boy," said Bob. And then, with slightly elaborate casualness, "Anything in it this week?"

"Just a feature article and a six-inch double gossip column about you, General," replied George, with ill-concealed jealousy. He did not mention Fiametta Fettini. Nobody ever did, in Bob's hearing. "You've certainly got a touch with the publicity boys. Sure you wouldn't like to read it?"

"I never read trash of that sort," said Bob sharply. "I can't imagine who buys it."

George's embarrassment in the face of this snub was mercifully covered by the arrival of Murray with Bob's various costume accessories, which he checked off with Margery Phipps as he presented them to Bob. There was the old raincoat, the shabby porkpie hat (which sold in thousands after the film had come out—"The Masterman Hat," as they called it), the heavy horn-rimmed spectacles, the gnarled pipe. Sam, for all his pose of art for art's sake, was certainly working to create a "Masterman image."

The big arc lamps had been swiveled around to face the platform, and electricians were working fast and smoothly under Fred's direction, moving other lights into position, so that the area of light—where Bob's stand-in was once more established—was now on the platform. The camera crew checked and adjusted and focused. Margery Phipps scribbled in her shorthand notebook. The make-up and hairdressing teams clustered around Bob like flies. The whole place had that air of approaching climax which always hovers over a set just before shooting starts.

"D'you want a run-through before we turn?" Sam asked

Bob.

"No, no." Bob sounded impatient. "It's just what we did yesterday, isn't it? Run down steps, ramming spectacles onto nose. Arrive full tilt on platform, pull up, pause, look round."

"That's it," said Sam. "How about you, Fred?"

"Naw," said Fred. He had spent some years in Hollywood, and lapsed into an American intonation when he was concentrating. "We can roll 'em straight away."

"Is the train standing by?" Sam asked.

He should not have had to. Gervase should have seen to it.

"Train and driver," shouted Gervase, hastily putting down a paper he had been reading.

"Train and driver," echoed his assistant.

"Train and driver ready," came a third voice from the recesses of the tunnel.

"I was carrying a newspaper yesterday," said Bob Meakin. "I don't seem to have one today."

"Mr. Meakin's newspaper. Quick, somebody. Margery, why didn't you point it out?" Gervase was obviously trying to put on a show of efficiency. I hoped that my earlier thrusts might have gone home. The property man appeared with the newspaper. Bob put it under his arm, straightened his shoulders, and stretched his neck forward in a characteristic gesture which he always used before a shot, and walked halfway up the staircase. I know it is easy to be wise after the event, but it is true that it did strike me at the time that his steps were not quite steady, and it flashed through my mind that his fall on the platform might have done more damage than he cared to admit. After all, he was not a young man. I noticed, too, that he held firmly onto the handrail as he mounted the steps. However, I said nothing. Bob moved to the center of the stairway, spectacles in one hand, newspaper in the other.

"Right," said Sam.

Gervase blew his whistle. "Quiet, everybody!"

Silence descended, like magic.

"O.K., Bob," said Sam. "Take it good and fast. Plenty of uncontrolled arms and legs."

"Ay, ay, sir," said Bob.

Again the whistle shrilled.

"Quiet, now! We're turning this time!"

In the dead silence, little Steve, the clapper boy, stepped in front of the camera, holding his blackboard. *"Street Scene,* Retake One-Nine-Four, Take One," he announced cheerfully. The clapper fell with a sharp click, and the light went on to signal the train. Steve removed the clapper board, and the camera concentrated on Bob as he began to run down the steps, hastily jamming on his spectacles with his right hand as he came.

What happened next will always remain a confused nightmare blur in my mind. There was the shriek of the train as it came roaring in from the tunnel. There was Bob, flying helterskelter down the stairs, shouting, reaching the platform, stumbling. There was Keith's voice behind me, shouting, "Bob! Stop him, for God's sake!"—and a screech of brakes. There was Fiametta Fettini screaming hysterically, "I didn't mean it! I swear I didn't mean it!" And Keith Pardoe vomiting in the corner and Biddy Brennan in tears, and Gervase Mountjoy, as might have been expected, out to the world in a dead faint. I am pleased to say that it was Sam and I who restored some sort of order and telephoned for doctors and ambulances— not that it was any use. Robert Meakin had fallen onto the line under the wheels of the approaching train, and he was quite dead.

3

I am sure I do not have to remind you of the sensation which Robert Meakin's death caused, coming as it did on the heels of the Fettini scandal. I will therefore leave you to imagine what I went through during the next few days. There seemed to be reporters everywhere, and the harder I slammed the door in their faces, the faster they came climbing in through the window. My artistic colleagues proved of very little help. I had not been counting on Biddy or Keith for much support, but I was surprised at Sam. After handling the situation at the Underground station with remarkable sense, and giving, at my request, a short speech to the technicians and actors, he had contrived to disappear into the streets of London like a needle into a haystack, and neither I nor the press were able to discover his whereabouts until the evening. I was left to cope alone.

Naturally, the police had to be notified, even though Bob's death was so patently an accident. This aspect of the affair worried me. Apart from the question of bad publicity, I was afraid that La Fettini might contrive to make some scandalous sort of scene if interrupted in the middle of her hysterics by a flat-footed London bobby; and I was acutely conscious of the fact that Sam Potman had simply disappeared, in spite of the fact that I had given instructions that nobody was to leave the Underground station. It was then that I had the idea of telephoning direct to Henry Tibbett.

This Tibbett character is quite a remarkable man. He's a Chief Inspector of the C.I.D., but you'd never think it to meet him. He's a mild, sandy-haired little chap in his forties, the sort of bird you'd pass in the street without a second glance. In fact, the first time I met him—at Lord Clandon's house, it was—I put him down as a junior partner in the family's firm of solicitors or accountants, or at the very best a poor and obscure relation. I was most surprised when I realized, later, that he was not only a great friend but an honored guest of the Clandons, which only goes to show that you never can tell by appearances. From then on I made something of an effort to cultivate him; I didn't want him to think I had been deliberately rude at our first meeting.

Between ourselves, I always found Henry slightly hard going. He seemed constantly preoccupied, if you know what I mean; always polite, but, I felt, not really interested in what I was saying to him. His wife was a far more attractive proposition—a splendid, plump, black-haired woman with a great sense of humor. I took to Emmy Tibbett straight away; I think everyone did. But I am straying from the point, which was that I suddenly had the bright notion of getting on to Henry personally instead of merely calling a policeman after Robert Meakin's death.

I was lucky. Henry was in his office and listened sympathetically while I told him what had happened. And then, believe it or not, he simply said quite coolly that he was afraid it was not a matter for the Criminal Investigation Department, and advised me to ring the nearest police station or go out and bring in a constable from the street.

"My dear Henry," I said, "don't you understand? This isn't any Tom, Dick, or Harry who's been killed; it's Robert Meakin, the film star."

"You say he stumbled on the platform and fell under the train."

"That's right."

"No question that it was anything but an accident?"

"Of course not."

"Then," said Henry, "it's not in my province at all, Mr. Croombe-Peters, I'm only interested in the poor devils who get murdered."

"You mean to say you're going to allow a lot of flat-footed bluebottles to come in here and question Fiametta Fettini . . . ?"

"I'm not trying to be difficult, Mr. Croombe-Peters," said Tibbett, in his most maddening way, "but I am extremely busy and it's not my department. What I will do is to ring Superintendent Wilcox for you, and get him to go along himself, but I'm afraid you'll have to put up with a certain number of bluebottles. We haven't all got flat feet, you know."

Well, it was unsatisfactory, but better than nothing. Wilcox turned out to be quite a reasonable fellow, and it was not long before he had taken all the details he needed. To my great relief he said he saw no reason for questioning Miss Fettini, and he accepted without comment my statement that Mr. Potman had been called away on urgent business. There were plenty of other witnesses to describe exactly what had happened to Bob. As soon as I had got rid of Wilcox, and deputed the various members of the unit to clearing up the equipment, I was able to get down to some constructive work.

The first thing I did was to bundle Fiametta off to the country to join poor little Palladio and the pet monkey. I rented a house for them, under an assumed name, in the wilds of Buckinghamshire, and transferred the whole ménage that afternoon. At first I thought that I had fooled the newspapermen, but no. Somehow—and I have my own ideas on the subject—the story leaked out, and the village was virtually besieged. But I am going too fast.

I called a Board Meeting of Northburn Films in my flat on the evening of Bob's death, having finally succeeded in contacting Sam at his Islington house soon after six. As soon as I had spoken to Sam, I disconnected the telephone and locked all the doors, and thanks to the fact that several sturdy policemen were on duty in the street outside, we were left in comparative peace. Later that night one enterprising journalist did manage to climb a water pipe from the gardens at the back, and got as far as my balcony, but fortunately he gave himself away by coughing and we called a bobby to eject him. Otherwise we were undisturbed.

Keith, Biddy, and Sam all arrived together, having run the gamut of crowds and photographers to get to the front door. Biddy was curiously subdued for her, and she was dressed all in white. I knew that this was considered by some people as a color of mourning, so I carefully did not comment on it. If her mourning was genuine, it was more tactful not to mention it. If, on the other hand, she was merely making a flamboyant gesture to invite comment, I decided to leave that to the newspapers.

Of the three of them, Keith appeared to have taken Bob's death the hardest. In fact—one does not like to have to say such things about a man, but the truth is the truth—he had broken down completely in the Underground station and wept quite openly. It was most embarrassing for everybody, and I was relieved to see that by the evening he had his emotions more or less under control, although once or twice his voice trembled suspiciously. He was wearing a dark gray suit of surprising neatness, and a black woolen tie. It was the first sign of sartorial respect that I had ever known him display.

I confess that I had had some misgivings about the kind of mood that Sam might arrive in. He had been curiously abrupt on the telephone, and I knew that he was perfectly capable of turning up either so drunk as to be useless, or in a maddening frame of mind in which he stubbornly refused to speak or think about the matter in hand. However, he seemed, mercifully, to be just as usual. He ignored my question about where he had spent the afternoon, accepted a drink, looked around him, and said, "Well, I suppose this is as good a place as any to bury the body. Let's get on with it."

Keith said, "Sam . . . must you?" in a choked sort of voice; and Biddy said, "What in hell do you mean?"

"Northburn Films, of course," said Sam. "It was fun while it lasted, but this is obviously the end of the line. Speaking personally, I'm not even going to suggest to Pudge that he put up any more cash. It would be throwing good money after bad. In any case, the sum would be astronomic. Reshooting all Bob's scenes so far, plus the extra time we'd have to keep Fiametta; it's just not on. Let alone the fact that we'd never find a new leading man right away, and the unit has to be either paid or disbanded. I'm sorry about it, but there it is. I suggest we draw a veil over Northburn Films and kiss it good-bye."

From the flippant way he spoke, you would never have guessed that he was pronouncing sentence of death on all his most cherished hopes, and resigning himself to financial ruin. In a strange way, he sounded almost relieved.

"But Sam, . . ." said Keith, and then checked himself.

There was a silence.

Biddy said, "I suppose Gervase Mountjoy's father wouldn't . . ."

Sam shook his head. "Not this much," he said. "A few thousand, perhaps. But not this."

"Then there's nothing to be done?"

"Not a thing."

"Bloody hell," said Biddy quietly. From there she went on, right through her repertoire, until she had run out of swear words both in English and in French. I did not interrupt; frankly, I was fascinated and repelled at the same time. At last she stopped and said, "I'm sorry. It's just that after all we've . . ."

I stood up. "Now that that display is over," I said, "perhaps you'll all listen to me for a bit." It was a new and, I must admit, pleasant sensation to be in control of the situation for once. I did not hurry. I took a sip of my drink and lit a cigarette. "For a start," I said, "Northburn Films is neither going to fold up nor go bankrupt."

"Pudge," said Sam, "I've already told you. I'm not going to let you or your father . . ."

I raised my hand. "*Just* a moment, if you please. Northburn Films will continue, and *Street Scene* will be completed, and I will not be paying for it. Nor will my father, nor, most certainly, will Edward Mountjoy."

There was no doubt about the sensation caused by that remark. I had never seen all three of them reduced to complete silence before, waiting for me to go on talking. I felt myself smiling, although it was a serious moment.

"I am well aware," I went on, "that some of you have never had a very high opinion of my capabilities as a businessman. Some of you have questioned my usefulness to Northburn Films."

Keith made a small, impatient movement and started to say something, but Biddy checked him.

"Nevertheless," I continued, "it is a fortunate thing for the company that at least one member of the Board had some experience of the ways of finance, however inadequate. You may remember that I once worked in an insurance office. My time there was not, I think, entirely wasted."

"But, Pudge," Sam looked up, enormously interested, "I thought . . ."

"I had the foresight," I said quietly, "to insure Northburn Films against various contingencies . . ."

"We had the routine insurance, of course." Keith spoke almost angrily. "Injury to technicians and actors, life insurance for everyone."

"I wonder who'll get Bob's?" said Biddy, thoughtfully.

"Fire and theft insurance," Keith went on. "The usual things. Not . . ."

"I would like to point out," I said, "that copies of all our insurance policies were sent to each of you for approval before I signed them on your behalf. I can only presume that you did not take the trouble to read them."

43

"I can't read *and* write," objected Biddy. "There isn't time."

Sam and Keith said nothing. Of course, they had never even glanced at the policies—just dismissed them as another piece of what Sam called Pudgery—initialed them and sent them back.

"I did take a look at mine," said Keith, at length. "I thought it was just the normal . . ."

"Well, it wasn't," I said. "I have a copy of the relevant policy here, and I shall read it to you . . ."

"Oh God, Pudge, don't do that," said Biddy. "Just tell us."

"Very well. The company is insured and fully indemnified against any production losses or extra expenses arising from the injury, illness, or accidental death of either Miss Fiametta Fettini or Mr. Robert Meakin, always provided that the injury, illness, or death is directly ascribable to the artist's work on the film and is not caused by any negligent or deliberate act on the part of . . ."

Sam said, "What exactly does 'fully indemnified' mean?" He sounded both excited and wary, like a man who dared not believe good news.

"What it says. Our entire production costs for shooting Bob's scenes—Fiametta's overtime, unit expenses, and so forth—will be met by the insurance company. In fact, we can wipe the slate clean and start again."

"And if we get decent weather and no hold-ups . . ."

"Exactly," I said to Sam. "We'll be doing extremely well."

There was a dazed silence, and then Keith began to laugh with an almost hysterical intensity. "How bloody funny," he said. I was aware that I had never heard him swear before. "Bloody funny. Here we all were, thinking we were ruined, and in fact poor old Bob's death has saved the situation. Better that one man should die for the good of all . . ."

"Shut up, Keith," said Biddy.

"But don't you see how funny it is? If we'd known, we could have pushed him under a train long ago."

"Keith!" Without warning, Biddy stood up and slapped her husband hard across the face.

Keith was suddenly silent. He raised his hand and rubbed his cheek in a surprised way. There was an extended pause.

Sam broke it by saying, bluntly, "Will they pay up?"

"They'll have to," I said. "If all goes well at the inquest, they haven't a leg to stand on."

"What do you mean," said Sam, " 'if all goes well'?"

"We need a verdict of accidental death," I said. "That's a foregone conclusion, of course. Then we want it clearly established that the accident took place while Bob was in the course of his work for us. No dispute about that, either. The only danger is any suspicion that his death might have been caused by negligence on the part of a member of the unit. For instance, if it was suggested that a make-up man had left grease on the bottom step, or . . ."

"That's ridiculous," said Biddy. "Of course nobody was negligent. I mean, we all saw what happened. He just ran onto the platform and stumbled and went over the edge onto the line. His knee must have given out. He'd obviously twisted it when Fiametta pushed him down the stairs."

"Biddy," I said severely, "I beg you never to make a remark like that again, even in the privacy of this room. Bob's quarrel with Fiametta, and her deliberate action in pushing him downstairs, are the only possible grounds which the insurance company could cite for refusing to pay our claim."

Sam looked at me with a certain amount of respect. "So that was why . . ."

"Yes," I said. "That was why I suggested that you talk to the unit before the doctors and the police arrived, and ask them not to talk about the squabble. Frankly, the avoidance of unpleasant publicity had very little to do with it. I suppose the story will leak out eventually, but if we can keep it quiet until after the inquest at least . . ."

"They're a good bunch," said Sam. "I don't think they'll talk."

"Mind you," I said, "I don't want to give the impression that we're suppressing facts in order to press a fraudulent claim. My own view is that the insurance company would have to pay anyhow. But they would be sure to raise the matter, and that would lead to dreary and unproductive wrangling. You do see what I mean?"

"Perfectly, Pudge," said Biddy. She looked straight at me as though she did not like me very much. I suppose she was annoyed at not being the center of the conversation for once in a way.

"All four of us," I said, "will probably have to give evidence at the inquest. I suggest we simply say that Bob stumbled on the steps—which is perfectly true—lost his balance, and over shot the platform. Are we agreed?"

After that, the discussion took on a more practical and distinctly more cheerful tone. We weighed up the merits and possible availability of other actors who might take on Robert Meakin's part. We replanned our schedule so as to waste the minimum amount of time. We drank coffee and ate sandwiches and became absorbed in the future, which is the best possible cure for depression. Even the incident of ejecting the nimble but bronchitic reporter from the balcony, which happened soon after midnight, became almost amusing. We parted at half-past one in a comparatively cheerful mood.

The very next day, however, we were meeting again in a blacker atmosphere. London was seething with rumors, and it had taken very little time for them to find their way back to us. In bars, restaurants, dressing rooms, and film studios, wherever the theatrical profession congregates, the whispers were growing louder every minute.

"My dear, haven't you *heard?* Well, I got it from Madge who heard from Harry who's a *great* friend of Keith Pardoe. I promised I'd say nothing, so don't tell a soul, but there's no doubt *at all* that Bob Meakin killed himself. Why? Fiametta Fettini, of course. Everyone knows he was madly in love with her, no matter how much he denied it."

"But of *course* it was suicide. Peter dined last night with Olive, who knows Fiametta Fettini's stand-in, who was actually *there*. And she says that he simply *flung* himself under the train—yes, my dear, *literally*—of course, they're trying to hush it up."

"Suicide? Oh, undoubtedly. But nothing to do with La Fettini. The truth—keep it to yourself, dear boy—is that he was dying. Yes, cancer, I'm afraid. I do know what I'm talking about, as a matter of fact, dear boy. His doctor happens to be a friend of Sidney's mother's doctor and . . ."

"Yes, no doubt at all, I'm afraid. You'll treat this as confidential, won't you? You see, he was in danger of *serious trouble*. Yes, the police. No, no, I wouldn't like to be specific—

de mortuis, you know—but one can hazard a guess. . . ."

It was that afternoon that the press discovered Fiametta's hide-out. I shall never be able to prove my suspicions about that, but the fact remains that several enterprising reporters got in, and the evening papers carried a headlined story of an alleged interview with Fiametta, in the course of which she pointed out at some length that she and Bob had been devoted to each other, but that their love was doomed owing to her religious scruples concerning divorce, coupled with Bob's high moral principles. She did not, I was gratified to see, claim any high moral principles for herself; in view of her notorious past, she could hardly have done so. She added that she was smiling bravely through her tears, and that the show must go on. She afterward denied to me having said any such thing, and it is really irrelevant whether or not she did. The fact remains that the article appeared and fanned the flames of the suicide rumor. And suicide, I knew, was not covered by our insurance policy.

So the Board of Northburn Films met again, and we decided that, in order to quash any suspicion of suicide, we would admit at the inquest that Bob had had a fall earlier in the day, which had undoubtedly affected his leg. We would not mention what caused him to fall. I also dispatched our resident dragon, Louise Cohen, to sit on La Fettini's head in the country until the inquest was safely over. I announced to the press that Miss Fettini was suffering from exhaustion and a bad cold. The cold was fictitious, but with Louise around the house, I felt sure that the exhaustion would be genuine, and the thought pleased me.

We were, I suppose, very lucky. The inquest went like clockwork. Various people were called to give evidence of Bob's happy disposition and successful career. Sam and I described the accident, supported by Fred Harborough and Margery Phipps. The driver of the train told the story from his point of view.

"He sort of stumbled, sir, and come right over the edge of the platform. I jammed on my emergency brakes, but it was too late."

Keith related, in a voice tense with emotion, how he had come out of Fiametta Fettini's dressing room and onto the platform just in time to see the accident; how he had shouted at Bob, but to no avail. "He was running so fast," he said, several times. "There was nothing he could do, you see, he was running so fast."

The surprise witness at the inquest was Bob's widow, whom nobody had seen before. The press had, indeed, unearthed the fact that he had been married at Caxton Hall some fifteen years previously to a lady named Sonia Marchmont. This was about a year before his appearance in *The Square Peg*, the film which had rocketed him to sudden success. We were all puzzled because at the epoch of *The Square Peg* there had been no Mrs. Meakin in evidence—nor had there been since. Bob was frequently referred to as "the screen's most eligible bachelor," and he had never repudiated that title. His name was constantly being linked with those of various glittering young actresses and socialites, and there was much speculation, some of it vicious, as to why he had never married. Now we knew.

Mrs. Meakin, having resisted all efforts of the press to discover her whereabouts during the past few days, appeared out of the blue at the inquest. She must have married very young, for she looked no more than thirty; she was blonde and demure and very appealing in a simple black dress; and, in an almost inaudible whisper, she told the coroner a strange story.

She and Bob, she said, had been a devoted couple for the past fifteen years. When he had achieved meteoric success as the young "lone wolf" of *The Square Peg*, it had been mutually agreed by Bob, his then agent—who had since died—and herself that his appeal to his fans would be greatly lessened if it were known that he had a wife. So she had been installed in a small cottage in the country, where Bob spent all the time that he could. Sometimes, she said, she came to London. She had a key to his house in Mount Street. Recently, she added, they had sold the cottage and bought a country house near Haywards Heath, so as to be nearer to London, and Bob spent as much time as he could there. The village knew them as Mr. and Mrs. Marchmont. When the coroner expressed surprise that Bob had not been recognized by his neighbors, Mrs. Meakin looked embarrassed and whispered that he dressed so differently in the country and wore heavy spectacles as a disguise. I understood at once, of course, what she meant. Remove the toupee, the discreetly applied grease paint, the lifts in the heels of the shoes, the—let us be honest—the corsets, and few people would have recognized Robert Meakin. As I discovered afterward, it was, in fact, something of a routine joke in the village that twenty years ago Mr. Marchmont must have looked very like Robert Meakin. I hope that it never got to Bob's ears when he was alive, because it would have upset him greatly.

In any case, Mrs. Meakin's appearance and her evidence suited us very well. Firstly, it confirmed that Bob had no possible reason to commit suicide; and secondly, it set the hounds of the press off after a new hare. The coroner, an elderly and impressionable man, was obviously much taken by Mrs. Meakin. He expressed the court's deepest sympathy at her terrible loss; he exonerated Northburn Films from any hint of negligence; he even recalled the doctor to the witness stand to make him confirm that Bob had not been suffering from any illness or disability at the time of his death. I was watching with great care and interest the reactions of the lawyer retained on a watching brief by our insurance company, and I was delighted to see him grow steadily glummer. It took the jury only five minutes to come back with a verdict of accidental death.

As soon as the proceedings were over, the pack of reporters converged as a man on to the focal point of Mrs. Meakin, and we were able to escape more-or-less unscathed. I was surprised, I must say, when in the course of the next few days I realized what a willing quarry Bob's widow had been. I dare say you read "What Life with Bob Meant to Me," by Sonia Meakin in the *Sunday Siren,* and the open letter which she wrote to Fiametta Fettini in the *Daily Smudge* under the title "I Have No Hard Feelings, My Dear . . . ," not to mention the ghosted autobiography which was serialized in the *Evening Scoop.* The strange thing was that Mrs. Meakin had no need to sell her soul for money. Bob died intestate—like so many actors he had never bothered to make a will—consequently, as his widow, she inherited everything. Everything included the life insurance policy which we had taken out for him, a little matter of forty thousand pounds. Even if Bob had left only debts otherwise, there would surely have been enough to see her through. I could only presume that, after so many years of deliberately shunning the limelight, Sonia Meakin found some sort of perverse pleasure in being the center of attraction. In any case, it was none of my business. My main feeling toward her was one of gratitude for diverting the attentions of Fleet Street away from Northburn Films for the time being.

My next step was to press our claim against the insurance company and get it settled, and although I was not looking forward to the job, there was a certain compensation in the flattering way that Sam, Biddy, and Keith behaved toward me at that time. I was regarded as the savior of Northburn Films, and I could do no wrong. Nevertheless, not having such boundless faith in my own abilities as was evinced by my fellow Board members, I took the precaution of consulting a good lawyer before proceeding with the claim. He gave it as his opinion that we had a cast-iron case, and undertook to handle it on our behalf. I left everything in his hands. I was only worried about one thing.

The following morning, I drove down to Buckinghamshire. It was a perfect summer day—it would have to be, since we were not shooting. One of the occupational hazards of film-making is that one tends to regard the weather as good or bad solely in relation to whether or not it serves the film's immediate purposes. I remember once spending a whole cloudless, sunny day in Richmond Park, paying two stars and a crowd of extras for doing absolutely nothing because Fred Harborough refused to shoot until there were some clouds in the sky. That is the sort of thing that drives Executive Producers into early graves.

Anyhow, this was a perfect summer's day, and I made good time to the village of Medham. It was midday as I drove up the narrow main street, and The Red Lion looked inviting. I dared not go in, however, for I knew it would be full of reporters, and I had no desire to be recognized. I kept straight on through the village, took the first left and first right, according to my instructions, and began to look for a driveway on the left marked "Meadow Croft."

I need not have bothered. Around the next bend in the lane, I had to jab at my brakes to avoid running down a crowd of people, both male and female, whom I had no difficulty identifying as reporters, and who were clustered in the middle of the road, oblivious to any traffic. I stopped the car, got out, and went to see what had caused the excitement.

In the center of the group stood Fiametta Fettini. She was barefoot, and wearing a floating black negligée made of some diaphanous material, and in her arms she was clutching a small, obscene-looking monkey with a naked pink behind. She was cooing to it and feeding it with bananas, as the flash bulbs exploded and the cameras clicked.

"Yais, I am ill, it is true," she was saying as I came up. "But not from a cold, like they say. From a broken heart. Yes, print it—a broken heart! My doctor say I must not leave my bed, and if my darling Peppi had not escaped into the road, I would never . . ."

The reporters were scribbling and shouting questions. "Miss Fettini, have you read Mrs. Meakin's open letter? What's your comment? Will you carry on with the film? Who is to be the new leading man?"

"I 'ave read that woman's letter," said Fiametta, with flashing eyes, "and my comment is that she can go and . . ."

I decided it was time to break up the meeting. I pushed my way through the crowd and said, angrily, "Fiametta! What on earth are you doing here?"

"Poo-ooge!" In her surprise, Fiametta dropped the monkey, which scampered off into the crowd and leapt on to the back of a particularly unpleasant journalist, the gossip man from the *Smudge*. Under cover of this diversion, I grabbed Fiametta's arm and said in an undertone, "Go in at once."

"But Poo-ooge . . ."

"At once," I said. She did not move, so I took her arm again, and very firmly. "Gentlemen," I said to the reporters, "and ladies, of course. Miss Fettini is, as you know, very unwell. I am afraid she cannot stay talking to you any longer."

"We were promised an interview," piped an indignant female voice from the crowd.

"Promised? By whom?" I looked sharply at Fiametta, but she shrugged elaborately and turned away.

There was a moment of silence, and then a laugh, and somebody said, "Short memory, Mr. Croombe-Peters, haven't you?"

"What are you talking about?"

"You telephoned The Red Lion half an hour ago, dear chap," said the man from the *Smudge*, "and promised us an interview and pictures. If you've changed your mind, you only have to say so."

This was so unexpected and outrageous that I let go of Fiametta and, I am afraid, gaped in sheer astonishment. By the time I had found the words to deny making any such telephone call, Fiametta had slipped away and run into the house, and the crowd of newshounds was dispersing. They had enough for a good story anyway. The last to go was the *Smudge* man.

"I dare say you'll want this," he said, thrusting something live and wriggling into my arms. "Good-bye for the moment, Mr. Croombe-Peters."

I found myself standing in the lane alone, with the repellent Peppi chewing a button off my shirt front. Furious, I followed Fiametta into the house.

She was standing by the window in the drawing room, looking out at the hollyhocks as though they were personal enemies and tapping her left foot dangerously; but I was too angry to be intimidated.

"Now, young lady," I said, "what is all this?" There was no reply. "Where is Louise?"

"Shopping."

"Where is Giulio?"

"In bed."

"In bed? Why?"

"Funnily enough, he has a cold. I expect he caught it from me."

"Who telephoned The Red Lion and staged this ridiculous publicity act?"

Fiametta shrugged again. Peppi, having detached the button, spat it out and began to demolish my tie. I tried to put him onto the floor, but he appeared to have developed a passion for my society, and merely clung to me with both arms, making plaintive noises. I realized that the wearing of a pink-bottomed monkey as a sort of feather boa did nothing to help my dignity, but that could not be helped. I rapped the question out again. "Who made that telephone call?"

A voice behind me said, "I did."

I wheeled around, causing Peppi's back legs to swing out in a centrifugal arc, which he enjoyed immensely. Standing in the doorway of the drawing room was Keith Pardoe.

I tried as best I could to remain calm and keep a grip on the situation. I wanted to make some crushing and memorable remark, but the best I could think of was: "Are you out of your mind?" To which he replied, "No," in a most reasonable tone.

"But . . . what the hell do you think you're . . . ?"

"Fiametta, darling," said Keith, "would you trot upstairs like a good girl and take that terrible monkey with you? I want a word with Pudge."

"O.K.," said Fiametta. I had never seen her so docile. "I take a drink to my poor little Giulio, no?"

"You know best," said Keith, "but I wouldn't, myself."

"It is good for his cold," said Fiametta with an air of finality, and left the room, leaving a disturbing aura of scent behind her. She did not take the monkey, which was now jumping up and down in my arms, chattering and begging to be swung again.

"Can't you stop playing with that animal?" Keith asked.

"Since you ask," I said, "no. It has taken a fancy to me and it is extremely adhesive."

"Oh, well then, keep it if you want to."

"I do not want to," I pointed out. "It is merely that . . ."

"Look," said Keith, "there are serious things I want to say to you, and you will keep on talking about monkeys."

"I am not talking about monkeys," I said with some heat. "It is you who . . ."

"Sit down," said Keith abruptly.

I did so. I was aware that the initiative had effectually passed out of my hands and into his, and I blamed the wretched Peppi. I made an attempt to recapture my lost momentum. "I am waiting for you to explain your extraordinary behavior," I said.

"Yes." There was a long silence. Keith studied the tip of his glowing cigarette. I wondered if he were ever going to speak again. I said nothing. At last Keith said, "I wonder if I can ever make you understand. Nobody was more upset than I about Bob's death. I think you'll agree to that." I made no comment. He went on. "A week ago, when Bob died, it seemed as though everything had come to an end. Now it is apparent that Northburn Films and *Street Scene* will continue, unless you succeed in bungling matters with the insurance company."

This seemed to me to be a pretty ungracious way of acknowledging my foresight and hard work, but again I said nothing.

"That being so," continued Keith, "we have to keep going, from all points of view. Heaven knows who we shall be able to get to replace Bob. It's far too short notice for any of the big names. Sam and Biddy and I have decided that we shall have to launch a new, unknown actor, which is a very risky thing to do. So, we are left with Fiametta as our sole asset, publicity-wise, and if we want to sell this picture, we've got to exploit her instead of locking her up down here with Louise as though she had the plague."

"You know perfectly well," I said, "that until the insurance claim is settled we have to be most careful . . ."

"My dear fellow," said Keith, "Fiametta's line is a hopeless love for Bob. She's the last person in the world who's going to tell the press that she pushed him downstairs. Sonia Meakin's story and the inquest verdict have finally killed the suicide rumors, I hope. What we have to do now is to cash in, and to keep ourselves and the picture in the public eye until we can get going again."

"You have still not explained how you came to use my name on the telephone."

Keith laughed. "My dear Pudge, I couldn't use mine. The Art Director does not organize publicity stunts."

"Exactly," I said with triumph. "And nor, in this case, does the Executive Producer."

"It was a very good stunt," said Keith. He sounded like a small boy, sulking. "Fiametta ill—the monkey escapes—she pursues it in her nightgown—leaves her sickbed to help her dumb chum . . ."

"It's repellent," I said, "and you know it. I thought you were supposed to be dedicated to art for art's sake."

"This isn't art," said Keith patiently. "This is publicity."

"Well, I'll thank you to leave me out of it in future."

"Oh, Pudge, Pudge," said Keith. "How can you be so wrong

all the time about everything?"

"I do not propose," I said, "to stay here just for the pleasure of being insulted."

"No," said Keith, "you're quite right. I should leave at once, if I were you. And you might take Louise with you."

"Why?"

"She wants a lift to London."

"She is supposed to be looking after Fiametta."

"We shall all," said Keith calmly, "be returning to London tomorrow. Life goes on, you know."

"Then you can bring Louise yourself," I said, and walked out, slamming the door behind me.

It was only when I had covered about fifteen miles in the car that I remembered that I had not carried out the original object of my mission to Medham. But since I heard the following day that the insurance company, on the advice of their lawyers, had agreed in principle to pay our claim in full, I was in no mood to bother. As Keith had said, life went on.

4

Life went on, and so did *Street Scene*. I suppose it sounds heartless, but I cannot deny that poor Bob's death did make all the difference to the film. Of course, the exact amount of insurance compensation was still being worked out by an expert accountant, but the bank made no difficulty about advances. A great weight seemed to be lifted from the unit. Typically, just because we were no longer fighting a financial rear-guard action, our luck seemed to turn and everything ran our way.

Keith had been quite right—there was no hope of replacing Bob with a well-known actor at such short notice, so we tried to make a virtue of necessity by running a public competition and auditioning anybody and everybody for the part. *"Your chance to star opposite Fiametta Fettini"* made an attractive slogan; and we had thousands of entrants, each accompanied by a recent photograph, details of experience (if any), and biographical details (to be written in the applicant's own handwriting). In point of fact, of course, we already had in mind a couple of likely actors—small-part players whose names were as yet unknown to the public. We had arranged to show the "finals" on television, and it was agreed that the short list would consist of two genuine amateurs plus our professional nominees. If neither amateur proved outstandingly good, we would then give the part to whichever of the professional actors seemed most suitable; and we would have the comfort of knowing that his name and his face were already widely known to millions of viewers and newspaper readers.

I am not suggesting for a moment that the competition was a pure publicity stunt. We had arranged to include the actors simply because you cannot be certain of getting anybody suitable out of a purely haphazard contest of that sort. Biddy, Sam, Keith, and myself were the judges, of course, and our decision was final; but we promised to give weight to the volume of applause which each contestant drew from the studio audience. It was perfectly open and above board, and there was every chance for a member of the public to win.

We started off by rejecting more than eighty percent of the entrants on their photographs and written applications alone. Some were obviously over sixty and others under twenty—we had laid down twenty-eight to forty-five as the age limits. Some were illiterate and some were hideous and some were much too beautiful and wrote in mauve ink on scented writing paper. Having whittled the possibles down to fifty, we started interviewing candidates at our London offices.

It was a depressing business. We had previously decided to limit actual screen tests to ten, but it was difficult enough to find even that number of remotely suitable applicants. Eventually, however, we dredged up ten names and arranged for studio tests. Among the ten were a couple of men whom I thought myself might be useful material—one of them a real-life university professor who looked too suave and elegant for the part but who spoke beautifully and easily and was as urbane and cultivated a man as I have met; and the other, a slow-spoken countryman from Dorset, whose appearance had just the right sort of genuine, English appeal, and who was certainly by nature as gauche and clumsy as Biddy could ever have envisaged Professor Masterman as being. I considered that if Sam could coax a spark of acting fire out of this rather dead wood, we might have a winner.

I was wrong. When it came to the point, the university don dried up completely in front of the camera and began giggling like a schoolboy. The beautifully modulated voice came out as a sort of frenzied squeak, and the lean, sensitive hands seemed to swell to twice life size and hang like bunches of bananas in the foreground. We did not even have to bother to tell the professor that we would let him know. He bolted from the studios like a scared rabbit, more shaken, I imagine, than he had ever been in his life. I was amused to read, not long afterward, a brilliant but spiteful letter which he wrote to the editor of *The Times,* protesting against the salaries paid to actors, and describing the theater as a profession "which requires neither learning nor discipline, training nor application, rightly described as the province of the mountebank."

By contrast, our slow, solid countryman turned out to be a king of melodrama. It was impossible either to stop or to control him. As a parody of a Victorian ham actor, his performance might have been a sensation in a revival of *Maria of the Red Barn;* for us, it was hopeless. Of the other eight candidates, only one was tolerable, a young sanitary engineer from Manchester, who had the right look of slightly worried abstraction and who, although no actor, was at least amenable to taking direction and capable of understanding what Sam said to him.

When it was all over, we had a glum little conference. We had promised the television people four finalists for their program. Two were our "seeded" actors. The sanitary engineer would do, in a pinch, for the third. But we simply dared not let any of our other hopefuls loose in front of an audience of several million viewers.

"We'll have to get another actor," said Sam.

"We can't," said Keith. "We've promised two genuine amateurs, and we've got to provide them somehow. Otherwise it looks like a put-up job."

I appealed to Biddy. "You wrote the beastly character," I said. "Didn't you perhaps base him on somebody you knew or had met? Couldn't you . . . ?"

Biddy laughed. "If you really want to know," she said, "I based Masterman on . . ." Her voice trailed off. She sat for a moment, considering, her small head tilted on one side like a bird's. Then she said slowly, "I don't see why he shouldn't bloody well do it."

"Why who shouldn't do what?" I asked. None of these people ever said what they meant straight out.

"Keith," said Biddy.

"Keith?"

For a moment we didn't grasp what she meant. She went on in a rush. "I had Keith in my mind all the time I was writing Masterman. I saw him as Keith—tall and lean and a bit stooping and shambling—not a bit like Bob Meakin. Bob Meakin was never right. He was too good-looking and too intense; when he tried to be vague, he simply gave the impression of sulking. Keith's the original Masterman as far as I'm concerned and, after all, he's not an actor; he's an artist, so he'd do perfectly well for the TV show, and he couldn't be worse than what we saw today, now could he? And think of the publicity gimmick we could make of that one!"

There was a pause, while we all thought it over.

At last, Sam said, "Well, Keith? Will you do it?"

"I think you're crazy," said Keith. He had gone very pale. "I can't act."

"It doesn't matter, darling," said Biddy. "It's only for the TV show. It's all arranged that Edward Myers should play the part anyway, isn't it, Pudge?"

"Nothing is arranged," I said. "It depends on the outcome of . . ."

"Oh stuff it," said Biddy. "You know very well what I mean. Will you do it, Keith?"

"Yes," said Keith. He swallowed hard. "If you want me to, I will."

What happened is, of course, a matter of history; but I welcome this opportunity of going on record to state once and for all that the outcome of our contest was *not* pre-arranged. That is to say, even though a certain result might have been—shall we say—expected by the company, the actual winner took us all by surprise. Keith had not even bothered to do a runthrough with Sam, apart from the lighting rehearsals at the television studios, where he walked the part, making the required movements and repeating his lines like a parrot. The most that I personally hoped for was that he would get through somehow without disaster.

On the program itself one of the professional actors came first, put up a creditable show, and got a fairly generous round of applause from the studio audience. He was followed by the sanitary engineer, who did as well as could be expected. He was obviously not a serious contender for the part, but I thought that the audience was a little mean; his amateur status, I felt, warranted a bigger hand. Third on the bill was Edward Myers, and he was good—authorative, polished, a sound professional performance which drew prolonged applause. At the judges' table, we pretended to be busy making notes, but the thing was a foregone conclusion. And then Keith came on.

In describing his performance I can only say that he *was* Professor Masterman. Before he opened his mouth the character was established—the walk that was almost a run, head thrust forward; the nervous gesture with the unlit pipe, a didactic movement trailing into indecision; the spectacles removed in order to study things more closely—these and a score of other tiny factors etched the man with blinding vividness. The voice matched—diffident, but with the diffidence that is born of a conviction of superior knowledge; vague with the vagueness of a man who sees all sides of a question, who dares not be precise because he appreciates the hugeness of the problem; and suddenly, at moments, splendid and strong. The audience went mad. Sam and Biddy and I exchanged worried looks, and then I pushed a piece of paper over to Sam on which I had written: "We can't let him win. What the hell are we going to do?"

Sam turned the paper over, scribbled on the back, and

pushed it back to me. He had written: "We can't let him lose."
I had no choice but to concur. I showed it to Biddy and she
nodded. Meanwhile, the producer of the program was having
difficulty with the audience. Not all the notices in the world
marked "Finish Applause" would keep them quiet. Against
the background of their fervor, the camera swung toward the
judges' table, and concentrated on Sam.

"Ladies and gentlemen," said Sam, very North Country,
"you haven't half put us in a spot." Delighted laughter and
more applause from the studio audience. "As you know, Keith
Pardoe is a colleague of ours who only stepped in at the last
moment because one of our finalists fell ill. We at this table
can't judge Keith; we know him too well. It's obvious that the
audience here liked him, but maybe they're all his friends and
relations." More laughter. "So I'm going to ask all of you
viewers who saw this program to send us *your* choice, on a
postcard, please. Just send it to me, Sam Potman, at Ash Grove
Studios. I think I'm right in saying that this will be the first
time that a star has been made *by the public;* whoever you
choose, it'll be *you* who put him up there in the limelight, and
it will be your support that keeps him there." And so on—all
good strong stuff.

The result of the ballot was overwhelming. More than eighty
percent of the thousands of postcards were votes for Keith. So
we found our new leading man, and Keith Pardoe, the Art
Director, became Keith Pardoe, the film star.

It was by the grace of God that our television program
proved such a success, because we had been deprived, at the
last moment, of the co-operation of Fiametta Fettini, who was
to have been its principal attraction.

The day after my visit to Medham, Giulio Palladio turned
up, unannounced, in my office. He looked not unlike the
wretched Peppi, with his melancholy monkey face and his
shiny black hair and the dark rings of dissipation under his
mournful eyes. I was annoyed to see him, for I could imagine
no reason for his visit except that he was seeking a lunchtime
drinking partner and I was very busy. As I have said, he
figured officially on our budget as Fiametta's manager, but
that was purely a courtesy title. I had never known him do
a stroke of work or interest himself in the film in any way.

Fiametta's English agent ran the business side of her affairs, and everything else she ran herself.

"I'm sorry, Giulio," I said, "not today. I'm busy."

"Pooge," said Giulio, looking like Peppi deprived ot a banana, "it is on business that I am come."

I did not even register the sense of that remark. I was engaged in reading over the typescript of a letter I had dictated, and I merely said, "I'm busy now and shall be all day."

There was a long silence. When I had finished checking through all my letters, and signed them, I looked up and saw with surprise that Palladio was still there. He was sitting absolutely still, never taking his big liquid eyes off me, saying nothing, obedient, passive, but utterly immovable. Suddenly, he infuriated me.

"Why are you still here?" I said angrily. "What do you want?"

"You can see me now?" he asked hopefully. "Business finished?"

"I can see you perfectly," I replied with some irony. "What I cannot do is go out and drink with you."

"You can hear me?" he asked tentatively. His English was not good.

"Of course, I can."

"Then I tell you. Fiametta go back to Rome tomorrow."

"She can't," I said. "Out of the question. She is due to appear in our television program. If she thinks she can take a holiday just . . ."

"This is not holiday."

"Not a holiday? Then what is it?"

"Is work. Cinecitta Studios in Rome."

"No. She is under contract to us. She has no right ιo accept other work."

"Is a contract from before," said Palladio. He smiled ingratiatingly, as if hoping to soften my heart.

"An earlier contract? She never told us about it. What does it involve? How much work?"

"Four weeks," said Palladio blandly.

At that I exploded. "Wait there," I said. "I'll see about this." I reached for my telephone and dialed the number of Fiametta's London agent. "She's trying to pull a fast one, and if she thinks she can bamboozle me by sending you here with a story of . . . Hello? Mr. Travers, please. Mr. Croombe-Peters. Yes. Hello, Dick? Croombe-Peters here. Never mind about how I am. What's all this about Fiametta Fettini having to go back to Rome to do four weeks' work at Cinecitta? You haven't? That's what I thought. Yes, by all means ask her. I shall be interested to hear what she says. Thanks old man. 'Bye."

I put down the receiver. "Well," I said to Palladio. "Mr. Travers has never heard of this mysterious contract and neither have I. So you may go home and tell Fiametta that she is being paid to stay in England, and in England she will stay. And that is all there is to it."

Palladio left, looking like a whipped monkey, and I went back to my work, feeling pleased with myself. I was considerably shaken, therefore, when I received a telephone call from Dick Travers in the afternoon, confirming that there was, indeed, a contract requiring La Fettini's presence in Rome.

"She never told me about it, old man," he said. He was obviously acutely embarrassed. "Of course, I suppose she imagined all her work here would be over long ago. No, I'm not sure what it is. Probably one of these Italian epics with every big star doing a cameo part. Yes, yes, I know it'll inconvenience you—I couldn't be more sorry, but I don't see what we can do—yes, quite watertight, I'm afraid—of course, she'll be completely at your disposal when she comes back—I do appreciate that you could fight it in a court of law, but then you'd only antagonize her, and you know what she's like. . . ."

We were at Fiametta's mercy, and she knew it. I personally never believed in the contract from beginning to end; she wanted to go to Rome for private reasons, and since she was our big star and we had already got a considerable amount of footage of her scenes in the can, she was in a position to dictate. I had to bow to the inevitable. The television program took place without her, and I rearranged the schedule so as to start our re-shooting with scenes which did not require Fiametta.

As it turned out, everything went very smoothly. Since we were now well into the summer, I had arranged to shoot the location scenes first, and leave the studio sequences until later on. For once in a way, the weather was ideal, and reel after reel of film was sealed safely away into the cans.

The weather, however, was only one of our reasons for rejoicing. Even more important was the spirit of vitality and enthusiasm which infused the whole unit. I think we had all harbored an unspoken fear that Keith's performance on television might have been just a flash in the pan. In fact, he got better and better. I have never seen a team working in closer harmony than that which existed between Keith, Sam, and Biddy during those few weeks. At last they were realizing to the full the dream which had been born that night in The Can; they were making a film which was truly theirs, with no outside factors to distract them. Biddy's script suddenly seemed to grow flexible, adapting itself to the vagaries of Sam's mood. Sam's direction became subtler; his analysis of character more meaningful; and his use of symbolism more controlled. Instead of having to hack an approximation of his vision out of the intractable material which was Robert Meakin, he was molding Keith's performance out of a living, responsive medium.

If you feel that that last paragraph does not sound like me, you are right. I was, in fact, quoting from the article which Ralph Tweeting, of the high-brow magazine *Artform*, wrote about Sam after spending some days on the set. I would not have put it quite like that, myself. As far as I was concerned, everyone seemed relaxed and happy, and work went ahead well. We kept up to schedule and within our budget for the first time, and the whole unit worked with a will.

As for Keith, he was thoroughly enjoying himself. I hope I do not sound spiteful when I say that he reveled in the personal publicity which his new role brought with it. I suppose it was only natural that he should. In any case, the three of them were entirely happy. At last all outsiders had been eliminated from the charmed circle—except for myself, of course. And they were prepared, in their exaltation, to tolerate me.

If I say that our troubles started again with Fiametta's return, I do not mean to imply that she was responsible for everything that happened subsequently. She merely triggered off the first of a series of misfortunes.

On the actual day of her return, we had no inkling of this. She came back in an apparently radiant mood, bringing her personal circus with her and attracting the usual bevy of journalists to the airport. We encouraged this publicity by sending Keith out to meet the plane, and several newspapers carried photographs of them embracing warmly. My only quarrel with Fiametta was that she had allowed her skin to get deeply suntanned in Italy, and I had some satisfaction in pointing out to her, when I welcomed her at the airport, that in consequence the make-up experts would have to be at her house by half-past six in the morning, in order to paint on her London pallor before the day's shooting began.

Even this, however, did not damp her high spirits and good temper, as she swept off with Keith in the Rolls-Royce which we had hired to take the two of them into town. She seemed to have forgotten poor Bob completely. In fact, sometimes I found it hard to believe that he had ever existed. Like a footprint blown from desert sand, he had passed into utter oblivion. Even the press had lost interest in him. Keith was the new star, the new story. At that time, none of us ever mentioned Bob, nor indeed, as far as I know, thought about him; and yet we should have remembered him constantly, and with gratitude. For by his death he had unwittingly made possible what promised to be a great film.

I have said that we had no premonition of trouble as we stood in the sun that day at the airport welcoming Fiametta back; and yet, I think, we ought to have foreseen something of the trials that lay ahead. It should have been obvious that emotions would run high when we were faced with re-shooting the scenes in the Underground station. We told each other laughingly that it was ridiculous to be superstitious, and I went ahead and arranged to hire the derelict station and the train once more. We were scheduled to begin shooting there the very day after Fiametta's return from Rome.

5

The call was for eight o'clock at the Underground station, but I was determined to be there well ahead of time, to make sure that everything went smoothly. It was a Friday morning, fine and sunny, and I found it no hardship to be up and about by seven. In fact, I walked across the park to Piccadilly before I hailed a cab to take me to my destination. By half-past seven, I was clattering my way down the motionless escalator, out of the balmy summer morning into the dusty subterranean cavern.

I was not, of course, the first to arrive. The electricians were already there, trundling their heavy arc lamps into position, and the Second Assistant Director was having some sort of discussion with the Property Man. I noted without surprise that there was no sign of Gervase Mountjoy. Admittedly, the call was for eight o'clock, but any decent First Assistant would have taken the trouble to be there sooner. Once again, I found myself faced with the job of assuming Gervase's responsibilities. I went up to the Second Assistant, a fresh-faced youth named Harry.

"Mr. Mountjoy not here yet?" I asked. One had to be sure.

"Haven't seen him, Mr. Peters."

"Well, . . ." I glanced at the Property Man, "what's up? A spot of bother?"

Neither of them answered me for a moment. They looked at each other shiftily, as though they were in some sort of an alliance against me, although I had distinctly heard them arguing as I came down the stairs. It annoyed me. "Well, come on, out with it," I said.

"It's the name card," said the Property Man at last. "It's a painters' job. I don't see as I can do it."

"What name card?"

"You can at least take the old one down, Props," said Harry. He had gone rather pink.

"It's not strictly speakin' my job," repeated Props, stubbornly but unhappily. "I'd like to help, but I don't want no trouble."

"What name card? Where?" I demanded.

Before either of them could answer, a new voice said, "Mr. Croombe-Peters," and I looked up to see that Margery Phipps, the Continuity Girl, had come onto the platform. She looked —I don't know just the right word—agitated and upset and at the same time curiously excited, the sort of anticipatory excitement that you see on the faces of spectators just before a heavyweight fight or a horror film. "Mr. Croombe-Peters," she said again, "can I speak to you for a moment?"

"Very well," I said. Margery was, as a rule, a most imperturbable person. If she was worked up about something, it must be important.

"This way," she said.

I followed her off the platform and into the corridor at the far end, and instantly I saw why she was upset, and I understood what Harry and Props had been arguing about.

It was Gervase Mountjoy's responsibility, of course, but I think I have made it fairly clear that he showed up extremely badly on the occasion of Bob's death. I suppose he cannot be blamed for fainting as he did, but on his recovery he had simply crawled, green-faced, into a taxi and disappeared, leaving the rest of us to do the necessary, if unpleasant, clearing up. As a result, nothing had been properly organized. I myself had supervised the loading of the lamps and electrical equipment into lorries, and Props had coped with his usual efficiency in the disposal of all the movable articles which were his responsibility. But in the general confusion, we had all overlooked the matter of dismantling the two plywood-and-canvas dressing rooms; and there they still stood, grimy relics of disaster. Worse, they still bore their boldly painted signs: "Fiametta Fettini" and "Robert Meakin."

Margery said, "Look, Mr. Croombe-Peters. Isn't it awful We must get them out of the way before . . ."

"We shall need the dressing rooms," I said, "but they must be spruced up and given new name plates. What are they like inside?"

"Horrible," said Margery. "Full of—well, go and take a look."

I pushed my way in through the canvas flap that served for a door to Bob Meakin's dressing room and looked around me. As I did so, it struck me that Margery had used exactly the right word. What I saw was horrible in the truest sense, the horror of ordinary, everyday objects charged with an unbearable load of emotion.

Bob's dresser had, of course, removed his employer's personal clothes, and the Wardrobe Master had collected the few items of studio-owned costume which Bob was not wearing at the time of his death; but nobody had touched the little, unimportant things. On the trestle table under the big mirror were enough poignant reminders of Meakin to send either Fiametta or Keith into hysterics if they should see them.

There was a half full bottle of whisky and a glass; there was an empty packet of a very expensive brand of cigarettes which Bob always smoked; there was a big pot of cold cream for removing make-up, and a lot of cotton wool, some of it unused, and some smudged with grease paint. There were the horn-rimmed spectacles, with one of their plain glass lenses miraculously unbroken, which Bob had been wearing when he died, and which I remembered having removed myself from his shattered body. A paperback detective novel, with the ironic title *Death Gives No Warning,* was lying open and face downward on the table, beside a small, empty leather box, whose black velvet lining was slashed into two deep slits, presumably to hold cuff links. In a plain cardboard box were disquieting reminders of Bob's battle against the encroachments of time: a tube of a most discreetly tinted foundation lotion, widely recommended to ladies for "smoothing away those wrinkles as if by magic" and a little bottle of the special spirit-gum preparation which I knew was used to keep a toupee firmly in position. In the center of the table, immediately underneath the mirror, there was a pad of cheap scribbling paper and a ballpoint pen of the kind that can be bought for a few pence. I am not by nature an inquisitive person, I hope, and so I cannot really explain what it was that made me lift the cover of the writing pad. The top sheet had been torn off, leaving a little ragged edge; but the sheet below bore the imprint of writing as clear and decipherable as if it had been in ink. Bob's writing had been bold and flamboyant, and the ballpoint had pressed hard onto the yielding surface below. My mind registered the first words. "Dear Sam, Nobody enjoys breaking a contract, but . . ."

"Fiametta's room is just as bad," said Margery's voice behind me. "Full of old lipsticks and things. We must get them cleared up or there'll be hell to pay."

"Yes," I said. "You're quite right, Margery. I'm very glad you called me."

"I simply had to," she said. "I mean, a scene would be too awful, wouldn't it?"

"It would indeed," I said. We looked at each other and smiled.

It occurs to me that I have not said very much about Margery Phipps so far, which is an undeserved omission. The trouble with living among tempestuous characters, or writing about them, is that the most admirable people tend to get pushed into the background; and so it has been with Margery. She was a pretty girl, but you didn't realize it straight away. She had none of Fiametta's obvious sex appeal or Biddy's eccentric brilliance. Her brown hair was always neat, but never dressed with fashionable extravagance. She wore just the right shade of light red lipstick and a little powder, but no other make-up. She dressed plainly but becomingly, usually in a crisply clean white shirt and a dark skirt. She always reminded me of the recruiting poster's ideal of a member of the women's services—and when I say that, I mean it as a very great compliment. She also possessed the efficiency without bossiness that should characterize a good officer.

Of course, if she had not been efficient, she would never have made a Continuity Girl. I thought suddenly of the job she had on hand that very day. Three months ago, in what seemed like another world, we had taken the shots of Fiametta leaving the little restaurant which had been built on Stage 2 at Ash Grove Studios. In the film we would cut straight from there to her arrival at the Underground station. Of course, she would wear the same costume, the same accessories; but it was for Margery to say exactly how the scarf had been knotted, the precise position of the brooch, in which hand she had carried her handbag, whether or not she wore a ring, the angle of the rose in her hair. Certainly, Margery had her Continuity Sheets to help her—her own summaries which she noted down in shorthand, shot by shot, and then typed in a multitude of copies to be distributed to various departments. The Continuity Sheets were the Bible of the film, but they could not tell you the angle of a rose. It occurred to me that the degree of observational power developed in a Continuity Girl would put most professional detectives to shame. And with that thought came a question—had Margery noticed the writing on the pad?

"Shall I clear up in here?" Margery asked.

"Let's take a look at Fiametta's room first," I said. I stepped aside to let her go first through the canvas-curtained door. As she went, I quickly picked up the little notepad and slipped it into my pocket. I didn't feel that Robert Meakin's executors were going to worry very much about a sixpenny jotting book.

Fiametta's room was, as Margery had said, in much the same state as Bob's. Her maid had cleared away everything usable, but the litter remained—old lipsticks, crumpled face tissues, an ash tray with lipstick-smudged butts still in it.

"All this must be swept up and tidied," I said. "The things in Bob's dressing room had better go to his widow, I suppose. One can't be too careful over things like that. Fiametta's nasty bits and pieces, she can have back. Can you cope here while I go and fix this business of the name signs?"

Margery nodded. "Certainly, Mr. Croombe-Peters," she said.

"Thank you, Margery. I'm really very grateful." I hesitated, and then, on impulse, I added, "If you're not busy today, perhaps we might lunch together." As soon as I had said the words, I regretted them, and cursed myself for a fool. Nobody knew better than I that discipline was impossible to maintain once senior executives started fraternizing with lower grades of technicians—and heaven knew, I had enough trouble that way with Sam. Well, I was stuck with today's date, I reflected grimly, but it would be the last.

Margery gave me a cool, serious look. It was almost as though she could read my thoughts and was lightly amused by them. I felt myself growing pink. Then she said, "It's very kind of you, Mr. Croombe-Peters, but I never go out to lunch. I always have so many Continuity Sheets to get typed, I'd never finish if I took a lunch break. I've brought sandwiches."

I didn't know, and I still don't, whether this was a simple statement of truth, or whether Margery was being supremely tactful. I only know that I was profoundly grateful, and that my liking and respect for the girl went up by several notches. She gave me a charming smile and began packing up Fiametta's disgusting litter. I went out on to the platform and into battle with the Property Man.

There was a certain amount of discussion, of course, but the situation was saved by one of the painters arriving early. In no time at all, the old name cards were safely out of the way and new ones of a different color put up. Margery made a most efficient job of tidying and cleaning the dressing rooms; when she had finished, she handed me packed up the sad little relics from Bob Meakin's room and the sordid bits from Fiametta's room, packed up neatly in a cardboard box. If she noticed the absence of the writing pad, she did not remark on it.

It was as well that we took prompt action, for Keith Pardoe arrived a good ten minutes early. For someone as constitutionally unpunctual as Keith, this was remarkable, and a fair indication of his state of mind. There was no doubt about it, Keith was in a wrought-up and near-hysterical mood.

He came running down the stairs in a parody of lightheartedness which deceived nobody. "God, what a marvelous morning," he cried. "Hello, Pudge! Here already? I've been up since six. Walked all the way. 'Morning, Harry. How are you? All set for the fray?"

We were all acutely embarrassed. The forced heartiness and brittle bonhomie were a million miles from Keith's usual slow, sardonic style. It brought back all too vividly the awkwardness and humiliation of Keith's breakdown at the time of the accident, and made it very clear to everybody that he had by no means recovered from that emotional strain.

There was an agonizing silence. At last, I said, "You're

early." A ridiculous remark, but the only one I could think of.

"I told you, I've been up since five—six—what does it matter? How's the schedule, Pudge? Still going well?"

"We're still two days ahead, as we were yesterday," I replied. I was beginning to get a little irritated. Keith, like everybody else, knew perfectly well that we had achieved the miracle of running two days in advance of our planned schedule. "We weren't supposed to be here till next Tuesday. I had quite a job changing the booking."

That was a mistake, of course. Keith picked it up at once. "Really?" he said. "London Transport are running excursions to the scene of the accident, are they? See the Tower of London, Buckingham Palace, and the spot where Bob Meakin was killed—all for sixpence on the Red Rover." His voice was rising dangerously. "I'm surprised the crowds aren't out today. What's happened before can happen again, after all. The greatest popular show since the last public execution."

It was only then that I realized, for the first time, that Keith Pardoe was not merely affected by emotional memories. He was frightened. It was hard to believe, but in some extraordinary and superstitious way he seemed to think that there was a real possibility of history repeating itself, this time with himself as the victim of the accident. It was so childish that I actually laughed.

"Don't be ridiculous," I said. "Today won't be an easy day for any of us, but for God's sake don't get morbid."

"No," he said, suddenly serious. "No, of course you're right, Pudge. That's your trouble. You always are. That's why nobody can stand you."

This was more like Keith's usual self. I was so relieved at his change of mood that I overlooked the insult, and smiled. "Where's Biddy?" I asked.

"She's," Keith hesitated, "she's not coming today. She had some rewriting to do on next week's stuff—the Hampstead Heath sequence."

So Biddy Brennan was not as tough as she liked to make out. For the past three weeks she hadn't missed a day's shooting, and if there was rewriting to be done, she had either scribbled in her battered notebook then and there, on the set, or had taken it home and presumably sat up all night working. There was only one explanation of why she was absent today, and while I didn't exactly blame her—I was not looking forward to the day myself—nevertheless I felt that she might have supported Keith by coming along. In any case, it showed that our iron butterfly had an Achilles heel, if I may mix my metaphors.

"Well, I suppose I'd better . . ." Keith hesitated. The nervousness seemed to be coming back. "Have we—I mean, are there the same dressing rooms . . . ?"

"Not the same," I said, quickly, "but in the same place. Yours is all ready. I'll show you."

"Thank you, Pudge," said Keith.

He followed me docilely down the platform and into his canvas booth. Inside, he looked around quickly, and I was devoutly thankful that Margery had made such a good job of cleaning up. The place looked like new.

"Good," said Keith. "Very nice. Good." He sat down on the plain wooden chair and regarded himself earnestly in the mirror. At that moment, a diversion was caused by the arrival of the Wardrobe Master with the clothes which Keith was to wear that day. I escaped thankfully, hoping but not really believing that the worst was over.

Sam was the next person to arrive. He came clattering cheerfully down the stairs at five minutes to eight, closely followed by Fred Harborough, the cameraman, and a giggling gang of girls from the make-up and hairdressing departments. Gervase Mountjoy arrived at two minutes past eight, thus contriving in his usual maddening way to be late, yet not late enough to constitute the basis of a serious complaint. The extras, stand-ins, and George Temple had all arrived by ten past. The place buzzed and hummed with work and chatter. Nobody mentioned Bob.

I was glad to notice that Sam appeared to be quite unaffected by morbid imagination. He came straight up to me and began arguing that I hadn't budgeted enough for extras in the Hampstead Heath sequence.

"I've got to have half-a-dozen pearly kings and queens, Pudge," he said, "and they come expensive. Be a good chap and unbelt a bit. After all, we're two days ahead."

This was Sam in his charming, persuasive mood. I noticed, however, that he never lost an opportunity of rubbing in those two days ahead, as though they were a rich gift from the director to the producer, a gift which ought to put me under a permanent obligation to him. Certainly it was a fine achievement and I did not want to belittle it, but I found that I frequently had to point out that the two main causes of our present happy position were generous scheduling and good weather, and that at any moment we might find our luck turning and be faced with the prospect of being two days behind schedule.

I put this to Sam now. "These two days certainly give us a reserve in hand," I said in conclusion, "but it's a reserve I have worked very hard to build up."

"Nothing to do with you," remarked Sam under his breath.

I ignored him. "Having built up my reserve," I went on, "the whole purpose is to keep it—quite literally—against a rainy day, not to squander it on unnecessary extravagances."

"I'm the one who says what's necessary and what isn't around here," said Sam, truculently.

I have—as I hope I have made clear—a great admiration for Sam's talents; but unfortunately, like all men of his class, he has never learnt how to conduct an argument without being rude.

"I'm prepared to go back to the office and study the matter," I said, "but I must warn you that I think it's highly unlikely that I will be able to increase . . ."

"You'll bloody well do what I tell you," said Sam.

"If you intend to take that attitude, there is little point in discussing the matter," I said. I felt tired, and I was sickened that the old arguments were beginning to develop again, just as before. For the last few weeks everything had been so pleasant. This seemed like a foretaste of fresh disaster.

Sam looked sharply at me, and suddenly put his hand on my arm. "Sorry, Pudge," he said. "That was unreasonable. Just bear it in mind, will you, though? We'll talk about it later."

That's what I mean about Sam. However outrageous he may be, it's impossible to go on disliking him for very long. Whether a sudden switch of mood like this was a genuinely friendly impulse or a shrewdly calculated move, I could never decide. But it was certainly disarming.

"I am absolutely prepared to . . . ," I began, but I was cut short by the arrival of Fiametta Fettini.

As soon as I heard the commotion on the stairs, I feared the worst, and I was right. Without any sort of authorization that I knew of, Fiametta had brought a gaggle of press and photographers along with her, and she was playing the scene for all it was worth. Amid a pyrotechnic display of flash bulbs, she stood poised at the head of the staircase, swathed in black chiffon. Then, with a richly histrionic gesture, she cried, "I cannot! *Mamma mia,* I cannot go down there!" and covered her face with her hands in what appeared to be a fit of uncontrollable weeping.

Sam was up the stairs in an instant. "What's all this?" he said, and I could tell from his voice that he was very angry.

"I cannot go down to that 'orrible place," sobbed Fiametta, removing her hands from her face to give the photographers a chance. "The 'orrible place where . . ."

"Gervase!" Sam called.

Gervase unwound himself from a canvas chair and went up the steps.

"Miss Fettini is rather upset," Sam went on drily. "Please take her to her dressing room."

There was a howl of protest from the assembled journalists, but Sam took no notice. "At once," he said sharply. "Go and lie down, Fiametta dear, and you'll feel better."

Fiametta shot him a look of intense dislike out of her black eyes—eyes which, I noticed, were completely dry; but there was nothing she could do but allow Gervase to lead her away in a fresh spasm of grief.

Then Sam turned to the journalists. "I'm sorry, ladies and gentlemen," he said blandly, "you see how it is. Miss Fettini is in no state to talk to you, and the rest of us have work to do. So perhaps you wouldn't mind going away."

And with that, he turned on his heel and went downstairs, leaving the members of the press to face Harry and his minions, who arrived at that moment with several large signs saying "No Admittance." One or two of the more enterprising journalists made feeble attempts to come down onto the platform, but they were outnumbered, and Fiametta was in purdah. Grumbling, they drifted away, and I went to find Sam and congratulate him.

I did not have far to look. As I came onto the platform, he emerged from the corridor where the dressing rooms were and hailed me. "Come here a moment, Pudge, will you?" he called. He looked angry and very grim. I joined him at the end of the platform.

"God, these bloody women," he said. "You'd better come and see if you can do anything with her. She's like a hellcat."

"Me?" I said alarmed. Generally, I avoided these scenes, and I could not imagine that I could be of any practical use.

"She's wild about being done out of her publicity stunt," said Sam, "and so she's latched on to some business about a lipstick case, just to make trouble. If anyone knows about it, you do. You cleared up here after—after last time, didn't you?"

Before I could answer or protest, he had propelled me firmly inside the dressing room.

The atmosphere in the little canvas booth was charged with dangerous electricity. Fiametta sat at the trestle table, looking like an avenging goddess of death. She was fully made up, for the make-up experts had been at her house since six; and her pale face, deep red lips, and heavily blackened eyes added to the dramatic effect. She was breathing heavily through her shapely nose and drumming her long carmine fingernails on the table. In a corner, little Giulio Palladio sat hunched up, looking more like a frightened monkey than ever. Gervase Mountjoy was draped spinelessly against the wall, smoking and looking bored. An elderly maid and a young hairdresser were both in tears.

As I came in, Fiametta swiveled on her chair, ostentatiously turning her back on me. To the mirror she remarked, "I can endure many things, but to be robbed—no. That I do not stand."

"What do you mean, robbed?" I said. I was determined to make an effort not to be intimidated.

She wheeled on me, her black hair flying like Medusa's snake locks.

"Solid gold, with rubies!" she screamed. "Stolen! Stolen by you treacherous, dishonest English! And don't speak to me of insurance," she added, in a low growl, although I had not attempted to speak to her of anything. "How can insurance replace it when *he* gave it to me? Is it not enough to humiliate me before the newspapers, but that you must steal my most precious possession as well?"

"Fiametta is trying to say," said Sam's sardonic voice behind me, "that she left a solid gold lipstick case in her dressing room on the last occasion that she was here. It was given to her by Bob Meakin and was such a precious possession that she has only just noticed she's lost it. Her maid must have overlooked it when she was packing up, and Fiametta thinks one of us has stolen it."

"Think! I know it! You all hate me, you all wish to destroy me! You cut my best lines and give me the worst camera angles. . . ."

We were off again. I had heard too many of these outbursts to attempt to check the flow until it had exhausted the worst of its venom. I stood quietly, waiting for the frenzy to die down, and looking forward with pleasant anticipation to the scene which must follow; for I had noticed what I took to be a gilt lipstick case studded with chips of red glass among the debris which Margery had cleared up that morning.

When we had all been accused of sabotaging her career, of brutality and heartlessness, and every crime in the calendar, Fiametta finally ran out of breath. In the silence, I said quietly, "Gervase, I wonder if you would ask Margery Phipps if she can spare us a moment?"

"Margery?" said Sam, surprised. "What has Margery . . . ?"

I raised my hand. "Please," I said, "just ask her to come along, and to bring the cardboard box with her. She'll know what you mean."

Everyone was looking thoroughly puzzled by now, and even Fiametta seemed at a loss for words. Gervase gave me a quizzical sort of look, and sloped off through the canvas doorway. I lit a cigarette. I was enjoying myself. Nobody said anything. A minute or so later Gervase came back with Margery. She was carrying the box containing the bits and pieces from the dressing rooms, and she looked positively scared, poor girl, and no wonder. I smiled at her reassuringly.

"Ah, Margery," I said. "May I see that box please?"

"Of course, Mr. Croombe-Peters." Margery spoke in little

more than a whisper. She held the box out to me.

I opened it, took out the lipstick case, and handed it to Fiametta. "Miss Fettini," I said, "do you recognize this?"

Fiametta barely glanced at it. She was simmering with fury. "Yes," she said. "It is my lipstick case. Where did you get it?"

"Margery," I said, "will you tell Miss Fettini where you found this and the other things in the box?"

"Of course." Margery was obviously relieved that there was no question of my blaming her for anything. She caught my eye and grinned. "These are the things which I found in these two dressing rooms when I cleared them up before the unit assembled this morning."

To my amazement, Fiametta wheeled on Margery with such venom that I thought she was going to attack her physically. "Thief!" she screamed. "How dare you! How dare you touch my things! Give me that box!" She snatched the box out of Margery's hands, slammed it down onto the dressing table, and stood there with her back to it and her hands outstretched, like an animal at bay defending her young. I had seldom seen a more ridiculous or unnecessary performance.

"So," Fiametta went on, "if I had not had the good sense to make inquiries and protect my property, this cheap little sneak thief would have got away not only with my lipstick, but God knows how many other valuable things as well!"

Margery, who had not unnaturally looked quite stunned under the first impact of Fiametta's fury, had by now recovered herself, and was beginning to look pretty angry. "Mr. Croombe-Peters," she said, "will you explain . . . ?"

Indeed, I had been about to remonstrate with Fiametta, but before I could say a word, La Fettini had launched a new line of attack, this time directed at me.

"And you're no better than she is," she went on, in a low growl that gave the impression of grinding teeth. "This morning? You mean to tell me that my valuable things were left lying about here until this morning? It's for you to safeguard our property, no? Let me tell you, I wouldn't trust you further than I could throw you. Any of you!"

"Miss Fettini," Margery began.

Fiametta turned to meet the fresh attack. "Get out of my room!" she shouted. "Dirty cheating little thief! Get out before I call the police!"

Margery went very white, but she behaved with great dignity. For a moment I was afraid that she was going to descend to a slanging match with Fiametta, which would almost certainly have ended in violence of the most degrading kind. However, the dangerous moment passed. Margery gave Fiametta a look that would have withered anybody less arrogant or more sensitive, and walked quietly out of the dressing room. Fiametta had paused to draw breath, and I took the opportunity of intervening firmly.

"Miss Fettini," I said, "that was a completely unwarranted attack on someone of the greatest integrity. It is utterly unfounded, as are your accusations of carelessness on my part." I would dearly have liked to take the opportunity of pointing out that the responsibility lay with Gervase, but I decided that, at such a moment, the unit should present a united front. "The responsibility for clearing the rooms," I went on, "lay with your maid and Mr. Meakin's dresser. Understandably, both were upset and may not have been as thorough as they should. Your maid must have overlooked the lipstick case because she did not realize its value; you will find nothing else in that box except worthless bits and pieces. Your property was never in any danger, because since we were last here, this station has been securely padlocked by the London Transport Authority. Margery's action in clearing up this morning was no more than a generous impulse to make things neat and pleasant for you. If you had not made this ridiculous fuss, you would have had your property back before now. In the circumstances, I trust you will withdraw your implications and accusations against the company and its employees."

I thought, I must say, that I had put the matter rather neatly, and I could not see how Fiametta could avoid climbing down and apologizing. The maddening thing about women of her type, however, is their utter lack of logic. As soon as she realized that she was beaten—which happened about halfway through my little speech—she simply lost interest in the subject and stopped listening to me. Before I had finished speaking, she was already sitting down with her back to me with the box on her knees, deeply engaged in going through its contents, murmuring to herself as she did so. "Ah, my eyebrow pencil, and my little roll of cotton wool—and here's that pretty pink nail polish, I wondered where that was . . ."

There was a sort of mesmeric quality about her sudden obsession with these trifles. We all stood around in silence, watching her, so absorbed that nobody noticed Keith coming in. It gave us all a start when he suddenly said, "What on earth are you doing, Fiametta?" in the same brittle voice that we had heard earlier that morning.

Fiametta looked up and held the box out to him with a ravishing smile. Her good humor seemed miraculously restored. "Look, Keith," she cooed, "all my little treasures, the kind Poodge has brought back to me. All the little things I left in here and had thought lost. But no, all are here."

To listen to her, you would think butter wouldn't melt in her mouth.

Keith was apparently not impressed. "I thought I heard you raising hell," he said, shortly.

Fiametta shrugged. "There was a little thing I thought I had lost." She turned to Keith and gave him that dazzling, toothy smile which is renowned from Rome to San Francisco. "But now I have found it, which means that all day we shall be lucky. You will see. Everything I lost is here, so everything will go right. I know it."

"Well, thank God for that," said Keith, in his normal voice. He sounded tired, but the strain had gone.

Like a sigh, the tension relaxed. After a moment of silence, everyone started talking, quietly. Sam kissed Fiametta on both cheeks, and said, "Be ready in half an hour, luv." He had evidently decided to take advantage of her present sunny mood, and not to refer to the unpleasant episode again. Gervase ambled out, calling for Harry. Keith and Sam strolled out together, discussing the motivation for the next shot. Fiametta, singing softly to herself, had already begun to remove her clothes in order to change into her costume for the day's shooting. I escaped thankfully from the overperfumed atmosphere of the dressing room and out onto the bleak platform.

As soon as I could, I went in search of Margery. I found her sitting at her typewriter, self-consciously isolated, and working with angry fervor. The fact that everybody else now seemed in good spirits had naturally done nothing but aggravate her sense of grievance.

"I'm sorry, Margery," I began lamely.

She looked up sharply, with unfriendly eyes. "Please don't mention it," she said icily. "Perhaps sooner or later somebody will take the trouble to explain to me what it was all about."

"Miss Fettini," I said, "thought she had lost her gold-and-ruby lipstick case . . ."

"Gold and ruby?"

"Yes. The one I handed to her out of the box."

Margery laughed shortly. "That's nonsense," she said.

"I agree, she was utterly unreasonable," I said, "but when one thinks that something valuable may have been stolen . . ."

"Mr. Croombe-Peters," said Margery, "I know something about jewels. My father was an expert. I can tell you categorically that that lipstick case was made of cheap gilt with a few chips of red glass set into it."

"Then why?" I began, and then stopped. If Fiametta chose to put a great sentimental value on some trifle simply because Bob Meakin had given it to her, it was hardly fitting for me to discuss the matter with a junior member of the unit. The important thing was that Margery had been accused of dishonesty, and deserved an apology.

"Why, indeed?" echoed Margery, in a strange, cool voice.

And before I could say anything more, she got up from the typewriter and walked away from me. I was about to follow her, when Harry came up and told me that I was wanted on the telephone. This turned out to be a call from the office, demanding my presence urgently for discussion with the auditors who were dealing with our insurance claim. I am afraid that this drove all other matters out of my head for the time being, and in fact the financial discussions went on all day.

I had arranged to spend the weekend at my father's place in Gloucestershire, and I drove straight there from the office that Friday evening. I had every intention, however, of contacting Margery first thing on Monday morning and putting matters right with her. I was not to know then that this would be impossible; for on Monday, Margery Phipps was no longer with us.

6

I found Margery's letter of resignation waiting on my desk when I arrived at my office on Monday morning. It was short and to the point. She regretted, she wrote in her large, looped script, that for personal reasons it was impossible for her to continue her work with Northburn Films, and that consequently she would not be reporting for duty today or any subsequent day; she enclosed, in cash, two weeks' salary in lieu of notice, and trusted that this would be agreeable to us. We would find all the Continuity Sheets typed up to date and filed in the Production Office; she did not think that her successor would have any difficulty in taking over the work. She was sorry that she had to take this step, as she had enjoyed working on *Street Scene,* but she feared that she had no alternative. She wished us luck with the film, and remained ours sincerely.

I read the letter twice, cursed Fiametta Fettini aloud, and told Sylvia, my secretary, to get me Margery's flat on the telephone. I was surprised and disappointed that such a sensible and level-headed girl as Margery Phipps should have taken Fiametta's rudeness so much to heart—for there was no other possible explanation for the "personal reasons." Bitterly, I regretted that I had not found time to talk to her and soothe her ruffled feelings, as I had intended. However, there was nothing to be gained by brooding over that now. All I could do was to try, belatedly, to remedy the situation by tactful handling.

The phone rang, and I picked it up to hear Sylvia's voice

saying, "Is that you, Margery?"

"Yes." The voice at the other end sounded sharp and edgy. If I had not known it was Margery, I wouldn't have recognized it.

"Mr. Croombe-Peters for you," said Sylvia. "Hold on. I'm putting him through."

"Hello, Margery," I said warmly. "Pudge here." It went horribly against the grain to use my nickname to an employee, but I realized that it was just the sort of small thing which might make all the difference. "Now look here, my dear," I went on, "I've read your letter and I'm really distressed by it. I don't know what your reasons are, but I can make a good guess, and if I'm right in thinking that they have something to do with that ridiculous scene on Friday, I want you to know that I was and am entirely on your side. It was a disgraceful display of bad temper and discourtesy, and if you'll reconsider your decision, I'm prepared to insist that Miss Fettini apologizes to you." My heart sank at the prospect of implementing this rash promise, but I simply could not afford to lose Margery.

There was no reply from the other end of the line, so I went on. "I'm sure that you're far too good a trouper to desert the ship at a moment like this." My metaphors were becoming tangled, but that couldn't be helped. "You're a key member of the unit, you know, and if you feel that perhaps we haven't appreciated you to the full, I can tell you now that I had already made plans to increase your salary, in view of the extra work you've had with all the retakes." This was, of course, quite untrue, but I hoped that I made it sound plausible. "Now, what I suggest is that you meet me for lunch at the Orangery, and we talk the whole thing over. What do you say to that?"

Margery's answer was short and eloquent. Without saying a word, she gently but firmly replaced her receiver, leaving me talking to myself, to the accompaniment of the dial tone. When I tried to call her back, the line was persistently engaged; and Sylvia, having reported the fact to the telephone exchange, came back a few minutes later with the information that the instrument had been left off its hook. It was abundantly clear that Margery Phipps was not prepared to speak to Northburn Films.

The next thing that happened, of course, was an urgent call from Sam. The unit had assembled at the Underground station; they were almost ready to begin shooting; and where was Margery, in God's name? When I told him what had happened, Sam grew deadly quiet, which I recognized as a more ominous sign than a healthy outburst of bad temper.

"I see," he said, in that flat voice of his in which fury was indistinguishable from ironic amusement. "My Continuity Girl has decided, at no notice at all, to leave for 'personal reasons.' My leading man is already half an hour late, which is perhaps a blessing under the circumstances. My leading lady is having hysterics because her pet monkey has caught a chill, my script writer has failed to deliver the alterations which were promised for this morning, and my lighting cameraman informs me that my next shot is technically impossible. All I needed to make my day complete was the news that you have undoubtedly bitched things up with Margery to such an extent that . . ."

"I resent that, Sam," I said. "I told you; I did my best. If you like, I'll go around and see her . . ."

"For God's sake," said Sam, "don't do that. You've done enough harm already. Give me her telephone number and I'll talk to her myself."

"That won't do you any good. I tell you, she hung up on me."

"So would any sensible person," said Sam, with what I thought was unpardonable rudeness. "I'll handle her, even if I have to go around there myself. Whatever you do, keep out of this. Don't attempt to contact her; leave it to me. What you can do is to get on to the studios and the union and have them send us somebody temporary, and the faster the better. We're bound to lose at least half a day's shooting, as it is."

"Perhaps you appreciate now," I said, "how fortunate you are to be two days ahead of schedule." I knew that Sam was having a trying time, but he had been gratuitously insulting to me, and I was determined to get a little of my own back. "It gives you just the leeway you need to cope with an emergency like this. If I had listened to you and allowed you to . . ."

"Oh, go to hell. Give me Margery's phone number and address, and get off the line," said Sam. And then, in a different tone, "I'm sorry, Pudge. I know it's not your fault. You'll have to bear with me. It's just that . . ."

I don't know what he would have said next, because his voice grew suddenly faint, as he obviously turned away from the telephone to speak to somebody at his side. I heard him say, "Oh, has he? Does he? Oh, my God. Very well. Tell him I'll be along in a moment." Then, into the phone, he said, "Keith has arrived at last. There's some sort of bother. Let's have that number, there's a good chap."

Time after time I had been fooled by Sam's sudden and disarming switches from rudeness to affability. Now, suddenly, I saw his famous charm for what it was—blatant, self-interested insincerity. Sam knew that he could push me so far and no farther, and each time as the red light showed danger, he would retreat and palm me off with a dab of flattery and good humor. At that moment I despised Sam Potman, genius or no genius; and I don't mind confessing that at the same time I felt a thrill of pleasure at the realization that, ultimately, he was in my power, even if that power was vested in my father's money.

"The number is Flaxman 08741 and the address is 716 Chelsea Mansions," I said coldly. "I will arrange for a temporary Continuity Girl. Good-bye."

I put down the receiver, being careful not to bang it. I wished to give an impression of dignity rather than bad temper. It was, I reflected with satisfaction, the first time that I had ever hung up on Sam.

I made no further attempt to get in touch with Margery, nor did I go near the location that day. I stayed in my office in what I hoped was a marked manner.

Whether or not Sam ever succeeded in contacting Margery, and what passed between them, I never knew. Frankly, after Sam's remarks, I washed my hands of the whole affair. At all events, Margery did not reappear, and from the fact that Sam was careful not to mention the matter again, I surmised, not without satisfaction, that he had, in fact, either telephoned or called on her and had been snubbed as flatly as I had been. The temporary Continuity Girl—a plain but bright little person named Diana—was quickly and tacitly accepted as permanent; and considering the immense difficulty of taking over the job in the middle of shooting, she managed very efficiently. The tempo of work went back to normal, and we were all glad when, two days later, the shooting in the Underground was completed and we were able to move up into the fresh air of Hampstead Heath. But once again I am going too fast.

The day after Margery's walk out, I put in an hour at the office, and then took a cab to the Underground station location, where I arrived at about quarter past ten. The first thing that hit me—and I mean hit—was the change in Fiametta's attitude toward me. Having parted from her on the worst possible terms after the episode of the lipstick case, I was amazed and not altogether pleased to be greeted with an effusiveness which was even more embarrassing than her earlier hostility.

Now, I don't wish to imply that, in normal circumstances, I would have been averse to one of the most beautiful women in Europe flinging her arms around my neck, kissing me on both cheeks, and dragging me off to her dressing room. Taken by itself, Fiametta's enthusiasm for my company was extremely pleasant; but taken in conjunction with other factors, it was distinctly disturbing. Perhaps I should explain a little more clearly what I mean.

In their efforts to build up film-making in the public imagination as a glamorous and exciting profession, the publicity experts have always taken great pains to play down the fact that the overwhelming sensation experienced by everyone—except perhaps the director—during the actual shooting of a film is dreary, frustrating, and seemingly endless boredom. Day after day, hour after hour, nothing whatsoever appears to be happening on the set. This is an illusion, of course; one man, or a small group of people, will always be working quietly and industriously among the electrical equipment or on rearranging the set or on painting a notice or working out a lighting plan. But while the few work, the majority wait. And wait. And wait.

These deserts of inertia, stretching yawningly between brief intervals of intense activity and emotional strain, make a dangerous breeding ground for the formation of cliques, for the fostering of petty politics, for the germination of spite and suspicion, and above all for the dissemination of gossip. Apart from the director himself, whose personality is bound to infect the whole unit, the man who can and should prevent an unhealthy and unpleasant atmosphere from forming on the set is the First Assistant Director, for he is in direct contact with everybody, from the stars to the humblest carpenters and plasterers, and the studio floor or location is his particular domain. In our case, I think I have made it clear that Gervase Mountjoy was about as much use as a sick headache as far as this—or, for that matter, any other—aspect of his job was concerned.

The very fact that Sam, Keith, and Biddy formed such an integrated group was in itself dangerous. Previously, Fiametta had identified herself—albeit somewhat tempestuously—with Robert Meakin. Patterns of friendship and suspicion, alliances and squabbles, had shifted kaleidoscopically among the key people on the set, that is to say, Fiametta, Bob, Sam, Keith, Biddy, and, to a lesser degree, myself. Now, Fiametta had returned from Rome to find herself very definitely the odd man out, excluded from the warm free-masonry of the hierarchy, and she was not only angry but, I suspected, genuinely hurt. So, inevitably, she cast around for an ally; and, equally inevitably, she picked on me. At least, that was my impression.

At all events she greeted me that morning with quite unnecessary effusion and bore me off to her dressing room. Fred Harborough was busy with a complicated lighting set-up that might take an hour or more to complete, leaving everyone else to the familiar occupation of waiting. I noticed that Sam, Keith, and Biddy were in a huddle at the far end of the platform, talking earnestly. Gervase, who should have been keeping Fiametta amused, was playing poker with George Temple and Fiametta's stand-in. Fiametta's hairdresser was flirting with the Property man; and Diana, the new Continuity Girl, was discussing plastic values in modern Italian films with the camera operator. It was no wonder that La Fettini felt neglected.

As soon as she got me inside her dressing room, Fiametta launched herself into a tirade against Margery Phipps, proclaiming the greatest possible horror at Margery's behavior and the greatest possible sympathy for me. What a dreadful girl! What disloyalty and ingratitude! Fiametta's heart bled for me and for the troubles I had to contend with. The fact that she herself was responsible for the greater part of these troubles had apparently not occurred to her. I made noncommittal noises. It was true that I had been angry and upset at Margery's behavior, but I could still sympathize with the girl over the humiliation she had suffered at Fiametta's hands. Fiametta appeared to sense a certain coldness in my manner and shifted her line of approach.

Her second gambit was to try to enlist my sympathy for Peppi, the monkey, who had apparently caught a bad chill and was languishing on the danger list in Fiametta's suite at the Belgrave Towers Hotel, ministered to by Giulio and the maids. The fact that the creature was being visited twice a day by London's most eminent veterinary surgeon was no consolation, I gathered, since two great Harley Street specialists, whom Fiametta had endeavored to consult, had politely but firmly declined to spend their time and talents treating a monkey. Growing tearful, she pointed out that she had offered them more money than most human beings could afford to pay for their services. It was, she maintained, monstrous and cruel of them to refuse.

If Fiametta was hoping to touch a responsive chord in me, she could hardly have chosen a more unfortunate subject. The memory of the visit to Medham was still green, and my own view was that a world which no longer contained the repellent Peppi would be a cleaner and sweeter place. However, I did my best to be polite.

"I hope he'll be better soon," I said with an effort. After all, Fiametta was our star, our only remaining one, as Keith had so pertinently pointed out at Medham. Incidentally, I had noticed, not without amusement, that this point of view no longer preoccupied Keith. Now that he himself had taken over the role of co-star, he was as vociferous as any of us in condemning Fiametta's less dignified attempts to attract publicity. Quite simply, Keith was hogging every scrap of notoriety for himself, and did not welcome competition. However, all this is beside the point. As I have said, I was doing my best to be polite.

"If Peppi dies," announced Fiametta, in a fine flush of melodrama, "it will be entirely Giulio's fault!"

"Giulio?"

"I told him this morning—'Murderer!' I said. 'That poor little creature's blood will be on your conscience for the rest of your life!' "

"But what had Giulio to do with it?" I said, although frankly I couldn't have cared less.

"What? Well may you ask, what! Taking the poor baby onto the balcony after midnight with that cold wind blowing! Giulio, of all people—Giulio, the great expert!"

"Expert? You mean Giulio is a vet?"

"Vet—what is this, please?"

"A doctor for animals," I explained.

Fiametta laughed shortly. "Not for animals," she said, "oh, no. Evidently he is not clever enough for that. Not animals, only people."

This was news to me. It had never occurred to me that Giulio had any function in life except to travel around the world at his wife's heels, providing employment for barmen wherever he went and drawing a salary from her employers.

"I had no idea that Giulio was a doctor," I said. It was not an enthralling subject of conversation, but anything was better than discussing Peppi's temperature.

"No longer. You don't imagine that Giulio would work when he can live from my earnings, do you?" said Fiametta spitefully. "Oh, yes, he has a fine life. Is it Giulio who has to be up at six o'clock for make-up? Is it Giulio who slaves at the studios all day? Is it Giulio who makes himself ill with emotion to give a great performance?"

I considered several replies to these rhetorical questions, and rejected them all. The last thing I wanted was to find myself in the middle if there were going to be a domestic upheaval in the Fettini household. As a matter of fact, it had occurred to me more than once to wonder why Fiametta bothered to drag poor little Palladio around the world on her apron strings, but I certainly had no intention of asking her. I said nothing, and Fiametta seemed to lose interest in the subject.

"Pah, Giulio!" she said. "He is not worth talking about. Tell me, Poodge—what of my costume for the ball scene? You don't make me wear that terrible blue thing, no? It should be white tulle or chiffon with sables. I have explain to Sam."

It seemed to me that Fiametta was going out of her way to pick awkward topics. The battle of the ball dress had been going on ever since Fiametta's return. Sam and Keith, on the one hand, were immovable objects. Fiametta, on the other, was doing her best to be an irresistible force. As usual, I was caught in the middle. I did my best.

"What you call the 'ball scene' is a Saturday night hop in a Palais de Danse in Bermondsey, Fiametta," I said, patiently. We'd been into it all a hundred times before. "We've got to have a little realism. The girls who go to that sort of affair just don't wear white chiffon and sables."

Fiametta snorted. "Realism! Realism! That's all you can say. Me, I am sick and tired to realism. You know what it mean? It mean that I must look ugly all the time!"

"My dear Fiametta, you could never look ugly," I began, in an attempt at gallantry, but she swept on regardless.

"Never do I complain! Never once! With all these hideous dresses, I never complain. But one scene there is when I may look pretty. What is a ball scene but for the star to look pretty? You think my fans will like to see me in that bit of blue sacking? You will see. I can sell a picture in two minutes in white chiffon and sables!"

I was aware of mixed emotions. The idea of white chiffon and sables was clearly ridiculous, but nevertheless I could not but concede that Fiametta had a point. All through the film, Sam and Keith had insisted that Fiametta's clothes should be ruthlessly shabby—no glamorous rags or artfully cut sackcloth, but genuinely cheap, tawdry, and ill-fitting garments. The dance scene was the one moment in the film when it might have been legitimate to allow her to wear something attractive, and to cheat a little—as most film-makers do—in providing her with a dress which would be, strictly speaking, out of the financial reach of the character she was portraying. But Sam was adamant, and he and Keith between them had evolved a really repellent little number in blue taffeta, of which they were inordinately proud—"Isn't it marvelous, Pudge? It's so *ghastly*." I could understand Fiametta's point of view in wishing for at least one costume which would show off the famous

Fettini curves to advantage; and I had a shrewd suspicion that she was right about her ability to sell a film to the public on the strength of her looks alone.

"I agree that the blue is unnecessarily ugly," I said. "I'll speak to Sam about it."

"You will speak to Sam! I have spoke to Sam! Everybody speak to Sam! What's the use? Sam, he is a monster. Sam do not care what happen to my reputation. . . ."

We were off again. By this time, I had grown fairly accustomed to these tirades of Fiametta's, and I had even developed a technique of composing my features into an expression of kindly sympathy, and then allowing my mind to wander to quite different topics, while the tide of indignant oratory rolled harmlessly over my head. But that was a technique which I used when there were several of us present—Fiametta did not usually waste her breath unless there was enough of an audience to make it worth while. As the sole recipient of a blast of Fettini temperament, it was harder to close one's ears.

Consequently, I was heartily thankful when, just as Fiametta paused to take breath for the first time, her dresser came in and said, "Excuse me, Mr. Croombe-Peters. You're wanted."

"Go away, Hilda," said Fiametta. "Mr. Croombe-Peters is busy. He is talking to me."

"Excuse me, Miss Fettini," said Hilda firmly. She was a stout, gray-haired woman who had had thirty years' experience of spoilt young actresses; she sometimes reminded me of a wardress in a women's prison. "Mr. Croombe-Peters is wanted. Important."

"What is it, Hilda?" I asked.

Hilda did not reply, and I was surprised to see that she looked embarrassed. I had not thought it possible. "If you'd just step outside, Mr. Croombe-Peters," she said.

"Sorry, Fiametta," I said. "I'll see you later."

Fiametta shot me one of her famous looks—the sort that can blister paint at a hundred yards—and turned her back ostentatiously. As I followed Hilda out into the passage, I was uneasily aware that we would have trouble with La Fettini for the rest of the day. Once outside, Hilda said to me in an urgent whisper, "I'm sorry, Mr. Peters. I couldn't say it in there. They've got her down at the other end of the platform. Mr.

Potman said to tell you to get her out of here at all costs."

"Hilda!" Fiametta's voice came in a pettish shout from her dressing room.

Hilda hesitated. "I'd better go," she said, and went back into the canvas booth.

I made my way onto the platform. There was an anxious little knot of people gathered at the far end of the station. I could see Gervase and Sam and Keith, and they were clustered around somebody, talking earnestly. As I approached, Sam looked up and saw me, and an expression of intense relief crossed his face.

"Ah, Pudge," he said. "Just the person we want. Mr. Croombe-Peters will be able to help you," he added to someone in the center of the group. "Just leave everything to him."

He stepped aside and I found myself looking straight into the limpid blue eyes of Sonia Meakin.

I was considerably taken aback, but I hoped that I did not show it. "What can I do for you, Mrs. Meakin?" I asked.

Before she could answer, Sam said, "Mrs. Meakin has come to collect Bob's things—the odd bits and pieces that were in his dressing room. You've got them, haven't you, Pudge?"

To tell the truth, I had forgotten all about the wretched things. Ever since the painful scene in Fiametta's dressing room the previous Friday, I hadn't given a thought to the cardboard box. Now, sickeningly, I remembered exactly where it was. It was still standing on a corner of Fiametta's table in her canvas booth. I suspected that Sam knew this as well as I did.

I was certainly in a fix. I could not possibly go back to Fiametta's room and collect the box without arousing her curiosity and bringing her out onto the platform; and if she were to meet Sonia Meakin face to face, and here, of all places, the fat would be in the fire all right. As it was, Fiametta might come out at any moment. Obviously, the important thing was to get Bob's widow out of the place as fast as possible.

I said the first thing that came into my head. "Oh, I'm most awfully sorry, Mrs. Meakin. I'm afraid your husband's things are not here."

Sonia Meakin looked at me steadily. "Where are they?" she asked. "I would like them."

"Well, as a matter of fact, . . ." I groped in my mind for a suitable lie. "As a matter of fact, Margery Phipps has them, our Continuity Girl. That is . . ."

"Then perhaps she would give them to me."

"Well, it's a little difficult—you see, she's no longer with us. It's rather a long story. I say," I added, with what I hoped was the enthusiastic note of someone who has just had a good idea, "I'll tell you what. Come with me to the coffee bar around the corner and I'll telephone her. We can have a cup of coffee at the same time. I'm terribly thirsty. How would that be?"

I could feel my cheeks burning, and the trickle of sweat from my brow. I have never been a very good liar, and I was acutely aware of the cool, steady gaze of those enormous blue eyes. The others, of course, had melted discreetly away, leaving me to cope alone, as usual.

For a moment Sonia Meakin looked at me in silence. Then she said, "This is where—it happened, isn't it?"

"Yes," I said. "I wouldn't stay down here if I were you. You'll only distress yourself. Come with me and . . ."

"That was the staircase, was it?" she asked. Her voice was deep and clear, like a dark river. "He ran down that staircase, and fell onto the track."

"Please, Mrs. Meakin," I said, "there's no sense in going over all this. Let's go up to the coffee bar and . . ."

"Was anybody near him when he fell?"

Sonia Meakin's question was so unexpected and apparently senseless that for a moment I just looked at her with what I am afraid must have been an idiotically vague expression. Then I said, "I don't know what you mean. Lots of people were near him—all around him. We were shooting a scene."

"I know that." She sounded impatient. "I mean, did any-one actually touch him, could anyone have pushed . . . ?"

This was dangerous stuff, and I began to get angry. Out of the corner of my eye, I saw that Gervase Mountjoy was lean-ing up against the wall nearby, ostensibly reading a paper, but actually listening intently to our conversation. I said brusquely, "Mrs. Meakin, I have no idea what you are driving at. Your husband stumbled on the stairway and fell onto the line. He did it in front of a crowd of witnesses, any one of whom will confirm that nobody could possibly have touched him. The coroner's inquest made it perfectly clear what happened. I think you are only causing yourself distress by staying down here. Come and have some coffee." And with that, I took her arm and fairly hustled her up the staircase and out into the sunshine.

Sonia Meakin did not say another word until we were installed in a mock-Tudor inglenook in the coffee bar around the corner. I had the impression that she was watching me carefully, sizing me up. It was not a pleasant sensation. She seemed altogether too cool and calculating, and I was uneasy in my mind about the real purpose of her visit.

When I had ordered coffee and biscuits, I settled down to make some sort of small talk until I could decently get rid of the woman altogether. The all-important thing, to my mind, was to prevent her from trying to go down to the location again. I was halfway through an admittedly feeble anecdote about an Englishman, an Irishman, and a Scotsman when Sonia Meakin suddenly said, "Hadn't you better go and telephone her?"

"Telephone? Who?"

"The girl who has my husband's things. Margery Phipps, I believe you said her name was."

I had completely forgotten my previous remarks, and this flustered me somewhat. "It's a slightly awkward situation, Mrs. Meakin," I said. "You see, the day after—I mean, when Miss Phipps had packed up all the things that your husband left behind—that is, the things from his dressing room, you understand—the day after—on Monday, I should say . . ."

"The day after what?" she asked. I had the feeling that she was laughing at me.

I pulled myself together. "Last Friday," I said with dignity, "Miss Phipps packed up all your late husband's belongings and took them home with her, intending to bring them to the office on Monday morning, whence they would have been returned to you. Yesterday, however, she was compelled for personal reasons to resign her position with the unit. It all happened rather suddenly, and I am afraid that I have not yet made any arrangements . . ."

"That is why I asked you to telephone her," said Sonia

Meakin gently.

Well, there was nothing for it but downright deception. I knew exactly where Bob's things really were, and I had promised Sam that I would not try to contact Margery. To put a good face on things, however, I went into the phone box, dialed TIM and listened for some time to the golden-voiced operator informing me that on the third stroke it would be eleven twenty-one precisely, and then went back to the table.

"You spoke to her?" Sonia Meakin asked, with, I thought, a note of anxiety in her voice.

"Yes, indeed," I said easily. "It's all arranged." I found that lying was not as difficult as I had anticipated. In fact, it was almost enjoyable in a curious way. "She is sending the box around to the office this afternoon; it will be there by six o'clock. Would you like to collect it then, or shall I have the things sent to you?"

Sonia Meakin gave me another of her long, cool looks. "I'll collect it, if I may," she said. "That's your office in Duck Street off Shaftesbury Avenue."

"That's right," I said. "Number 38, fourth floor. Just ask for me. Any time after six."

By the time we had finished our coffee, and I had seen her safely into a taxi, it was getting on for midday. I hurried back to the location, and was surprised to find nobody there except Harry, Props, and a couple of electricians—all busily engaged in packing up.

"Good Lord," I said, "finished already?"

"We only had the one scene to shoot," said Harry. "Seems all yesterday's stuff went like a dream, and we got Fiametta into the can in three takes. Sam broke early for lunch, and he's given the boys the afternoon off."

"What's that?" I asked sharply.

"Well," said Harry, "it stands to reason, doesn't it? We're finished here and we can't start on Hampstead Heath until tomorrow, when we've got the pearlies called. That's what the boys appreciate so much about Sam, getting the odd few hours off like this."

"I am sure it is," I said grimly. I was very angry indeed. For a start, Sam knew that I considered it extremely bad for discipline, this habit of his of letting people go free during working hours just because there was nothing in particular for them to do. Secondly, I had expressly forbidden him to employ the large numbers of costermongers, "Pearly kings and queens," that he wanted for the Hampstead Heath scene; clearly, he had arranged it all behind my back. Something else occurred to me.

"I don't think I have received a copy of my call sheet for tomorrow," I said.

Harry looked far too innocent. "Haven't you?" he said. "Oh, I am sorry, Mr. Croombe-Peters. I'll have one sent to your office straight away."

It was obvious, of course. Sam had deliberately instructed Harry to forget to send my call sheet, because he did not want me to see that it featured a dozen unauthorized "pearlies." I was so annoyed that I had turned on my heel with the intention of striding out of the station, when Harry said, "Oh, Mr. Potman said to tell you that there'll be rushes at four at Duck Street."

This meant that the more senior members of the unit would be assembling at four o'clock in the small private cinema in the basement of our offices—a cinema, I may add, which was shared by the numerous small film companies occupying the building—in order to see the first prints of the previous day's filming. Sam never seemed very keen on my presence at "rushes," so I was slightly mollified that he had sent me this message.

"Thank you, Harry," I said. "I'll be there."

It was then that I realized that I had been on the point of leaving the Underground station without picking up the box of bits and pieces which had already caused so much trouble. I went quickly to Fiametta's dressing room, found the box, and tucked it under my arm. Then, having made sure that Props was arranging for the final dismantling of the dressing rooms, I emerged into the light of day and walked back to the office.

The afternoon passed uneventfully. I saw no signs of the other executive members of the unit. Louise Cohen, whose office was next to mine, wasted an hour of my time over some fiddling details connected with the hiring of a car to take Fiametta to the location the following day; but my irritation at this was more than assuaged by a telephone call from our lawyer shortly before four o'clock, telling me that the actuaries' figures had been accepted by the insurance company and that we could expect a check in settlement within a few days. It was in a very cheerful frame of mind that I took the lift down to the theater for "rushes."

To my surprise, only Sam, Fred Harborough, and the new Continuity Girl, Diana, were there. Normally, everybody comes to the rushes—the Art Director, the actors, the sound crew, the hairdressing and make-up experts, the script writer, and the editor—everybody, in fact, whose work is involved directly in what appears on the screen. As soon as I appeared, Sam said, "Ah, here you are, Pudge. Good. Let's start."

"Where are the others?" I asked.

"Keith wasn't feeling too good," said Sam. "I've packed him off with Biddy for a day in the country. Fiametta is mooning over that terrible monkey and refuses to appear. Since I've given everyone else the afternoon off, and the sun is shining, I excused them all from rushes. If there's anything we don't like, we'll tell them tomorrow."

This was, of course, exactly the sort of thing of which I disapproved, but I said nothing. I sat down next to Sam, and we watched the previous day's takes in silence. There was one interruption. We'd hardly seen a couple of rushes before Sam was called away to speak to Biddy on the telephone. He came back looking extremely cheerful, but did not volunteer any information about the conversation. He merely settled back into his chair, lit a cigar, and said, "Right, let's get on."

It was exactly five minutes past six when Sylvia, my secretary, came into my office to tell me that Mrs. Meakin had arrived and was asking for me.

"Oh, yes, that's right," I said. "Show her up."

I had already sorted out Bob's things from Fiametta's, and the cardboard box was on my desk all ready for Sonia Meakin to collect. I felt fairly proud of the way that I had handled what might have been an extremely tricky situation that morning.

Sonia Meakin came in quickly, and said, "Mr. Croombe-Peters, I'm most terribly sorry. I don't want to worry you . . ."

I beamed. "You're not worrying me at all, Mrs. Meakin," I said. "You see? Margery was as good as her word. Here is your box, all present and correct."

"You mean . . . ," she faltered, and then went on. "She actually sent it here—I don't believe it."

"Don't believe what?" I felt a slight tremor of alarm. Was my deception going to come to light after all?

"Haven't you seen? Don't you know?"

"Don't I know what? I'm afraid I don't understand you, Mrs. Meakin."

"This," she said, and thrust a copy of the late edition of the *Evening Standard* under my nose. On the front page was the headline "London Girl Falls to Her Death," and a large photograph of Margery Phipps. Feeling numb, I began to read the story.

"Soon after four o'clock this afternoon, passers-by in Dredge Street, Chelsea, were horrified to see a young woman falling to her death from the window of a seventh-story apartment. She has been identified as the tenant of the apartment, Miss Margery Phipps, aged 27. Police were called in, but have stated that foul play is not suspected. Miss Phipps, who was (*Please turn to Page 3*) . . ."

"I never dreamt—I mean, that wasn't why." Sonia Meakin was saying something, but I did not take it in.

"Forgive me, Mrs. Meakin," I said, as politely as I could manage. "This is rather a shock. I think I should speak to Mr. Potman right away. Your box is on the table. Please take it. Everything is there."

"But, Mr. Croombe-Peters . . ."

"Anything you want, ask my secretary," I said, and hurried out and down the corridor to Sam's office. It was only much later that I realized that there were several questions that I could profitably have asked Sonia Meakin.

7

Sam was sitting in his office with his feet up on the desk, doing a crossword puzzle. He read through the newspaper report quite impassively, with no emotion of any sort on his face. Then he looked up at me and said, "Poor Margery, I wonder what the trouble was."

"That doesn't concern me," I said. "What concerns me is that . . ."

"Joost as well she'd left the unit," said Sam phlegmatically. He pulled out one of his little black cigars and lit it. "I thought she must be worked oop over soomthing. She'd never have flown off the handle and given notice like that, just because of a tiff with Fiametta. Enjoyed working on *Street Scene,* she said, and so she did. So she should have. No, there was something else. Something we don't know about."

"It's all very well for you to say it's as well she'd left the unit," I said crossly. "If you think that's going to save us from publicity of the worst sort, you can think again. It'll come out in no time that she was working for us up until last Friday, and coming on top of Bob's death . . ."

"There's nowt we can do about it," said Sam shortly.

"There's something I can at least try," I said. "With your permission, I'm going to get on to Scotland Yard and ask them to keep our name out of it."

Sam gave me a lazy, incredulous grin. "Good luck, chum," he said, "I'm sure Scotland Yard is ready to obey your faintest whim."

"I happen," I said, "to have one or two fairly influential

friends. Have I your permission?"

"Go ahead," said Sam. I could tell that he was laughing at me.

"Thank you," I said, "I will."

I went back to my own office, where I noticed with relief that there was no sign either of Sonia Meakin or the wretched cardboard box. I sat down at my desk and told Sylvia to get me Chief Inspector Tibbett of Scotland Yard on the telephone.

Frankly, I was not relishing the prospect of ringing Henry Tibbett, after the way in which he had snubbed me over Bob's death. But presumably Margery's fall had not been accidental, and I felt that Henry could hardly say that suicide was none of his business. In any case, however distasteful the task, it had to be done for the sake of the film.

Henry sounded surprised to hear from me. "Margery Phipps?" he said. "Oh, yes. I heard about that. A routine suicide case, I believe."

"Routine or not," I said, "the fact remains that we can't afford any more publicity of the wrong sort. If it gets out that she was working for us, and left the unit after a row with Fiametta Fettini . . ."

"That would hardly drive her to suicide, would it?" asked Henry mildly.

"Of course not, but wait till you see what the press do with it."

"I don't really see what I can do for you, Croombe-Peters," said Henry. "I can hardly prevent the press from finding out where the girl used to work, and if they feel they're on to a good story . . ."

"I tell you, we shall be besieged by reporters and . . ."

"I think, you know," said Henry, "that you're taking an unnecessarily gloomy view. I can't believe that the newspapers will be vastly interested in the fact that the girl once worked for you in a not very glamorous capacity. It may be good for a small paragraph, but no more. And as for her having had a row with Fiametta Fettini, I don't see how they're going to find that out unless one of you tells them."

"But . . ."

"In any case, I assure you that the thing is quite outside my control. The only cases in which we can ever request the press not to publish certain facts are those connected with national security and the Official Secrets Act, and I hardly think that this would apply . . ."

"Now look here, Henry . . ."

"So, if you'll forgive me—I'm extremely busy just now. Good-bye, Croombe-Peters."

There was a sharp click, and then the telephone began to buzz like an impatient wasp. As I put it down, I had no kindly thoughts in my head for Henry Tibbett.

As it turned out, however, he was right; and this was perhaps the most infuriating aspect of the affair. In fact, to my surprise no newspaper even mentioned the fact that Margery had worked for us. As Henry had predicted, her death was treated as a routine suicide. A note had apparently been found, addressed to her mother, and although the text of it was not published, it clearly gave some sort of explanation for her drastic action. One or two neighbors remarked that she had seemed agitated on the morning of the day she died. A girl friend, a Miss Sarah Prentiss, told the press that she had not noticed anything out of the ordinary in Margery's behavior recently, but added, "You never could tell what she was thinking. Still waters run deep, that's what I say. We used to go to the ballet together, and sometimes concerts, but I never felt I really knew her. I believe she'd recently lost her job, but she never told me anything about that either."

A date was fixed for the inquest, and the newspapers promptly lost interest. Whereas Bob Meakin's demise had at least been a nine-day's wonder, poor Margery was wiped out of the world with as little fuss and bother as a chalk mark cleaned off a blackboard. Once again, life went on.

Within the unit itself, of course, people talked a lot about Margery's suicide, and speculated on the reasons for it; but it appeared that Miss Prentiss had given an accurate picture of Margery to the journalists. Everybody on the unit had liked Margery and been on amicable terms with her, but nobody could say that she had been a friend. None of her colleagues had ever been invited to her flat, or met her out of working hours. She had always seemed, as Biddy put it, "as self-contained as an egg." So, after a bit, people stopped talking about

Margery, for there was nothing to say. A few of the more excitable and superstitious members of the unit—I am thinking of Amy, the Assistant Hairdresser, in particular—amused themselves by indulging in pleasurable tremors of horror at the thought that the film might lie under a curse, like Tutankhamen's tomb, and that the members of the unit were destined to die violently, one by one. Fortunately, however, most of our people were sensible enough to pay no attention to any such nonsense, and the whole matter was soon enough forgotten.

As for myself, the only thing that really rankled was my double humiliation at the hands of the insufferable Tibbett. I cursed myself for the moment of stupidity and weakness which had led me to telephone him, and I decided to avoid him socially for a bit, if I could. Mind you, we did not see each other frequently; but, as I have indicated, we had a number of mutual friends in whose houses we were apt to meet. He knew the most surprising people.

In view of all this, I was none too pleased when, about a week after Margery's death, Sylvia informed me just after lunch one day that Chief Inspector Tibbett was on the telephone and wished to speak to me.

For a moment I hesitated. Then I reflected that Henry would hardly ring me up during the course of a busy day merely to gloat over me. The very fact that he was calling me seemed to indicate that I was, for once, in a commanding position. This time, he must want to ask a favor of me.

"Put him on," I said.

"Mr. Croombe-Peters?" Tibbett's voice was almost diffident. "I'm extremely sorry to bother you. I know how busy you are."

"Not at all," I replied cordially. "What can I do for you?"

"You can give me an hour or so of your time, if you will," said Henry. "I have a problem, and I think you may be able to help me."

"Naturally, I'll be pleased to give you any help I can," I said. His tone of humility was most gratifying. "I'm afraid I can't possibly get away this afternoon, though. I trust it's not a matter of life and death."

"Not in the metaphorical sense," said Tibbett enigmatically. "I'll tell you what. Could you possibly come round to my place for a drink this evening? Emmy would be delighted to see you again, and we could talk quietly."

"I'd enjoy that very much," I said, and meant it. I think I have mentioned before how much I liked Mrs. Tibbett, and I looked forward to seeing her. "This isn't an official matter then?"

Tibbett hesitated. Finally, he said, "Yes and no. It's a little hard to explain."

"Dear me," I said, in mock alarm, "you're not going to arrest me, I hope."

"I hope not, too," he said, and there was surprisingly little humor in his voice. I concluded that he was piqued by my flippant tone. Like so many people who are deeply absorbed in their work, he was inclined to be a little pompous about it.

"Well," I said, "be that as it may, what time would you like to see me?"

"Can you manage half-past six?"

"I think so."

"You have the address?"

"Wait a minute—yes, it's here in my book."

"Good. I'll be seeing you, then. And—Croombe-Peters . . ."

"Yes?"

"Perhaps you'd be good enough not to mention to anybody else that I called you."

"Oho," I said, "the plot thickens. Cloak-and-dagger stuff, is it?"

"Not really." Tibbet sounded embarrassed. "It's just that, well, I'll explain this evening. Good-bye for now."

The Tibbetts lived on the ground floor of a rather shabby Victorian house in that part of Fulham which is now described by house agents as Chelsea. It was an unassuming flat—just a large living room, a small bedroom, a miniscule kitchen and a bath built in to what had apparently, from its size, been a broom cupboard. However, it was cheerful and comfortable, and the living room at least had the merit of being enormous and high-ceilinged, with a big open fireplace and French windows opening onto a rather straggling garden. I arrived at twenty to seven, and rang the front doorbell.

Emmy Tibbett answered the door, as warm and welcoming

as ever. She was wearing trousers, and I noticed that she looked rather plumper than I remembered, which was comforting for me. When one is constitutionally stout, it so often seems that the rest of the world is inhabited exclusively by walking skeletons.

"Pudge!" cried Emmy. Unlike her husband, she always used my nickname, and had done so since our first meeting. "How lovely to see you. Do come in. Henry's not home from work yet, but you will have a drink and stay to see him, won't you? He'd be awfully upset if he missed you."

"You weren't expecting me, then?" I asked, as I followed her in.

Emmy shook her dark, curly head. "No. Should I have been? You know I've got a memory like a sieve . . ."

"Henry phoned me this afternoon and asked me to come round this evening," I said. "I think it's something to do with his work. He said he wanted to ask me something. You've no idea what about?"

"Not the faintest," said Emmy. "Henry really is a monster. He should have rung me and told me. You must think me hideously rude."

"You couldn't be rude if you tried," I said. "And I certainly can't imagine you trying."

Emmy laughed. "Bare-faced flattery," she said. "I shan't listen or I'll get too big for my boots. What will you drink?"

"A whisky and soda, if I may," I said.

As she poured drinks, Emmy went on, "Now, you must tell me all about Fiametta Fettini. Is she really as gorgeous as she looks on the screen? And what about your Keith Pardoe becoming such a celebrity? You do have an exciting life, Pudge."

"Rather too exciting sometimes," I said.

Emmy was instantly subdued. "You mean Robert Meakin. Yes, that was terrible. Were you actually there when it happened?"

"I saw it."

Emmy shuddered. "I couldn't believe it when I read about it," she said. "Robert Meakin seemed like—like an institution. I suppose he wasn't very old, really, but I can't remember the time when he wasn't around. When I heard he was dead, it was as though I'd lost a personal friend. I think lots of people felt like that."

"The older people, perhaps," I said, and then realized that it was not the most tactful of remarks. However, Emmy didn't mind. She was in her early forties, and looked younger, and she didn't care who knew it. In any case, it would not have occurred to her to take such a remark personally.

She answered, thoughtfully, "Yes, you're right. Robert Meakin wasn't at all what the teenagers are after these days. He was the epitome of feminine taste in men about fifteen years ago. Now, Fiametta Fettini . . ."

". . . is a spoilt, selfish guttersnipe and a bloody nuisance, if you want the truth," I said.

Emmy opened her eyes wide. "Is she really? She looks so adorable, like a fluffy black kitten."

"She's got the brains of a fluffy kitten and the claws of a full-grown, bad-tempered tigress."

"How disillusioning you are, Pudge. I wish I'd never asked you about her. Surely she must have *some* good qualities?"

Before I had time to answer, there was the sound of a key in the front door, and Emmy said, "There's Henry." A moment later Henry Tibbett came in.

I have already mentioned that he looked as little like a great detective as any man could, with his slight physique, undistinguished features, and mild blue eyes. However, people who were better qualified to judge than I apparently had the highest opinion of his talents, and I presumed that he would not have reached his present position without a certain amount of ability. I can only say that he did not give much outward sign of it. He came into the room quietly, almost diffidently, poured himself a drink, and chatted about the weather.

At last, when we had established that it had been a cool day for the time of year, but might easily rain tomorrow, Henry Tibbett settled himself in a large, shabby arm chair and got down to business.

"I'm really very sorry to worry you with this, Croombe-Peters," he said, "but, frankly, I don't know quite what action to take, and I hope you can help me."

"Certainly, if I can," I said politely. It was, I considered, a pretty shilly-shallying way for a senior detective to go on, but that was none of my business.

"The other day," said Henry, "you telephoned me about a girl who committed suicide. Your ex-Continuity Girl, Margery Phipps."

"That's right. I'm glad to say that your guess was correct; we haven't been bothered by the press at all."

"That," said Henry, "is because nobody knows that she used to work for you."

"Oh, rubbish," I said. "Everybody must know. We all . . ."

"She was apparently a very secretive character," Henry went on, ignoring my interruption. "She had few friends, and those that she had knew very little about her. The closest friend she had, it seems, was a girl named Sarah Prentiss, who used to go to theaters and concerts with her. All that Sarah Prentiss knew was that she worked for a firm in Soho, and that she had recently given up her job. The detectives who searched her flat after the suicide found absolutely no personal papers whatsoever, just the suicide note. I presume that she must have been a member of a trade union to be allowed to work on a film?"

"Most emphatically," I said with feeling.

"Well," Henry went on, "we couldn't even find a union card among her things. It was all rather mysterious."

"I don't think so," I said. "Margery was a quiet, secret sort of person, but there was no mystery about her that I know of. The union will have all her particulars." There was a short silence.

As Henry did not seem inclined to start the conversation going again, I could not resist putting bluntly into words what had been in my mind ever since his telephone call that afternoon. "The last time I spoke to you," I said, "you described Margery's death as a routine suicide. Why are you suddenly so interested in her?"

Henry was filling his pipe, and spun this operation out with unnecessary attention to detail. For the first time in my acquaintance with him, he seemed to be at a loss for words.

At last he said, "Well, I know it all sounds rather silly, but it's because of this woman."

"What woman?"

"I'll try to explain it to you as best I can," said Henry. "As you know, Margery Phipps left a note addressed to Mrs. Cyril Phipps, at an address in Kensington. Mrs. Phipps was contacted at once, and proved to be a charming, intelligent, and well-educated woman in her late fifties, a widow. The Superintendent told her the news and gave her Margery's note. She was apparently very upset. She said that although she did not see a great deal of Margery these days, she and her daughter had always been devoted to each other and kept in touch by telephone. She could not imagine why Margery should have killed herself. It was true that the girl was moody and even her own mother found her secretive and sometimes difficult to understand. Mrs. Phipps could only presume that there had been some tragedy—probably an unhappy love affair—but she could not supply any details."

"Wait a minute," I said. "What about the note?"

"Ah, yes," said Tibbett. "The note. I'm coming to that. In fact, I'll show you a transcript of it. It's a suicide note all right —no doubt about that—but it's couched in pretty vague terms, as though Margery had expected her mother to know all about the affair—whatever it was. But Mrs. Phipps maintains that she has no inkling about what drove the poor girl to kill herself."

"I don't see what all this has to . . ."

"Please," said Henry. He sounded tired, and also embarrassed. "Let me explain it in my own way. Superintendent Wilcox was in charge of the inquiries, and it was he who interviewed Mrs. Phipps and generally coped with the case. If it hadn't been for your telephone call, I would never have heard of the girl at all. It had nothing to do with me. But then this woman turned up."

"What woman? You keep talking about a woman . . ."

"Mrs. Arbuthnot, her name is. From Lewisham."

"My dear Tibbett," I said—I could not repress a smile— "this is becoming most delightfully complicated. Who or what is Mrs. Arbuthnot, and how does she come into the affair?"

Tibbett grinned. "She comes into it," he said, "because she literally camped outside my office for two days and refused to budge. She simply turned up at the Yard, demanding to see me and nobody else, and refused to say what it was about. She informed the Duty Sergeant that she had taken the train up from Lewisham to come to Scotland Yard direct, because, as she put it, she knew a thing or two about the local police, thank you very much. When she was told that she could not see me, she simply produced a package of ham sandwiches and a Thermos flask and proceeded to lay siege to the Yard. The Sergeant interviewed her again, and this time she volunteered the information that her visit concerned what she described as 'the mysterious death of Miss Margery Phipps.' The Sergeant was in a dilemma, poor chap. He's a kindly soul, and Mrs. Arbuthnot's dogged determination had impressed him. Besides, he was haunted by the idea that she might have something important to say. Anyhow, to cut a long story short, he came to me very apologetically this morning and told me all about it, and I agreed to see the woman. . . ."

One thing I will say for Tibbett, he has a gift for telling a story. As he spoke, I could almost see Mrs. Arbuthnot, in her crushed black straw hat and shabby black coat, following her sharply pointed nose warily into Henry's office. So I'm proposing to tell you about the interview just as Tibbett told it to me.

She came in, he said, as though she were expecting an ambush. She could not have been much more than fifty years old, but her face was deeply lined and her hands roughened by hard work.

"Chief Inspector Tibbett, is it?" she asked distrustfully. Her voice was not Cockney. It had, rather, the mournful whine of the southern suburbs of London. There was even a distressing attempt to be genteel. Henry admitted his identity, and proffered a chair.

"It's taken me a good two days to get to see you," said Mrs. Arbuthnot accusingly. She sat down and pulled the black coat tighter around her skinny waist. "Obstruction, all the way."

"I'm sorry," said Henry. "These things have to go through what are called the normal channels. You see, Mrs. Arbuthnot, it's rather unusual for a member of the public to insist upon seeing . . ."

"If you don't have the right to see a detective when your daughter's been murdered, I don't know when you do," said Mrs. Arbuthnot.

This took Henry aback, as can be imagined. "Your daughter's been murdered?" he repeated, rather foolishly.

"Yes. My daughter. Margery Phipps. Murdered. Don't you understand English?"

"Just a minute, Mrs. Arbuthnot. First of all, Margery Phipps committed suicide. There's no doubt about that. And secondly, she was not your daughter. She left a note addressed to her mother, Mrs. Cyril Phipps of . . ."

"Foster mother," said Mrs. Arbuthnot with scorn. "Wanted to adopt her, but I wasn't having any of that. So she got Margery's name changed to Phipps, so as to look better. But Margery was my girl, and I'm telling you she was murdered."

At this point Henry took a pull at his pipe, and said, "I may as well telescope things a little here, and tell you that Mrs. Arbuthnot's story was perfectly true, at least as far as Margery's birth was concerned. I checked up at once, and found that Margery had been taken in as a foster child by Mrs. Phipps at the age of six months. It was also true that Mrs. Phipps and her husband, when he was alive, had made great efforts to adopt the child legally, but had always been foiled by the iron determination of the real mother not to relinquish her right to her child. However, all this appeared to have nothing to do with Margery's death, and I said as much to Mrs. Arbuthnot.

"I explained all the circumstance to her. Margery's work on *Street Scene*—she seemed to know all about that—and her resignation from the job. It was perfectly clear that for some reason she had decided to take her own life. At this point Mrs. Arbuthnot interrupted."

"For some reason! What reason would *that* be, I'd like to know?"

"We don't know the precise reason, Mrs. Arbuthnot, but she left a note addressed to her mother—that is, to Mrs. Phipps—making it clear that . . ."

"And she wrote a note to me, her real mother, the very same day!"

Mrs. Arbuthnot fumbled in her enormous, well-worn handbag, and produced a letter, written in the same definitive hand that Henry recognized from the suicide note.

"Dear Mum," it read, "Just a line to tell you that I'm doing well, so don't worry. In fact, I'm on to something pretty big and exciting, and I just wish Dad were here to see me in action. I'll write again soon—I may need your help. Love, Margery."

Henry read the note carefully, and then looked up. "Well?"

he said.

"Does that sound like a girl who's going to throw herself out of a seventh-story window?" Mrs. Arbuthnot demanded aggressively.

"I'm afraid, Mrs. Arbuthnot," said Henry, "that it's useless trying to make sense of the way people behave. Here at Scotland Yard, we have to go on facts; and the fact is that your daughter killed herself. It's a great tragedy, and you may be sure we are all very sympathetic, but . . ."

Abruptly, Mrs. Arbuthnot sheered off onto a new line of thought. "What about the will?" she asked.

"That's quite outside my province, I'm afraid," said Henry. "If there was a will, it must have been found among your daughter's belongings. If not, it would be a matter for lawyers to decide whether you or Mrs. Phipps should inherit. I would say that your claim would be stronger in law, but I'm only guessing."

"You mean, I'd get everything?"

"I think so."

"What I mean," said Mrs. Arbuthnot, with a strange mixture of diffidence and cunning, "I read the other day about a man left a fortune by his uncle and couldn't lay hands on a penny of it. Lipstick or some such name, it was."

Henry said, "I think you must mean Alexander Lipovitch, the novelist."

"I dare say. It was some sort of foreign name."

"That case was quite different, Mrs. Arbuthnot. The uncle committed suicide, leaving a will which directed that the nephew should inherit the proceeds from a large life insurance policy; but there was a clause in the insurance policy rendering it null and void in the case of suicide. I hardly imagine that your daughter . . ."

"Not that the Lipstick man needed the money, from what it said in the papers. Rolling in the stuff already. Not like most of us."

"Really, Mrs. Arbuthnot," said Henry, "this isn't my line of country at all. I would advise you and your husband to go to a solicitor . . ."

"My husband's dead." Mrs. Arbuthnot sounded irritated at the fact. "Six months ago, he went. That cold snap in March.

Bronchitis turned to pneumonia. I did at least think I'd have Margery to look after me in my old age. What's going to happen to me now, I'd like to know?"

According to Tibbett, as he told me the story, it was at this point that he managed to get rid of Mrs. Arbuthnot as tactfully as possible. I can imagine what this involved, the usual Tibbett mixture of stubbornness and flattery which would have charmed the birds off a tree and left them no time to reflect that they had left a nest and fledglings on the topmost branch. I often wondered why Henry Tibbett had not become a confidence man. He would have been a huge success.

"Well," I said, "that's all very amusing and interesting, but I don't see what it has to do with me."

"Have another drink," said Henry. He got up and refilled our glasses, and then he said, "I was somehow intrigued by Mrs. Arbuthnot. I suppose it was my—a sort of instinct."

I knew him well enough to know that the word he had avoided using was "nose." Tibbett's admirers maintain that he has a sort of sixth sense when it comes to crime, a facility to which he refers as his "nose." I knew, too, that he had an understandable reluctance to talk about this nonsensical and totally imaginary attribute. On this occasion, he sidestepped it quickly and went on. "Purely on impulse I sent for all the papers concerning Margery Phipps. As I've told you, they confirmed Mrs. Arbuthnot's story. Margery was the daughter of Lily Arbuthnot of 12 Inkerman Terrace, Lewisham. On the birth certificate, the father was entered as 'unknown.' There were documents to prove that when the child was six months old, she had been handed over to foster parents, Mr. and Mrs. Cyril Phipps of Barons Court. There had never been an official adoption order, but at the age of sixteen Margery's name had been changed by deed poll from Arbuthnot to Phipps. After I'd studied all these papers, I decided to have another word with Mrs. Arbuthnot."

"Why?" I asked. Frankly, I was beginning to get a little bored by the whole thing, and I had a dinner appointment at nine o'clock.

"Because of the inconsistency," said Henry.

"What inconsistency? Apparently everything that the woman had said was true, and she was just . . ."

"No," said Henry. "There was that small entry 'father unknown.' It was perfectly reasonable and probable that Mrs. Arbuthnot—or, more correctly, Miss Arbuthnot—would invent a fictitious and defunct husband; but it seemed rather unlikely that she would have placed his death a mere six months ago, and supplied me with details of his last illness. Besides, it appeared from the letter she had that Margery, too, had known her real father. Of course, the obvious explanation was that after the child's birth, her mother had settled down to an illegal state of domestic bliss with some other man, whom Margery had regarded as her father. Still, I wasn't entirely happy. So I telephoned Mrs. Arbuthnot and asked her for a few details about her husband.

"At first, she sounded quite taken aback. Then she told me that his name was Fred, Frederick Arbuthnot. I asked what his profession was, and she said he was an undertaker. Then, rather surprisingly, she said, 'Fred wouldn't have stood for it, if he'd been here. He'd never have nothing to do with murder, Fred wouldn't.'

"The next thing I did was to put through a call to the police station at Lewisham. I know the Superintendent there quite well. A nice fellow, and very good at his job. I told him that I'd like some information from him and that it might take some time to dig it out. I wanted a bit of background on one Frederick Arbuthnot, undertaker of 12 Inkerman Terrace, who had died of pneumonia last March. To my surprise, the Super began to laugh.

" 'What's so funny?'

" 'What's the idea, Inspector?' he asked. 'Intelligence and initiative tests for local forces?'

" 'Certainly not. I merely asked . . .'

"The Super gave a great guffaw. 'Undertaker!' he rumbled. 'That's rich. Not a bad description, either. Reckon there wasn't much he wouldn't undertake. But he liked his clients alive and kicking.'

" 'I'm told he didn't hold with murder.'

" 'Dear me, no. He was the old-fashioned type of criminal, very set in his ways. He had his own set of morals, and very rigid they were. You don't get 'em like that any more.' Believe me, the Super sounded really regretful about it. 'Layabouts, the new young crowd are, ready to dabble in any sort of dirt going, including violence. Indiscriminate. The day of the specialist is just about over.'

"I asked what Fred Arbuthnot's specialty had been. The Super sounded really surprised. 'You mean you don't know? You weren't pulling my leg?'

" 'I certainly wasn't. I can't be personally acquainted with every criminal in the country, specialist or not.'

" 'Still, I did think you'd have heard of Doctor Sam, as the papers called him.'

" 'Of course I've heard of Doctor Sam. But his name wasn't . . .'

" 'He changed his name about once a week,' said the Super. 'Very confusing, it was. But his favorite alibis were nearly all some sort of variation on Samuel Johnson. I've known him arrested as Sir Samuel Johns, Colonel Samson Jobson, Doctor St. John Samuel, and so on. It's really rather interesting. It wasn't until he died in Wormwood Scrubbs last March that we found out what his real name was. You'll never guess.'

" 'Frederick Arbuthnot?'

" 'No, no, no. James Boswell. What d'you think of that?'

" 'Not very much. Where does Frederick Arbuthnot come in?'

" 'Arbuthnot was the name of the woman he lived with down here in Lewisham. He never married her. She seemed quite a respectable type, and never got into trouble herself; but of course she couldn't put on the high-society act that he used when he was working. In between jobs, as you might say, he lived quietly at Inkerman Terrace, calling himself Fred Arbuthnot. He never sullied Samuel Johnson's name with that rather sordid suburban establishment. Still, he stayed faithful to the woman all his life, which is more than you can say for most of them. That's what I mean by principles. She's still living here, in the same house.'

" 'With her daughter?'

" 'Daughter? I never heard anything about a daughter. There were no children, as far as I know.'

"After I'd spoken to the Superintendent," Henry went on, "I called the people who were dealing with the girl's death. They told me that she had left no will, but that her only apparent possessions were her personal clothes and trinkets, and twenty pounds in the bank. It was then that I telephoned you."

I glanced at my watch. It was after eight o'clock. Emmy had disappeared into the kitchen, thus removing the only inducement I might have had to stay longer.

"My dear Tibbett," I said, "I can't help feeling that we're both wasting our time. Of course, it's fascinating to hear about the girl's background, but it obviously has nothing whatsoever to do with . . ."

He interrupted me. "Margery Phipps' real father," he said, "was an expert blackmailer and confidence man. Margery wrote to her mother that she was on to something big, and that she wished Dad were there to see her in action. That very same afternoon she died, leaving only twenty pounds. Doesn't that suggest anything to you?"

"Nothing," I said firmly. My voice sounded rather louder than I had intended. "And now, if you'll forgive me, Tibbett, I have an appointment. It's been so nice seeing you again . . ."

Tibbett saw me to the door. "I hope you won't take it amiss, Croombe-Peters," he said, in that annoyingly diffident way of his, "if I get in touch with you again. There may be more developments in this matter. Perhaps you'd also turn over in your mind the possibility that Margery Phipps might have been blackmailing somebody in your unit, and, if so, who? That's the way our cases build up, you know, little by little."

"I'll certainly consider what you've said," I replied. One has to be polite after all. "But I somehow don't think—ah, taxi! Good-bye Tibbett. Hope we'll meet again one of these days. . . ."

With which blatantly untrue statement, I climbed thankfully into the cab and told the driver to take me to the Orangery. I was surprised to find that I was sweating, even though the evening had turned chilly.

8

The following morning I decided to go up to Hampstead Heath and see how shooting was progressing. I should perhaps explain that I had been keeping away from the location quite deliberately for a day or so, as a result of a stupid and unpleasant incident with Sam Potman.

It had happened on our first day on the Heath, the day after Margery's death. I suppose it was natural that we should all be a little upset, and I more than suspected that it was the fact of a second death on our doorstep, so to speak, which was making Keith Pardoe behave like a prima donna.

When I arrived, there was a blazing row going on between Keith on the one hand, and the entire make-up and hairdressing departments on the other. Keith was shouting at Anton, the chief hairdresser, calling him a miserable frog and an officious little pansy, and a lot of equally unsavory names. There was no sign of either Sam or Biddy, and Gervase Mountjoy was, as usual, evading his responsibility by pretending not to notice that anything was going on. I had no option but to intervene.

When I had managed to calm Keith and Anton sufficiently to get a coherent story out of them, I found out the cause of the trouble. Apparently, Keith had spent a part of his free afternoon the day before in visiting a barber, and had had his hair cut. Now, this may not sound like a deadly sin to an outsider, but to a film-maker it is inexcusable behavior. It was the job of Anton and his department to insure that Keith's hair remained precisely the same length throughout the film;

as I have explained, scenes are inevitably shot out of chronological order, and you cannot have a man going out through a door with long hair and emerging on the other side with a crew cut. I am not saying that Keith's case was as bad as that, but his hair was noticeably shorter than it had been the day before, and rather differently shaped. I was entirely on Anton's side, and I was saying so in no uncertain terms when Sam's car drove up and he and Biddy got out of it and came over to us.

The first thing I noticed was how ill Biddy looked. There were black circles under her eyes, and her little heart-shaped face was positively haggard. I felt sorry for her. She was not having an easy time with Keith these days, and I am sure that she frequently regretted having suggested that he should take part in the television audition. He had changed fundamentally since he started his new career, and the change had not been for the better.

Any sympathy that I felt for her evaporated at once, however, when I heard her say to Sam, "Oh, God, Pudge is upsetting the bloody apple cart again."

I turned on her. "I heard that," I said, "and I consider it not only unjust but typical that you should leap to conclusions and put the blame on me when you haven't even heard what the trouble is."

"Well, what is it?" she said unpleasantly. "I suppose somebody's spent six sodding unauthorized pence on something."

"It's nothing of the sort," I said. "Anton is very angry with Keith, and he's entirely justified. I'm the person who is constantly being accused of being an amateur, but for Keith to go to an outside barber and have his hair messed about and cut is just about as unprofessional as . . ."

"If you say another word, Pudge, I shall walk out. Here and now. I'm not going to be spoken to like that." Keith's voice was rising hysterically.

"I was not speaking to you," I replied. To Biddy, I added, "And you're as much to blame. You must have known what he was up to. Why didn't you stop him?"

To my surprise, Biddy looked confused. Then she said, shortly, "I wasn't with him."

"Oh, weren't you? I understood that Keith was feeling ill

and that Sam had packed you both off to the country for . . ."

Before I could finish, Sam intervened. He spoke quietly, in that dangerous tone of voice that I was getting to know only too well. "This nonsense will now stop," he said. "We are starting a new sequence and it doesn't matter a damn about Keith's hair. I suppose Professor Masterman visited a barber occasionally, like everybody else. As a matter of fact, Keith asked for my permission to have it done, and I gave it."

At this, Anton broke into a protesting stream of mixed English and French, and I said, "I consider that to be irresponsible and unprofessional behavior on your part, Sam."

Sam turned on me. He was absolutely furious. "I would be grateful, Pudge," he said, "if you would go away and stay away. We don't need you on location, and every time you come you stir up trouble of some sort."

The monstrous injustice of this took my breath away. Perhaps the worst thing of all was that Anton, whose cause I had been championing, did not come to my rescue, but merely sniggered and turned away. I considered several replies, but none of them seemed as devastatingly crushing as I would have wished, so I decided to stick to dignified silence. I simply turned on my heel and walked away to my car without a word, and for the next couple of days I did not go near the scene of the shooting. However, Sam had evidently repented to a certain extent, for he made a point of sitting next to me and chatting in a friendly way during rushes the next evening, and actually suggested that I might enjoy watching the filming of the fun fair sequence the following day. And so it was that on the morning after my talk with Henry Tibbett, I decided to bury the hatchet and go out to the location. Besides, I had a strong suspicion that Sam was being wasteful in the matter of extras and overtime. He was like a child in many ways; I could never trust him not to be up to some mischief the moment my back was turned.

I arrived at the location at ten o'clock. As I had feared, the place was crawling with unauthorized pearly kings and queens, fairground men, spivs, beatniks, onlookers and dogs—all of whom were being paid at the exorbitant rate now demanded as the minimum for film extras. However, the sun was shining, and the whole scene was so colorful and alive and full of fun that I decided to postpone my remonstrations until later. In any case, it was by then too late to send any of the extras away unpaid, and—to be frank—our insurance claim had put us into the happy position of not being compelled to watch every halfpenny. Not, mind you, that I would have admitted this to Sam to save my life.

The camera was set up for the first shot of the day—Keith and Fiametta trying their luck at the coconut shies. I was in time to see the final rehearsal, and then Sam nodded and Gervase called, "Quiet, everyone, please! We're turning!"

Steve, the clapper boy, stepped forward with his blackboard.

"*Street Scene,* two-eighty-five, take one!" he chanted, and let the clapper fall.

I should explain that Sam had insisted on shooting all the sound "live," rather than dubbing it afterward in the studio. He maintained that it was more immediate and lifelike in its effect. As far as I was concerned, it was much cheaper, so everyone was happy. Consequently, an open-air scene like the one we were shooting today was not being filmed silent, but with all the paraphernalia of the sound camera, booms, and microphones. It remained to be seen whether the results would be usable.

At a signal from Gervase, the background noise began—the hurdy-gurdies, the shouts of the stallkeepers, the babble of the crowd.

Keith turned to face Fiametta. "What about trying your luck?" he said.

She gave him a smoldering look as the camera tracked in to a close shot of her face. "When I hit a coconut," she said, "I always think—suppose it was a head that was falling off and rolling in the sand, a man's head . . ."

"Cut," called Sam. He walked over to Fiametta and began talking to her quietly. If Sam disapproved of his actors' performances, he did not, like some directors, pillory the wretched creatures in front of a circle of smirking technicians.

When he had finished talking to Fiametta, Sam said, "Right. Once again."

"*Street Scene,* two-eighty-five, take two." The clapper fell again.

This time Fiametta spoke lightly, throwing out the remark

as a toss away pleasantry, quite devoid of any sinister meaning. Sam grinned at her.

"Fine," he said. "That's it. Once again for luck."

I glanced at Biddy. She generally showed a partiality for the more purple patches in her script, and resented the way in which Sam insisted on playing them down. Today, however, she did not appear to notice what was going on. She was sitting hunched up in the canvas chair marked "Sam Potman"—it's a curious sort of tradition among film people that they never use their own carefully labeled seats—and gazing at nothing with a brooding intensity in which worry and anger seemed to be about equally divided. Keith, I thought, looked more relaxed than he had for some time; Sam, as usual when on the set, was utterly absorbed in his work.

For the third time the tiny scene was played through.

"Cut," said Sam. "O.K. Print two and three."

At once, bustle and babble broke out. Keith put his arm around Fiametta's shoulders and said something that made her laugh immoderately. Sam and Fred Harborough were already conferring about the next shot. The Continuity Girl's typewriter began to chatter. The extras lit cigarettes and brought out newspapers, ready for another long wait. Electricians switched out lamps and began to trundle them on their heavy bases to new positions. And a voice at my elbow said, "Mr. Croombe-Peters, can you spare a moment?"

I turned and saw, to my surprise and annoyance, that Henry Tibbett was standing just behind me. Heaven knew how long he had been there. When one is filming in a public place on location, a crowd invariably collects, and Gervase and his assistants had put up rope barricades to keep the over-inquisitive at bay; Henry had presumably invoked my name in order to get past the barriers.

"What on earth are you doing here?" I asked.

"Sightseeing," Henry replied, with an unconvincing smirk. "I wanted to see you, and your secretary told me on the telephone that you were here. It seemed an ideal opportunity for taking a look at how a film is made, and a perfect excuse for getting out of the office for a bit."

"I'm afraid we don't encourage visitors," I said. I suppose it sounded very rude, but, frankly, I was only concerned with getting rid of the man as soon as possible. Any moment, Keith or Sam or Fiametta might come up and start talking to me, and if they discovered who Henry was, and blamed me for introducing him to the set, there would be hell to pay. "You must remember that we are working. We're not here as a peepshow for the public."

"I am not exactly the public," said Henry, in a spuriously pleasant voice that reminded me of Sam in his more dangerous moods. "And I, too, am working."

"I think it would be better," I said, "if we went to my office."

And then the very thing that I had feared happened. Sam came up and said, "Ah, there you are, Pudge. What did you think of that, eh? Just three takes and printing two. I hope you're pleased."

Before I could say a word, Henry said, "Mr. Potman, may I introduce myself? Henry Tibbett of Scotland Yard, an old friend of Mr. Croombe-Peters, and a great admirer of yours."

There was a tiny pause while Sam's bright, calculating eyes flickered over Henry's face, summing him up. Then Sam said, "Come to have a bit of a look round, have you? Well, that's champion. I hope you'll show Mr. Tibbett everything he wants to see, Pudge. Oh, Keith . . ."

As Keith and Fiametta walked past, Sam caught Keith's arm. "Come and be introduced," he went on. "Mr. Tibbett of Scotland Yard. Miss Fettini and Keith Pardoe, the local boy wonder. Mr. Tibbett wants to see genius at work. I hope you'll both oblige."

Keith looked taken aback, to say the least of it. "I hope it's just a friendly visit, Inspector," he said with a nervous little laugh.

Fiametta, to whom the words "Scotland Yard" meant nothing, apparently took Henry for a journalist, and immediately went into a big act. She grabbed Henry's arm, and began to enthuse in the most nauseating way about the fun fair, claiming that she had never before seen anything like it, and that she was enraptured by everything—the simple pleasures of the British proletariat, the gaiety, the *fun!* She insisted on climbing onto a hobby horse to prove her point, thus creating the opportunity of striking several fetching poses with her short skirt hitched higher still above her knees. It was nearly ten minutes before she suddenly asked, in a different and sharper tone, "But where are the photographers? You have no photographers with you?"

"Not today," said Henry. He sounded amused.

"You wish photographs from my agent for your article?" Fiametta pursued, mystified.

"I think you've made a mistake, Miss Fettini," said Henry. "I'm not a reporter. I'm a policeman."

"Carabiniere?" There was absolutely no doubt about Fiametta's reaction. The film-star veneer dropped away like old paint flaking off under a chisel, and left the white-faced, wide-eyed, frightened waif from the slums of Naples, the child brought up to steal and cheat in order to live, the child to whom every policeman was a deadly enemy. For a moment, it almost looked as though she would take to her heels and run in sheer, instinctive terror. Then she recovered herself and lifted her small head defiantly. "You can't do anything to me," she said in Italian.

To my surprise, Henry answered in the same language. "My dear child," he said, "why should you imagine that I should want to?"

At the time, of course, I did not understand either remark. Keith translated them for me later on. All that was obvious to me, as a bystander, was that Fiametta underwent another of her abrupt changes of mood. She grinned and winked at Henry, and suddenly became what she really was—an impudent, fascinating guttersnipe. She held out both her hands to grasp one of Henry's and one of Keith's, and marched them both off to eat candy floss. The three of them were soon joined by Sam and Biddy, and then by Gervase. Henry appeared to be a great success, and I felt distinctly out of things. I also felt uneasy. Heaven knew what indiscretions Henry was wheedling out of these irresponsible young creatures. However, there was nothing I could do except wait until Henry Tibbett deigned to come back and tell me the real purpose of his visit.

It was some twenty minutes later that the others were called away for a preliminary run-through of the next shot, and Henry came over to where I was sitting chatting to Diana, the Continuity Girl. Once again, Henry insisted on being introduced, and showed considerable interest in Diana's work. She was obviously pleased and flattered, and explained in some detail how she recorded everything in shorthand—even the tiniest deviations in dialogue or movement from one take to the next—and how she then typed the data on to her Continuity Sheets in sextuplicate, which were distributed to the production office, the cutting rooms, the property and art departments, and the hairdressing, make-up, and wardrobe sections. It seemed an age before I finally managed to detach Henry from her earnest explanations and get him to myself.

"Now," I said, "what's all this?"

"You sound like a policeman," said Henry. "That's what I'm supposed to say to people."

"You know very well what I mean," I said. "Don't tell me that this is just a social call. You told me you were working. Well, what's up? What do you want?"

"I want to talk to you," said Henry—"about Margery Phipps."

"You've already done that," I said. "I've told you all I know, which is very little. Really, there's no need to come and disturb the whole unit, simply because some idiot of an old woman from Lewisham . . ."

Henry interrupted me. "Last time we met," he said, "I promised to show you a copy of the note that Margery left for her mother. Somehow I forgot. I've brought it for you to see today."

"I'm not very interested," I said. "Apparently the coroner was satisfied. There seems no reason why I should read it."

"Nevertheless," said Henry, "I'd be grateful if you would."

He handed me a paper. It was a photostatic copy of a letter. I recognized Margery's handwriting without difficulty; it had been a large and distinctive hand, with widely looped letters.

"I am sorry I have to take this step. I sincerely feel that it is the only thing. There is no need to tell you the reasons, Dear." At the bottom, it was signed with one word— "Margery."

"Well?" said Tibbett.

"Well, what?" I answered. "This seems a perfectly ordinary suicide note to me. What else did you expect her to say in it?"

"It was on the table in her apartment," said Henry, "in an envelope addressed to Mrs. Cyril Phipps. The envelope was typewritten on Margery's typewriter."

"Well?" I said again.

"Doesn't anything strike you as—unusual—about that note?"

"No," I said. "Nothing."

"When you compare it," said Henry, in that almost diffident way he has, "with the other note I told you about, the one to her real mother, the style is so entirely different."

"That's not surprising," I said. "One was to her real mother, and the other to her foster mother. And then, I dare say, she wasn't worrying too much about literary style when she was about to jump out of a seventh-story window. In any case," I added, "I can reassure you on one point. That's certainly Margery's handwriting."

Henry gave me an odd, sharp look. "Yes," he said. There was a pause.

I looked at my watch. "Well," I said, "if you'll forgive me— and if you've seen all you want to—I think I ought to be getting back to work. My office doesn't run itself, you know."

"I haven't quite finished yet," Tibbett said. "Tell me, did you ever receive a letter from Miss Phipps, written in her own handwriting?"

"Yes," I said. "Her letter of resignation was handwritten. That's why I was able to recognize her writing at once."

"Where is that letter now?" Henry asked.

"In the appropriate file in my office, of course," I said, with some impatience. It seemed to me that Tibbett's questions were getting more and more futile.

"If you're going back there now," he went on, "perhaps I might come with you. I'm rather interested in seeing that letter."

I could hardly refuse without seeming churlish, although the last thing that I wanted was Henry Tibbett rooting around in my office among my private papers. I did not like the turn that things were taking.

"I'll send my car away and ride with you, if I may," said Henry. "I don't want to give your office a bad reputation."

"What do you mean by that?"

"I just thought you might prefer not to have a police car parked outside."

"Look here," I said, with a certain amount of heat, "just what is going on? Are you here on official business or aren't you? What authority have you to demand to look at the firm's private correspondence?"

I suppose my voice must have risen more than I intended, for Gervase Mountjoy, who was as usual reading a newspaper, looked up and gave both of us a long, hard stare as we walked past, and I saw Amy, the hairdresser, whisper something to Anton and giggle.

I went on in what was little more than a whisper. "If this is a police investigation, we surely have a right to be informed officially. Just because I happen to have met you socially, that's no excuse for trading on our acquaintance in order to . . ."

Henry laid a hand on my arm. "Mr. Croombe-Peters," he said, "I do appreciate your point of view. Believe me, my only object in approaching you unofficially is to cause you and your colleagues the least possible embarrassment and inconvenience."

"If you'd just explain," I began.

"I'll explain soon enough," he said, and then fell silent. In fact, he scarcely opened his mouth while we were in the car. I found a free parking meter close to the office, and we went up in the lift together. As we walked through the outer office, where Sylvia sits with her typewriter and files, I said to her, "Oh, Sylvia. Look out Margery Phipps's letter of resignation and bring it in to my office, will you?"

I ushered Tibbett into my office, closed the door behind us, and offered him a chair. Then I sat down at my desk, lit a cigarette, and said, "I suppose it's your job to make mysteries out of perfectly ordinary events, but it seems to me you're carrying it a bit far this time. What on earth is on your mind?"

Instead of replying to my question, Henry said, "Can you remember offhand what Margery said in that letter?"

"Nothing very much. Just that she was sorry that for personal reasons she would have to resign her job. A very typical letter—short, concise, and to the point. You'll see it in a moment."

The door opened and Sylvia came in. She's a calm little person as a rule, and extremely efficient, and I could see at once that she was upset about something. "Mr. Croombe-

Peters," she said, "I—I'm terribly sorry—if you can wait just a moment . . ."

"I rather imagine that Sylvia can't find the letter," Henry said. He grinned encouragingly at Sylvia, who smiled back as if relieved to have found an ally.

"I just can't understand it," she said, more to Henry than to me. "I know I filed it the day it came in, but it's not there. The only thing I can think of is that Mr. Potman's secretary must have borrowed it for the address or something. I'm just going along to ask her now. I mean, it *can't* just have disappeared, can it?"

"By all means ask," said Henry, "but I doubt if you'll find it. It's all right," he added, rather quickly, "it's not your fault, Sylvia. Run along now and see if you can locate it anywhere in the offices."

Sylvia vanished, still red in the face and thankful to escape. Henry turned to me. "This is just what I expected, and feared," he said.

"I don't see what . . ."

"Just supposing, Mr. Croombe-Peters," said Henry, "that for some reason you wanted to forge a note in someone else's handwriting. Not being an expert forger, how would you set about it?"

"I—what a preposterous idea. Why should I want to forge anything?"

"My question," said Henry blandly, "was purely hypothetical. How would you set about it?"

"Well—I suppose I'd try to get hold of a specimen of the person's handwriting and copy it."

"Do you think that would deceive anybody?"

"That," I retorted with a certain amount of sarcasm, "would depend on my skill as a forger, wouldn't it?"

"Forgery," said Tibbett, "is a highly specialized craft; you could almost call it an art. I very much doubt if you, as an amateur—and I'm assuming you *are* an amateur—would be able to produce anything that would pass muster. Can't you think of a better way?"

"No," I said shortly, "I can't." I could see the trend of his questions and I did not like it.

"In your position," Tibbett went on, "I would try to get hold of some fairly long document handwritten by the person in question—a letter, for instance—and then compose my forged note entirely of words and phrases which occurred in that letter. In that way, instead of copying I could actually trace complete words and sentences. You see, most forgeries are given away by the lack of flow with which the individual letters are put together. Do you agree with me that it would be a pretty ingenious idea to do as I've suggested?"

"I think it would be nonsense," I said.

Tibbett put a hand into his breast pocket and brought out Margery's suicide note again. "Well," he said, "you may not think much of the idea, and maybe you're right; but it was undoubtedly the method used to forge this. Or so our experts say."

"Are you trying to tell me . . . ?"

"Margery Phipps," said Tibbett, "did not write this. It is an amateur but quite competent piece of forgery. Normally, of course, a suicide note isn't subjected to the scrutiny of handwriting experts, and this particular piece of trickery would almost certainly have passed unnoticed if it hadn't been for the fact that Mrs. Arbuthnot had roused my interest sufficiently to make me take a second look at it. Quite apart from the difference in style between this and the letter that Margery wrote to her real mother, it struck me, on a more careful reading, that this note was composed of the sort of phrases which would be likely to occur in a business letter—'to take this step,' 'There is no need,' 'Dear,' 'sincerely,' and so forth." He paused.

I said nothing.

"So," Tibbett went on, "I visited Margery's apartment yesterday, and had a bit of a hunt around among her things. I told you before that our people found very little in the way of personal papers, and nothing whatever to connect Margery with Northburn Films; but I had a good idea of what I was looking for, and sure enough, by great good luck, I found it."

"Found what?"

"This," said Henry. He extracted a folded sheet of paper from his wallet. "It's almost certainly a draft copy of her letter of resignation. I'd like you to read it, and tell me if it corresponds to the one which your secretary has so carelessly mislaid."

I unfolded the paper without enthusiasm. It had no superscription, and several words had been crossed out and others substituted.

I am sorry to have to tell you that, for personal reasons, I am compelled to resign my position as from today. I regret that I have to take this step as I have enjoyed working on *Street Scene,* but I am afraid that it is the only thing I can do. I am enclosing two weeks' salary in lieu of notice, and hope you will feel that this arrangement is satisfactory. If you agree, there is no need for any further correspondence between us.

Reluctantly I said, "Yes, that is certainly a draft of the letter she sent to me."

"You will notice," said Tibbett, "that every phrase in the so-called suicide note occurs in that letter, with the exception of the words 'Dear' and 'sincerely,' which presumably were in the final copy."

"That's all very well," I said, "but what about the envelope addressed to Mrs. Phipps?"

"What about it, indeed?" Henry echoed. "If you remember, I told you that it was typewritten; that was another inconsistency which made me think."

"Typewritten on Margery's own machine," I pointed out.

"Yes," said Henry. "And the typewriter was in Margery's flat. It was a very audacious and cool-headed bit of work. We don't know whether the apartment was broken into and the envelope prepared beforehand, along with the note, or whether the person in question actually had the effrontery to sit down and type the envelope after . . ." He stopped.

"After what?" I asked. My throat felt curiously dry, and my voice sounded to me like a sort of croak.

"After Margery had been murdered," said Henry.

9

There was a tingling silence. I suppose I had known all along what Tibbett was going to say, but it still gave me a numbing shock to hear the actual words. I was as incapable of speech as if I had just fallen through thin ice into a freezing pool— literally, physically breathless. Then I became aware that Henry was smiling easily, sitting back comfortably in his chair, and I made a tremendous effort to concentrate on what he was saying.

". . . could have had access to the files?" he ended, on a note of interrogation.

"I—I'm sorry. What did you say?"

"I was asking you who could have got at that file?"

"I don't know. Anybody. Things here aren't treated as top secret, you know." I took a cigarette, and it seemed to steady me.

"I'm still very much in the dark over the case," said Henry.

It made my blood curdle to hear him use that word, with all its associations of investigations, questionings, clues, dossiers, scientific experiments, fingerprints—and then the arrest, the trial, the verdict, the sentence. I forced myself to listen again.

"One thing that seems obvious," Henry was saying, "is that the murderer was in some way connected with Northburn Films, firstly, because an outsider could hardly have taken the letter, and secondly, because of the deliberate removal from Margery's flat of any papers connecting her with the company. That gives me a very narrow field to work in."

"What do you mean, a narrow field?" I asked. "There are more than fifty people in the unit, one way and another, counting the principal actors. You must have seen that for yourself today."

"Ah, yes," said Henry, "but most of them have perfect alibis."

"What do you mean?"

"Margery Phipps was killed at seven minutes past four last Tuesday afternoon," said Henry. "She fell to her death in full view of several people who were walking in Dredge Street. They naturally assumed that she had jumped from the window. In fact, in the words of the old song, she didn't fall, she was pushed—*by somebody who was in that apartment with her*. Naturally, there was pandemonium in the street below, and it was quite some time before it was established who she was and just which apartment she came from. Plenty of time for the murderer to slip quietly out of the building by another door. The wretched place has no less than four exits, all leading onto different streets, and, of course, all the staff had come rushing out into Dredge Street to gape at the disaster. Do you know the place, by the way? Chelsea Mansions?"

"I know it from the outside, of course," I said. "A monstrosity, an artistic abortion in dirty concrete."

"I'm not competent to judge it architecturally," Henry said, with a slight smile, "but it's a detective's nightmare. A rabbit warren with more than four hundred flats in it, and, as I said, four separate entrances. The main foyer is always full of tenants and visitors coming and going, and there's only one porter on duty. Even so there might have been a faint hope that he'd have been able to pick out a familiar face among your people; but, of course, he was called at once and went rushing round to Dredge Street, which is the little road at the back of the building. All the murderer had to do was to come down in the lift, mix with the crowd in the foyer, and walk out. The only risk was of meeting somebody on the seventh-floor corridor, but it was a remote one. Margery's flat is just opposite the lift."

"You said that most of our people had alibis," I remarked. "What did you mean by that?"

"Simply," said Henry, "that nobody can be engaged on

shooting a film in a disused Underground station in the City
—as I believe you were that day—and simultaneously be pushing young ladies out of windows in Chelsea. The technicians
and actors who were actually on the set are in the clear. The
same goes for anyone who was working here in the office all
the afternoon, and can prove it. That leaves us with the members of the unit who tend to . . . move about from one place
to another."

He was looking at me curiously now, and I felt a sudden
surge of real anger. How dared he pick on me like that? Anger
brought warmth, and with warmth came common sense. The
numbness had passed, and I was able to lean back and give as
good as I was getting in the matter of slow looks and quizzical
smiles.

"My dear Tibbett," I said, "I am afraid that you are very
badly informed. What can our much-vaunted police force be
coming to?"

His face did not change, but I could sense that he was
annoyed. "Badly informed?" he said. "About what?"

"About the movements of the members of this unit."

"Your secretary told me on the telephone this morning . . ."

"Doubtless," I said, punctuating the words with puffs as I
lit a cigarette, "you asked Sylvia where the unit had been
operating on the day in question, and she told you—quite
correctly—that our location had been the Underground station. What she did not tell you—because you did not ask—
was that we finished early. In fact, the unit broke up for the
day soon after half-past eleven, and everyone went their separate ways. So, you see, any of us could have been at Chelsea
Mansions at seven minutes past four."

"Oh, hell," said Henry. He said it so simply and with such
obvious dismay that I could not help smiling. When he wished,
he had the same disarming straight-forwardness as Sam Potman. There was a little pause, and then he said, "Any of you?"

"Well, now you come to mention it, no. Rushes were shown
at four o'clock in the private cinema in the basement here, but
they weren't very well attended. The only people there were
Sam Potman, Fred Harborough, the cameraman, and the Continuity Girl, Diana. And, of course," I could not resist another
quizzical smile, "yours truly."

"So," said Henry, "anybody else on the unit could have . . . ?"

"Precisely," I said.

There was a short silence. Then Henry said, "I'm going round to Chelsea Mansions after lunch. Would you care to have a bite to eat and then come along there with me?"

"I'm rather busy this afternoon," I said. I had a feeling that it sounded unconvincing.

"I wish you would," Henry said. "You might be able to help me a great deal."

My instinct was to refuse, but then a small warning bell seemed to sound at the back of my brain. If this were going to develop into an unpleasant affair, it would look very bad if Northburn Films had not co-operated up to the hilt right from the beginning.

"I'll come," I said.

We had a quick lunch of cheese and sausages in a nearby pub, during which Henry did not mention Margery Phipps at all but spoke about his wife, Emmy, her prowess as a cook, and the delicious recipes she had brought back from their summer holiday in Spain. I listened as politely as I could. At half-past two, we took a cab to Chelsea.

Chelsea Mansions was a vast new concrete structure with no apparent raison d'être except to provide a minimum area of square footage in which to house a maximum number of people. It was, however, tricked out with the garnish of so-called luxury—a word frequently bandied about by those who, poor devils, have no conception of its real meaning. "Luxury" was here represented by a hall porter in over-elaborate uniform, a worn and dirty carpet in the foyer—where linoleum or tiles would have been infinitely more attractive and practical—and a couple of immense vases filled with plastic lilies and carnations. Henry approached the porter, produced his official card, and was given the key to No. 716. Then we went up to the seventh floor.

Margery's flat was small but beautifully furnished. It consisted of a single large room, which was approached through a minuscule hallway. The room had two windows, both overlooking Dredge Street. To the right, a door from the main living room led into a box-like kitchen; to the left, an identical door gave access to a dwarf-size bathroom. These necessary offices boasted a window apiece, giving the occupant of the flat two more opportunities of viewing the narrow and sordid pavements of Dredge Street, the garish posters of the small and arty cinema opposite, and the rear court yards of a row of Regency houses whose frontages stood on the more fashionable length of Flaxman Avenue. The flat had the depressing, heavy atmosphere of disused premises. I walked over to the right-hand window.

"So she jumped from here," I said, for want of something to say.

Henry replied seriously, "No, she didn't."

Remembering his earlier hints, I amended, "I should say, it was from here that she was pushed." I did not intend to be caught out in any inaccuracies, whether of fact or of grammar.

To my surprise, however, Henry went on. "No. Not from here. From the kitchen."

"The kitchen? What an extraordinary thing."

"It's not the only extraordinary thing about this case," said Henry, with more than a touch of gloom.

"But how do you know . . ."

"I haven't been able to find any witness who actually saw her come through the window," said Henry, "which isn't surprising. Very few people walk about the streets with their eyes fixed on seventh-story windows. But once she had fallen, and the crowd had collected down below, everyone agrees that it was the kitchen window which was swinging open. And my men found some strands of wool from her cardigan caught on the window latch."

"But why . . . ?" I began, and then realized that I was talking to myself. Henry, with that peculiar self-contained expression that I have often noticed when he is concentrating hard, had wandered off into the bathroom. I decided to take a look in the kitchen, since it appeared to have been the center of the affair.

The first thing that struck me was that Margery had certainly been anxious to do things the hard way, if she had, in fact, thrown herself out of this window; I also reflected that, if Henry's fantastic theories were true and she had been murdered, the murderer must have been a maniac to choose this room for his defenestration. The kitchen was, as I have indicated, extremely small. It possessed three features—a sink, a refrigerator, and an electric stove—and each of these occupied the whole of one wall, the fourth wall being taken up with the door from the living room. The window, set high and with a broad sill, could only be reached by clambering over the electric stove; but a small wooden stool, liberally scuffed with the marks of stiletto heels, was placed so as to indicate that this was the method Margery had used to reach the window when the kitchen needed ventilation. The window itself was of the casement type, divided vertically by a metal bar into two sections, each of which opened like a door onto the dusty Chelsea equivalent of fresh air. The more I looked, the more baffled I felt. In the living room, a window seat ran along the length of the Dredge Street wall, giving easy access to the large, low windows. Whether the thing had been suicide or murder, it was almost inconceivable that anybody should have chosen the kitchen window when the other was available.

"This was a very expensive flat, you know. Still is, in fact." I became aware of Henry's voice behind me, and turned. He was standing in the doorway which separated the kitchen from the living room. "I'd be interested to know how she was able to afford it."

"She was a key member of a film unit," I replied with a certain sense of pique—if we are to be forced by the unions into paying fantastic salaries to our technicians, we might as well be given credit for it. "Such people are not underpaid, you know."

"All the same," Henry gestured vaguely. "Have you looked around? Brand new television set, pure silk interlined curtains, latest model of electric stove with all the gadgets, quilted satin bedhead, deep pile carpet in white of all ridiculous colors— isn't it frightful?"

I could not make him out. "It is a very luxurious and well-appointed flat," I began.

"Isn't it?" said Henry. "That just about sums it up. Did she really have such appalling taste?"

"Margery Phipps had very good taste, and I think that her apartment shows it," I said rather coldly.

I remembered Tibbett's shabby Victorian abode, and decided that he must be suffering from understandable jealousy. After all, he was near the top of a difficult and competitive profession, and it must have been galling to reflect that he was almost certainly not earning as much as a Continuity Girl.

"You may consider," I said, "that people like Margery are overpaid, but I can assure you that in terms of value for money a good Continuity Girl is . . ."

Henry seemed to have lost interest in the subject. He had walked into the kitchen, and was examining the gleaming electric stove.

"I wish," he said, "that I could afford something like this for Emmy. She has a terrible time with ours; it's about fifteen years old. D'you know how these things work?"

I went over to the kitchen doorway. Henry was looking admiringly at the battery of knobs, switches, clocks, and levers.

"I can see that it has one of these new eye-level ovens with a fireproof glass door," I said, "and a built-in clock that has stopped at a quarter to four. As to the dial that's set at three-quarters of an hour, I suppose it's some sort of timing device, but don't ask me how it all works. It looks to me like the sort of monster that wakes you in the morning with a boiled egg, a cup of tea, and the weather forecast."

"Um," said Henry. "Yes." He began opening cupboards above and below the sink. As far as I could see, there was nothing remarkable in them, just neat glass jars of tea, coffee, sugar, and rice; packets of dried fruit, matches, and detergent; a half-burnt candle and several pieces of string; some plastic bags and a selection of dishcloths. Henry, too, seemed to find the exercise unrewarding.

He straightened up, turned to me, and said, "Now you can tell me something. I've asked you before. Which member of your unit might have been blackmailed by Margery Phipps, and what about?"

"Nobody," I said. "It's a preposterous idea."

"I can't agree that it's preposterous," said Henry. "It seems to me to be obvious. Margery was the daughter of a professional blackmailer, and her letter to Mrs. Arbuthnot makes it plain that she was dabbling in her father's old game. A lot of wealthy people work in films, and some of them must have secrets. I'm fairly sure that this wasn't her first excursion into crime, though her note indicates that it was her most important one to date. Frankly, I don't believe that this flat was bought and furnished out of her legitimate earnings."

I laughed. "My dear Tibbett," I said, "I have no idea what Margery may or may not have done in the past, but I can assure you that there is nobody on the *Street Scene* unit who would be worth five minutes of a blackmailer's time. You surely must know that we're making the film on a shoestring. Why, at one time we were very nearly bankrupt. If what you say about Margery is true, then her victims must have been previous acquaintances."

Henry looked thoughtful. "What about Fiametta Fettini?" he asked.

"Fiametta must be pretty rich, certainly," I said with some feeling. "At least, judging by the amount we've had to pay her. But I can't imagine that there's any sort of publicity, however distasteful, that she wouldn't welcome with open arms. She's married to that poor little Palladio man, and yet look how she openly pursued Bob Meakin when he was alive. And she makes no secret of the fact that she got her first chance in films by sleeping with some director or other. She's nothing but a cheap little tart, and her publicity agent trades on it."

"There are other things besides a disreputable sex life," Henry began.

I cut him short. "I defy you," I said, "to mention anything which could harm Fiametta. She's written newspaper articles about how she was arrested for stealing in Naples when she was thirteen, and seduced by her uncle when she was fourteen, and set up in a love nest by this film director when she was sixteen. The only hold Margery might possibly have had over her would have been a threat to expose that in fact she was perfectly respectable and had been reared in a convent."

Henry sighed. "All right, you win," he said. "What about the other people on the unit?"

"Sam Potman," I said, "has no assets in this world except his remarkable talent. The little bit of money he did manage to save has all gone toward making this film. He's not married; he's perfectly respectable; and he cares about nothing except his work. The only thing I can think of that would upset him would be to be deprived of the chance of doing his job, and no power on earth could do that. Even if *Street Scene* had gone bankrupt, Sam would've got a job straight away with one of the big companies. He's good and they know it."

"Keith Pardoe," said Henry, "struck me as being rather an unstable character."

"Well," I said, "he's artistic. One has to make allowances."

"Does one?" Henry said with a smile.

"Yes, I think one does. You can't expect a man of Keith's brilliance to behave quite like other people." Having said this, I felt I could let go a little bit. "I won't pretend," I went on, "that Keith doesn't infuriate me sometimes. Especially since he took over Bob's part, he seems to think of nothing except his personal ambition. He has become vain and self-opinionated and—however, all this is beside the point. Of all of us, Keith is the poorest. He has absolutely no money except what he is earning on *Street Scene,* and he appears to be spending most of that in ostentatious living."

"Would you say," Henry asked carefully, "that his prospects were good?"

"My dear Tibbett, far be it from me to start predicting the future. Anybody who could tell in advance whether a picture was going to be popular or not would be a millionaire long since. All I can say is that *if* things go as we hope, Keith Pardoe will be an international star. Even if the film doesn't make the impact that we expect it to, his name is already well enough known to guarantee him good parts in the future. I believe he's already had several tentative offers, but he's wisely not accepting anything until *Street Scene* has been shown."

"I see," said Henry. "What about his wife?"

"Biddy is a splendid girl," I said quickly. "I know some people are upset by the way she swears and so forth, but I assure you . . ."

Henry smiled. "I liked her," he said. "But that wasn't what I meant. She's a successful writer, isn't she? I was just wondering whether she might have a lot of money or a guilty secret or both."

I shook my head. "She's not wealthy," I said, "and, like Sam, she put all she had—the proceeds from her first book—into the film. As for guilty secrets—can you imagine Biddy standing for blackmail? 'Publish and be damned' would certainly be her attitude, but she wouldn't say anything as mild as 'damned,' not if I know her."

"Hm," said Henry. "That leaves you."

"Me? What do you mean, me?"

"You are wealthy, and you have a social position to keep up. I don't imagine you'd say 'publish and be damned,' would you?"

I admit that I was very angry at the insolent tone in Tibbett's voice. "I won't even bother," I said coldly, "to defend myself against your insinuations. I hope it will be enough to satisfy you if I point out that I can account for every minute of my time throughout the day when Margery—died. And I have witnesses to prove it."

Henry had pulled out a small and shabby-looking notebook and a ballpoint pen. "I'd be very interested to hear what you did that day," he said. "Forgive me if I jot it down. It's not an official statement, you understand. This is just to help my memory, which isn't very efficient."

"All right," I said. "I'll tell you. I got to my office at nine A.M. and dictated letters to my secretary for an hour. Then I took a cab to the Underground station, where the unit was shooting. I went immediately into Miss Fettini's dressing room, where I discussed various matters with her, including her costume for the ball scene. She will certainly remember. It must have been soon after eleven that I was called out by Hilda, Miss Fettini's dresser, to go and speak to Mrs. Robert Meakin."

Henry looked up sharply. "Sonia Meakin?" he said. "What was she doing there?"

"She had come to collect some odds and ends that had been left behind in her husband's dressing room," I explained.

"And so you gave them to her?"

"Well, no, not exactly. I couldn't lay hands on them for the moment. Sam was anxious for Mrs. Meakin to leave the location; he was afraid she might be distressed by the associations of the place. And then . . ."

Henry grinned. "And then there was Fiametta Fettini," he said.

"Quite."

"Did they meet, in fact?"

"No. I suggested to Mrs. Meakin that she might like some

coffee, and I took her to the Olde Tudor Espresso Bar around the corner. We were there until nearly midday. I told her to come to my office during the afternoon to collect Bob's things, and then I saw her to a taxi. She can confirm all this."

"Good," said Henry. "What did you do then?"

"I went back to the station, and found that the unit had packed up for the day and that Sam had given everyone the afternoon off. Typically wasteful. Just because we were two days ahead of schedule . . . Anyhow, there was nothing I could do about it."

"And how did you spend your afternoon off?"

I laughed, a trifle bitterly. "Afternoon off?" I repeated. "I certainly couldn't afford any such luxury. I went straight back to my office and carried on with my work. Sylvia went out and got me some sandwiches and coffee at about half-past one. Miss Cohen, the Production Manager, was in my office from soon after two until about three. After that, I worked on my schedules until five minutes to four, when I went down to the private cinema in the basement for rushes. I think I told you that nobody else showed up except Sam, Fred Harborough, and Diana, the new Continuity Girl. By the time we'd seen the rushes and had some fairly lengthy discussion about them, it was getting on for five. I went back to my office to finish things up, and I was just on the point of leaving, at five past six, when Sonia Meakin arrived to fetch her husband's things. It was she who told me about Margery's death. It was already in the papers."

I paused to light a cigarette, and became aware that Henry was looking at me steadily.

"Why?" he said.

"Why? Well, you know how fast these things get reported . . ."

"I didn't mean that. I meant why did Sonia Meakin tell you?"

"Because—I don't know." I reflected with irritation that Henry was pushing me into a position where I would have to go into the whole dreary and irrelevant story of how I had pretended that Margery had the cardboard box, when in fact it was in Fiametta's dressing room.

"What made Mrs. Meakin connect Margery Phipps with

Street Scene?" Henry pursued. "She'd never been on the set before, had she?"

"No. I don't know how she knew. I suppose Bob must have mentioned Margery's name. It wasn't a secret, after all."

"What exactly did Mrs. Meakin say to you?"

"I can't remember. Something like 'Have you seen this?' And then she showed me the paper."

"And what happened then?"

"I was naturally rather upset. I gave Mrs. Meakin her box and got rid of her as quickly as I could, and then I went to Mr. Potman's office and told him about Margery. Then, if you remember, I telephoned you."

"So you did," said Henry. "Was that Mr. Potman's idea, by any chance?"

"It certainly was not. In fact, Sam behaved very callously about the whole thing, I considered. Merely remarked that it was a good thing Margery wasn't working for us when it happened. But that's Sam all over. The film is all that matters. I sometimes think he has liquid celluloid in his veins instead of blood."

Henry was reading over what he had written in his notebook. At length he said, "So, from about eleven in the morning, when you took Mrs. Meakin out for coffee, you didn't see any of the senior members of the unit except Mr. Potman?"

"That's right."

"Have you any idea how the others spent the afternoon?"

"None at all. Sam told me that he thought Keith and Biddy were both looking tired and that he'd sent them off to the country. Oh, and Keith had his hair cut. There was quite a row about it the next day. Thoroughly unprofessional. If Biddy had been there, she'd never have allowed him . . ."

"So she wasn't with him during the afternoon?"

"She said she wasn't, when this row blew up about his haircut," I said.

"Then where was she?"

"I've really no idea," I said, with some irritation. "I know she telephoned Sam here soon after four—rushes had just started."

"Did she, indeed? What about?"

"My dear Tibbett, how should I know? You'd better ask

her."

"That's just what I intend to do," said Henry. "Shall we go back to your office?"

"Why to my office?"

"Because," said Henry, glancing at his watch, "I have a rendezvous there with some of your colleagues when the day's shooting is over, which I imagine should be any moment now. I hope you don't mind."

"I should have thought it only common politeness to ask my permission before . . ."

"I'm sorry, Croombe-Peters," said Tibbett. He sounded genuinely abashed. "I really didn't get a chance to speak to you this morning, you were so busy. And I'm afraid it slipped my mind afterward. You do understand that all I want to do at this stage is to have a friendly chat with one or two people."

"Since you intend to do it in my office," I said, "I presume you will have no objection to my being present."

Henry looked at me again, in that steady and disconcerting way that he has. Then he said, "By all means. I should be delighted. Shall we go?"

I was outside in the passage, pressing the button to call the lift, when I realized that Henry was not with me. I went back into the flat in time to see him climbing down from the stool in the kitchen. He had evidently been taking another look at the fatal window.

"The lift's here," I said.

"Sorry," he replied, "just coming. Wanted to see something . . ."

He came back into the living room, brushing a speck of something white from his sleeve.

"What's that?" I asked. "Fingerprinting powder?"

"There's quite a lot of it around, I'm afraid," said Henry. "I've had the flat thoroughly tested for prints. No good, of course."

"You mean, there aren't any?"

"Only Margery's own. And not many of them."

"What do you mean? Do you think somebody wiped them off deliberately?"

Henry sighed, a littled impatiently. "Either that," he said, "or else Margery Phipps was house-proud and kept everything well polished."

"She surely wouldn't have bothered about housework on the day she killed herself," I said.

"No," said Henry, "but she might well have on the day she was murdered." He took one last look around the apartment, and then said, "Right. Let's go."

10

Sam Potman, Fiametta, Biddy, and Keith were all in my office when Henry Tibbett and I got back to Soho. I could hear them laughing and chattering as soon as I got into the reception hall. Certainly, it did not sound as though any of them was particularly worried about the thought of a police investigation. I remembered Henry's deceptive bonhomie on Hampstead Heath earlier in the day, and decided that he must have lulled them all into believing that his inquiries were the merest routine. I felt quite certain that nobody but myself was aware of the threat of a murder case hanging over us. I opened the door of my office and went in.

Fiametta was sitting on my desk, showing a yard or so of shapely leg and laughing in an exaggerated way at something Keith had said. Sam was sitting in the big arm chair opposite my desk, smoking his inevitable cigar and looking as though his thoughts were miles away, which they probably were. This was the time of day when he liked to retire to his own office in order to plan the next day's shooting. Biddy, to my annoyance, was standing behind my desk reading Sylvia's typescripts of the letters I had dictated that morning. Not that there was anything secret about them, but I felt it was an unwarranted liberty. There was a moment of silence as Henry and I came in, and then everybody began to talk at once.

Fiametta, typically, threw herself into Henry's arms and kissed him soundly, crying, "Ah! My favorite little policeman!"

Sam stood up and said, "Right. Let's get this over. I've work to do."

Keith said nervously, "What's it all about, anyway? I thought . . ."

Biddy said, "Oh, shut up, Keith."

Henry disentangled himself from Fiametta, beamed at everyone, and said, "I'm really very sorry to disturb you. It's just that we're making a few more inquiries about Margery Phipps."

"Margery? But it's all over and done with. The coroner said," Keith's voice rose, and he ran a hand through his newly cropped hair. It flashed across my mind that if Keith had been trying to create the impression of a man with a guilty conscience, he could hardly have done it better. Knowing him as well as I did, I put it down entirely to his hysterical temperament, but I wondered what Tibbett was making of it. It certainly seemed to register, for Tibbett gave him a sharp look and said, "It won't take long. Perhaps the rest of you would wait outside while I talk to Mr. Pardoe. Mr. Croombe-Peters is going to sit in with me, to see fair play."

By now, it seemed to be getting through to the others that this was a serious business rather than a social call. Sam, Biddy, and Fiametta went out in a subdued silence. Henry motioned me to sit down at the desk, while he himself perched on the edge of it with his little notebook. Then he invited Keith to take the large arm chair.

"No, thanks. I'd rather stand," said Keith. "What is all this about?"

"What I'd like to know," said Henry, "is exactly what you did after shooting finished on the day that Margery Phipps died. If you'd just run through . . ."

"It's no business of yours," Keith said, hotly. He appealed to me. "Pudge, what right has this man to . . . ?"

"He has every right, I'm afraid," I said. "He is an officer of the C.I.D. and he has reason to believe that Margery Phipps was murdered."

I had not been briefed by Tibbett whether or not to disclose this information, but I did not believe that he could hope to keep it a secret for long. He betrayed no emotion at my remark, but went on making notes. Keith, however, reacted violently.

"It's not true!" he shouted. He seemed on the point of losing all control, and put his hand out to grasp the edge of the desk in order to steady himself. "I swear it's not true! She killed herself! They said so at the inquest! You can't come here raking it all up now! I don't know anything about it!"

For the first time, Henry looked up. "I'm sure you don't, Mr. Pardoe," he said. "All I want from you is an account of your movements that day. Nobody is accusing you of anything."

I could see Keith making a great effort to get control of himself. After a moment he swallowed, and said, "I'm sorry, Inspector. It came as a bit of a shock—what Pudge said. This morning you didn't mention . . ."

"I know." Henry grinned disarmingly. "We policemen have to be horribly discreet. As yet I'm only working on the merest of suspicions, and I wouldn't have used the word 'murder' if Mr. Croombe-Peters hadn't come out with it so impetuously. However, now that it has been said, I may as well tell you that I'm not entirely satisfied about the circumstances of Miss Phipps' death."

I was furious, as may be imagined. Earlier, Henry had told me quite categorically that he was treating Margery's death as murder and had ridiculed me when I protested. Now, he made it sound as though I was the one who had leapt to rash conclusions. Certainly, he had deliberately engineered matters so that I should be the one to mention murder, and not he. I had to admit, however, that the device served its purpose. Keith relaxed visibly, and said that he thought he would sit down after all. He lit a cigarette and then began to talk.

"There's really very little I can tell you," he said. "Sam got the shot in the can at about half-past eleven and broke for the day. He suggested that Biddy and I might like to have an afternoon in the country. He thought we'd both been working too hard."

"And did you go to the country?"

Keith hesitated for a moment. "Yes and no," he said.

Henry grinned. "Just what does that mean?" he asked.

"Well . . ." Keith looked embarrassed. "I suppose Biddy will tell you if I don't. We set out in my car and drove to Henley, where we stopped for lunch at some pub or other. We'd intended to take a boat out on the river afterward, but it didn't work out like that."

"Why not?"

"I'm afraid we had a row. If I'm to be absolutely frank, Inspector, I'm afraid that Biddy is jealous of me. Up to now, she's been the celebrity of the family, you see. She doesn't seem to realize that I've got a certain position to keep up these days. She can't expect me to—but I'm boring you. All this is unimportant. The only thing that matters to you is that we had a fight which ended in my walking out of the pub and driving off on my own."

I saw Henry's eyebrows go up a fraction of an inch. "How did Mrs. Pardoe get back, then?" he asked.

"I offered her the car," said Keith quickly, "but she wouldn't take it. She hates driving. She said she'd take a train."

"I see. And what did you do?"

"I drove back to London."

There was a pause. "Well," said Henry, "go on."

"I had my hair cut," said Keith.

"Where?"

"At the Belgrave Towers. They have quite a reasonable barber."

"Can you remember what time this was?"

To my surprise Keith answered promptly. "Yes. Ten past four exactly. I was in the barber's shop until half-past. It was Alfredo who cut my hair. He can confirm it."

Henry looked interested. "Have you any special reason for remembering all this so accurately?" he asked.

Keith smiled ruefully. "I have plenty of reason to remember that haircut," he said. "There was enough of a row about it the next day. And Sam said . . ."

"You remember, Henry," I put in, "I told you about that. Our unit hairdresser was furious with Keith, and quite rightly in my opinion. But then Sam said he'd given Keith permission, and there was nothing more that anyone could say. I still think . . ."

"Oh, wrap up, Pudge," said Keith. "Can't you ever stop making trouble?"

Henry intervened quietly but firmly. "And what did you do after that, Mr. Pardoe?"

"I went and bought some shirts at Peal's in Burlington Arcade. Then I went home. Biddy was already there. We made it up, and went out to dinner together at the Orangery."

"And when did you hear about Miss Phipps's death?"

"Not until the next day. Neither Biddy nor I bought a paper that evening."

"I see." Henry frowned slightly as he read quickly through his notes. "You didn't see anybody else during the afternoon, anybody who would remember you?"

"Just the barber," said Keith firmly.

"Right," said Henry. "I think that's all. Thank you very much, Mr. Pardoe. Would you mind asking your wife if she could spare me a moment?"

I felt that I must intervene. As Keith was walking toward the door I scribbled on a piece of paper "Fiametta is staying at the Belgrave Towers," and pushed it under Henry's nose. He glanced at it, but said nothing.

As the door closed behind Keith, I said, "He must have gone there to see her. Now he'll warn her to say nothing . . ."

Henry put a finger to his lips. "Not so loud, please," he said.

"But don't you see?"

"Of course I see your point. But you really must let me do as I . . ."

He got no further before the door opened and Biddy walked in.

She was wearing a white dress, shaped, as far as I could see, exactly like a potato sack and made of some coarsely woven material. The fact that it looked both charming and striking I can only put down to Biddy's vibrant personality, which I have tried, rather lamely, to convey before now. The dress had a scooped-out neckline that showed off her suntanned throat most attractively. I imagine that most girls would have embellished it with a necklace of some sort, but Biddy wore no jewelry except for a knuckle-duster ring on her right hand. Her left, as usual, was bare. I suppose she would have considered a wedding ring as some sort of a sign of bondage. Her shoes fascinated me. They were made in shiny patent leather, the color of a mole's fur, with squat heels and little black bows. They made her feet look like two tiny animals creeping across the carpet. This was not a pleasant conceit, but once the thought had crossed my mind, I could not get rid of it. I shrank instinctively from those small, neat feet, as one does from a mouse—not because the animal is dangerous, but because of the speed and unpredictability of it.

I became aware that the preliminaries were over, and that Biddy was speaking.

"It was the Black Bull in Henley," she said. "I suppose I was bloody silly, but Keith makes me mad sometimes. I blew my top."

"Will you tell me exactly what the quarrel was about, Mrs. Pardoe?"

Biddy looked straight at Henry. "No," she said, "I'd rather not. And my name is Miss Brennan."

"It's not, you know," said Henry pleasantly, "not legally."

Suddenly Biddy grinned widely, like a guttersnipe. "Why don't you call me Biddy?" she said. "Everyone else does."

"I'll call you whatever you like," said Henry. "Why won't you tell me what the fight was about?"

"Because I bloody well won't," said Biddy, exactly like a spoilt child.

Henry did not press the point any further. He went on, "So you quarreled. What happened then?"

"Keith said he was going. He stumped out of the dining room, and then put his head around the door and said did I want the car? He knew very well I'd say 'No.' He only did it to make us both look conspicuous. Everyone else stopped eating and turned to look. I was livid. I said I'd be perfectly happy to take a train—which I did."

"Straight away?"

"No. I went for a walk by the river. I was pretty damned upset, what with—with everything. I suppose I walked for about an hour. Then I went to the station and took the first train to London."

"Can you remember the time of the train?"

"About half-past two, I suppose. I was in London by half-past three. I went to the pictures."

"What did you see?"

"An old Marx Brothers film, *Duck Soup*."

Henry registered no emotion whatsoever. "Have you ever visited Miss Phipps's apartment?"

"Certainly not. I don't even know where she lived."

"Did you enjoy the film?"

"Enormously. I'd seen it often before, of course. I missed the first ten minutes, and the projector jammed halfway through reel two, but it didn't matter. It was still wonderful. It finished about half-past five, and I took a cab home. I got in a few minutes before Keith did. We—we decided to kiss and make up, and he took me out to dinner. Is that all you want to know?"

"That'll do for the moment," said Henry.

While we were waiting for Fiametta to come in, I made another attempt to say something on the subject of Keith and Fiametta. I could not imagine why Keith should be hiding the fact that he went to see her, if indeed he did. There was no scandal attached to their friendship. If he was concealing the visit, I pointed out, it must be for some ulterior motive. Perhaps . . .

To my annoyance, I realized that Tibbett was not listening. He had picked up an evening paper from my desk and was doodling on it with his ballpoint pen. Knowing from experience that there are none so deaf as those who don't want to hear, I stopped talking. After a moment or so Fiametta came in.

She sat down, hitching her short black skirt as high as she could, and exhibiting a very pretty leg to Henry. I noticed that she had left the top button of her chiffon blouse undone, and she now maneuvered her supple young body in such a way as to make this fact obvious. I was intrigued, for she did not, as a rule, take such pains to exude sex appeal to the ordinary run of mortals. This was the sort of thing that she normally reserved for the gentlemen of the press.

"Miss Fettini," said Henry, apparently unmoved by the exhibition, "how well did you know Miss Phipps?"

Fiametta stopped squirming and looked angry. "I knew 'er enoof," she said, in her low husky voice, "to know that she was a thief."

"A thief? What makes you say that?"

"A thief and a cheat. She take my gold lipstick with rubies. Then Pooge make her give it back, so she walk out on 'im. Pooge will tell you I say true. Isn't it, Pooge?" She flashed her dark eyes at me hopefully.

"It's not so at all," I said, "and you know it. You made a ridiculous and unjustified fuss . . ."

"I was robbed," said Fiametta. Her voice had sunk to a dangerous growl. "Isn't it enoof I am robbed, without you insult me also? Any more, I go back to Rome. Sue me if you like. I do not stay for . . ."

"My dear Fiametta," I said, "nobody is insulting you. I just think you were mistaken about Margery, that's all. You know that we all think the world of you . . ."

"Then why you not let me wear chiffon with sables in the ballroom scene?"

"I've explained. Sam feels . . ."

"Do forgive me for butting in," said Henry, "but isn't this rather off the point? Can we get back to your lipstick case, Miss Fettini? Why should you accuse Miss Phipps of stealing it?"

"Because she did," said Fiametta sulkily. Then suddenly she added, "She was a thief. I 'ave been a thief myself. I can tell."

"Look here, Tibbett," I said, "this is all nonsense." I told him briefly about the things which Margery had found in the dressing rooms, about Fiametta's ridiculous outburst, and how the precious lipstick had been produced. I did not tell him what Margery had said about it being made of tin and colored glass, because I did not want my office to be broken up, and I knew that when Fiametta got really angry her first instinct was to smash things. I made a mental note, however, to tell him later.

Henry behaved very tactfully. He listened to my story, sympathized with Fiametta, and said he absolutely understood how she felt, and that he'd noticed how people failed to appreciate the great sentimental value of small objects. In a few minutes he had her purring instead of growling; whereupon he quickly led her to the events of the day of Margery's death.

Fiametta confirmed that she had spent most of the morning with me. She could hardly have failed to do so, but nevertheless I was relieved. She was feeling far from kindly toward me, and would have been quite capable of lying just to put me in an awkward position. When the unit broke for the day at twenty to twelve, she said, she had gone back to her hotel, where her husband was nursing her sick monkey. She added, to my disappointment, that Peppi had now quite recovered.

"And the rest of the afternoon?" Henry inquired.

"I 'ave lunch sent to my suite. I stay with Giulio and my poor Peppi."

"You didn't leave the hotel at all?"

"Never once. Never till eight o'clock in the evening, when Giulio and I go for dinner to Dick Travers, my agent, at his home. He is very funny man," she added enigmatically.

"Did anyone," Henry asked, "visit you during the afternoon?"

Fiametta shook her head positively. "Nobody."

"Mr. Pardoe," said Henry, "told us he was in the Belgrave Towers during the afternoon."

Fiametta looked surprised. In most people the surprise would have passed as unmistakeably genuine; but I remembered that Fiametta was an accomplished actress in her own rather limited way. It was certainly within her powers to register surprise convincingly.

" 'E was? Then why he not come to see me?"

"I don't know," said Henry. "By the way, might I see the famous lipstick case?"

For a moment Fiametta looked really put out. Then she said, "No. Again I 'ave lose it."

"Again? That is unfortunate. How did it happen?"

Fiametta had evidently decided to carry the thing off with a flourish. " 'Ow should I know?" she demanded. "My maid is careless. All the maids in the 'otel are thieves, everyone know that. This time, it is gone, and I look for it no more. The past is the past, and what are a few small rubies? I 'ave 'undreds of rubies—and diamonds—and sables—and mink . . . You poor little man, you think I care over a little thing like a lipstick? Let the maid 'ave it! I don't will be bothered. My poor little policeman. If you find it, you shall 'ave it—as a gift from Fiametta Fettini . . ."

Whereupon she bestowed a resounding kiss on the top of Henry's head and swept out of the room, gurgling with laughter. Henry rubbed his head reflectively and said, "How very interesting."

"Pay no attention to her," I said. "She's preposterous."

"She's frightened," said Henry.

"Frightened?" I could not help laughing at that. "La Fettini isn't frightened of anything or anybody in the world."

"Oh, well," said Henry, meekly, "I may be mistaken. Ah, there you are, Mr. Potman."

"Now," said Sam, "let's get this over. We're busy people, you know."

"I know you are," said Henry, apologetically. "It won't take long."

"I gather from the oothers," said Sam, North Country accent well in evidence, "that you want to know wot we did all that day. Well, I can tell you, and fast. I broke the unit at twenty to twelve and came back here. I had a bite of lunch in my office with the costume designer. I had some things to talk over with him. Two to three, or thereabouts, I went for a bit of a walk, to do some thinking. Pudge will tell you it's a thing I'm partial to doing."

I nodded. "A very annoying habit," I said to Henry, but not, I hope, with any malice. "He just disappears. I remember the day Bob Meakin was killed; nobody could find him for hours. Just walking around the streets."

"I like London," said Sam shortly. "Anyhow, I was back here before half-past three, and I got through a bit of office work with my secretary till four, when we had the rushes. Pudge was there, and Fred Harborough and Diana; nobody else that I remember. Then I came back to my office and did a bit more work. It must have been a bit after six when Pudge came in and told me about Margery. Then I went home and spent the evening planning the next day's work."

"You had dinner at home?"

"I never go out in the evening when I've got a picture on the floor," said Sam.

"You're not married, are you, Mr. Potman?" said Henry. "Do you have a housekeeper, or . . . ?"

"No, I don't. I have a char who comes each morning. I like to do my own cooking of an evening. It helps me to think."

"By the way, Mr. Potman," said Henry, "did you ask your secretary to look out Miss Phipps's letter of resignation for you?"

Sam looked surprised. "Certainly not," he said, "why ever should I do that?"

"It's just that we can't lay hands on it at the moment," said Henry, "and Sylvia suggested that you might have . . ."

Sam shook his head. "Sorry, Inspector," he said, "can't help you. Never set eyes on it. It was addressed to Pudge, you know."

"I know," said Henry.

That seemed to be all that Sam could contribute, and he kept on looking at his watch in a marked manner until Henry told him he could go. As the door closed behind Sam, I breathed a sigh of relief.

"I'm glad that's over," I said.

"I'm afraid it's far from over," said Henry. "Still, I won't be bothering you people again for the time being, I hope. I've got other people to see, and—well, I'll be in touch. Thanks for the use of your office."

With that he left, saying "good-bye" most politely to Sylvia as he went.

I sat on at my desk unable to concentrate on the work which I knew I should be doing. We might have a short respite, but I knew Henry Tibbett well enough to be sure that once he had started something, he would go on with it to the bitter end. Heaven knew where the bitter end of this affair might lead him to. In an effort to distract my thoughts, I picked up the paper which Henry had left on the desk. It was open at the section headed "What's On in Town," and I noticed that Henry's doodling had taken the form of making inked rings around the announcement of the program at the New Forum Cinema. Idly, I read the advertisement. "New Forum, Chelsea. Marx Bros. *Duck Soup*. 2.15, 4.00, 6.15, 8.00." There did not seem to be anything very remarkable in it. It merely confirmed what Biddy had said. It was at that moment that my telephone rang.

"Mr. Croombe-Peters," said Sylvia's voice, "I've got Mrs.

Meakin on the line. Will you speak to her? She says it's very urgent."

I can't pretend that I was pleased. However, I could not imagine that Sonia Meakin could have anything vitally important to say, and speaking to her would at least give me the excuse I wanted for shelving my work for a few minutes longer.

"Very well," I said, "put her through."

A moment later Sonia Meakin's voice floated down the line. "Oh, Mr. Croombe-Peters. How kind of you to speak to me. I'm so sorry to disturb you—listen, I must see you. At once. I simply must."

This was more than I had bargained for. "I don't think I can manage," I began.

"You must. Oh, you must. I'm telephoning from the Olde Tudor coffee bar, you remember. Please be here in ten minutes."

"I'm sorry, Mrs. Meakin. It's out of the question." I could not imagine what the woman wanted, but I was certainly not prepared to go treking around to Covent Garden to find out.

"All right then. I'll come to you. I'll be outside your office in five minutes. Please."

"No."

"Mr. Croombe-Peters," she said softly, "Inspector Tibbett has been to see me."

"Has he really? I don't think that is any concern of mine."

"I didn't realize that the police were—that they . . ."

"You must forgive me, Mrs. Meakin. I'm very busy and . . ."

"Very well." Her voice had suddenly changed, grown hard. "Very well, Mr. Croombe-Peters. The next time I see Inspector Tibbett, I shall tell him the exact circumstances of my husband's death."

"You'll what?" For a moment, I was too taken aback to think. "I don't know what you mean."

"Don't you?" she answered, quietly. "Will you be outside your office in five minutes' time?"

There was nothing I could do. "Yes," I said, and rang off.

11

Sonia Meakin was waiting for me when I came out into the narrow Soho street five minutes later. She was on the opposite pavement, with her back to the door of our offices, and she was making a pretence of studying the menu of a scruffy-looking Italian restaurant. I crossed the street and came up behind her.

"Well, Mrs. Meakin," I said, "what do you want with me? I can't spare more than a few minutes."

She turned around and gave me the benefit of a long look from her limpid blue eyes. It was difficult to believe that anybody could look so innocent and appealing, while indulging in a particularly nasty form of blackmail.

"Oh, Mr. Croombe-Peters," she said, in a melting voice, "how good of you to see me."

"It's not good of me at all," I replied crossly. "I have come here simply because I intend to get to the bottom of the extraordinary remark which you made to me on the telephone."

She looked down demurely. "Well," she said, "we can't talk here in the street, can we? Shall we have a cup of coffee somewhere?"

"Very well." I looked at my watch. "But it'll have to be quick. There's an espresso bar around the corner in . . ."

"I was going to suggest the Casablanca in the King's Road."

"In Chelsea? Are you out of your mind? We can't possibly go all that way just to . . ."

She smiled, like a Madonna. "Oh, but we're going to Chelsea in any case, Mr. Croombe-Peters," she said, and before I could

152

say a word she had hailed a cab and climbed into it. There was nothing I could do but follow her.

I made one or two attempts to say something during the taxi ride, but Sonia Meakin merely sat gazing serenely out of the window, presenting me with a graceful quarter profile. I do not mind admitting that I was growing more and more depressed and agitated. I had no idea of what she knew, or thought she knew, but it was evidently something that could be unpleasant, if not dangerous, to us all. It was also apparent that she was one of the coolest and most ruthless people I had ever had the misfortune to come across. It made me furious to think that I had been taken in by her outward artlessness not once but twice before; first at the inquest, and again— when I should have known better—on the day when she turned up at the Underground station. I reflected grimly that I would not be caught in the same way again, but the thought brought me little comfort. Manifestly, it was now too late.

We found a secluded corner in the near empty restaurant and ordered coffee. When it had arrived, I said, "Well?"

Sonia Meakin hesitated. She had had plenty of time to think up exactly what to say to me, so I judged this apparent indecision to be part of a prearranged plan designed to influence me in some way. At last she said, "Mr. Croombe-Peters, I'm going to be frank with you."

"Good," I said as unpleasantly as I could.

"You see," she went on, in that gentle, cooing voice, "I have a favor to ask of you."

"Oh, have you? Well, the answer is 'no.' "

She did not appear to have heard. She went on, "I happened to be passing Chelsea Mansions today and I saw you going in with Chief Inspector Tibbett. You went to Margery Phipps's flat."

"How do you know," I asked, "what flat we went to? And how do you know who my companion was? I suppose you've had dealings with the police before, have you?"

She wrinkled her pretty nose and smiled, like a doll. "Oh, Mr. Croombe-Peters, how could you think that? No, I'll be perfectly honest. I'm afraid I was rather naughty."

"That doesn't surprise me."

"I followed you in, and I heard the Inspector talking to the porter. The porter called him by his name, that's how I know it. I also heard you asking for the key to seven-one-six, Margery Phipps's flat."

"You seem extraordinarily well informed," I said coldly. "May one ask whether you knew Miss Phipps personally when she was alive?"

"I had met her, yes."

"Had you been to her flat?"

"Yes, once."

"Why?"

Mrs. Meakin looked at me with that devastating candor. "To have tea," she said.

"When was this?"

"Oh, I don't remember. Shortly before she died."

"Just a friendly call?"

"Of course."

"You didn't tell me this last time we met."

"There was no reason why I should."

There was a silence.

Then I said again, "Well? Get on with it."

"It so happens," said Sonia Meakin delicately, "that Margery had something of mine, something which I—I prize, and I would like it back. Of course, the porter wouldn't give me the key, but he'd surely recognize you as having come in with the Chief Inspector this afternoon. He'd give you the key." She looked at me hopefully across the coffee cups.

"I'm sorry," I said, "it's out of the question. I am interested to hear that Margery Phipps was blackmailing you, but I can only say that it was no more than you deserved."

"Blackmail? What a horrible word."

"Yes, isn't it? I should keep well clear of it, if I were you. In any case, you've surely nothing to fear now that Margery is dead."

"This—thing—I want to get back is nothing valuable, just sentimental. I'm sure nobody would mind if I went in and took it."

"How do you know that the police haven't already confiscated it?"

"Oh, I don't think—they wouldn't know—I mean, I told you, it's just a question of sentimental value . . ."

"And I told you some time ago that the answer would be 'no'; it still is. Now, if you'll excuse me, I'll be off. I have an engagement."

"You won't help me?" Her voice quivered and a suspicion of tears appeared in the huge blue eyes.

"No, to put it in a nutshell, I won't."

She sighed. "Then there's only one thing for me to do. I shall have to ask Inspector Tibbett to let me in."

"Yes," I said, "why don't you?"

"Of course, he couldn't be expected to do it for nothing. And there's really nothing I can offer him, except perhaps some little pieces of information that he might find useful."

"I am getting very bored with this, Mrs. Meakin," I said. "For God's sake, stop being coy. You made a definite and threatening remark to me on the telephone. You said that if I wouldn't see you, you would tell the police how your husband really died. Now, you'll have to put up a better bluff than that, you know. I was just one of about thirty people who saw the whole thing happening. Nobody was near him. Nobody touched him. He slipped and . . ."

"Yes." She gave me another of those looks. It was like drowning in cold, clear blue water. "Poor Bob. He slipped."

"There was no negligence of any sort on the part of the unit. That was proved by the coroner's court. If you have anything to add, I shall be most interested to hear it."

"Mr. Croombe-Peters, you made a lot of money out of Bob's death, didn't you?"

"I certainly did not. Whatever do you . . . ?"

"I'm sorry. I put it badly. I didn't mean you, personally. I meant your film company. Bob told me a few days before he died that he thought the whole concern was going bankrupt, but then he had that sad accident, and the insurance company paid up, didn't they?"

"I'm afraid," I said icily, "that Bob was misinformed. The company has always been in a perfectly healthy financial state. After all, it is backed by my father. Certainly, the insurance claim was met, as was right and proper. We have had to reshoot practically half the film, and that was precisely the contingency against which we insured ourselves. You are talking utter nonsense."

"Please, Mr. Croombe-Peters." She smiled at me and put a gentle hand on my arm. "Don't let's quarrel. After all, we're both in this together."

"What on earth do you mean?"

"*I* made a lot of money out of Bob's death, too."

"You inherited his estate," I said, "but when Bob was alive he was earning big money. I don't imagine you lacked for anything. You must be even more callous than I thought if you prefer a few thousand pounds to a live husband."

"You don't understand. Bob was certainly earning a lot, but, well, you know what actors are like. He'd got behind with his income tax years ago, and latterly it was just a question of earning enough to keep the vultures happy from day to day. Then, he was fearfully extravagant. Heaven knows how he got through the money as he did, but I suppose spending just comes easily to some people. It was terrible, Mr. Croombe-Peters. We were always broke, and always trying to keep up appearances. Worse than that, I couldn't see how I was going to keep on paying the children's school fees . . ."

"Children? I didn't know . . ."

"I have two boys. They're both at prep school, the younger one started last term. Oh, I'm not surprised you hadn't heard of them. I was determined at all costs to keep *them* out of this sordid business."

"Really? You showed very few signs of wanting to keep out of this sordid business yourself at the time of the inquest."

"You mean those terrible newspaper articles? Oh, of course I'd never have done it, if I'd known . . ."

"Known what?"

"That Northburn Films had taken out that marvelous insurance policy on Bob's life. It seemed to me that the only way I could provide for the future was to sell my story to the press. It was horrible." She gave a little reminiscent shudder. "But I couldn't have faced telling the boys they'd have to leave school. Harry's in the first eleven this term and Tom's— oh, but I mustn't bore you."

Believe it or not, I very nearly fell for it again. She sounded so natural and plausible, and I suppose it is always a temptation to think the best of an attractive woman. I had to keep a tight hold on myself as I said, "Please get to the point."

She sighed. "It's so difficult, isn't it," she said, "to know exactly what is ethical and what isn't. After all, the insurance companies can well afford it."

"What can they afford?"

"The money they paid to me, and to you. I didn't refuse my share, and I notice that you didn't either."

I stubbed out my cigarette. "Once and for all, Mrs. Meakin," I said, "I will not have you making these insinuations. Northburn Films has done nothing that is not perfectly above board and legal. That claim . . ."

She interrupted me. "Both policies, yours and mine," she said, "depended on certain conditions. To qualify, Bob's death had to take place when he was in the employment of your company, and not to be due to any previous illness or weakness of Bob's. Do you agree?"

"Certainly I do. There is no dispute about any of those things. The coroner went out of his way to emphasize that Bob was in perfect health . . ."

She smiled. "Oh, I know all that," she said. "The only thing is—he was not, strictly speaking, in the employment of Northburn Films when he died."

"He was not—what?" This really astounded me. Then I remembered the scribbling pad in Bob's dressing room, and I felt cold with fright. Could it be that Sonia Meakin was right? I became aware that she was still talking.

"Bob was really upset by Fiametta Fettini, you know. He told me that she was simply using him to bolster up an unsavory publicity campaign of her own, and he had already made up his mind to walk out if she made another scene, whether or not it meant breaking his contract. I warned him that you'd sue him for thumping damages, but he said, 'They haven't the money for a law suit. They're practically broke already.' Between ourselves, he'd had a very good offer from Superb Films to star in the musical of *Oedipus Rex*." Sonia Meakin leaned across the table toward me, speaking softly but with immense conviction. "Mr. Croombe-Peters, I spent the last night of Bob's life ..ith him, in the Mount Street house, and the whole of the next morning. He told me he'd made up his mind. He said he'd only managed to keep his temper and get through the previous day's shooting by sitting in his dressing room drafting his letter of resignation to Sam Potman. I know all this, you see. That's why there can't be any question of a forgery."

"A forgery of what?"

Sonia Meakin looked straight at me. "Margery Phipps," she said, "showed me a letter, or rather a draft note in Bob's handwriting. She said she found it in his dressing room. It was an unequivocal letter of resignation. Something about not liking to break a contract, but that it had become impossible to work under the sort of conditions that had arisen, and so forth. The letter is dated August 15th, and on top of it Bob had scribbled, 'This is a copy of my letter to Sam Potman.' I need hardly point out to you that it was on August 16th that Bob died."

I lit a cigarette. I kept reminding myself that there was no need to panic. When I spoke, I tried hard to keep my voice very calm.

"Mrs. Meakin," I said, "I can quite understand your anxiety, but I can assure you that it is unfounded. Margery Phipps evidently got hold of the draft which your husband told you he had written the day before he died. But there is no reason to suppose that he actually wrote out a fair copy and handed it to Mr. Potman. If he had, Mr. Potman would have said so."

"Would he?" The cool blue eyes looked at me contemptuously.

Ignoring this, I went on. "I think I can tell you what must have happened. I have no doubt that Mr. Meakin was angry and upset, as you say, and may have decided to walk out on us. He might even have written the letter, intending to deliver it to Sam Potman during the afternoon. But I can testify personally as to what happened. When Bob arrived at the location, there was a—a little scene with Fiametta, which obviously fanned his resentment to a boiling point. However, Sam Potman and Biddy Brennan can be extraordinarily persuasive when they try, and my guess is that they calmed Bob down to such an extent that he thought better of delivering his note. After all," I concluded reasonably, "the moment Mr. Potman received that note, he would have suspended shooting and had a talk with Bob and . . ."

I became uncomfortably aware of the steady gaze of the

blue eyes, and found myself floundering for words. There was a moment of silence, while I tried to sort my tongue out from my ganglia, and then Sonia Meakin said, "You are a very brave man, Mr. Croombe-Peters."

"What do you mean?" I had seldom felt less brave.

"You are banking on the fact that even if that draft letter fell into the hands of the insurance company they would take no action but would allow the claims to stand. You are so confident that you are prepared to risk the possibility that someone—maybe the police, maybe a relative of the Phipps girl—will find it in her flat and put two and two together. You are absolutely confident that, in a court of law, you could demolish the validity of that letter, and prove beyond any reasonable doubt that Bob was still in the employment of Northburn Films when . . ."

"I'm reasonably confident that I could, yes," I said. "I certainly won't be intimidated into . . ."

Sonia Meakin gave what sounded exactly like a genuine sigh of relief. "Oh, well," she said, "if you really feel like that, then I needn't worry, need I? After all, we're both in this together. Either both our insurance claims stand or they both fall. I have seen and handled that letter. I know that it is in Bob's handwriting, and I know that it is in Margery Phipps's flat. I even know where to look for it, and I doubt whether the police have found it. But since you're convinced that it's of no importance at all, then I can relax; how wonderful." She smiled dazzlingly at me. She was like someone who has consulted an expert on a torturing problem and been reassured that there are no grounds for anxiety. Her sudden switch to my point of view made me extremely uneasy. I had been putting up a bluffing defense to what I thought was attempted blackmail. Now, for the first time, it occurred to me that what she had said was true. We were both in it together. None of us could sleep easily until that letter was destroyed. The insurance company would certainly take action, and even if we won, the law suit would cripple us.

It was at that moment that I realized that Sonia Meakin herself had provided the solution to the problem. It was she who had pointed out that, as a friend and companion of Henry Tibbett, I would have a good chance of bluffing my way back into that apartment and finding the letter for myself. There was no need, I told myself, to make any sort of fuss. Once I had got rid of this tiresome woman, I would go quietly to Chelsea Mansions, get the key from the porter, and all would be simple. Except, of course, that I had no idea where the miserable letter was hidden.

"I dare say," said Sonia Meakin softly, "that you think I am a very silly woman to get so worried; but then, perhaps you don't know what it means to me."

"I can guess," I said.

She stood up. "Thank you for a very nice cup of coffee, Mr. Croombe-Peters," she said. "The letter is on top of the curtain valance over the kitchen window."

"The kitchen window!" My exclamation was involuntary, and I could have cut my tongue out for allowing it to escape. Sonia Meakin gave me a curious, cool look.

"Yes," she said. "The kitchen window. Good-bye, Mr. Croombe-Peters. And thank you. You have saved me so much trouble."

She turned and walked out of the restaurant, leaving me to pay the bill. As a matter of fact, I hardly noticed her leave. My head was full of this new idea. If Margery's cache of incriminating documents—or even some of them—had been kept in that particular hiding place, then her death became very much more understandable. Climbing up onto that narrow sill to get something, slipping, the window unlatched, flying open—for the first time, it all made sense. Then I remembered the forged suicide note. *If* it really was forged, if Henry Tibbett was not barking up the wrong tree with typically ham-handed enthusiasm, if, if . . .

I pulled myself together. All this was pure speculation, and meanwhile there was work to be done, and quickly. I paid the bill and went out into the street.

There was no sign of Sonia Meakin. King's Road, Chelsea, was milling with its usual evening throng, a mixture of well-to-do residents hurrying home from work, and dissipated beats crawling out into the evening sunshine to start their night's career. I was glad to turn off into the comparative peace of Flaxman Avenue. I walked the few hundred yards up its shady pavement, and arrived at the main entrance of Chelsea Mansions.

My luck was in. The foyer was busy, for, as I have indicated, it was the hour when late-comers returning from work tend to collide in the hall with early diners-out; but I spotted the porter who had the key.

The porter was poring over some sort of a register of parcels received for residents, but he straightened at once when I spoke to him—from his general smartness and turn-out, I had already written him down as an ex-NCO—and he saluted respectfully and asked what I wanted. It was all most reassuring. I reminded him that I had called earlier in the day with Chief Inspector Tibbett, and he replied that he remembered me very well. I then said, with as much plausibility as I could muster, that I was sorry to bother him, but that the Chief Inspector had left a document behind in the apartment, and had asked me to drop in and collect it for him, so if I might have the keys for a few minutes?

He made no bones at all about it, the splendid fellow. No awkward questions or hesitations. He grinned, said, "Certainly, sir," produced the keys, saluted me again, and remarked that if by any chance he should have gone off duty when I came down, I should leave the keys with his colleague. It was all absurdly easy, and I think I whistled a little to myself as I waited for the lift.

Margery Phipps's flat looked exactly as it had done after lunch, except that the low-slanting westward sun was now gilding the windows and throwing its rosy fingers of light into the living room, giving a pinky-gold tinge to the white carpet. The whole effect was, I suppose, very attractive; but I was in no mood to hang about. I made straight for the kitchen, pulled out the stool, and climbed onto it. I am not very tall—about the same height as Margery had been—and even from the stool I could not see up onto the top of the valance board. I had to stand on tiptoe and run my hand along the dusty board to find whatever might be there. Twice I felt carefully all along the length of the window. There appeared to be nothing up there at all, and the thickness of the dust and dirt did not suggest that the valance had recently been used as a shelf. At the third attempt, however, my fingers came into contact with something at the very furthermost end—a piece of paper. I had just managed to get a grip on it without overbalancing onto the electric stove when I heard a key turning in the front door lock.

I froze into immobility. So far as I knew, only the management of the block of flats had access to the apartment. Surely, I told myself in desperation, this must be some porter dropping in for a routine check, or to read the meters, or—my invention failed. I could not imagine why anybody should possibly want to enter the apartment for any legitimate reason. I tried to keep my head. Whoever it was and whatever they wanted, there was no particular reason why they should come into the kitchen. If I stayed perfectly still, I might remain undetected.

The front door closed quietly behind the newcomer, and I heard footsteps coming into the living room. Then came the unmistakeable sounds of a search. Drawers were being opened and closed, books pulled out from shelves, papers sorted. The person, whoever it was, moved quietly and without hurry. I tried to stop breathing, horribly aware that my heartbeats sounded like a drum tattoo, at least in my own ears.

My head was in such a position that I was gazing down through the window into the street, but such was my absorption in my own predicament that it was several minutes before I registered a curious fact. I was, in fact, looking straight down onto the façade of the New Forum Cinema. So Biddy had not only been in Chelsea but very close to Chelsea Mansions when Margery died.

I suppose it was the fact that my mind was diverted onto this fresh line of thought that made me relax my concentration for a moment. Anyhow, just at the moment when the search next door was drawing to a close, and I was beginning to feel that the intruder would surely beat a retreat, a bit of fluff got up my nose, and before I knew what I was doing I sneezed loudly.

For a moment there was dead silence. Then purposeful footsteps came toward the kitchen door, and a very determined voice said, " 'O's that? Come out at once, *if* you please."

I knew who it was before the door opened and the shabby

black hat came accusingly around it. "Mrs. Arbuthnot!" I said.

She stood there, looking up at me. I felt a considerable fool, perched on a kitchen stool, faced by this small, relentless figure. Mrs. Arbuthnot was grasping an umbrella in a menacing sort of way, and I felt that tact and charm were called for if I was to extricate myself undamaged. Unfortunately I could think of nothing to say. We eyed each other with mutual suspicion for some moments.

"Well," said Mrs. Arbuthnot at last "so you know my name, eh? *Most* interesting. Now, if I may be so bold, who the hell are you and how did you get in 'ere?"

It was clear that Mrs. Arbuthnot scorned the use of either tact or charm, and it suddenly occurred to me that attack might be the best form of defense. My conversation with Henry Tibbett had put me in a strong position with regard to inside information on my opponent.

"I think, Mrs. Arbuthnot," I said, as suavely as I could manage, "it is you rather than I who should explain what you are doing here."

I made a move to come down from the stool, but she foiled it with a quick jab of her umbrella, which caught me painfully in the calf. "You stay where you are," she said savagely. "Don't think you can come that on me. This is my daughter's flat and I'm 'er sole heir and I've got me own key. I've got every right to be here, not like some."

Well, of course, I had to admit the force of her argument, but having committed myself to the policy of attack, there was nothing for it but to follow it up. "It so happens," I said with cool dignity, "that I am working with Chief Inspector Henry Tibbett of the C.I.D. I understand that you know him."

Mrs. Arbuthnot snorted. "Tibbett!" she said. "About as much use as a sick headache. He knows as well as I do that Margery copped it. Someone did her in, that's what, but Mr. High-and-Mighty Tibbett is too busy to worry. Oh, yes. And what about me, that's what I want to know?"

"Did Inspector Tibbett give you permission to come to this apartment?" I asked. I began to ease myself slowly down from the stool.

"Did 'e you?" she riposted.

"I was here with him this afternoon," I said. "You can check with the porter."

This seemed to impress her. She made another jab with the umbrella, but it was half-hearted and ineffectual. I managed to lower myself to the floor without further let or hindrance.

"I've more right to be here than you," she said, but I could tell from the surly and slightly whining note in her voice that she had moved onto the defensive. I decided to press home my advantage.

"You must realize, Mrs. Arbuthnot," I said, "that we in the police force have to be careful. After all, your long association with the late Mr. Arbuthnot—or should I say James Boswell—hardly qualifies you to be regarded as one hundred percent trustworthy by ordinary decent citizens."

This went home, all right. She turned and snarled at me. "Bloody perlicemen," she said, making what looked like an obscene gesture with her umbrella. "All alike. Prying nosey-parkers, busybodies, . . ." and so on, a lot more in the same vein. But the great thing was that she no longer questioned either my identity or my right to be in Margery's apartment. I felt, I must say, justifiably pleased with myself. Intelligence, after all, will always triumph over mere cunning, however unpromising the circumstances.

I cut short the stream of abuse to say sharply, "And now, I should like an explanation of what you are doing here."

She gave me a scowl and said, "I've every right. I'm the legal heir. The solicitor said so."

"You were looking for something."

"What if I was?"

"What was it?"

"None of your business."

"Did you find it?"

Mrs. Arbuthnot's thin mouth clamped into a stubborn line. "I'm saying no more. It's none of your business."

"Mrs. Arbuthnot, you seem to think that your daughter was murdered. You may be right. We are investigating the case. We can't do it if you don't co-operate with us." I had switched to what I hoped was a convincing imitation of Tibbett in one of his beguiling moods, but I seemed to lack his touch. She remained uncharmed, merely shaking her head so that the dusty black feathers in her hat quivered in the sunset, and said, "I'm saying nothing."

I decided to have one more try. "If you will do nothing to help me in my inquiries," I said coldly, "I shall have to get in touch with Inspector Tibbett and . . ."

"That won't be necessary," said a voice from the doorway. I looked up breathless with horror. Henry Tibbett was standing there. He did not look amused.

"I was just," I began.

Tibbett ignored me, and addressed himself to Mrs. Arbuthnot. "Good evening, Mrs. Arbuthnot," he said, "I see that you have met Mr. Croombe-Peters."

"Yes, I 'ave, and I can tell you I've got as much right to be here as he has."

"You have every right," said Henry gravely. "If Mr. Croombe-Peters said you hadn't, he was mistaken. All that I have asked of you, as you know, is that you shouldn't remove any of your daughter's possessions without my permission. That's clear, isn't it?"

Mrs. Arbuthnot looked uncomfortable. "Yes, Inspector," she said.

I could not resist putting in a word. "She was searching for something, Tibbett," I said. "I heard her. She . . ."

"Well," said Mrs. Arbuthnot with an air of finality, "I'll be getting along then."

She shot me a look brimful of malice, and directed her quivering hat out through the front door. Henry and I looked at each other. There was a lengthy pause.

Finally, Henry said, "The porter telephoned me at once. He had his orders. You see, I was half-expecting you. You, or somebody else."

There seemed nothing I could usefully say. One thought, and one only, was uppermost in my mind. I was still clutching that piece of paper in my right hand. So far, I had managed to keep it behind my back, but the problem now was to transfer it unobtrusively into my trouser pocket. I waited until Henry's attention seemed to wander for a moment, and then tried to slip the paper into my pocket; but he was too quick for me.

"What's that?" he said.

"Oh—nothing . . ."

"May I see it?"

There was nothing I could do except hand the thing over. I had already seen that it was an envelope, unaddressed. Reluctantly I gave it to Henry. He opened it, looked inside, then gave me the ghost of a grin.

"You're perfectly right," he said. "It is nothing. A perfectly plain empty envelope. Shall we go?"

Unhappily, I followed him out of the door and into the lift.

12

When we were out in the street, Henry said, "By rights I ought to take you to the police station."

"But I . . ."

"However," he went on, ignoring my agonized interruption, "I think I'll probably get more sense out of you if I take you home with me. If you have any engagements for this evening, you'd better cancel them."

"Fortunately, I happen to be free," I said with an attempt at dignity.

Tibbett gave me a long appraising look. "Let's hope you stay that way," he said, and suddenly laughed.

"I don't see anything funny in that," I said.

"I'm sorry. I was just thinking of Mrs. Arbuthnot catching you in that apartment. I wish I'd been there."

"I see nothing funny in that either."

"Come on, Pudge," said Tibbett. He had suddenly become suspiciously friendly. "A number nineteen will take us home."

"Please allow me to call a taxi," I said. "I'm quite prepared to pay for it."

"Just as you like," said Tibbett. He seemed quite oblivious to the fact that I was trying to insult him. We found a cab and drove in silence to the ugly Victorian house near the World's End.

Emmy Tibbett came out into the hall as we were shutting the front door behind us, and she threw up her hands in mock dismay.

"Henry!" she said, accusingly, "This is the second time you've done this to me!"

"Done what?"

"Brought Pudge home without letting me know. Everything is in the most awful mess, and I haven't even combed my hair . . ." Then she turned to me with that marvelously open, sweet smile of hers and said, "Pudge, it's lovely to see you. Do please stay to supper. I've made the most enormous dish out of lamb and eggplant and things that I got out of one of the papers, and . . ."

"Emmy," said Henry severely, "you've done it again."

Emmy looked abashed. "Well," she said, "it's the only way I can . . ."

Henry turned to me. "Emmy," he said, "has no culinary instinct whatsoever. She's a splendid cook, so long as she can have a book to follow. So what happens? She finds these things and follows the recipe slavishly, and of course the last thing that she reads is how many people the dish is supposed to serve." He looked accusingly at Emmy. "How many?" he demanded.

"Eight," said Emmy in a small voice.

"In that case," said Henry to me, "I trust you will stay to supper."

By this time I was feeling most uncomfortable. I dare say that Tibbett intended that I should.

"I think," I said, "that you should explain to Emmy why I am here."

"Oh," said Emmy, "business?"

Henry grinned at me. "Certainly not pleasure," he said, "from Pudge's point of view, that is. Actually, Emmy love, I happened to meet old Pudge—quite by chance—and I asked him back here because there *are* one or two business things that I'd like to talk over with him."

Suddenly I saw that Emmy's eyes were twinkling with suppressed laughter. "I can imagine," she said.

"What on earth do you mean?" Henry asked. He sounded genuinely taken aback.

"I meant to spring it on you later," said Emmy, "but I can't resist telling you now. I've just had a visitor."

"A visitor? Who?" Henry spoke with unusual sharpness.

"An absolutely splendid lady called Mrs. Arbuthnot," said Emmy. "She said she was just looking in on her way back to Lewisham to register a protest. She said I was to tell you that Croombe-Peters or no Croombe-Peters, *she* wasn't having policemen climbing all over *her* kitchen window. I managed to keep a straight face and said I'd deliver the message, but it did make me think that there'd been some sort of a contretemps and . . ."

"There was a certain amount of confusion," said Henry. I could see that he was suppressing his laughter. "If you don't mind, darling, Pudge and I really do want to talk."

"Of course. I'll be in the kitchen," said Emmy, and disappeared.

Henry ushered me through the door into the big, untidy living room.

"What will you have to drink?" he asked.

"Really, Tibbett, this is all most embarrassing. I don't . . ."

"Whisky? Gin? Beer?"

"Whisky and soda, please."

There was silence while Henry poured two drinks and handed me one of them. Then he sat down in an arm chair and motioned me to do the same. He took a swig of his drink, and then said, "Well, whatever it was that you were looking for, I imagine you didn't find it."

"I would like," I said, "to tell you the whole story."

Henry nodded approvingly. "I'd like to hear it," he said.

I had been doing some hard thinking in the taxi, and I had decided that the best way out led between the Scylla of complete truth and the Charybdis of utter falsehood. I had, in fact, worked out a story which was very nearly true and which seemed to me to be not only plausible, but capable of being checked independently at several points. It involved, however,

making myself out to be something of an impressionable fool
—and this I now proceeded to do.

"It all comes back," I said, "to the old saying *cherchez la femme.*"

"Does it?" Henry did not sound very interested.

"Call me an idiot if you like," I went on, "but I've never been able to resist a pretty face. You'd think I'd have learnt, after all these years, but I fall for it every time, just as hard as I did when I was an undergraduate."

I paused. Henry said nothing. It was a little unnerving, not being able to tell whether or not my story was getting across; however, there was nothing for it but to take a deep breath and press on.

"This afternoon," I said, "Mrs. Meakin telephoned me at my office. About five, it must have been, an hour or so after you left. Sylvia can confirm that. She took the call and put it through to me."

Still Henry said nothing. He was leaning back in his chair with his eyes closed. I went on.

"She begged me to see her at once on a matter of great urgency. I could hardly refuse. I met her outside my office, and at her request we took a taxi to the Casablanca in the King's Road, Chelsea, where we had coffee. The waitress there can bear me out. We were almost the only people in the place. I still had no idea why Sonia Meakin wanted to see me so much, but over coffee she explained. By the merest coincidence, she had happened to see me going into Chelsea Mansions with you earlier on, and this gave her the idea that the porter might be willing to entrust me with the key to Margery's apartment, since he knew me to be connected with you. She said that there was something in the apartment which she was desperately anxious to recover—a paper of some kind."

"Of what kind?" Henry asked. He did not open his eyes.

"I've no idea. She didn't tell me, and I hardly liked to ask. It seems pretty obvious to me that Margery had been blackmailing her in some way."

"Didn't it occur to her that by this time we—the police, I mean—would have removed any sort of incriminating document?"

"That's just what I said. But she said that the police

169

wouldn't realize the significance of this paper even if they found it, which was unlikely as it was kept hidden on the valance above the kitchen window. Well, I know I'm a fool, but she's a damned attractive woman, and she wept a good deal and told me her life would be ruined if she didn't have that paper, and in the end—I feel a fool having to admit it—but I agreed. I know it was wrong of me, but I hope you'll understand that I was behaving like a sentimental idiot rather than a criminal." I paused hopefully.

All Henry said was, "And you didn't find it?"

"I found an envelope," I said. "The one you saw in my hand. I had just picked it up and hadn't even had time to look at it when Mrs. Arbuthnot arrived. I'd be interested to know what *she* was doing there. How did she get in?"

"She's Margery's legal heir," said Henry. His eyes were still closed. "We've searched the place thoroughly and taken our fingerprints and our photographs. There was no longer any valid reason for keeping her out, and her key was handed to her this afternoon. I must say, though, that I didn't realize she would use it so promptly."

"Well, she did," I said, "and she must have thought or hoped that the police search was not as efficient as it might have been, because she was quite definitely looking for something. I heard her." Henry made no comment. I went on. "Anyhow, as you saw, the envelope I found was empty. So I can only assume that the police *did* find the precious paper, whatever it was, after all."

I hoped that I did not sound too eager, but, as you can imagine, I was most vitally interested. I prayed that Henry would either confirm or deny my statement. Instead, he remarked drily, "I had no idea you were so chivalrous. Now I suppose you'll have to report your failure to the lady."

"Yes," I said. "I'm meeting her tomorrow. I'm afraid she'll be very disappointed." I lit a cigarette, and then said, as casually as I could, "It would be something if I could tell her whether or not the police had found her precious bit of paper."

Henry grinned at me. "It would, wouldn't it?" he said. "I'm afraid I can't tell you. We found quite a number of interesting pieces of paper, but since you have no idea what this one referred to, it's a little difficult to identify it."

He had me neatly trapped there, but I did my best. "There would surely have been only one document connected directly with Sonia Meakin," I said.

"How do you know," Henry asked, "that it was directly connected with her?"

I opened my mouth and then closed it again. I had put myself in such a position that I could not possibly tell Tibbett that I knew the contents of the missing document; and, apart from sensing that he was laughing at me, I could get no real idea of what was going on in his head, that is, of whether or not he had believed my story and whether or not he had Bob's draft letter in his possession. I realized that I would get no further with Tibbett, and it seemed to me that my next and most urgent move should be to consult Sam. It was vitally important to know whether or not Bob's note had been delivered; and, if it had, to find what had become of it and to ascertain our legal position. In fact, I was inclined to believe that Bob had repented of his decision and had never written the actual letter of resignation, for I could not imagine that either he or Sam would have continued so calmly with shooting the film after a bombshell like that; but one had to be sure, and I knew that a good lawyer could make a case out of the mere existence of the draft letter.

I looked at my watch. "Well," I said, "that's my story and I hope you're satisfied. I know I behaved very foolishly, but fortunately there's no harm done. And now, if you don't mind, I won't accept Emmy's kind invitation to dinner. There are one or two things that I have to . . ."

"Oh, please don't go," said Henry, and I had a nasty feeling that behind the politeness was a definite order which I was in no position to disobey. "There are several other things I'd like to discuss with you and, besides, I'm expecting another visitor. Someone you'll be interested to meet."

"Who's that?" I asked.

Before Henry could reply, the front door bell jangled. He got up and looked out of the window. "Here she is now," he said. And a moment later the door opened, and Emmy ushered in Sonia Meakin.

To say that I was staggered is to put it mildly. I was rather relieved to notice that Mrs. Meakin seemed as surprised to see me as I was to see her, but it soon became obvious that her surprise had given way to anger. The look she gave me would have cut through steel plating, and her voice was like dry ice as she said, "Mr. Croombe-Peters. *What* a surprise."

"Yes," I said, "isn't it?"

"I gather," said Henry, and I could hear the amusement in his voice, "that you two are old friends. No need for introductions."

"None whatsoever," said Sonia grimly.

There was a silence.

"Well, Mrs. Meakin," said Tibbett, "what did you want to see me about?"

It was only then that I tumbled to the fact that this meeting was of Sonia Meakin's seeking. Stupidly, I had assumed that she had been summoned for some sort of questioning; now, the affair took on a more sinister aspect. It seemed as though the wretched woman was about to make good her threat of exposing information to the police. And yet, I asked myself, what information? What could she possibly know that would interest Scotland Yard? The question of whether or not Bob was legally in our employment when he died was not a police matter, and it seemed hardly feasible that Sonia Meakin would risk ruining herself as well as Northburn Films out of pure spite. After all, as she had remarked, we were in the thing together.

I am glad to say that she had the grace to look very uncomfortable.

"My business is private, Inspector," she said, looking at me in a pointed way.

"I understood," said Tibbett delicately, "that Mr. Croombe-Peters enjoyed your confidence."

Sonia Meakin gave me a look that was very different from the melting, peaches-and-cream technique she had used earlier in the day. "What has he been saying?" she demanded.

"Oh, nothing in particular. We were just chatting about you, funnily enough, and the previous occasions on which you two had met."

There was a moment of palpable indecision, quite unlike the artificial pauses and hesitations to which I had been subjected before. Mrs. Meakin was evidently undecided as to her next move. Then, suddenly, she made a decision. She spun around to face Tibbett, turning her back on me, and she said, "Very well, Inspector. Since what I have to say concerns Mr. Croombe-Peters, perhaps it's best to say it to his face. There is something which I think you ought to know."

"And what is that?" Henry asked. He sounded, if anything, faintly amused.

"Mr. Croombe-Peters," said Sonia, still with her back to me, "was in Margery Phipps's flat this evening. He tricked the porter into giving him the key, and I can only imagine he went there to steal something. Ask him, and see if he denies it!"

I opened my mouth, and then shut it again. I decided to leave the handling of the situation entirely to Tibbett.

"I should be most surprised if he denied it," said Henry. "He could hardly do so, since I was there with him. We were also accompanied by a lady called Mrs. Arbuthnot from Lewisham. It was quite a little gathering."

"In that case," said Sonia Meakin, with a certain satisfaction, "you must have caught him red-handed . . ."

"Mrs. Meakin," said Henry reasonably, "if I had caught Mr. Croombe-Peters doing any thing nefarious, is it likely that I would have invited him back to my house for dinner?" Turning to me, he added, "You are staying, aren't you, Pudge?"

Well, it seemed sailing fairly close to the wind of truth for a Chief Inspector, but it did the trick, and I was profoundly grateful to Tibbett. "Yes, thank you very much, Henry old man," I said as easily as I could.

Sonia Meakin swung around as if to attack me, and I feel sure that she would have equaled one of La Fettini's onslaughts if she had been able to get going, but Henry interrupted her.

"As I said before," he remarked, "we were just talking about you, Mrs. Meakin. And Mr. Croombe-Peters was explaining to me that you had asked him to break into that apartment in order to abstract a document you wanted."

Sonia Meakin said nothing.

"He further explained," Henry went on, "that he had agreed to do so, and was on an errand of selfless chivalry when . . ."

173

"That's not true!"

"In any case," I said, unable to hold my tongue any longer, "how do you know what I did this evening, or where I went?"

"I followed," she began, and then stopped abruptly, realizing her mistake.

"You see?" I said triumphantly to Henry.

Sonia Meakin did the only thing possible to retrieve the situation from her point of view. She began to cry, sniffing into a small lace handkerchief. "He broke into that apartment. I saw him myself. I only came to tell you because it's the duty of every citizen to help the police, and now you won't believe me."

"Now, now, Mrs. Meakin," said Henry, "nobody's disbelieving you." He then went on, in the nicest possible way, to make it quite clear that in his opinion Sonia Meakin was talking through the back of her beautiful neck. He suggested that, if she wished to make a complaint, she should do so the following day, through the proper channels; but he was not quite clear, he added, what she was complaining about. Politely, he pressed her to take a drink before she left.

By all the rules, this was the point at which Sonia Meakin ought to have crept away, probably tearful and certainly defeated. It was a development to which, frankly, I was looking forward with pleasurable anticipation.

I was somewhat taken aback, therefore, when she blew her nose loudly, straightened up, and said, "All right, Inspector. I don't know why you're taking this attitude, but I think it's my duty to tell you that Mr. Croombe-Peters has been concealing important information from you."

Henry and I both reacted sharply. In fact it was in unison, like a well-trained chorus, that we said, "What?"

The Meakin woman looked at Henry. "Has Mr. Croombe-Peters told you," she asked, "that he had a long telephone conversation with Margery Phipps at about half-past eleven on the morning of the day she died?"

Henry faced me. "Is this true?" he demanded.

"No," I said.

"It is," said Sonia Meakin.

"She thinks it is, but it isn't," I said clumsily. "If you really want to know, I was listening to a golden voice telling me that on the third pip it would be eleven twenty-one precisely."

Sonia said, "You told me you were going to phone Margery Phipps. You went into the booth, and you came back and said you'd spoken to her."

"I know I did," I said. I was alarmed to detect a desperate note in my own voice. "But, actually, I didn't. I'm sorry I had to deceive you, but . . ."

"Then how do you account for the fact," she said, "that by six o'clock that evening you had in your office a box which was in Margery Phipps's flat at noon?" She turned to Henry. "Inspector Tibbett," she said, "this man is lying. I don't pretend to know why, but he is."

This made me really angry. "Don't you dare put on that holier-than-thou attitude with me," I shouted. "What about trying to persuade me to break into Margery's flat and steal . . ."

The blue eyes opened more widely than ever. "What *do* you mean?"

"You surely aren't going to deny that we met this afternoon, and that you . . ."

"We certainly met this afternoon for a cup of coffee."

"And what did we talk about? I challenge you to tell Inspector Tibbett!"

Sonia Meakin wrinkled her nose, as if in an effort at recollection. "I don't really remember. I think we mentioned Bob. And—oh, yes—I was telling you about my two boys at prep school, and how Harry's got into the first eleven . . ."

"And what else?" I rapped out the words.

Coolly, she said, "Nothing, that I remember."

"That's a lie! Perhaps you'll explain to the Inspector just why you telephoned me and insisted on seeing me and . . ."

"Please, Mr. Croombe-Peters, there's no need to shout. The Inspector has made it quite clear that he is not really interested in anything I have to say. I imagine he is waiting to hear your explanations. I am sure he is anxious to hear all about your visit to Chelsea Mansions, and the telephone call and the cardboard box. Well, I must go now. You two have so much to talk about." And with that, she left.

Henry saw her to the door, and I stood by the window and watched her walk off down the street. I was furious, both with

Sonia Meakin and with myself. She had set a trap, and I had walked into it like a fool, when all the time I had imagined I was being clever. Of course, there had never been any note of resignation from Bob. Sonia Meakin had invented it, in order to lure me around to Chelsea Mansions. She had followed me and watched me go in, and then come around here to denounce me to Tibbett. But why . . . ? Why should she do such a thing? And then, there was the writing impressed on the scribbling pad in Bob's dressing room. *"Dear Sam, Nobody enjoys breaking a contract, but . . ."* The scribbling pad was still in my coat pocket. Somewhere, the top sheet on which Bob had written must exist. Where was it? And what would Sonia Meakin plan next?

I was roused from these uneasy speculations by the sound of the sitting-room door opening again, as Henry came back.

"Well," I said, with as light a laugh as I could manage. "After *that* little exhibition, you'll be in a position to appreciate what I've been going through. And now, I really must be off."

"But Pudge," said Henry, gently, "you're staying to dinner. Had you forgotten?"

It amounted to an order. "Oh, very well," I said.

"Sit down," said Henry abruptly. He poured me another drink in silence, took one himself, and then said, "Now, one good turn deserves another. Supposing you tell me the truth."

"I really don't know what you . . ."

He raised his hand impatiently. "Please don't waste time," he said. "If it's any consolation to you, I don't think that either of you were telling the truth, but I think that your story is closer to the facts than hers. I think there was a document in that apartment that both you and Mrs. Meakin wanted. It had presumably formed the basis of an attempt at blackmail of Mrs. Meakin by Margery Phipps. If it was so important for you, I'm wondering whether you, too, had been asked for money?"

I laughed, sardonically. "There never was any document," I said. "I can see that now. It was just a dirty trick to put me in the wrong. Making me go around there . . ."

"Pudge," said Henry quietly, "I have extricated you from a very nasty hole this evening. You could still be charged with burglarious entry, you know, and I'm making myself an accessory by not turning you over to the rozzers. I'm doing this because I believe that you are not wicked but merely stupid."

This stung me. "Thank you very much," I said. "In that case, there seems little point in continuing this discussion. I shall go." I stood up.

"Sit down," said Henry. He sounded tired. "You should be gratified that I consider you stupid rather than criminal. Because if ever I should change my mind . . ."

"Oh, all right," I said sitting down again. "What do you want to know?"

"She told you what this alleged document was, didn't she?"

"Well . . ."

"Or was she speaking the truth when she said she never mentioned it?"

"She certainly mentioned it. She told me all about it, if you must know."

"Yes," said Henry, "I must."

Reluctantly, I outlined the contents of the alleged letter. "Personally," I went on, "I don't believe it would stand up in any court of law. Meakin was legally in our employment when he died, any judge would support that. There's absolutely no proof that Potman received any such letter, and after Mrs. Meakin's display here this evening I'm more than ever convinced that the wretched bit of paper never existed at all."

"Then why did you risk so much to go after it?"

"Well," I hesitated, and I could feel my face reddening. "Well, I thought I might as well be sure. And, as I've told you, she was very persuasive. Naturally, the thing meant nothing to me, one way or the other . . ."

Henry gave me a sceptical look and then closed his eyes.

I went on. "It did occur to me," I said, "that Bob Meakin might have written a draft and a copy of such a letter in a fit of temper, and then thought better of it and destroyed the original."

"But not the duplicate?"

"My theory was that he threw it into his wastepaper basket, and that Margery Phipps found it there. I've told you how she cleared up the dressing rooms. Being her father's daughter, she'd have realized the possible value of such a document.

You'll notice that the clearing of the dressing rooms didn't take place until we'd returned to the location, by which time the insurance claims had been paid out and Margery would realize . . ."

Henry opened his eyes. "Claims?" he said. "More than one?"

"Claim, I should have said," I amended quickly, "Mrs. Meakin's insurance claim. It's quite true that the policy we took out on her husband's life was contingent on his being in our employment at the time of his death. It all sounded very possible, and she worked a great sob-stuff act about her sons and so forth, and—call me foolish if you like—but I was touched and sorry for her and . . ."

"Now," said Henry, "tell me about your telephone call to Margery Phipps."

"If you're going to take that woman's word against mine . . ."

"I said nothing about taking her word. I only want to hear your side of the story. Why were you listening to TIM, and what was in this mysterious box?"

Feeling considerably foolish, I outlined to Henry the events of that unfortunate morning. Mrs. Meakin's arrival, the necessity for getting her away from the location without a clash with La Fettini. I admitted my duplicity in pretending that Margery had the box, and my further trickery in telephoning TIM. Henry listened to what I had to say, quietly, making no comment. I had a very strong feeling that he did not believe a word of it.

When I came to the end of my story, there was a pause, and then Henry said, "What was in the box?"

"Oh, a lot of unimportant trifles." I ran through the items I could remember. "The book Bob was reading at the time. His cold cream for removing make-up, and . . . well, other things like that." It seemed mean to mention the cosmetics. "A half-bottle of whisky. Some cotton wool. Quite trivial things. Fiametta had already removed her nasty debris, fortunately."

"Her things were in the same box, were they?"

"Yes. Originally. Everything was together in the box, the day that Fiametta attacked Margery—I told you about that, didn't I?"

"Yes," said Henry, "yes, you did. Tell me, did Meakin have a dresser or valet or whatever it is these people have?"

"Yes," I said, surprised. "A little man called Murray. Been with him for years."

"I suppose you've got his address somewhere in your office?"

"I suppose so."

"I'll come around in the morning and get it," said Henry cheerfully. "There are other people I'd like to see as well. Where are you shooting tomorrow?"

"We're in the studios now. Finished with location work. We're out at Ash Grove, near Wimbledon."

"I'll probably drop in there, too," said Henry. "I hope that'll be all right?"

"If you must," I said coldly. He knew very well that I could not stop him. I could not resist adding, "But I hope you won't come and upset people. Actors and directors are temperamental creatures, you know, and if . . ."

Henry beamed at me. "I don't think this part of the investigation could possibly disturb any of your people," he said. "After all, the company is backed by your father, isn't it?"

"What do you mean by that?"

"Just that you must be prepared for the fact that Sonia Meakin's story may be true, in which case your insurance company may decide to fight the case."

"I said nothing about our insurance company," I said.

"I know you didn't," said Henry. "Nevertheless, I'm warning you. They may re-open it and contest the claim. Still, that won't worry you, will it?"

I was mercifully spared from having to reply to that question by Emmy's announcement that dinner was ready.

I dare say that the concoction of lamb and eggplant for eight was delicious, but I was in no mood to do it justice. I have seldom spent a more wretched evening, in spite of the fact that Henry put himself out to be charming, and that Emmy was her usual delightful self. The conversation ranged over a host of subjects—politics, the theater, new books and films, mutual friends—everything, in fact, except the topics uppermost in my mind and, I suspected, in Henry's.

As soon as I decently could, after coffee had been served, I excused myself on the pretext of an early start in the morning and left. I was obsessed with one thought—the urgency of getting in touch with Sam Potman before Henry Tibbett could do so.

Out in the balmy air of the King's Road, I made my way to a telephone box and dialed Sam's number. I did not really expect any reply. I knew that, while working on a film, he stayed at home every evening and planned the next day's shooting, with the telephone unplugged from its wall socket. I was encouraged, therefore, to hear the "engaged" signal. It implied that Sam was not completely incommunicado. I decided to go as far as Sloane Square and try again from there. As luck would have it, I couldn't find a cab, so that it must have been a good quarter of an hour later that I tried Sam's number again, but my second attempt produced nothing but an interminable, unanswered ringing tone. There was only one thing to be done, and that was to go to Islington. I hailed a taxi and gave Sam's address. By half-past nine, I was ringing the doorbell of his beautifully restored Carolean house.

Once again, I was not unduly surprised when the doorbell was not answered; but I was surprised when I stepped back into the street and looked up at the first floor. Sam always worked in the big first-floor drawing room, which ran from front to back of the house. Now, I could see clearly that the room was unlit. The curtains had not been drawn, and moonlight streamed whitely into the shadowy corners of the empty room, throwing the furniture into grotesque silhouettes. Indeed, the whole house was in darkness, and it was quite untypical of Sam to switch the lights out simply because he had decided not to answer the doorbell. I was forced to the conclusion that for once, because of some exceptional circumstance, he was out.

Dispirited, I made my way home. It was not feasible to start combing London for the man, especially since his favorite recreation was to walk at random, usually in the East End and around the docks. My best course seemed to be to make contact with him early in the morning, and I could only hope that I would get to him before Tibbett did.

As I came into my own apartment, I was surprised to see a line of light under the drawing-room door. Hedges, my man, would be off duty and in bed by now. I concluded that he had simply forgotten to switch the light off. I pushed open the door without going in, found the light switch, and flicked it down.

Simultaneously with the darkness came an indignant exclamation. "Oi!"

In a flash the light was on again, and I was in the room. There on the sofa, with a beaker of whisky in his hand, was Sam Potman.

"Sam!" I exclaimed. "I've just been to Islington looking for you! Why weren't you there?"

"I wasn't there," replied Sam calmly, "because I found a dead man on my doorstep."

13

I suppose that by then I was past surprise. At any rate, I know that my voice was completely matter-of-fact as I said, "Oh, really? Anybody you know?"

Sam gave a great laugh. "Pudge," he said, "you're much too good to be true. Yes, as a matter of fact, somebody we both know."

"Who?"

"You remember Bob Meakin?"

"Of course. I'm not likely to forget him. But he's been dead . . ."

"His dresser, that funny little man, Murray."

I took a deep breath. "Now," I said, "let's get this straight. How did Murray die, and how does he come to be in your house?"

"How he died is very simple," said Sam. "He was hit over the head with our old friend the blunt instrument. A piece of lead piping, to be precise. It was lying beside him."

"When you say 'was'—do you mean that you've moved it?"

"Oh, yes." Sam smiled and lit a cigar. "I moved it, and I intend to move him, too. With your help."

This was too much. "Now, look here, Sam," I began.

"Wait a minute, Pudge. Just hear me out. I'll tell you exactly what happened this evening. I was at home, working, as I always do. At about eight o'clock the front doorbell rang. Well, I didn't answer it, of course, because that's one of my rules, as you know. A couple of minutes later it rang again, loud and long. I still didn't go down, but I thought it might be you or Keith or Biddy, so I opened the window and looked out. I just caught a glimpse of the rear light of a car vanishing around the corner, no chance to identify it. And then I saw that there was somebody sitting on my doorstep, looking as if he were either dead drunk or very ill. Nobody else in sight. I thought I'd better go and investigate. Well, when I opened the front door, there he was. I managed to get him inside into the hall. Then I saw the lead piping. I put on a pair of gloves and an overcoat and I slipped the piping inside my coat and walked around to a derelict building I know of, where I ditched the piping. Then I came on here."

"But Sam . . ."

"As you know very well, I haven't got a car. Don't like them. But you have, and between us we're going to get Murray into it and drive him to a bombed site I know, down by the docks. Any objections?"

I had so many that I could not put them into words. All I said, ridiculously, was, "I've never been able to understand why you don't buy a car."

"I admit," said Sam, "that it would have come in handy tonight. But fortunately you have one, so, what do you say?"

"I say 'No,'" I replied emphatically. "I shall ring Inspector Tibbett immediately, and tell him . . ."

"Pudge," said Sam quietly, "do you want to ruin us all?"

"I'd rather be ruined than jailed for life."

"Listen to me, Pudge." I could hear the fatally persuasive note in Sam's voice, and I tried to stop my ears to it. "Listen. We've had a run of the most horrible bad luck on this picture. First of all, the weather. Then, poor old Bob having that accident. Then, Margery Phipps throwing herself out of a window for no reason that anybody knows. Now this." He paused. "It's as though somebody—somebody indescribably evil was determined that the film should never be made. But it's going to be made, get that straight." Sam's jaw was out, and his North Country accent marked. "Nobody's going to stop me now. The locations are in the bag, and Keith's giving the performance of his life. Just another week and the whole thing'll be in the can. I'm not giving up."

"But still," I protested, "if we call Tibbett . . ."

Sam interrupted me. "I don't pretend to know," he said, "who killed Murray, or why; or why he was dumped on my doorstep, unless that was a bit of gratuitous spite. What I do know is that there's nothing in particular to connect him with us, unless he's found where he is now. I remember Bob mentioning that he was a bachelor and lived in lodgings, so he probably won't be missed for quite a while."

I gave what was intended to be a sardonic snort, but it sounded more like a sob. "That's where you're wrong," I said. "Chief Inspector Tibbett is coming to the office tomorrow morning with the express purpose of getting Murray's address so that he can interview him."

"Is he, indeed?" said Sam. After a pause, he added, "Does anybody else know this?"

"No," I said. "Henry mentioned it to me this evening, while I was dining with him. There was nobody else there, except Mrs. Tibbett."

"Then," said Sam thoughtfully, "if Murray had some damning information to disclose, and was about to be interviewed by the police, you were the only person who might logically have taken steps to get him out of the way."

"I resent that. If you're implying . . ."

"I'm implying," said Sam, "that Murray may well have had information that could put us all in the cart. I don't know who killed him, but whoever it was, Northburn Films ought perhaps to send him a vote of thanks." And he gave me a long, speculative look.

"Sam," I said, "I'm sick and tired of all this. Tell me what you mean. I've done nothing that wasn't above board and legal and . . ."

'Now come, Pudge," said Sam, settling himself comfortably on the sofa, "you don't believe that that insurance claim should have been paid without a big fight, do you?"

"Of course I do. It was perfectly legal. Even if Bob's letter of resignation did get to you before . . ."

"Letter of resignation? I don't know what you're talking about. No, what I meant was a small, black box that was in Bob's dressing room."

"His cuff-link box?" I said, surprised. "But it was empty . . ."

"Exactly," said Sam.

"I haven't the faintest idea what you . . . ?"

"Well, perhaps it's joost as well that you haven't. But I warn you . . ."

"Just a minute, Sam," I said. I had remembered my original mission of the evening. "Did you receive a letter of resignation from Bob, just before we started turning on that last shot?"

Sam looked really surprised. "Certainly not," he said. "There'd been a bit of talk, of course, but Biddy fixed all that. Meakin was really fond of her, you know. As for resigning his part, well, there was no question of it. None at all. Is that clear?"

"It is to me," I said. I was, in fact, greatly relieved at Sam's positive denial. "The trouble is, can we make it clear to Tibbett?" And I outlined what had happened that evening. That is to say, I did not mention Sonia Meakin, nor did I touch on my somewhat ignominious encounter with Mrs. Arbuthnot. It seemed unnecessary. I merely told Sam that I had reason to suspect the existence of the draft note, that I had bluffed my way into Margery's flat to try to find it, but had failed. I had subsequently seen Tibbett, I added, and had by devious means ascertained that he, too, suspected the existence of the document, and intended to follow it up the following day. By the end of the recital I was uncomfortably aware that, without meaning to, I had given an impression of myself as something like an intrepid hero of fiction, and, knowing how undeserved this was, I hoped that Sam would not embarrass me by fulsome congratulations. I need not have worried.

"Proper little sleuth, isn't he?" he said, in his most unpleasant manner. "Lord Peter Wimsey to the life."

"I was only doing my best," I began.

"Never mind that now," said Sam. He stood up. "Coom on. Get the car going."

"Once and for all, Sam," I said, "the answer is 'No.' We must ring the police . . ."

At once, the rudeness vanished, and Sam was all charm. "Now look, Pudge," he said, "I can see your point of view entirely. In fact, it's the reaction of any honest man, and I'd say just the same if I hadn't had this diabolical trick played on me of dumping a murdered man at my door. Just look at it this way. Murray's certainly been moved once since he was killed—I told you, I saw the car driving away. What difference does it make if he's moved again? He'll certainly be found tomorrow at the bombed site . . ."

"And supposing we're seen putting him there?"

"We won't be. This place I'm thinking of is perfectly safe. Been deserted for years."

"Then he won't be found tomorrow."

"If it makes you any happier," said Sam, "you can telephone the police anonymously in the morning and tell them to look there. But I'd think twice about doing that, if I were you. I mean, if the call were traced to you . . ."

My hand was on the telephone. "I'm not interested," I said. "I'm ringing Tibbett."

"Oh, God, Pudge," said Sam. He suddenly looked completely defeated, and put his head in his hands. "If I'd had any idea . . ."

I put down the telephone. "What do you mean?"

"Don't you see? If I hadn't been so sure that you'd help me, I'd have left the man where he was, and I might just have got away with it. Now I've moved him inside my hallway and locked the door on him. If you call Tibbett now, how am I ever going to explain that away? I swear to you that I had nothing to do with killing the man, but nobody's ever going to believe that if he's found where he is now." He paused. Then, with a trace of his old grin, he said, "Well, if you're going to telephone, do it and get it over with. Just tell me one thing first. Do you believe that I had nothing to do with it?"

"Yes, Sam," I said. And I meant it. I picked up the telephone again. I even dialed the first digits of Tibbett's number.

Then I put the receiver down, and said, "Oh, hell. I can't do it. Come along to the garage, then. We'll shift poor Murray to temporary quarters for tonight, and tomorrow I'll phone Scotland Yard anonymously. It's all I can do."

Sam stood up. "Thanks, Pudge," he said.

"Don't thank me," I said crossly. "And don't ever do such a damned idiotic thing again." But even as I said the words, I could hear the exasperated affection in my own voice. It was like dealing with a beloved, irresponsible child. "Come on, and God rot you," I said, and led the way downstairs to the car.

As we turned into the narrow street where Sam lived, it was immediately obvious that we were too late. The road was blocked with ambulances and police cars, and to reverse rapidly out again at that stage would merely have been to invite pursuit. In fact, there was not even time to slam the car into reverse gear before a policeman appeared at the window, asking us who we were and where we were bound.

Sam answered at once. "I'm Sam Potman," he said, "and I live here."

"Oh, yes sir? Which number?"

"Twenty-three."

The policeman had one of those clay faces on which it is almost impossible to register emotion, but it grew more impassive than ever, which is always a bad sign.

"Indeed, sir?" he said. "Would you drive on a little and pull in to the curb? Thank you, sir. One moment."

One moment later Henry Tibbett was grinning at me through the car window. "Pudge!" he said. "This *is* a surprise. What are you doing here?"

"I would be driving Sam Potman home," I replied, "if it weren't for all your minions cluttering up the road."

"Hullo, Henry," said Sam in a cheerful, friendly voice. "What's going on?"

"You live at number twenty-three, don't you?" Henry asked.

"Yes, I do. What of it?"

"Well, I'm afraid something rather unpleasant has happened. A man has been found murdered in your hallway."

"Good God!" I swear that, knowing all I did, I was almost taken in by Sam's incredulous exclamation. "But when did it happen? I've been out all the evening . . ."

"I think we'd better go indoors and talk about it, if you don't mind," said Henry. "You can leave the car here. Just a formality, you know, a statement about your movements this evening . . ."

We climbed the steep staircase to the first floor drawing room.

Murray looked extraordinarily peaceful. He was lying on the sofa as though in a deep sleep. The injuries were presumably on the back of his head, which was not visible.

The first thing that Tibbett said to Sam was, "Do you recognize him?"

I glanced quickly at Sam, ready to take a cue from him as to whether we should admit Murray's identity or not, and my look was intercepted by Tibbett, who frowned slightly. Without as much as a flicker of the eyelids in my direction, Sam said, "Yes, of course I do. It's poor old Murray, Bob Meakin's dresser."

"You're sure?"

"Certain. You recognize him, don't you, Pudge?"

I swallowed. "Yes," I said.

Henry was looking closely at Sam. "Did you know him well?" he asked.

"I didn't know him at all," Sam said. "Except for the fact that he was on the set every day. He was privately employed by Bob, and we all knew him by sight. Didn't we, Pudge?"

"Yes," I chimed in miserably.

"Have you any idea," Henry went on, speaking to Sam, "why he should have come here this evening?"

"Yes," said Sam promptly. "He must have been looking for work. With Bob dead, he'd find himself out of a job, and most stars have their own dressers. I'd say he must have come along here to ask me whether I knew of a vacancy."

"You were out this evening?"

"Yes, as it happens, I was. I came home and started working, as I always do; but about a quarter past nine, I came up against a technical problem that I couldn't solve without the help of old Pudge here. I telephoned him, but there was no reply. I understand he was dining with you."

Henry nodded.

"So," Sam went on, "I tried to work on alone, but about half-past nine I realized it was hopeless. I reckoned Pudge wouldn't be late home, and I decided to visit him in person. I had to walk quite a bit before I picked up a cab to take me to Pudge's flat. His manservant let me in, but told me that the young master was still out on the tiles. 'All right,' I said, 'I'll wait.' And I did. At last he came in; we cleared up our knotty problem; and he gallantly said he'd drive me home—and here we are."

I could not help admiring Sam, especially when I remember his near despair in my flat. He had pulled himself together and done some fast thinking. The result was a story which was beautifully near the truth, and could be checked at every point. The only thing he had failed to mention was that Murray's body had already been on his doorstep when he left the house.

Tibbett was looking thoughtful. "You're the sole occupant of this house, aren't you, Mr. Potman?"

"Yes, I am."

"Then how could anybody have put Murray's body into your hallway after you'd gone out?"

This was the very question Sam had been dreading, but he merely beamed, and said, "Because I didn't lock the front door. I hardly ever do. When I'm working, I lock the door of the room I'm working in—this one. The rest of the house is always open, isn't it, Pudge?"

"Yes," I said again.

"The front door was locked when we arrived, Mr. Potman," said Tibbett.

"Well, of course it would be." Sam sounded irritated. "It's only a Yale lock, and whoever lugged poor Murray into my hall, he wouldn't want to think that the door was open for anyone to walk in, now would he?"

"And you think that Murray came to consult you about getting a job?"

"I told you," said Sam, "that that's my guess why he was here, if he came voluntarily. But from what you say now, it sounds to me as if he didn't come voluntarily at all. It sounds to me as if someone did him in and brought him here after he was dead, just so as to make trouble for me."

In spite of the uneasy circumstances, I could not help being fascinated, watching the two of them. Both were skilled to a high degree in creating an apparently artless effect upon an audience, and, knowing what I knew, I wondered with lively apprehension which was succeeding the better. It seemed, for the moment at least, as if Sam were winning. Henry seemed to relax in the face of that blunt, honest good humor. He asked Sam a few more questions about Murray, to all of which Sam replied with a bluff, "I don't know, Inspector. He was Bob Meakin's dresser, and that's all."

At last, Murray was carried away, the photographers and fingerprinters withdrew, with injunctions to Sam not to touch anything in the hallway. Tibbett said good night and left, mentioning ominously that he would be seeing us again soon. Sam and I were left alone.

As the engines of the police cars faded in the distance, Sam poured a stiff drink for each of us, and said, "That was unfortunate. But you were champion, Pudge."

"I'm glad you think so," I said.

"Yes, I'm sorry now I moved the poor old fellow, but there's no real harm done. It was all much easier than I expected." He paused, turning his glass thoughtfully in his hands so that the golden spirit swirled like a lazy whirlpool. Then he said, "You know, I suppose, the question that you'll be asked before long."

"I've no idea what you mean," I said.

Sam looked at me with pity. "You'll be asked," he said, "how many pairs of spectacles we provided for Bob Meakin in his role as Professor Masterman. The correct answer is 'one.'"

I suppose my face must have betrayed my mystification, for Sam went on, "Bless me, I don't think you've got it yet. Let's hope that your Inspector Tibbett is as dumb as you are, but I doubt it. Meanwhile, just remember that the correct answer is 'One pair, with clear glass lenses.'"

"But," I protested, "that *is* the correct answer. I signed the order form myself. One pair of horn-rimmed spectacles with clear glass lenses."

Sam came over and laid a friendly hand on my shoulder. "Pudge," he said, "I love you. Now go home and go to bed and don't worry. See you on the set in the morning."

I drove home, slowly and far from happily. Sam seemed to

have taken leave of his senses, and I was really worried in case the events of the past few weeks had deranged his mind in some way. Why on earth should anybody ask me about Bob Meakin's spectacles? What on earth could they have to do with Margery Phipps or Murray? I was much more concerned with the fact that Tibbett might discover that I had visited Sam's house in Islington after leaving Chelsea that night. Taxi drivers can be traced, after all, and tend to have good memories. If it came to the point, I supposed I would have to tell the truth—that Sam had been out and that I had not noticed Murray's body in the hall. But would Tibbett believe me?

I was still preoccupied with these thoughts when I arrived home. Hedges, having been roused from his well-earned slumber by the coming and going, was up and about in his dressing gown, obviously agog for news. I merely told him that I had driven Mr. Potman home, and asked him to pour me a whisky and soda. It was while I was sipping this that the telephone rang. I picked it up.

"Croombe-Peters?"

"Speaking."

"Tibbett here. There's just one small thing I wanted to ask you. I understand that Mr. Meakin wore a pair of horn-rimmed spectacles in the role of Professor Masterman. Can you tell me how many pairs he had?"

I felt exactly like the victim of a card trick, who is told, triumphantly and correctly, that the card he was thinking of was the five of spades. I suppose that this accounts for the fact that I hesitated for a moment before replying, "Yes, of course I can tell you—one pair."

"You're sure of that?"

"Absolutely."

"And they were fitted with plain glass lenses?"

"Of course."

"I see. Well, that was all. Thanks, Pudge. Good night."

I went to bed, but I couldn't sleep. Something, something I could not quite grasp, kept intruding between my conscious mind and the bliss of unconsciousness. At five o'clock I got up and had a glass of cold milk from the refrigerator. This seemed to calm and refresh me, because I dropped into a dreamless sleep almost at once. It seemed to take me hours to drag myself out of it when Hedges appeared with my early morning cup of tea at half-past seven; but, with consciousness, came the realization that in sleep I had solved my problem. Somehow, I had remembered quite clearly signing a petty-cash slip for five guineas, made out in favor of Robert Meakin, the purpose of which was "Purchase of extra pair of property spectacles (private use)." I could not imagine what bearing this had on Continuity Girls falling from high windows or dressers being coshed at dead of night, but the fact remained—it seemed that there had, in fact, been two pairs of spectacles. And, so far as I knew, after the accident at the Underground station there had only been one—the plain glass pair that I had myself removed from Bob's body. As for the second pair, they must have been taken from Bob's dressing room and that meant that they were in the possession of one of two people, Murray or Margery Phipps. I was completely in the dark, but I was aware of some sort of plot thickening like a béchamel sauce all around me. I left for the office in a gloomy frame of mind.

14

I was greeted at the office by Sylvia, who seemed in an indecently cheerful frame of mind. Of course, the girl had no idea of the trouble we were in. I had scanned the morning newspapers very carefully, and they merely reported, in small paragraphs, that the body of a man called Murray had been found in Islington and that the police suspected foul play. No more. I doubt if Sylvia had ever heard Murray's name, and if she had, she would never have connected him with Bob Meakin or the film. So, as I say, it was with terrible nonchalance that she said, as I came in, "Good morning, Mr. Croombe-Peters. Oh, Mr. Croombe-Peters, Mrs. Meakin is waiting for you in your office."

"What?"

"Mrs. Meakin. She arrived about ten minutes ago and said she'd wait."

I went into my office, not knowing what to expect. Sonia Meakin was sitting there, very quiet and composed. As I came in, she looked up at me and said, "Ah, Mr. Croombe-Peters. This is a very bad business, isn't it?"

"What is?" I tried to sound unconcerned.

"Murray being killed. I think the time has come to put our cards on the table."

"You can put all the cards on the table that you like," I said. "Personally, I'm dealing off the top of the pack. I have no idea what is going on."

"Haven't you really?"

"None at all."

She lit a cigarette and looked at me, speculatively. I could see that she did not believe me. After a long pause, she said, "Very well. You must have known that Bob was not as young as he liked to make out. You must have known that he wore a toupee, and that most of his teeth were false, and that he'd had his face lifted."

"I suppose," I said, "that you are working around to telling me that he also had to wear glasses. That is something that I didn't know until, . . ." I checked myself. I had been about to say, "Until last night." Instead, I finished lamely, "Until recently."

"Yes." Her voice was slightly unsteady. "Don't you understand? Don't you see what it means?"

"No," I said, "I don't. People have been hinting . . ." Once again I stopped. I was determined not to say too much.

Sonia Meakin sighed impatiently. "It means," she said, "that Bob's death was not an accident. It was deliberately contrived."

"But . . ."

"Bob," said Sonia Meakin, "hated anybody to know that he had to wear glasses. Normally, he wore contact lenses. When he found that he had to wear spectacles anyway for this part, he had a pair made up to his own prescription, as well as the pair with clear glass lenses that you, in your innocence, provided for him. Murray was the only person who knew about the two pairs and who substituted the real spectacles for the clear glass ones whenever there was a long or medium shot. Bob didn't dare use his own for close shots, because the lenses were magnifying and might have shown on the screen. Murray also looked after Bob's contact lenses."

"Go on," I said.

"The day he was killed," said Sonia slowly, "somebody had deliberately switched the glasses. Bob wasn't wearing his contact lenses . . ."

"How do you know that?" I demanded.

"I'll come to that in a minute. Anyhow, for that last shot he had to run down a flight of steps to the platform, ramming his spectacles on his nose. He took them from Murray, believing them to be the pair made to his own prescription—and they weren't. He was virtually blind. Of course, he stumbled and fell, and with the train coming in . . ."

"I really don't see the point of all this, Mrs. Meakin," I said.

"Well, you see," she said, "Margery Phipps was blackmailing me."

"You don't say."

"She telephoned me the day before she died, and asked me to go and see her at her flat in Chelsea. She said she had some things which had belonged to my husband. Not only did she show me the draft note of Bob's resignation, and demand money from me, but she also hinted about Bob's eyesight and the two pairs of spectacles."

"Did she produce the second pair?"

"No. She just talked. She said that if it could be proved that Bob's death was due to negligence on behalf of an employee of the company, the insurance claims would be null and void."

"If she said that," I said, "she was mistaken. The truth is . . ." And I stopped abruptly. The truth was that if negligence —or worse, design—could be proved against a member of the unit, it would not affect Sonia Meakin's life insurance policy at all. But it would invalidate ours. I became aware that Sonia Meakin was talking again.

". . . just laughed it off," she said. "Nevertheless, you can understand why I came around the next day to collect the things from Bob's dressing room. I wanted to know the truth. What I found was the clear glass spectacles, smashed; obviously he'd been wearing them when he died. There was no sign of the other pair. Still I was not too worried. I assumed that he'd been wearing his contact lenses at the time. And then, yesterday, Murray telephoned me."

"Did he really?" I liked the sound of this less and less.

"He said," went on Mrs. Meakin, "that he found he still had Bob's contact lenses and imagined that I'd like them back."

"More blackmail?"

"I suppose so. It's hard to believe that Murray—but there it is. He said he was very hard up. He gave me the address of his lodgings, and I said I'd go there last night. And so I did, after I left Inspector Tibbett's house, but I was later than I had promised and Murray was out. It was then that I decided I ought to warn Mr. Potman."

"How very charitable of you. Why?"

She looked at me out of those limpid innocent eyes. "Well, he is in charge of the film, isn't he? I thought he ought to know, and be on his guard in case Murray started blackmailing him. You had been so unsympathetic . . ."

"I still am," I assured her.

"So I went to Mr. Potman's house. I rang the bell, but there was no reply. Then I looked in through the glass panels of the front door, and in the moonlight I saw something—a man, hunched up on the floor as though he were dead. It was horrible. I ran straight to the nearest telephone and rang Inspector Tibbett."

"You did, did you?" I said icily. It had been bothering me, how Henry Tibbett had found Murray before Sam and I got back. "Well, what do you expect me to do about it?"

"I don't know," said Sonia, with another of those melting looks. "All I know is that the second pair of spectacles and the contact lenses are about somewhere, and I have an idea that Inspector Tibbett is looking for them."

"If he is," I said grimly, "it's because you told him."

"I couldn't help it," said Sonia, in a voice trembling with tears. "I had to tell the truth. It was my duty. But I thought I must come and warn you . . ."

"It occurs to me, Mrs. Meakin," I said, "that you have very

cleverly succeeded in implicating Mr. Potman with the poor man, Murray. And of all the people who had both motive and opportunity for killing Margery Phipps and Murray, I can think of no more likely suspect than you."

She looked hard at me. Her eyes were dry now and her expression unfriendly. "Or you, Mr. Croombe-Peters," she said.

And before I could reply, she had gone.

It was impossible to settle down to any work. The more I thought about the situation, the murkier it looked. The whole thing seemed to hinge on that miserable second pair of spectacles, and until I had located and destroyed them, the future of Northburn Films would hang in the balance. I made a great effort to think clearly.

If Margery had found the spectacles and had realized their implications, then they must have been in her flat; in which case, they were now in the custody of the police or of Mrs. Arbuthnot or of the murderer, if indeed such a person existed. The fact that Henry Tibbett had telephoned me to ask about them made it unlikely that the police had them. If Mrs. Arbuthnot had found them, we would surely have had some sort of a blackmailing approach from her by now; but we had not. I remembered how I had heard her searching in the Chelsea Mansions flat; very likely she had been looking for them, unsuccessfully. On the other hand, it was even more likely that Murray had both the spectacles and the contact lenses. It seemed odd that he had waited so long to start his blackmailing activities, but that was no concern of mine.

What was my concern was that Murray had been killed and left on Sam Potman's doorstep. By whom? Sonia Meakin? She seemed the obvious person, and yet, she looked so frail. It was hard to imagine that she had the strength to commit two murders, let alone push bodies out of windows and lug corpses around London at night. Sonia with an accomplice then? This, also, seemed unlikely. In my dealings with her, she had been playing a lone hand.

For a moment I toyed with the idea that Sam might have killed Murray himself, but that hypothesis, too, seemed absurd. For one thing, he could have disposed of the body quietly himself, instead of leaving it there and coming around to see me. For another, Sam was one of the few people who could not possibly have had a hand in Margery's death, for he was watching rushes at the time when she was killed. To presuppose not one but two murderers within the unit was carrying things altogether too far. And then there was the case of Bob Meakin . . .

I had got as far as this in my very haphazard analysis of the facts when the telephone rang, and Sylvia informed me that Henry Tibbett was on the line. I was not surprised. I had not been taken in by his hearty friendliness the night before. I was well aware that we were in for another—and much more unpleasant—session with him in his official capacity. This time, there was no argument about it being a case of murder.

I picked up the phone gingerly. "Croombe-Peters here."

"Oh, Pudge." Henry sounded as chummy as ever. "I was wondering where your unit is shooting today?"

"At the studio," I said briefly. "The café scene."

"Were you thinking of going out there yourself?"

"Not today, no. I have a lot of work in the office." This was not true, but I didn't intend to make things too easy for him. I could see exactly what was coming, and I was right.

"I'd be most awfully grateful," he went on, in that almost boyish way he has, "if you'd change your plans and come down there with me. I have to interview one or two people, and I know they're a temperamental bunch. You did ask me before to try not to upset them, and somehow you seem to make a very effective buffer between your own people and the rather austere approach of the law."

"What if I refuse?"

There was a slight hesitation. "If you refuse," said Henry, "I shall have to go anyway, and upset them. That's all. I really think it would be in your own interest to come along."

"Oh, very well," I said crossly. "I'll see you at the studio in half an hour."

Henry was waiting for me in the production office when I arrived at Ash Grove Studios. Under the malevolent eye of Louise Cohen, he was studying a batch of continuity sheets, and he looked up with a friendly grin as I came in.

"Ah, Pudge. Glad to see you. Can you tell me one or two things about these—whatever they are?"

"Continuity sheets," I said shortly.

Louise had stood up. "Mr. Croombe-Peters," she began, in her most dragonish manner, "I do think that I might be told beforehand if we're going to have detectives rummaging around the office . . ."

"I didn't know," I said. "Chief Inspector Tibbett did not honor me with his confidence. I thought he wanted to go on the set."

"So I do, later on," said Henry amiably.

"He really is a Chief Inspector, is he?" said Louise suspiciously. "Coming in here, demanding to see . . ."

"Yes," I said, "he really is a Chief Inspector."

"Oh, well. If you say so, I suppose it's all right. Mr. Potman will be furious, I can tell you that." Louise flounced out of the office, banging the door.

Henry grinned again. "You see?" he said. "One word from you, and I'm accepted."

"If you call that accepted," I said.

"Well, tolerated at least. Now, do explain these things to me."

"I thought Diana had already done that."

"She gave me an idea, but I'd like to check it with you. These," Henry indicated the pile of colored papers on the desk, "these are the sheets made out by Margery Phipps on the day of Robert Meakin's death."

"So I see."

"Now, each is marked with a number. I presume that's the identifying number of the shot."

"That's right."

"And these numbers, taken consecutively, show the order in which the scenes were actually filmed, do they?"

"Yes," I said. "They have nothing to do with the sequence of the script itself."

"This one," said Henry, "is unfinished. It appears to relate to the actual shot in which Meakin died."

"Let's have a look," I said. I took the pink paper from Henry's hand. "Yes, that's right. Margery had noted down the basics of the shot—the location, action, props, and so forth—beforehand. Afterward, if all had gone well, she'd have recorded any differences between one take and another; actors vary their movements slightly each time and maybe alter dialogue a little . . ."

"I see," said Henry, "that it's marked 'Retake One-Nine-Four.' And further back, in the previous day's sheets, there's a shot called 'One-Nine-Four,' which sounds exactly the same."

"That's right," I explained patiently. "We took that shot the day before and we thought we had it in the can, but it was spoilt in processing. I never did find out," I added, "whose fault it was—ours or the laboratories." The old grievance returned, niggling. "Anyhow, we were all set up for the next shot, or nearly so, when this message came through and we had to retake."

"And what was the next scene, the one you should have been shooting?"

"As a matter of fact," I said, "it was the one immediately before the other in the script—Masterman running down the staircase."

"I see," said Henry. He studied the sheet again in silence. Then he looked up and said, "Now, tell me about these spectacles."

"What spectacles?" I hoped I did not sound nervous.

"I'm just checking on everything," he said. "You told me last night that Meakin had just one pair of spectacles that he wore in the film."

"That's right. The same ones that Keith is using now—with very heavy horn rims. They're a sort of signature of the character."

"Surely not the *same* ones?" said Henry, with a curious emphasis.

"Not identical, of course," I said. "Bob's were broken when he—in the accident. Naturally we had a new pair made for Keith."

"That wasn't exactly what I meant," said Henry. "I meant that Mr. Meakin's were made up to his own prescription."

It seemed to be more of a statement than a question, so I said nothing.

Henry went on, "It was only last night that Mrs. Meakin explained to me about her husband's bad eyesight. I can quite understand that he wanted to hush it up. According to Mrs. Meakin, he wore contact lenses as a rule, but for this film he had these spectacles made up with his own lenses. She says he had just the one pair, so he must have been wearing them when he died."

I could hardly deny it. "By Jove, yes," I said. "I am an idiot. I'd quite forgotten that old Bob had his own glasses."

"They were pretty powerful, weren't they?"

"I suppose so."

"When you told me last night," said Henry, "that Meakin's glasses had clear lenses, it occurred to me to wonder whether, by any chance, there might have been two pairs of spectacles. I understand that you had the unpleasant job of removing them from the body. Were they smashed?"

"One lens was broken. The other had somehow escaped intact."

"So," persisted Henry, "you'd have noticed if they'd been plain glass?"

In a flash I realized how clever Sonia Meakin had been; I just wished that she had been a little more explicit in my office, for I nearly missed my cue. Just in time, however, I saw it. Sonia had mentioned one pair of glasses only, with magnifying lenses. The remains of the clear glass pair were in her possession, and must have been safely destroyed by now. If another pair of prescription lens glasses should turn up, they could be explained away as a spare pair, privately ordered by Bob. All that was needed now was a small and easy lie from me, and one of our worries would be over.

"Why, of course," I said. "I do remember quite clearly, now you come to mention it. I noticed how the one remaining lens distorted everything. No doubt about it. Sorry I misled you last night—I was rather wrought up, I'm afraid, what with Murray's death and . . ."

"You knew about Meakin's disability?"

"Of course," I said easily.

"Oh, well." Henry stretched, and smiled at me. "Wrong again. Bang goes a perfectly lovely theory. I shall have to start all over again. By the way, you don't happen to know what became of those broken spectacles?"

"They were thrown away months ago," I said, truthfully I hoped.

"And Meakin's contact lenses?"

"I thought Murray," I began, and then checked myself.

Henry nodded. "Mrs. Meakin thought he might have them," he said, "but they weren't on him, and we couldn't find them at his lodgings. Oh, well, I dare say he lost them." He paused for a moment, in thought. Then he said, "Fiametta Fettini."

"What about her?"

"Was she genuinely fond of Meakin, or was it just a stunt?"

I shrugged. I was feeling much more at ease. "My dear Tibbett," I said, "don't ask me. La Fettini is publicity mad, as you know, and I'm fairly certain that's how the whole thing started. Whether, later on, she grew genuinely attached to Meakin, God knows. I would doubt it myself, but it's true that she made a ridiculous fuss about that lipstick case. I notice, however, that she's now lost it again."

"You say she came, quite literally, from the slums of Naples?"

"I should have thought that was obvious."

"Has she a lot of jewelry?"

I laughed. "I can see you don't study the gossip columns," I said. "She adores it. Festoons herself with it. It's rather pathetic in a way. I think it gives her a sense of security, not that she needs any such thing by now."

"You can never be sure," said Henry, enigmatically. "What about her husband?"

"Poor little Giulio? He's more of a nonentity than her wretched monkey. For one thing, he's never sober. Personally, I can't understand why she bothers with him at all."

"Perhaps he has some sort of hold over her?"

"Over Fiametta?" I laughed. "My dear Tibbett, what hold could a whipper-snapper like that have over a . . . ?"

"He is her husband," said Henry.

"I know, but . . ."

"And they are both Italians. No question of a divorce. I should call that a pretty firm hold."

"Nonsense. Fiametta doesn't obey any rules. She makes them up as she goes along."

"I wonder," said Henry. "Well, never mind. Tell me about the fascinating Mrs. Pardoe—I'm sorry, Miss Brennan."

"You've met her," I said.

"Yes." Henry lit a cigarette. "Have you any idea what she and her husband were fighting about in that pub in Henley the day Margery was killed?"

"My dear Tibbett, I'm not psychic."

"I just thought you might have some suggestions to offer. You are in such a good position for observing all these people. Has there been any friction lately?"

"If you want the truth," I said, "there has; but it has no possible bearing on anything else. The fact is that Keith has become intolerably swollen-headed since he took on this part, and Biddy doesn't like it, quite understandably. After all, a few months ago she was the celebrity of the family. If you ask me," I went on, warming to my theme, "that marriage won't last much longer. Not that it's ever been a real marriage, as far as I can see. It's not my idea of . . ."

"Don't you think so?" Henry was looking at me in that curious, quizzical, amused way again. "I think that Biddy Brennan would cheerfully perjure her soul for . . ."

"If you're implying that she lied to you," I began. Ever since Biddy's interview with Henry in my office, I had had a sneaking suspicion that Henry had disbelieved her, and I thought it only right to try to put in a good word for her. I went on. "I had a feeling at the time that you didn't believe her evidence. Well, I can assure you that Biddy is as straight as a die. If anybody lied, it was Keith. He's shifty and devious and ambitious and . . ."

Henry was smiling again. "No need to get so worked up, Pudge," he said. "I have no doubt that Biddy was telling the truth. None whatsoever. In fact, I've checked with the cinema, and the projector did break down at that performance. Her evidence was completely accurate."

"Then why . . . ?"

"Sometimes," said Henry slowly, "truth can be misleading."

And before I could work out what he meant by this, Henry got up and said, "Well, let's go along to the set and talk to these people to their faces instead of behind their backs."

We went out into the cheerless concrete corridor and along to the heavy, soundproof double doors of Stage 2.

15

Stage 2 was a dark, lofty cavern of a place, the size of a small-ish aircraft hanger. A lot of people seemed to be hanging about doing nothing in particular, and miscellaneous pieces of electrical equipment, furniture, sections of sets, rostrums, camera trucks, and so forth gave one the feeling of having strayed into a disorganized warehouse of some sort. Over at the far side of the stage, activity was centered on a small, tight-knit group of people, and here, too, was a focus of brilliant lights, a small, dazzling island in a sea of shadows.

"This way," I said to Henry, and took his arm to pilot him across the stage.

We had only just reached the outskirts of the group when it became clear that things were about to happen. I motioned to Henry to stand still, and we waited quietly, watching from the ringside, as it were, while the familiar routine of film-making unfolded in front of us.

The small, brightly lit area represented a corner of a big popular café. From the many painted flats and extra tables and chairs piled up around the place, it was obvious that the set, in its entirety, represented the whole restaurant; but for this shot, the camera was concentrating on the particular corner table occupied by the two stars of the film, so that the rest of the set had been roughly dismantled and pushed aside, accounting for much of the confusion on the stage. The lighting set-up consisted of batteries of arcs and spots clustered around the little table, in its angle of walls, where Keith's and Fiametta's stand-ins were sitting, languidly, looking as bored as only stand-ins can look.

As Henry and I approached, Gervase Mountjoy shrilled his whistle, and comparative silence ensued. "Miss Fettini and Mr. Pardoe, please!" called Mountjoy officiously. "Quiet, everybody! We're rehearsing!"

Two figures detached themselves from the shadows, and as they came forward into the light I saw that they were Keith and Fiametta, who had evidently been having a tête-à-tête behind one of the discarded bits of scenery. They seemed in high spirits, both of them; in fact, Fiametta was giggling immoderately, and the two of them kept up some sort of bantering conversation in undertones as they sat down in the seats vacated by their stand-ins. Murder or no murder, Murray or no Murray, there was a splendid atmosphere on the set that day. I could sense it at once.

Sam, who had been talking earnestly to Fred Harborough, now strolled across to the table and squatted down on his haunches between Fiametta and Keith. In defiance of all the studio regulations, he was smoking another of his horrible little cigars, and of course nobody raised a finger to stop him. It made me very angry. Sam knew as well as I did that we would get no compensation in case of fire if there had been people smoking on the set, and if the director persistently breaks the rules, it is difficult for his First Assistant to enforce them with other members of the unit. Not, of course, that Gervase Mountjoy could have enforced a hot knife onto a pat of butter.

I became aware of Tibbett's hand on my arm. "What's happening now?" he whispered.

"Sam's giving them an idea of how he wants the scene played," I answered in a normal voice. "No need for whispering yet. We're not shooting."

"Quiet over there! Rehearsing!" yelled Mountjoy, looking most pointedly in my direction.

I ignored him.

Meanwhile, Sam was talking quietly to his two actors, and all three of them were laughing and looking as relaxed as one could wish. This was the sort of day when everything goes right and the picture gets ahead of schedule. After a minute or two, Sam stood up and said, "O.K. Let's have a run-through."

After an unnecessary delay, caused by Gervase blowing his whistle and shouting at people who were making no noise anyhow, silence finally prevailed. Fred Harborough and his camera operator signified that they were ready for a tryout, and Sam said, "Right. Let's have it."

This was to be a "tracking shot," that is, it started as a double shot of Keith and Fiametta, taken from some feet away; but during the dialogue the camera crept in on rubber wheels toward the table, until it ended up as a big close-up of Keith. This maneuver, of course, involved adjusting the focus and moving the microphone as well; in fact, quite a crowd of people accompanied the camera on its journey; but the whole thing was accomplished in such dead silence that nothing registered on the sensitive recording apparatus except the voices of the actors.

At a signal from Sam, they started.

Fiametta glanced at her watch. "I must go, Tony," she said.

The camera crept in toward Keith. "But Rosa," he said, "I—I've got tickets for the zoo . . ."

"I have to go."

The camera was closer now. "Where? Where do you have to go?" By now, we were on a big close-up of Keith. He leant forward and snatched off his spectacles. "Rosa! You must tell me . . ."

"O.K." said Sam. "How was it, Fred?"

"O.K. by me," said Fred.

"O.K. for sound," came another voice from the shadows.

"Right, let's shoot it," said Sam.

Mountjoy's whistle shrilled. "Quiet, please! We're rolling! Red light on! Quiet everyone! We're turning this time!"

A big red light glowed above the door and an almost uncanny silence descended on the set. Steve stepped forward, with his usual grin, carrying the clapper board.

"*Street Scene,* Seven-Six-Eight, Take One," he called. The clapper fell with a thud.

Fiametta looked at her watch. "I must go, Tony," she said.

An hour later Steve was saying, "*Street Scene,* Seven-Six-Eight, Take Eleven."

For the eleventh time Fiametta looked at her watch. "I must

go, Tony," she said for the eleventh time.

For the eleventh time the camera crept silently toward Keith.

"But Rosa," said Keith. "I've got tickets for the zoo . . ."

"Cut it!" said a voice from the camera truck. "Boom shadow."

Keith jumped up. "Goddamn it!" he shouted.

I must say I sympathized with him. Take One had been spoilt because the sound recorder accused the camera truck of squeaking. This had been remedied, only to have Take Two wrecked by an arc lamp fusing in the middle of the shot. Take Three had come to grief because the camera jammed, and Take Four because a property man knocked over a chair. By Take Five, Fiametta was growing restless and nervous, and she exaggerated the gesture of looking at her watch to the extent of upsetting a wine glass on the table. During Take Six another lamp had fused, and Take Seven was ruined by a low-flying aircraft passing overhead and drowning the dialogue. Take Eight was possible, but Sam naturally wanted to cover himself and asked for another, and the camera had run out of film in the middle of it. Take Ten came to grief because the focus puller sneezed, and now Take Eleven was invalidated by the shadow of the moving microphone intruding into the picture, one of the commonest of pitfalls but one which had so far been avoided. All this time Keith had continued to give an impeccable and unchanging performance of his scrap of dialogue, and that takes some doing eleven times in succession. It was no wonder he lost his temper.

Sam was at his elbow in an instant. He said something to Keith, and then called Mountjoy over, and the next moment Mountjoy's whistle was shrilling, and he was announcing a tea break, some ten minutes early. This was obviously a sound move. Sam had one take in the can, and the best possible thing at this stage was to give everyone a chance to relax and get a second wind before starting again. Mentally, I took a gloomy look at our schedule. We were by no means keeping up to the amount of work planned for the day; however, things could have been worse. I have heard Alfred Hitchcock describe how it once took him eleven days to get forty-five seconds of screen time into the can.

Henry's voice at my elbow said, "This might be a good opportunity for me to have a word with some of your people."

"For God's sake," I said, "leave them alone. Sam's only called a tea break because everyone's getting wrought up. Once you pass Take Ten, you can always expect trouble."

"Well," said Henry pacifically, "we can perhaps start with somebody who isn't actually on the set. Like Miss Brennan."

"What in hell do you mean, not on the set?"

Biddy's dusky voice came mockingly from the shadows, and as she stood up I saw that she had been sitting within a few feet of us, huddled into a basketwork chair. She is, of course, a small person, but even so she has a capacity for melting into a background when she wants to which is, in my experience, unrivaled. She stood up now, five-foot-one of compact nervous energy, and grinned at Henry.

"What's the master sleuth up to now?" she asked.

"Did you see a paper this morning?" asked Henry.

"No."

"Then you haven't heard about Murray's death?"

Biddy seldom makes a mistake, but she did so now. She hesitated palpably, and her eyes strayed for a moment to the lighted area of the set where Sam and Keith were talking. It was plain that she would have liked to deny any knowledge of anything, but since Sam must obviously have mentioned his bizarre experience of the previous night, she could hardly fail to admit knowledge of the event.

"Sam said something," she began, and then stopped.

"Mr. Potman had a very nasty experience, I'm afraid," said Henry easily. "It's not a nice thing to find a corpse on your doorstep."

Biddy said nothing.

Henry went on, "You knew Murray, of course?"

"By sight. We all did."

"Have you any idea why somebody should want to kill him?"

"None at all. He always seemed an inoffensive little chap. Couldn't it have been an accident? I mean, supposing he'd been hit by a car which didn't stop, and that he just managed to crawl into the doorway before . . ."

"There might be a chance of that," said Henry, "except for one thing. The front door was shut and locked when we got there. Mr. Potman says he left it open . . ."

"It's always open," Biddy said. "Everyone knows that."

"Well, there you are," said Henry. "Somebody shut it and released the Yale lock. Murray could hardly have done that himself, if he'd crawled in there dying."

Inwardly, I cursed Sam. It had suddenly occurred to me that Biddy's explanation might well be the correct one. Sam, as I knew, had actually found Murray outside the front door, and had been idiotic enough to lug him in and lock the door on him, instead of informing the police straight away. Then I remembered the piece of lead piping and the fact that somebody had twice rung Sam's doorbell, at a time when Murray was, presumably, already dead. It was chilling to consider the degree of vindictiveness behind that person's actions. In fairness, I tried to keep an open mind about the murderer's identity; but, in my heart, I acknowledged that it could only be one person—Sonia Meakin. Only she had had both motive and opportunity. Only she would have been prepared to jeopardize the film—perhaps she had some twisted idea of avenging poor Bob's death. And, to clinch the matter, she had admitted calling the police to Sam's house. Presumably, she had been lurking somewhere nearby to watch Sam's reactions and was afraid, when he left the house, that he might indeed be able to dispose of the damning evidence of a body on his doorstep. I knew all this, and the frightful thing was that I could not as much as hint it to Henry without giving away Sam's criminally foolish actions and my own condoning of them.

I became aware of Biddy's voice, answering a question of Henry's.

"Last night? Yes, of course I can. Keith and I spent the evening at the Belgrave Towers with Miss Fettini and her husband."

Henry grinned. "That seems straightforward enough," he said. "If you were all together all the time, it looks like killing four birds with one stone. Can you remember what time you arrived there?"

"About half-past nine. We had dinner at home and went along afterward."

"And none of you left Miss Fettini's suite all the evening?"

"No. We were all there together. Her maid can confirm it,

and so can the waiter who brought us drinks. We left at half-past twelve. I remember, because I suddenly noticed how late it was. Keith has to be up so early, you see, when he's on call. We don't usually go out in the evenings when he's working."

"This was a long-standing engagement, was it?" Henry said casually.

Biddy hesitated for a moment. "No," she said. "Actually we went along on the spur of the moment. There was something Keith wanted to—to discuss with Miss Fettini."

"I see," said Henry, in the slightly absent-minded voice which always means that his brain is ticking over with more-than-average energy. "Well, that seems to let all four of you out, doesn't it?"

Biddy raised her eyebrows. "Let us out?" She laughed. "Surely Inspector, you never seriously thought that any of us might have . . . ?"

"No, no," said Henry. He rubbed the back of his neck with his hand. "Half-past nine. According to Mr. Potman's account, he was still at home then, and there was no sign of a corpse."

"I can confirm that," I said quickly. It had suddenly occurred to me that I could help to bolster up Sam's story. "That he was at home, I mean. You see, I telephoned Mr. Potman from the public call box near your house, just after I'd left you."

Henry looked interested. "Did you? That's very helpful. You left us at ten past nine, I remember. So it must have been about a quarter-past when you spoke to Mr. Potman."

"Oh, I didn't speak to him," I said. "I couldn't get him."

"You mean there was no reply? Then he must have been out already."

"No, no. I was expecting no reply, frankly, because I know he generally unplugs the telephone when he's working in the evenings. But when I rang last night, I got the engaged tone. So I knew he must have been there. As a matter of fact, he must have been trying to ring me at my home at the time."

"I see," Henry looked hard at me. "Why were you trying to contact Mr. Potman?"

I laughed. "Some sort of telepathy, I suppose. Funnily enough, the very same problem that was bothering him had occurred to me. I thought we ought to discuss it . . ."

"And what problem was that?"

He had me there. Sam had not, in my hearing, specified what we were supposed to have discussed. Heaven knew whether he had gone into details with Henry on the subject. I felt cold with alarm. "Oh, just a technicality to do with the film. It wouldn't interest you."

"But it does. Film-making fascinates me. It was something to do with today's shooting, so I gathered from Mr. Potman."

I looked around wildly for Sam, but he was deep in discussion with Mountjoy and Fred Harborough. He had not even noticed Henry's presence on the set, or, if he had, he gave no sign of it. There was nothing for it but to plunge, and hope for the best. Desperately, I tried to remember Sam's words to Henry—something about a problem that only Pudge could solve. Well, the only problems I solved around the studios were financial ones, and Henry knew it.

"It was—a question of—of more extras for the big café scene. . . ." I sounded to myself to be babbling incoherently. "I had to authorize the payment, you see. Everything comes down to a question of filthy lucre in the end. I knew Sam wanted twenty or so other diners, to fill in the background, as it were, and I had only budgeted for six . . ."

Henry was looking puzzled. "Surely it was a bit late to hire them? After nine o'clock in the evening? Did you succeed?"

"Er—no. No, we didn't." I knew that if I said "Yes" Henry would demand to be shown the extras, who, of course, were not there. "It was too late. We re-arranged the schedule of shooting so as to do all the close-ups today and leave the general establishing shots for tomorrow, when we can get the people."

This seemed pretty neat to me. We were, in fact, shooting the close-ups that day, as Henry could see for himself. However, it was now vitally important for me to have a quiet word with Sam before Henry started questioning him again. So I was much relieved when, instead of asking for Sam, Henry suggested that he might have a very quick word with Keith and Fiametta, just in order to confirm Biddy's account of their movements during the evening.

I left the two of them with him, Fiametta explaining earnestly that she knew it was exactly twenty-five past when Keith and Biddy arrived, because she had been on the point of going to bed—normally she always went to bed at nine when she had an early call the following morning.

I slipped away and went over to Sam and Fred Harborough. They were deep in a technical discussion about the next shot and neither of them looked at all pleased to see me.

"Sam," I said, "can I have a word with you?"

"If you must," he said snappily. And when I said nothing, he added, "Come on, man. Out with it. What's up?"

"A word in private," I amended, looking hard at Fred.

"Sorry, I'm sure," said Fred, obviously offended. "I'll make myself scarce."

"You'll do nothing of the sort," said Sam. And to me, "I don't like secrets on film sets. Anything you have to say, you can say it in front of Fred."

"Very well," I said. "Henry Tibbett is over there, talking to Keith and Fiametta."

"Oh, is he? Well, what of it?"

"He was asking me about our conversation last night, when you came to my house. I was explaining to him that it was about the extra bit players for the big café scene tomorrow."

"For the—but we're due to finish the café today," protested Fred. "What's all this about a big café scene? Has the script been changed?"

Sam looked at me and shook his head almost imperceptibly, but as if in despair at my stupidity. A most ungracious attitude to take, I considered. I was rather proud of my improvisation. Then, in a voice full of anger, he said, "Really, Pudge. Do you mean you haven't yet informed the unit about the new scene and the change of schedule?"

Furiously I said, "Well, no. Not yet."

"Then I suggest you do so at once," said Sam offensively. "After all, we fixed the whole thing up last night, didn't we? I dare say you haven't even booked the extras yet. God, does one have to do everything oneself to be sure of getting it done?"

I must say I was speechless. It seemed to me to be the meanest attack I had ever had made against me. It was only afterward, in the production office, that I simmered down enough to realize that Sam had saved the situation brilliantly. Sure enough, I was the scapegoat, as usual, but it certainly never crossed Fred Harborough's mind for an instant that Sam and I had not, in fact, rearranged the shooting schedule the night before. And Fred would purvey this impression to the rest of the unit.

My only trouble was that I had no lead from Sam as to where the famous rewritten and interpolated scene was supposed to occur in the script. All I could do was to write in another long shot more or less at random during the café scene, and then I got Louise Cohen onto the job of hiring the extras and doing all the paper work involved in a change of schedule. For the first time, I blessed the fact that the director's word, however unexpected, is law, and that Sam was in the habit of making these last-minute snap decisions. Louise and Fred and Props and the head carpenter all grumbled about the extra work and last-moment change, but it did not strike any of them as bizarre or unusual. I breathed again, and went back to Stage 2.

By the time I got there, work had started again, and Take Twelve was about to start. I saw that Henry was sitting beside Sam in the chair marked Fiametta Fettini, apparently absorbed in all that was going on. Sam was explaining something to him, and I could sense a warm feeling of mutual respect between the two men. Each, in his own sphere, was a perfectionist, and each admired the other.

Then came the whistle, the cry, "Red light on! We're rolling!" And for the twelfth time Fiametta looked at her watch and said, "I must go, Tony."

It went beautifully. Sam beamed and said, "Print Eight and Twelve"; the red light went out; and the stage began to buzz with chatter as the army of electricians and scene shifters and property men moved in to organize the next set-up. I walked over to Sam and Henry. They were still sitting side by side in their canvas chairs, talking earnestly. As I came up, I heard Sam say, "That's right. I tried to phone him, but there was no reply. About a quarter past nine, it must have been."

"So you decided to go over to his flat and wait for him?"

"I did."

"Wasn't it?" Henry hesitated. He sounded diffident. "Forgive me—I'm no expert in this business—but wasn't it rather unusual to have left something as important as the hiring of extras until the last moment?"

I must confess that I saw my opportunity, not only of confounding Mr. Nosey-Parker Tibbett but of getting my own back somewhat at Sam. "Not at all," I said. Both men wheeled around in their chairs to look at me. "Not," I went on, "when you're dealing with a director like Sam, who never makes up his mind until the last moment, and then wants to change everything. You can ask anybody on this set, Tibbett, and they'll all tell you the same thing."

I could see that Sam was furious, but there really was nothing he could do, except give in gracefully. "I'm afraid Pudge is right," he said. "Until one day's work is in the can and you've seen rushes, it's difficult to get a complete mental picture of what one wants for the next day. I know that it's this sort of thing that produces expensive films, but it also produces masterpieces." And he glared at me.

Henry laughed. "Oh, well," he said, "heaven forbid that I should get into an argument on something I know nothing about. I'll take your word for it." He stood up. "Well, Mr. Potman, you've been very helpful and patient, and I don't think I need worry any of you any longer." He glanced at a small notebook. "I've got details here on the movements of all the important members of your unit last night. Have you any idea where I can find Miss Fettini's husband, by the way?"

"Yes," said Sam, "in a bar."

"Any idea which?"

"I should start at the Belgrave Towers and work outward from there."

"I see. Thank you." Henry turned as if to go, hesitated, and then said, "Oh, there was just one more thing, Mr. Potman. I understand you always have a run-through of the previous day's filming in the evenings."

"That's right. Rushes, we call it. Six o'clock in the cinema here."

"I was wondering if you could arrange for an extra piece of film to be shown for my benefit."

Sam looked surprised. "What extra film?" he demanded.

"Well," said Henry, "it occurred to me that the camera was already—what's the word you use—rolling, that's it, isn't it—

was already rolling when Robert Meakin had his unfortunate accident. I dare say it has nothing to do with Murray's death, but it's unusual, to say the least, that an accident of that sort should have been recorded on film. I suppose it must exist somewhere, and I'd like to see it."

Sam wheeled on me. He seemed really rattled. "Does it exist, Pudge?" he asked. "What happened to it?"

"I expect it was destroyed," I said, hoping that I didn't sound as nervous as Sam did. "I'll make inquiries, of course, but there would have been no reason to keep it. If it does exist, I suppose it's in the cutting room. I'll have a look."

"That's very kind of you, Pudge," said Henry. "Well, I'll get back to London now and see you at six."

When Henry had gone, Sam and I looked at each other in silence for a moment.

Then Sam said, "That film doesn't exist, does it, Pudge?"

"I don't know."

"I'll put it like this," said Sam. "I hope it doesn't."

"Sam," I said, "if you're asking me to go and find it and destroy it . . ."

"I never said . . ."

"Never mind what you said." I was speaking in an urgent sort of whisper, even though there was nobody else within earshot. "What with last night—and now this—for God's sake, Sam, what are you playing at? I'm not a murderer, and I'm damned sure you're not, but you've got us into such a false position with the police by now that there's no knowing what they might think if . . ."

"Oh, Pudge." Sam looked at me with that quizzical grin that he gives to actors who still can't get it right after ten takes. "Dear, misguided Pudge, don't you *see?* Don't you understand?"

"I understand nothing, except that I am being expected to conceal evidence and to lie . . ."

"If we're going to get this film safely in the can," said Sam, "we've got to protect him. Until the last day's shooting. When that's over, I don't care. He can fend for himself. This is my film, and I'm seeing it through."

"Protect whom?" I was completely bewildered. "What are you talking about?"

"You poor idiot," said Sam, "I'm talking about Keith Pardoe. Now, go to the cutting room and get that can of film and burn it."

16

The cutting room is a world quite apart from the rough and tumble of the rest of the film studio. Here, only the finished product is considered. The agonies of the "floor" have been resolved into neat lengths of film and this is the raw material from which the editor works. It is nothing to him that the star was having hysterics, or that the performing dog failed to turn up and the set collapsed during Take Three. He sees only the successful takes, and, in collaboration with the director, he constructs the film from them.

I approached this austere and orderly world without too much trepidation. I had always enjoyed hanging around the cutting room, and I was greeted amiably by the editor and his assistants; and when I said that I wanted to take a look at a certain can of film, nobody expressed surprise—or any other emotion, come to that. I was merely motioned to go into the storeroom and look for what I wanted. The editor did offer me the services of one of his minions to help me, but I declined them. For this job, I preferred to be alone.

It took some time, but I found the can in the end. It was buried deep at the back of a lot of rejected material, which is never thrown away in case the director might decide at the last moment to make use of it. I extracted the film, and came back into the cutting room, looking as unconcerned as I could.

"I'd like to run this through the viewer," I said.

"Help yourself," said the assistant editor, and went back to his work.

The viewers are like miniature film screens, designed to be watched by one person at a time. On them, you can watch a miniscule but moving film show, your eyes jammed into a rubber eyepiece reminiscent of "What the Butler Saw" on Brighton Pier in the old days. I inserted my strip of film into the viewer and pressed the button.

Of course, there was no sound, but I saw Steve step forward and display his clapper board with its chalked legend "*Street Scene*, Retake One-Nine-Four, Take One." Then he dodged out of range, and there was Bob Meakin running pell-mell down onto the platform, jamming his spectacles onto his nose, and then suddenly swerving, and coming straight at the camera, with an expression of horror on his face which I dimly remembered from the actual event but had not expected to see so agonizingly re-enacted. He rushed, out of control, at the camera, then seemed to swerve again, and went out of picture at the same moment as the film cut to blackness. It was a horrifying experience to see it all again, but perhaps the most unpleasant thing about it was that it was abundantly clear, as Bob came close to the camera, that his spectacles were made of perfectly plain glass. There was no question of any distortion. I remembered, sickeningly, what I had said to Henry Tibbett about noticing the strong distortion in the glasses Bob had been wearing. Sam was right. This piece of film would have to be destroyed.

I straightened up from the viewer. "Well, thanks very much," I said.

"Anything more you need, Mr. Croombe-Peters?" asked the assistant editor politely.

"No, thanks. I've seen all I want to."

"Shall I take the can back for you?"

"No, no. I'll do it."

It was only then that I realized my dilemma. I could easily enough cram the film into my pocket and dispose of it; but the large canister was clearly marked as containing that particular take, and if it should be found empty, it would be—well—odd, to say the least. I knew Henry Tibbett well enough to feel sure that he would insist—in the nicest possible way—

on searching the cutting room himself, if I reported that the film was not there.

I glanced again at the canister. There was a broad strip of white adhesive tape stuck across the center of the lid, and on this was written in ink the name of the film and the number of the shot. I breathed again. Things were not going to be so difficult after all.

In the comparative dimness of the film store, I ripped the damning piece of tape off the can and crammed it, together with the film itself, into my jacket pocket. The can, now anonymous, I buried carefully underneath a mountain of old, rejected material. Then, with a jaunty "So long" to the editor and his staff, I stepped out into the sunshine of the studio grounds.

"Grounds" is perhaps too grandiose a word for the straggling lawns and flower beds which interlace the various buildings at Ash Grove. We have none of the spaciousness of Pinewood; being so close to London, every square foot represents valuable and expensive territory, and the best that Ash Grove can do is to try to brighten up its paths with a few nasturtiums. I knew that the large conglomeration of nasturtiums, trained carefully up a trellis-work screen near the river, was designed to conceal the least attractive of the Ash Grove buildings, the rubbish incinerator. And it was there that I made my way.

The incinerator was housed in a small, ugly red-brick structure. I took a look to see if there were anybody about, but the place seemed deserted. Quickly, I dodged behind the trellis-work fence and into the dark building, where the furnace snored sonorously. I pulled the length of film and the piece of adhesive tape out of my pocket, opened the burner door, and was about to throw them in, when I suddenly heard a voice behind me saying, "Just a moment, if you please, sir."

Partly from the heat, and partly from sheer fright, the sweat was streaming down into my eyes. I had to brush it away before I realized that a very large, solid, and unemotional police sergeant was standing in the doorway.

"May I see wot it is you are about to dispose of, sir?" he asked ponderously.

Curiously enough, the emotion that I remember taking precedence over all others at that moment was that Sam would never forgive me for being so inefficient.

I was not formally charged with murder. I was taken to the police station "to assist the police in their inquiries," which meant that I was ushered into a bleak, white-washed room and questioned mercilessly for hours on end by a seemingly tireless detective. I was horribly and persistently aware of the young, fresh-faced policeman who sat unobtrusively in the corner, taking down every word in shorthand.

My first impulse was to refuse to say a word until I had consulted my solicitor. And this I did. A fat lot of use it was, too, as I might have known. My solicitor was an old school friend of mine, and when I tell you that he was generally known at school as "Loony" Lawrence, you can form your own opinion of his mental ability. I had employed him in the past simply because I felt sure that old "Loony" needed the work, and the few simple things I had asked him to do, such as drawing up a will and transferring small sums of money here and there, should, I felt, be within the grasp of the feeblest intellect.

When "Loony" finally turned up at the police station, he was gray with fright, and could do nothing except babble about reserving my defense, which hardly applied since I had not been charged with any crime. He also urged me to say nothing which might incriminate me, adding paradoxically that I should tell the whole truth. He ended by exhorting me to remember that British justice was the finest in the world and that innocence was the best defense. He then withdrew in some disorder to consult with abler colleagues. I was left alone.

My next move was to demand to see Henry Tibbett. Humiliating though the interview might be, I would at least be dealing with somebody I knew, a reasonable man, prepared to understand the quirks of fate which might land a chap in this sort of a jam. I was told, icily, that Chief Inspector Tibbett was busy and would see me at his convenience. The unpleasant detective then resumed his summing up of the damning evidence.

I had been apprehended, he said—I use his own words—in

the act of depositing in an incinerator a length of film and a piece of adhesive tape, marked in ink, of the type used to identify cans of film at Ash Grove Studios. This film showed the last living moments of the late Mr. Robert Meakin, and also showed conclusively that the late Mr. Meakin was wearing clear glass spectacles at the time of his death. I had told Inspector Tibbett that I distinctly remembered the deceased wearing strong magnifying lenses. Could I account for this discrepancy?

I said feebly that I must have made a mistake.

The detective did not comment. He merely made a note, and went on to recall that I had mentioned to Inspector Tibbett that I was well aware of Meakin's bad eyesight. Did I stand by this statement?

Miserably, I said I did—what else could I say? The detective then pointed out that I was, it seemed, the only person in the unit who had possessed this interesting knowledge. He then switched to the subject of the telephonic communication which, according to Mrs. Meakin, I had had with Miss Phipps at approximately eleven-twenty on the day of Miss Phipps's death. I had denied this. Had I anything to say about it?

I repeated my story, well aware of the detective's disbelief.

To proceed, he continued, I had given no good account of my whereabouts at half-past nine the previous evening, the time when Murray was presumed to have been murdered. He read to me my statement that, having tried unsuccessfully to contact Sam on the telephone from Sloane Square, I had returned to my own apartment. Could I provide corroboration for this statement?

I said, fervently hoping it to be untrue, that I supposed the taxi driver who drove me might be traced.

Indeed, yes, said the detective, to my dismay; he already had been. And the curious thing was that he maintained that he had driven me not to my own home, but to Mr. Potman's house in Islington. Another driver remembered picking me up a little way from Mr. Potman's house about ten minutes later and driving me home. Had I any comment to make?

It seemed pointless to deny it. I said that I had quite forgotten to mention that I had passed by Sam's house on the way home, in the hope of finding him in. I denied that I had seen or heard anything of Murray, dead or alive, although presumably he had, at that time, been lying in the dark hallway. The detective remarked that it was odd that Mrs. Meakin, coming along a little later, should have seen the body, whereas I had not. I agreed, with emphasis which seemed lost on the man, that it was indeed extremely odd.

The detective then asked me to confirm that Margery Phipps's letter of resignation had been addressed and delivered to me personally and was easily accessible to me at any time while it was in my files. I could not but agree.

He then switched the conversation to the various insurance policies carried by Northburn Films, about which he was astonishingly well informed. I was forced to agree that our policy did not cover the death of Meakin if caused by suicide, deliberate negligence, or malice on the part of the company or its employees; and that it was also null and void if Meakin were not in the employ of Northburn Films at the time of his death.

The one point on which I felt utterly secure was when the detective started asking where I had been at the time of Margery's fall from Chelsea Mansions. I had plenty of witnesses, I said, to prove that I had been watching rushes at a private cinema in Soho. To my surprise, the detective did not seem unduly put out by this. He concentrated, rather, on questioning me about my movements earlier in the afternoon, and I hoped that I had convinced him that I had been in my office, although, of course, I could not produce witnesses for every moment of the time.

Finally, he got around to my clandestine visit to Chelsea Mansions, and I replied rather stiffly that I had already explained all that to Chief Inspector Tibbett. The detective consulted his papers, and to my amazement, smiled. I had not thought it possible.

"Ah, yes," he said. "The Chief Inspector explained all that."

And he leered at me and practically winked. I don't think I have ever hated Henry Tibbett more than I did at that moment.

The detective then went on to put several questions to me, the meaning and drift of which escaped me completely. He asked me, for example, whether I knew what make of electric stove Margery had used in her kitchen. I replied that I had no idea, but that it was certainly an elaborate one, with a battery of clocks and dials on it. He corrected me, pedantically pointing out that there was only one clock, and he asked me if I could remember what time it was reading when I visited the flat with Henry. I closed my eyes and thought hard, and then said that it had read a quarter to four. The detective looked extremely surprised when I said this; for some reason, I seemed to have caught him off his guard. He asked me if I were sure, and I said that I remembered clearly, because I had checked the time with my own watch, unable to believe that it was so late; and, indeed, it was only half-past two. It was then, I said, that I tumbled to the fact that this was not an ordinary clock but one which could be set to fulfill some function, like switching the stove on or off at a certain time. The detective made a note, and said that no doubt I was perfectly right.

He then asked whether I had given my manservant the evening off the previous evening. I replied that he knew very well that I had not, since Hedges had admitted Sam to the flat. He gave me a sceptical look and made another note. Then he changed his line of attack and asked whether I had heard any rumors that Robert Meakin intended to break his contract and walk out on his part as Masterman. I replied as confidently as I could that I was convinced there was no truth in any such gossip. I felt very glad that I had burned the little writing pad which I had found in Bob's dressing room, even though it contained nothing more compromising than the faint imprint of a ballpoint pen.

At this point the detective thanked me for my co-operation, and asked if I would like a cup of tea. I looked at my watch and saw that it was half-past four. I was, in fact, ravenously hungry, having refused the offer of a cold lunch from the police canteen when I arrived at the station. However, I replied frigidly to the offer of tea by saying that it was not worth the trouble, as I would be leaving the police station shortly and intended to have a substantial meal then. The detective looked embarrassed, shuffled a few papers, and said that unfortunately that would not be possible.

"Not possible? What do you mean?"

"My orders are that you're not to leave here for the time being, sir."

"That's ridiculous," I protested. "You can't hold me here. Either you must charge me or let me go."

"We can hold you for questioning so long as we think fit," he said stubbornly.

"Well," I retorted, "you've questioned me and I've answered. If you've any more to ask, fire away and get it over."

"It's not a matter for me, sir," said the detective, not very chirpily. "The Chief Inspector wants to see you himself."

"About time, too," I said sharply. "I hope you have it on record that I have already requested permission to speak to him."

"Yes, indeed, sir. It's all written down."

"And so," I went on, "until he sees fit to turn up, I intend to leave this place and have a meal."

I spoke with considerably more bravado than I felt. One thing only gave me courage, the fact that I had not yet been charged with any crime. Obviously, there was a link missing somewhere in the chain of police evidence, and I imagined that Henry was at that moment ferreting for it, either in my office or in the studio or at the Underground station or heaven knew where.

I had hardly got into my stride about the rights and privileges of a free citizen, when the young shorthand writer reappeared with a sheaf of typed papers in his hand, which turned out to be the transcript of the interview. The detective read it through quickly, handed me a copy so that I could do the same, and then asked me to sign it. I considered shouting for my solicitor again, but the thought of old "Loony" blundering around and putting his foot in things was too much to bear, and so I signed meekly. I could not deny that it was a completely accurate report of what had taken place. Having signed, I again announced my intention of leaving.

The detective had started bleating again about his orders, and I was preparing to assert myself in a big way when the situation was eased—if that is the right word—by the appearance of Henry Tibbett in person. He looked extremely tired and harassed.

He greeted me briefly, dismissed the detective and the shorthand writer, and settled down at the desk to read through my statement. I sat fidgeting slightly in my chair, growing steadily more irritated. I might not have been there, for all the notice he took of me. Once or twice I opened my mouth to put a well-worded protest to him, but each time he silenced me, without even looking up, simply by raising his right hand in a gesture of such authority that there was no gainsaying it. He reminded me of the headmaster of my prep school, engaged in reading an adverse report on one of his pupils in the unhappy presence of the victim.

I fully expected him, when he had finished his reading, to look up, fix me with a hawk-like and pedantic eye, and demand, "Well, Croombe-Peters. What have you to say for yourself?"

Instead, he closed the dossier, sighed, and then grinned at me and said, "This is a bad business, Pudge."

"If by 'business' you are referring to the fact that I have been kept here since midday with no food . . ."

"No food?" Henry sounded full of concern. "That's most irregular. Didn't anybody offer . . . ?"

"Oh, yes. It was offered, all right. I was in no mood for eating it. I don't know what you're up to, Tibbett, but if you suspect me of murder, for God's sake say so straight out. Arrest me. Charge me. You can't just keep me here like this . . ."

"We can, actually," said Henry. "You're helping us in our inquiries." There was a little pause, and then he went on, "How much more shooting is there to be done on *Street Scene?*"

"Three days. We should finish on Friday, if all goes well."

"And then, I suppose, there's the editing and dubbing and . . ."

"You're very well informed technically," I said coldly.

"I've been learning a bit about film-making," said Henry.

"Well," I said, "there certainly is editing and dubbing and post-synching, and so on, but in our case it shouldn't be a very complicated job. Sam is a director who constructs his picture on the floor, not in the cutting room. All the editor has to do is to follow Sam's instructions and the script, and there it is."

"I see," said Henry thoughtfully.

"And now," I said, "I would like to get back to my office.

I still have time to do a little useful work, before . . ."

"I'm sorry," said Henry, and he was not smiling. "You're staying here."

"What do you mean?"

"You will sleep the night here . . ."

"But . . ."

"Helping us with our inquiries."

It was at that moment that I chanced to catch sight of an evening newspaper which was sticking out of Henry's raincoat pocket. It was a late edition and the headline was, "Film Producer at Police Headquarters."

As quietly as I could, I said, "May I please see that newspaper?"

"Certainly," said Henry, and handed it over.

They had devoted the whole front page to the story. There was a photograph of Bob Meakin and another of Margery Phipps and a vague blur which might have been anybody but was captioned, "Murder Victim Alfred Murray." There was also a large and glamorous picture of Fiametta, and a promise of more on Page 6. Worst of all, there was a most unflattering likeness of myself entering the police station in company with the ponderous sergeant, who was carrying the fatal can of film under his arm.

I started to read the report. "At twelve-fifteen this morning," it began, "The Hon. Mr. Anthony ('Pudge') Croombe-Peters, a Director of Northburn Films and Executive Producer of the Fiametta Fettini film *Street Scene*, went to Blunt Street Police Station, accompanied by a Detective Sergeant who carried a canister of film (see picture). Mr. Croombe-Peters, only son of Lord Northburn, is believed to be helping police in their inquiries into the death of Mr. Alfred Murray, found last night battered to death at the Islington home of Mr. Sam Potman, Director of the film. *Street Scene*, now nearing completion at Ash Grove Studios, has been dogged by tragedy. Only a few weeks after the accidental death of the film's star, Robert Meakin, came another disaster when Continuity Girl Margery Phipps committed suicide by throwing herself from a seventh story window. Now, comes the death of Mr. Murray, formerly Mr. Meakin's dresser; a death which the police, according to Chief Inspector Henry Tibbett, are treating as a case of murder. Mr. Croombe-Peters, who was wearing a gray suit and a dark red silk tie, was apparently (please turn to Page 6)" . . .

I looked up, almost speechless with fury. "You did this," I said.

"I did what?" Henry asked innocently.

"You drew the attention of the press to my—my—my being here. You tipped them off, so that they could get pictures. You've been talking to them . . ."

"My dear chap," said Henry, "you can't stop the press from nosing out a good story."

"You can and you know it." I don't know which emotion was uppermost in my mind at that moment—anger or fear. "You did this deliberately, and if you keep me here all night, it'll be as good as saying that I'm arrested. What do you think that'll do to my reputation? What'll happen to the film?"

"I should have thought," said Henry, quite seriously, "that it would be very good publicity indeed."

17

I prefer not to think about the events of the next two days. I cannot deny that I was adequately fed and accommodated at the police station, that is to say, if you can call a prison cell adequate accommodation. The fact that the door was left unlocked and comfortable bedding brought in did nothing to dissipate the essentially penal atmosphere, and in my position I was acutely aware that the door might not remain unlocked for very long.

I saw little of Henry. It was obvious that he was engaged in a lot of activity outside, presumably connected with the case. The glimpses I did have of him were confined to a few minutes conversation in his office, during which he munched at sandwiches and drank cups of coffee. Clearly, he was working too hard to take time off for meals.

During these conversations, he chatted about the case and asked a few apparently meaningless questions. He seemed to have developed a great interest in Keith Pardoe, and wanted to know all about how I had originally met him in the army. He got the whole story about the formation of Northburn Films out of me, and he also seemed intrigued beyond reason by the story of Keith's haircut. Remembering what Sam had said to me, I began to get seriously perturbed. Pleasant though it would be to be released from suspicion myself, it would be sheer disaster for Northburn Films if Keith were arrested. Could he be guilty of murder? I found myself considering the question quite seriously, and coming up with the reply that he certainly could; but I could not for the life of me think of any motive that would make Keith kill Murray and deposit him on Sam's doorstep.

Another time, Henry talked to me for some time about Fiametta Fettini, and her scurrilous background of the Naples slums; he also seemed interested in her wretched little husband, and even in Peppi, the monkey. I told him about my experience at Medham, and he looked thoughtful and said it was indeed most remarkable. Then he finished his last sandwich and said that he must be off.

"Look here, Henry," I said, "I've been here since midday yesterday, and it's now six o'clock in the evening. Do you mean to say you're going to keep me here another night?"

"I'm sorry, old man. I'm afraid I must."

"Now look here," I exploded. "You surely know me well enough to believe that I wouldn't try to run away. Obviously, you haven't enough evidence against me, or you'd have arrested me by now."

"That's perfectly true," said Henry, quietly and ominously.

"Well, then, by any common standard of justice, you must let me go."

"Pudge," said Henry, and he sounded almost apologetic, "please be patient. Tomorrow is Friday, the last day of shoot-

225

ing, isn't it? It'll all be over by tomorrow."

"The film will be in the can, if that's what you mean."

"That's not what I meant. I meant that I shall have the evidence I need."

"You mean you're going to keep me here—illegally—until tomorrow, and then arrest me for murder."

"Pudge," said Henry very seriously, "I dare not let you leave here." And with that he was gone.

One thing that he did do, each time he visited the place, was to bring me a newspaper. The case had certainly hit the headlines, and I was forced to admit that it was magnificent advance publicity, so long as the scandal of an arrest did not besmirch the company itself. Fiametta—or her publicity agent —gave interviews right and left; so did Keith, which made me laugh with some irony. Sam and Biddy had both behaved with dignity, refusing to comment. Even Mrs. Arbuthnot had got into the act as Margery's mother, and there was a very unconvincing, obviously posed photograph of her taking a cup of tea in her parlor at Lewisham, which was captioned, "Bereaved Mother's Long Heartbreak." All this, however, caused me scarcely a tremor; what really hurt was the fact that, without a doubt, the reporters' pin-up boy of the moment was none other than the Hon. Anthony ("Pudge") Croombe-Peters.

I could only dimly guess at my father's frame of mind. It had taken the press no time at all to unearth details of my birth, my family, my education, and my career. They had also tracked down an old nurse of mine—a Nanny Bates whom I had always disliked—and from her obtained disreputable "reminiscences" of the boyhood pranks and foibles of the young Croombe-Peters, together with some nauseating snapshots. *The Smudge* had somehow laid hands on a copy of a flashlight photograph which had been taken some weeks ago, very late at night, when I had been dining at the Orangery with Keith, Biddy, and Fiametta. It contrived to make me look thoroughly debauched and more than half tight.

The newspaper stories were couched in the usual cautious manner of the British press, scrupulously careful never to risk contempt of court or defamation of character or prejudging a case; nevertheless, the meaning that screamed out from between the lines was absolutely unambiguous. The Hon. Anthony ("Pudge") Croombe-Peters had now been helping the police with their inquiries for more than twenty-four hours. His solicitor had visited the police station on three occasions. It was known that Chief Inspector Henry Tibbett of the C.I.D., in charge of the case, had had several interviews with Mr. Croombe-Peters. In fact, it was a foregone conclusion that the "imminent arrest" about which Henry had so injudiciously talked to reporters could refer to one person only—me.

The bit about my solicitor was perfectly true. Old "Loony" was fairly haunting the place. On his second visit, he brought with him an older and more experienced character, who seemed to be of equally little use. Mind you, at that stage, before I had been charged with anything, I suppose there was not much they could do, except warn me against making statements which could be used against me.

In the meantime I played patience and talked to the sergeant, a pleasant chap whose great hobby was the keeping of cage birds. There was very little I didn't know about the budjerigar in sickness and in health, by the time Thursday evening came around. And with it, at about nine o'clock, came Henry Tibbett again.

I was ushered into the now familiar office, and noted with relief that Henry and I were alone. No shorthand-writer perched discreetly in the corner. This encouraged me to think that the moment of the actual arrest had not yet arrived.

Henry looked absolutely exhausted, but he seemed to perk up a bit as he dug into the inevitable sandwiches and coffee which the sergeant had provided. He motioned me to sit down, and then, between mouthfuls, he said, "Now, Pudge. I want you to tell me the truth."

"I have told you the truth."

"Not all of it. I want to know why you lied about Meakin's glasses. I want to know exactly what you found in those dressing rooms. I want to know the real truth of your conversation with Mrs. Meakin before you broke into Margery Phipps's flat. I want to know what you and Potman really talked about in your apartment the night Murray was killed. I want to know the truth about Fiametta Fettini and Robert Meakin, and I want to know what in hell you thought you were doing, trying to destroy that reel of film. I want to know more about Miss

Biddy Brennan and a couple of phone calls, and about Mr. Keith Pardoe and his haircut. I want you to remember verbatim conversations as far as you can. I also want to know what it is you're so frightened of, but I think I can guess."

"I see no reason for telling you anything," I said. "I dare say you've never been chief suspect in a murder case, but I can assure you . . ."

To my surprise, a tired grin lit up Henry's face. "You're wrong there," he said. "As a matter of fact, I have—once. In Switzerland. I agree, it wasn't pleasant. But then, you see, my case was rather different. The officer in charge of the case really suspected me." *

"You mean—you don't . . . ?"

"I told you before," said Henry, "that I thought you were stupid rather than criminal, and I still do. And I am the officer in charge of this case. If it weren't for that fact, you'd have been arrested long ago."

I felt acutely embarrassed. "Thank you," I said awkwardly.

Henry went on. "I'm on your side, Pudge. I have a certain sort of—of instinct, I suppose; some people call it my 'nose.' "

"If it tells you I'm innocent," I said, "it is perfectly correct."

Henry rubbed the back of his neck with his left hand. "That's what I think," he said. "But although I'm in charge of the case, I'm not the only person at Scotland Yard, you know, and I have my superiors. Frankly, Pudge, I'm under a considerable amount of pressure to arrest you at once. And, of course, the fact that I know you socially doesn't help matters. Time is getting horribly short. I've got a theory, but it's only a theory, and it'll never be more if you don't co-operate. Meanwhile, the opposition have a perfectly lovely case against you, all worked out and tied up in blue ribbon. You can take your choice."

There was a horrible silence that seemed to go on and on. If I told Henry all he wanted to know, and if something I said confirmed his theory, it might mean the arrest of a friend or a colleague. It seemed a pretty mean way of saving my own skin. On the other hand, I am not a hero and have never set out to be.

Henry seemed to read my thoughts. He said, "Murray was

* In *Death on the Agenda*.

an old man, Pudge, and he had his head bashed in and was left to die. Margery Phipps, according to our latest pathologist's report, was first drugged and then thrown out of a seventh-floor window. There's no reason on earth to cover up for the person who did those things."

"Northburn Films involves more than one person," I said.

"Tomorrow is the last day of shooting," said Henry. "Even if the insurance company does decide to fight the claim, the film is in the can and the worst that can happen is that they'll have to be repaid out of the profits. If it's as good as I think it is, it should be box-office magic."

I opened my eyes wide. "How do you know how good it is?" I asked. "And where did you pick up that Wardour Street jargon?"

"I've spent a lot of time at the studios these last few days," said Henry. "I've seen the rough cut. Potman is a genius. He's got sensational performances out of both Keith and Fiametta. The camera work is brilliant. The script is as good as anything the French have done." He sounded curiously regretful. "There's one more day's shooting. I won't interfere with it, if I can help it. Well?"

I took a deep breath. "All right," I said. "I'll tell you everything I know. You can use it how you like."

"Thank you, Pudge," said Henry. He smiled at me. "Fire away."

It was very late that night when I finally went to bed in my cosy cell. I was exhausted. At the same time I felt a wonderful sense of relief at having unburdened my soul. I had no idea—for Henry had given me no clue—as to whether my evidence had, in fact, served to support or clinch his theory. I had left him still hard at work as the dawn began to streak the sky. My last waking thought was that I was now, indeed, "helping the police in their inquiries," but not in the sense that the newspapers understood the phrase. It gave me great satisfaction.

The sergeant called me at eight, with breakfast and the morning paper. The headlines screamed "Croombe-Peters"— they had dropped the respectful "Hon." by then—"Still at Police Headquarters. Arrest Imminent." The sergeant put down the breakfast tray and settled down for a chat.

"If you want 'em to talk," he said, "you 'ave to 'ave just one alone. Two birds, and you've 'ad it. I 'ad one called Charlie— proper little character, he was. Of course, it's unkind, wot some people teach 'em. Friend of mine 'ad Charlie for a week or two while I was on holiday, and the poor little blighter came back saying 'Charlie is a proper twirp,' pleased as punch with 'imself, too. Crool I call it. Everyone laughed, of course. Well, your budgie's a sensitive bird. Takes it to 'eart, bein' laughed at. In the end, I got 'im to change it to 'Charlie is a proper treat,' but it took time, poor little feller."

The sergeant sighed, and poured himself a cup from my coffee pot. It was just then that Henry arrived, spruced up and shaven, but still looking deadly tired. I don't imagine he had been to bed at all. The sergeant departed with his cup of coffee, and Henry sat down on my bed and said, "Will there be a full day's shooting today at Ash Grove?"

I cast my mind back to the schedule. I had not even considered it for the last couple of days, and it required an effort to conjure up the mental picture of those graphs and charts which had so recently been my whole life.

"If they've kept up to schedule," I said at last, "they should be through by lunchtime."

"What are you shooting today?" Henry asked. I was grateful for the word "you." It made me feel that I was not entirely cut off from Northburn Films; at that moment, I realized fully how desperately important *Street Scene* had become to me personally. Nothing to do with money, I mean, nor even kudos. It was something I had worked for, and I wanted it to be good. I wanted Keith's performance to be great, and I even wanted La Fettini to be acclaimed as an actress at last. I wanted Sam to crown his already shining reputation, and I wanted Biddy's script to be seriously compared to the work of Cocteau or Marguerite Duras. Curiously enough, at that moment I wanted nothing for myself except the satisfaction of knowing that no film can be made without reasonably efficient administration, and that I had achieved it.

I shook myself back to reality. The schedule charts were clear before my eyes now. "Today," I said, "if they've kept to schedule, there are just two shots left. Both of them are in the interior set of Rosa's lodgings in Limehouse, a tatty sort of boarding house. It's the scene on the landing. Rosa and Masterman have quarreled and she comes running out of her room, down the stairs, and out through the front door. He follows her. That's all. It sounds a tame sort of thing to end up with, but film making is like that. You end wherever is convenient for the schedule, not with a bang but a whimper."

"This," said Henry, "just may be a bang, after all. I think it would be interesting to be there, don't you?"

"What do you mean?" I asked.

"I mean," said Henry, "that you and I are going to visit Ash Grove Studios—together."

When we came out into the yard behind the police station, I was surprised to see a small dark green van standing there, looking as unofficial as possible. Henry led the way to it.

"Not very comfortable, I'm afraid," he said, "but anonymous. I'm anxious that nobody should see us leave. Between ourselves, I'm not very popular in some quarters for insisting on this—this experiment."

He smiled, but his face was full of strain. I suppose I had been too preoccupied with my own problems up to then to realize just what I owed to Tibbett, and how he was virtually staking his reputation in order to save my neck. Or was it to see justice done? Or both? I was about to try and thank him, when he said abruptly, "Well, we'd better not hang about. Get in."

He held the back door open. As I climbed in, he said, "By the way, can you drive one of these things?"

"Of course I can. I may take a little while to get used to the gear box, but . . ."

"It'll only be a question of a few hundred yards," said Henry. "In you get." He closed the door.

It was dark inside the van, and so it was a couple of seconds before I registered the fact that I was not alone. I had a fellow traveler. Another second and I had identified her as Sonia Meakin. My heart leapt, unpleasantly. It was true enough that in my talks to Henry I had hinted as openly as I dared that I was convinced of her guilt. How much store Henry set by my opinions, I had no idea; but her presence here was sinister, to say the least. It was not a comfortable sensation, having to share the back of a small van with a person who, I was fairly sure, had killed two human beings; nor, from a different point of view, was it pleasant being confronted at such close quarters with someone whom I had virtually denounced to the police.

Before I could say anything, Henry had climbed into the front of the car, behind the wheel, saying cheerfully, "Sorry to keep you waiting, Mrs. Meakin. Have you brought what I asked for?"

"Yes," said Sonia Meakin in a voice like dry ice. "I have."

"So we meet again, Mrs. Meakin," I said, trying to emulate Henry's cheerful tone. It seemed the only thing to do. I sat down beside her on the hard wooden bench.

Sonia Meakin did not answer me. More eloquently, she stood up and crossed to the other side of the van, practically drawing her skirts aside as she passed me. Evidently, the prospect of our shared ride was as distasteful to her as it was to me. A moment later we were speeding through the streets of London.

A few hundred yards from the studio gates, we stopped. Henry got out, came around to the back, and opened the doors.

"Well, Pudge," he said, "this is where you take the wheel."

"But what . . . ?"

"I shall keep out of sight in the back of the van," said Henry. "I'm relying on you to get me into the studios un-noticed. Mrs. Meakin will sit in front with you—if you have no objection, Mrs. Meakin?"

"If you say I must, Inspector," said Sonia.

You'd have thought Henry had asked her to sit next to a dead rat.

"Just forget all about me, Pudge," Henry went on, as he helped me out of the back of the van. "As far as you're concerned, the police have questioned you pretty thoroughly but have now let you go, much to your relief. Mrs. Meakin wanted to see over the studios, so you have brought her on a visit. That's all. Is that clear?"

"I suppose so," I said unhappily.

"Good," said Henry briskly. "Now, Mrs. Meakin, may I have it?"

I saw Sonia Meakin open her handbag and give Henry a

small parcel wrapped in brown paper. She looked extremely reluctant about the whole thing, but Henry just said, "Right. Thanks. Now, in you get!" And she climbed silently into the front seat beside me. After a little experimentation with the unfamiliar gears, I drove the van around the corner to the studio gates.

The guard on the gate seemed both surprised and gratified to see me, and didn't even glance into the back of the van. He was obviously bursting with curiosity, and tried to keep me talking, but I waved him aside and drove on down the main drive toward the administrative buildings. I became aware of Henry's voice in my left ear.

"Drive around to the back of Stage 2 and drop me there," he said. "Then park the car, wait ten minutes, and take Mrs. Meakin onto the set."

"Really, Henry," I said, "I do think you might explain . . ."

"Please do as I say."

"Oh, very well." I pulled up at the back entrance to Stage 2. "But where will you be if I . . . ?"

"I'll be around," said Henry. Then I heard the back door of the van open and slam shut, and I realized that he had gone.

Dutifully, I drove to the car park, parked the van, and offered Sonia Meakin a cigarette, which she declined. We sat in frozen silence for a few minutes, and then I said, "Well, orders is orders. We'd better go down to the set."

Suddenly she turned to me. For the first time she sounded natural, human, and really scared. "Mr. Croombe-Peters," she said, "do you know why we have been brought here?"

"If I know anything about Henry Tibbett," I said, "it's to catch a killer."

"Oh, my God." Her voice was all at once quite flat, as if all emotion had been drained out of it. Then, with another complete switch of mood, she said almost gaily, "All right. What are we waiting for?"

"We're not," I said. I leant over and opened the car door for her to get out, and together we walked down to Stage 2.

They were setting up for the very last shot of the film when we arrived. We slipped quietly onto the stage, and stood for a moment in the shadows. As I have explained, there is not a lot of light on a film set outside the actual area of shooting, and the very contrast between the brilliance of the set and the dimness of its surroundings makes it easy for a visitor to remain unobserved.

It seemed extraordinary to me to be back on the floor again. My ghastly days at the police station seemed to have cut me off completely from the world I knew, and I gazed around the set with the fresh, wondering eyes of a convalescent returning to well-known haunts after a long spell in hospital. After what I had been through, it seemed somehow callous that things should be going on absolutely as usual; but, of course, they were. At least, when I say "absolutely as usual," that is not quite true. This was the last shot of the film, and there was a gay, party atmosphere on the set. Not just atmosphere. Bottles of champagne had already been opened, which surprised me, because such celebrations are usually delayed until the film is finally in the can.

Fiametta, who had completed her last shot, was drinking what looked to me like a slightly ironic toast to Keith, who was submitting to the ministrations of the make-up man; Sam was standing with his arm around Biddy's shoulders, talking to Anton, the chief hairdresser; Gervase was raising his glass to, of all people, the shop steward. Everybody looked excited and happy, as one does on the last day of shooting. Suddenly it swept over me, in a mixture of anger and hurt, that apparently nobody was giving a thought to my situation. As far as they knew, I was languishing in jail, with a murder charge hanging over my head; and they couldn't care less. I remembered how Robert Meakin and Margery Phipps had been forgotten, and I felt cold. Would it be the same with me? Henry had told me that he did not suspect me—or had he? He had implied it, but he was as wily as a fox and I didn't trust him an inch. Perhaps he was luring me into a sense of false security. Perhaps he really was about to arrest me. And if he did, I imagined that Northburn Films, Ltd., would heave a sigh of relief, go about its business, and forget me entirely.

The spurt of anger which this thought occasioned was, in fact, helpful. It obliterated my moment of embarrassment, and I stepped forward into the light of the set, like a demon king entering a pantomime stage in a flash of green cordite.

"Good morning, everybody," I said.

I couldn't make out whether the first, silent, stunned reaction to my appearance was caused by surprise or by dismay. At any rate, it was Sam who recovered first, and he stepped up to me with a warm, welcoming smile and an affectionate handshake.

"Pudge!" he said. "It's good to see you! They've let you out at last, have they? Back to the fold without a stain on your character?"

Taking their cue from Sam, Keith and Biddy now clustered around me, assuring me that they'd all been terribly worried about me. Fiametta flung her arms around my neck and kissed me warmly, and Gervase brought me a glass of champagne.

Typically, Sam wasted little time on congratulations, but started straight away talking shop.

"This'll please you, Pudge," he said. "Joost when we thought we were all through, and the champagne opened, we heard from the labs that this morning's first shot was spoilt in processing. So we've got a retake for the very last shot. How d'you like that?"

"I don't like it at all," I said. I was rapidly returning to normal and a very pleasant sensation it was, too.

"But don't forget," Sam added impishly, "we're still two days ahead."

"If you really want to know," I said, "I don't care a hang about anything. The picture's finished; I'm out of that terrible prison cell; the insurance has paid up; and we're two days ahead. It'll take more than one spoilt shot to depress me."

It was at that moment that Gervase came up to tell Sam that Fred Harborough was satisfied with his lighting and that we could start the camera rolling for the last time. The set consisted of a section of shabby hallway and a flight of stairs which led up to what looked like a first-floor landing, but was actually no more than a platform on scaffolding. Anybody foolish enough to open one of the solid-looking doors which led off it would find himself confronted with a fifteen-foot drop to the studio floor below. Keith's stand-in was at the top of the stairs, in the circle of light.

Gervase blew his whistle, and the usual tense atmosphere which immediately precedes shooting made itself felt. Keith had not engaged a personal dresser, and I noticed that it was

Gervase who handed him his props, in this case, pipe and spectacles. The Continuity Girl checked him over for details of costume. As the stand-in came down the stairs and Keith took his place, Fred Harborough peered up into the dimness of the stage ceiling and shouted a last-minute instruction to an electrician working on the high gallery among the arc lamps. Then the whistle shrilled again, and for the last time on *Street Scene* the familiar cry rang out, "Quiet everyone! Red light on! We're rolling!"

The clapper fell with its usual sharp click, and the camera swung up to focus on Keith, as he came running down the stairs. Suddenly, it reminded me horribly of that similar re-take in the Underground station. Just as Bob Meakin had done, Keith was ramming his spectacles onto his nose as he ran downstairs. As he got them on, he gave a sort of shouting scream. His arms flailed wildly, trying to find the banisters, and failing. For a long moment, he seemed to be poised in mid-air. Then he fell.

Everybody surged forward. Keith was lying at the foot of the staircase, looking extraordinarily peaceful. All at once, the general confusion was topped by a scream from Fiametta, a long, banshee-like wailing.

"Keith, I didn't mean—he's not—he can't be—Keith, darling, I didn't mean . . ."

I was near enough to the center of things to see that Fiametta had broken through the ring of people surrounding Keith and was preparing to go into a big act. She was about to fling herself to the ground beside Keith's prostrate body, when Biddy stepped out of the shadows and caught her a sharp slap across the face.

"Get the bloody hell out of here, you bitch," said Biddy.

Fiametta, a hand to her cheek, was too surprised to reply.

"You didn't mean—you didn't mean," Biddy went on, in a fair imitation of Fiametta's voice. "You didn't mean it with Bob Meakin either, I suppose. He died. Keith might have died, too, for all you cared."

"But Bee-dee . . ." Fiametta was falling back on her wide-eyed charm.

I could have told her it was useless.

"Get your filthy hands off my husband," said Biddy. And

when Fiametta didn't move, she added, "Have I made myself clear? Bugger off."

I don't know the exact extent of Fiametta's knowledge of English, but she certainly understood the import, if not the meaning, of Biddy's last words. With a final attempt to save her face, she swung her black hair out from her neck with a theatrical gesture of the head, and said, "Little man. Silly, stupid, foolish little man. You can 'ave 'im." And she flounced off toward her dressing room.

On the floor, Keith was stirring. He was obviously not badly hurt. He had knocked himself out momentarily, but there was no real harm done. He sat up, slowly, rubbing his head. On her knees beside him, Biddy said, "It's all right, darling. It's nothing. You just fell downstairs."

"But . . ." Keith looked up, slowly. There was an expression of real horror in his eyes. "The glasses, Bob's glasses; it happened; I knew it would; it happened to me . . ."

"Shut up, Keith." Sam Potman stepped into the ring of bright light and picked up the horn-rimmed spectacles that had fallen from Keith's nose. Even from where I stood, I could see that the lenses were made of strong magnifying glass. Sam examined them carefully for a moment, and then said. "Where did these come from?"

"They were in Keith's dressing room with all his other things." Gervase's voice sounded high-pitched from nervousness. "I went in and got his spectacles and his pipe. They were on his dressing table . . ."

"These aren't Keith's spectacles," said Sam impatiently. "Where did they come from?"

A cool voice said, "I brought them." Everybody craned to peer into the shadows. It was not necessary. Sonia Meakin stepped out into the circle of light.

"But . . ." Even Sam seemed at a loss for words.

"They belonged to my late husband," said Sonia Meakin. "Made up to his prescription. Mr. Croombe-Peters asked me to bring them with me. Then somebody took them away from me, and I don't know what happened to them. However, I can identify them positively."

Before I could protest against this appalling lie, Sam said, "I see. Right. Break for half an hour. Mr. Pardoe will need a bit of time to recover. Everybody back on the set at half-past eleven." Then, as chatter broke out and people began to drift off the set in ones and twos, he went over to Sonia Meakin, and said, "I'm sorry about that, Mrs. Meakin. Some sort of a mix-up. Would you care to come to the canteen for a cup of coffee with us?"

"Yes, do, Mrs. Meakin," said Biddy. "And then you'd probably like to see around the studios, while you're here."

"I'll show you around." Unexpectedly, it was Keith who spoke. He was on his feet and looking none the worse for wear.

"You'd best lie down, Keith," said Sam.

"Nonsense. Never felt better." Keith spoke with a sort of reckless light-heartedness. "Let's all have a coffee first anyhow."

They all walked off, with Sonia Meakin in the center of the group. One by one the lights went out, the electricians climbed down from the high gallery, the carpenters and property men and make-up experts and hairdressers and plasterers and stand-ins and camera crew and sound men drifted in gossiping groups off the set. Last of all, I saw the small, slight, and insignificant figure of Henry Tibbett slipping out through the soundproof door. And still I stood there, in the dark, alone and forgotten.

I don't mind admitting that my thoughts were pretty bitter, as I sat and smoked a cigarette in the dark. I could have put some lights on, but the blackness seemed more in tune with my mood. I had stubbed out my second cigarette when the door from the corridor opened and a stream of light poured in, silhouetting two figures. I could not identify them, but I was not left in doubt for long.

"Oh, isn't it dark?" cried Sonia Meakin coyly.

In answer her companion flicked a switch, which brought up the spotlights and arcs that stood on the floor, circling the set. A second switch clicked, and the high arc lamps on the gantry sprang to life. There was a murmured conversation which I did not catch, and then the sound of footsteps climbing the iron ladders which lead to the high gallery. Evidently, Sonia Meakin was being taken on her promised tour of the studio. An essential part of this was always to persuade visitors—so long as they had a good head for heights—to ascend to the gallery which ran around the stage at roof level, some hundred feet high. From there, the illuminated set below looked like a doll's house on a nursery floor. Personally, I suffer from vertigo, and had never enjoyed going up there.

Sonia Meakin, apparently, had no such qualms. I could hear her fluting voice exclaiming with delight as each fresh landing platform was reached. Suddenly, a soft voice spoke out of the darkness at my elbow.

"Pudge?"

I had not seen or heard Henry coming back onto the set. He must have moved as quickly and quietly as a cat.

"Henry," I began, but he clapped his hand over my mouth. In an urgent, anguished whisper, he said, "They gave me the slip. I never . . . How do we get up there?"

The hand was removed. "There's a ladder in each corner of the stage," I whispered.

"You go up this one, I'll take the next one," Henry breathed. "Your job is to grab Sonia Meakin, and for God's sake don't let her go."

"You mean—but who's with her?"

"Potman, of course." Henry sounded impatient, as if I should have known. But it was Keith who had offered to show her around. "This was to be the fourth. Quick. Take your shoes off. Creep up behind her, and then grab. Leave the rest to me. Good luck."

I slipped off my shoes and began to climb the iron ladder. So I had been right all along. Sonia Meakin was a killer. She had cheated and killed for money; she had lied and blackmailed; and now she was planning to kill Sam. Any differences I might have had with Potman vanished in the face of my cold fury. How dared she? How *dared* she?

Above my head the dulcet voice came, chilling my spine. "It's terribly high, isn't it? Oh, Mr. Potman, do come over here and look at this . . ."

I was in a cold sweat. Should I shout, warn Sam of the danger he was in? Henry had told me to keep quiet, but if Sam's life was in danger—I climbed faster and faster.

"Oh, look, it's just like being in an airplane—Mr. Potman, do come and look . . ."

I was on the gallery now, and most determinedly I was not looking down, for I knew that if I did, I would be lost. It always made me feel dizzy even to watch from below as the electricians sat so casually on the catwalk, reading their papers and swinging their legs over the abyss. Even when they stood up to work, the one safety bar at waist level had never seemed to me to be an adequate protection. Now, I was sure of it.

A great arc lamp was burning fiercely a little further along the gallery, and between me and it I could see Sonia Meakin's silhouette, as she leant recklessly and provocatively over the safety bar.

"Look down there . . ."

Gritting my teeth, I lurched forward and grabbed her, pinioning her arms behind her back. She let out a shriek, and I yelled, "I've got her! Henry, can you hear me? I've got her!"

She fought like a tiger, kicking and scratching and screaming. How I kept my footing on that narrow platform, as well as my hold on her, I shall never know. I suppose it was because I was, to say the least of it, otherwise engaged, that at first I was not aware of the sound of another scuffle going on further down the gallery, in the black darkness beyond the arc lamp. The first I knew was a shattering, wrenching sound, and then a terrible dull thud. Sonia Meakin went limp in my arms. Nerving myself, I looked down. In the middle of the garishly lit set, so far below, Sam Potman's body lay quite still, like a broken toy.

I was so horror struck that I was hardly aware of the fact that Sonia Meakin had stopped struggling. I only wrenched my gaze from that pathetic, smashed body on the floor below when Henry put his hand on my arm, and said, "Are you all right, Pudge?"

"I'm all right," I said.

"And Mrs. Meakin? I hope she's . . ."

"Oh, yes," I said, and my voice was harsh with anger and grief. "She's all right. Your murderess will face her trial, and be pronounced medically fit to be hung. That's all you care about, isn't it? It's nothing to you that Sam is lying down there dead because of your inefficiency? You're like all policemen. So long as you can convict the criminal, you don't give a damn about the victims. You deliberately allowed her to . . ."

"You've got it all wrong, Pudge," said Henry. He sounded

very tired. "I haven't caught my criminal, and I'll never convict him now. He's lying down there with his neck broken. It was one of the worst moments of my life, when I realized that Potman and not Pardoe was taking her around the studio. If you hadn't been here to help me, she'd certainly have been killed."

"You mean—you mean that *Sam* . . . ?"

I had somehow forgotten that Sonia had heard the whole of this conversation. She was lying so quietly in my arms that she might have fainted. Now, however, she began to cry. At least, it was so dark that I couldn't be sure whether she was weeping or laughing, but what she was saying was, "But I thought it was Pudge—I was sure it was Pudge—I was sure . . ."

"You thought it was Pudge," said Henry, "and so did a lot of other people. Pudge thought it was you. I've known for sometime that it was Potman, without being able to prove it. And now . . ."

There was no time for any more. The technicians had started coming back onto the set, and, as though in a peepshow, we could see from the high gallery the discovery of Sam's body—the horror, the near panic, the uproar.

"I think," said Henry, "that we'd better go down. There'll be a certain amount of explaining to do."

As we moved along the gallery toward the ladder, I realized that my arm was still around Sonia's waist. She didn't seem to object, so I left it there.

18

It seemed a very long time later, though in fact it was only a few hours. The agonizing formalities were over, and Henry had assembled a few of us for a private talk in the production office—Keith and Biddy, Fiametta and Giulio Palladio, Gervase Mountjoy, Sonia Meakin, and myself.

Henry came in. He didn't sit down, but perched on the edge of the big desk, lit a cigarette, and looked around at us. Then he said, "I imagine that the coroner's court will return an open verdict on Mr. Potman. That or accidental death. Nobody can say exactly what happened. Mrs. Meakin was with him on the gallery; he was showing her around; but it was very dark up there. Mr. Croombe-Peters and I happened to be up there as well, taking a look. It took us all by surprise when he fell. He must have lost his footing."

Henry looked around, blandly. Nobody spoke.

"As for the cases of Robert Meakin, Margery Phipps, and Alfred Murray," Henry went on, "there is little that anybody can do now. The verdicts of accident and suicide, respectively, on Meakin and Miss Phipps will stand. The case of Murray, which is being treated as murder, will remain open; but I doubt whether any more will be heard of it."

There was another silence. Keith looked uncomfortably at Fiametta, who turned away.

"However," said Henry, "for the benefit of the people in this room, I intend to give you an outline—perhaps fanciful —of my own theory about what might have happened, behind the scenes, as it were. I don't think that I need bother to ask you to keep it to yourselves. Please remember that my story is pure conjecture. You can, if you wish, correct me if I go wrong."

Silence again. Henry looked at me. "The crux of the matter," he said, "was Robert Meakin's death. And the crux of *that* was money."

Unexpectedly, Fiametta said, "No. No, you are quite wrong."

"I don't think I am, Miss Fettini," said Henry.

Fiametta looked at him with contempt. "You think I am poor? You think I need money? I am rich. I have jewels and . . ."

"I'm not saying," said Henry, "that you did what you did for money. I think you did it out of spite."

"Love," said Fiametta. There was suddenly a curious sort of dignity about her. "For love."

"I doubt it," said Henry cheerfully.

"I wish you'd get on with it." Keith sounded near hysterics.

"Sorry," said Henry. "Well, we start at the point where Northburn Films is on the point of bankruptcy, due to delays because of bad weather and—" he glanced at Fiametta—"illness . . ."

"You're putting it rather strongly," I said "We had enough money to carry on . . ."

"But not enough to survive a disaster. And the biggest possible disaster was threatening. Your male star was on the point of breaking his contract and walking out on you. Correct?"

"Perfectly correct," said Sonia Meakin quietly.

"Now," said Henry, "somebody else besides Mrs. Meakin knew this. My guess is that it was Miss Brennan. Meakin liked and respected her, and probably confided in her, and I think she was working hard on him to persuade him to stay on. I also think that she passed the information on to Mr. Pardoe and Sam Potman."

Nobody said anything. So it was true.

"Really, Biddy," I burst out. "You might have told *me* . . ."

"Oh, stuff it, Pudge," said Biddy.

Well, at least it explained the feeling of conspiracy of which I had been aware in the days before Bob died. I simmered quietly to myself as Henry went on.

243

"It seemed as though Miss Brennan had succeeded. However, various—em—personal matters finally led Mr. Meakin to decide once and for all to quit the film. This happened the evening before his death." This time Henry was looking at Fiametta, who shook her black hair defiantly at him, as though proud of the mess she had made of things.

"Mrs. Meakin knew of this decision," said Henry, "but of course she was nowhere near the Underground station that day. Miss Fettini also knew about it. She and Meakin lunched together, and it's quite clear from remarks she made that she knew . . ."

"He insult me," said Fiametta smolderingly. "He say I make his life hell. He say he do not love me . . ."

"Which," said Henry, "naturally hurt your pride. You told all this to Mr. Pardoe in your dressing room on the platform, didn't you? And you planned a mean little revenge. Apart from Murray, the dresser, you were the only person on the set who knew about Meakin's bad eyesight and the second pair of spectacles. While he was out of his dressing room, you slipped in and substituted the clear glass spectacles for the ones with special lenses in the pile of accessories which Murray had already laid out, ready. The interesting thing is—why didn't Keith Pardoe stop you?"

"You killed Bob. You killed my husband." Sonia had gone as white as a sheet.

"Mrs. Meakin," it was Keith who spoke, in a tone of deep earnestness, "I swear I never meant—nor did Fiametta . . ."

"That's quite true, Mrs. Meakin," said Henry. "Nobody meant to kill your husband. It was an accident."

"How could it have been? They knew he'd be blind without his glasses, and he was running down stairs and onto the platform with the train coming in . . ."

"You probably don't know, Mrs. Meakin," said Henry, "that the shot was switched at the last moment, owing to previous takes being spoiled in processing. Everybody on the set knew this—with the exception of Miss Fettini and Mr. Pardoe, who were together in her dressing room when the switch took place. Robert Meakin was intended to have a nasty fall down stairs —and maybe even break a leg, but no more. No question of his running onto the platform with the train coming in. I think that is why, at the time, Miss Fettini cried out that she hadn't meant it, and why Mr. Pardoe was so unduly upset at the death of a man he had never particularly liked. The question still remains—why didn't Keith Pardoe prevent Miss Fettini from carrying out her unpleasant trick? At first I thought it might have been because of Meakin's friendship with Mrs. —I'm sorry—with Miss Brennan. Then I decided that it was not that. The reason was far more practical. Wasn't it, Mr. Pardoe?" he ended, looking hard at Keith.

"Yes," said Keith. It was little more than a whisper.

"In fact, when your wife told you about the possibility of Meakin walking out on the picture, I think you studied that insurance policy pretty carefully, although later you denied doing so for obvious reasons."

"What is this insurance policies?" demanded Fiametta. "Keith never say . . ."

"You knew very well," Henry went on, still addressing Keith, "that Northburn Films would be finished if Meakin walked out. No clause in any policy covered that contingency, and there wasn't enough in the kitty for an expensive lawsuit. On the other hand, if he should be forced to give up his part through injury—injury incurred during his work for you, but not due to negligence on the part of the unit—then the insurance company would have to pay up in full. The sum involved runs into hundreds of thousands, doesn't it?"

I nodded.

"So, in Miss Fettini's spiteful idea of revenge, Keith Pardoe saw a hope, a slender one, of saving the company. He could count on the fact that negligence would not be mentioned, for Robert Meakin was much too intent on preserving his youthful public image to bring up the matter of the spectacles. He would be sure to agree that he had stumbled accidentally. So, the spectacles were switched; but so, unfortunately, was the shot. And Meakin died—accidentally."

In a quiet, calm voice, Sonia Meakin said, "Thank you for explaining, Inspector."

Henry smiled at her, and then went on. "When the directors of Northburn Films met that evening, Mr. Potman and Miss Brennan really believed that the company would have to fold up. Mr. Pardoe knew that it wouldn't, but apparently he had the grace to be conscience-stricken, if not a little hysterical, about the part he had played in Meakin's death. Mr. Croombe-Peters knew about the insurance cover, but was convinced that Meakin's death was accidental. Everything went smoothly. The inquest verdict was accidental death, the insurance claim was paid, and the film went on. It was an ironic chance that Pardoe himself took over Meakin's part. It must have been quite a nervous strain for him. Of course, the fact of a guilty secret shared brought him closer to Miss Fettini. She was not unduly sensitive to pangs of conscience, and undoubtedly did her best to—to take his mind off it. All the same, when Mrs. Meakin appeared on the scene, Miss Fettini prudently removed herself to Italy until she was quite sure that there would be no unpleasantness. There was none. The film went on, and it seemed as though Meakin was forgotten. And then the bombshell exploded."

Henry paused. "Margery Phipps," he said, "was the daughter of a notorious blackmailer. She had been sent to foster parents at an early age, when her father was in prison and her mother could not support her; but she was never adopted, and never lost touch with her real parents. She thus grew up in two entirely different worlds—the respectable Kensington atmosphere of the Phipps household, and the seedy, cunning, and criminal one of Lily Arbuthnot and James Boswell. Mrs. Phipps saw to it that Margery took secretarial training and got a good job; her real parents determined to take advantage of Margery's social polish and her place in the film world to launch her in her father's profession. Whether or not she had started her nefarious activities earlier, I don't know. There's no proof. But what is certain is that when Boswell died in prison this year, Mrs. Arbuthnot appealed to Margery for financial help, and the two of them naturally decided on blackmail as the best way of raising funds.

"Mixing with film people, Margery was well placed for the job. The only trouble is that you can't blackmail people until you have some sort of damning evidence against them. So Margery was keeping her eyes skinned for just that. It must have seemed a Godsend to her when she went into Meakin's dressing room that morning and took a thorough look at what was there. She'd probably been considering the insurance angle as a possible source of blackmail, and there, in the waste-paper basket, was a crumpled draft of a letter which seemed to indicate that Meakin had, in fact, resigned his part just before he died. That, she realized, could be used both against the company and against Mrs. Meakin, for both had collected large sums in insurance.

"It had also, presumably, occurred to her that Meakin's death was most opportune. Like all Continuity Girls, she was acutely observant, and had almost certainly noticed that Meakin sometimes wore plain spectacles and sometimes an identical pair with magnifying lenses. In his dressing room, she found the box which had contained his contact lenses . . ."

"It was empty," I put in. "I thought it was for cuff links . . ."

"Yes," said Henry. "I doubt if even Margery, in fact, realized what it was. The lenses themselves, of course, had been removed by Murray. However, in Miss Fettini's dressing room, probably hidden in a drawer, Margery found the magnifying spectacles. At once, she realized that the spectacles had been switched and that Meakin had been virtually blind when he died. She pocketed the spectacles and the draft letter. She must have felt extremely pleased with herself."

"I told you she was a thief," said Fiametta triumphantly. "I told you then, before . . ."

"All this happened on a Friday, if you remember," said Henry. "Margery went straight home and wrote to Mr. Croombe-Peters, resigning her job. Then, over the weekend, she contacted her selected victims, by telephone I imagine. Mrs. Meakin has already admitted that she went to Margery's apartment and paid her a considerable sum of money. I'd be interested to hear details from Miss Fettini and from Mr. Pardoe."

Henry looked around hopefully. Nobody said anything. Then Fiametta shouted, "All right. She telephone me, and I send Giulio to her with money. She was a mean little thief."

Henry said politely to Palladio, "When did you go to Miss Phipps's apartment with the money, Signor Palladio?"

Giulio looked mutely at Fiametta, begging for instructions.

"Tell 'im," she said. "What does it matter?"

"It was Monday," said Giulio wretchedly. "I go and I give five 'undred pound, cash. I say what Fiametta tell me. 'Ere is money. But next time . . ." He made a sudden vivid gesture, cutting his own throat with a pointed finger.

Fiametta turned on him and swore at him in rapid Italian.

Henry said, "So you threatened Miss Phipps with violence?"

"I say what Fiametta tell me," said Giulio sulkily.

"Well, that seems fairly clear," said Henry. "Now, Mr. Pardoe."

"I don't know why you pick on me." Keith was growing hysterical again.

"You were the obvious choice. You were in Miss Fettini's room at the time of Meakin's death, and must have known about the spectacles. If you won't tell me, I'll tell you. Margery telephoned you, and you made an appointment to go and see her on Tuesday afternoon, taking the money with you . . ."

"But . . ." I could not keep silent any longer. "I thought that it was Sam, and now you're accusing Keith . . ."

"Mr. Pardoe made the appointment," said Henry. "He didn't necessarily keep it."

"What do you mean?"

"As soon as he had spoken to Margery, I think that Mr. Pardoe decided to tell the whole story to his fellow directors and ask for their help and advice."

"He didn't tell me," I protested.

"No," said Henry, "he didn't. But he told his wife and Sam Potman, and it was arranged that one of them should go to Chelsea Mansions to keep that appointment. In deciding which one it was, I naturally had to reckon with the alibis, or otherwise, of the three people concerned. They all seemed pretty good. Mr. Potman was watching rushes in Duck Street with Mr. Croombe-Peters. Mr. Pardoe was having his hair cut at the Belgrave Towers Hotel. Miss Brennan's case was more interesting. She told me that she had been to see the film *Duck Soup* at the New Forum."

"And so I had," said Biddy. "You can check . . ."

"I have checked. You undoubtedly did go to that cinema."

"Well, then . . ."

"The cinema," said Henry, "is immediately opposite the

pavement where Margery fell to her death. The film started at four o'clock. You missed the first ten minutes. Therefore, you were in Dredge Street when Margery fell, and yet you denied knowing anything about it until the next day. In fact, you saw what happened, and immediately and very naturally you telephoned Mr. Potman from the cinema and told him."

Biddy said nothing. Fiametta suddenly came to life. "She telephone me, too," she said spitefully. "She telephone my suite and ask for speak to Keith, and Keith run off to 'ave his hair cut, and tell me to say he has not been with me."

"Yes," said Henry, "I know. It's all perfectly simple. I realized some time ago that it was Potman who had agreed to take Keith's place at the interview with Margery. He urged the others not to worry, to leave everything to him. They had no idea that he intended to kill the girl. He laid his plans very carefully. Everyone was to have a complete alibi. The Pardoes nearly wrecked matters by coming back from the country—he thought he had them safely out of the way. He told Biddy to contact Keith and impress upon him the urgent need to establish an alibi, which Keith did by rushing down to the barber's shop."

"But if he was with Fiametta," I began.

"Sam Potman," said Henry, "wanted Fiametta kept strictly out of this. Because, you see, it was from Fiametta and her doctor husband that he had obtained the drug he needed to knock Margery out—I presume it was the same barbiturate as was used in Miss Fettini's unsuccessful suicide earlier this year."

"You know too much, my little policeman," said Fiametta.

"I know enough," said Henry. "Right. To proceed . . ."

"You can't proceed," I said. "It all sounds very plausible, I agree, but you haven't explained how Sam Potman could be seeing rushes in Soho at the same moment that he was . . ."

"Yes," said Henry, "yes, that puzzled me for some time. Potman gave himself away, you see, when he talked to you, Pudge, about Margery Phipps alleging she had enjoyed her work on *Street Scene*. That was a straight quotation from her letter to you, which he swore he had never seen. That, plus his personality, and what my—my instinct told me . . ."

"Don't tell me you used your famous nose," I said, "to break his alibi."

"Yes, actually, I did." Henry sounded almost apologetic. "There was a very faint smell in Margery's kitchen. I investigated it and found a half-burnt candle. If you remember, Pudge, I came out with some white powder on my coat."

"Yes," I said, "fingerprinting powder."

"No," said Henry, "candle wax."

"But . . ."

"You noticed, being observant, that the clock on the electric cooker was set at a quarter to four. The next-door dial was set for three-quarters of an hour. That meant that things had been so arranged that the electric oven would come on at a quarter to four, and would remain at full heat until half-past, when it would switch itself off. You'll remember that it was an eye-level oven, right beside the window. Potman, of course, visited the flat soon after lunch, ostensibly to pay Margery the money she was demanding. He slipped her the drug, and then propped her, unconscious, on the kitchen window sill, leaving the window unlatched, but sealed up with candle wax. The kitchen window was certainly inconvenient, but it was the only one which opened outward. He had previously taken Margery's letter from the office files and traced a suicide note from it. As soon as she was unconscious, he typed the envelope in her apartment, and left the letter on the table. Then he went back to Duck Street. By four o'clock, the oven was fully heated, and gave out enough warmth to melt the wax which was holding the window shut. The window swung open, and Margery fell out. By then, Sam Potman was back in Soho, watching rushes. It was a very good alibi, on the face of it, especially as there was no suggestion of foul play. If Mrs. Arbuthnot hadn't stirred up trouble and made me curious about the whole thing, Potman would have got clean away with it. I should mention, I suppose, that before he left Chelsea Mansions, he found and removed the second pair of spectacles, the draft letter of resignation, and anything else which might have connected Margery with Northburn Films. He also removed the money which Margery had been paid in cash, for which Mrs. Arbuthnot was searching so avidly when —you remember when, Pudge."

"Indeed I do," I said grimly.

"Well," said Henry, "so far, so good. Margery is dead, the evidence is out of the way, and the film proceeds once again. Potman is worried about one person only."

"Who?" I asked. "Murray?"

"No, no," said Henry. "You, Pudge. You are innocent. You have no idea of what has really happened. You are also a friend of mine, and my interest has been aroused. Keith, Biddy, and Fiametta—not to mention Signor Palladio—all know enough to keep their mouths shut. Potman has made sure of that. You, on the other hand, may blurt out anything to the police. And so may Mrs. Meakin. Perhaps we should talk about Mrs. Meakin for a moment."

Sonia went very red. Henry went on, "Her interest in coming to collect her husband's things from the Underground station was, of course, to try to find the original of that draft letter, just as Miss Fettini's professed interest in her worthless lipstick case was to try to locate spectacles which she had hidden and could not find again. Fortunately, Mrs. Meakin told me the whole truth at an early stage, and I am afraid I misled her a little in order to enlist her help. It was at my suggestion that she laid a trap to induce Mr. Croombe-Peters to break into Margery Phipps's apartment—and he fell for it. His behavior confirmed my suspicions that the Northburn Films insurance policies were at the root of the whole matter. It also left Mrs. Meakin with the impression that Mr. Croombe-Peters was the culprit, and vice versa. Of course, at that point, nobody had reckoned on poor old Alf Murray."

"Yes," I said. "What about Murray? Where does he come into it?"

"That's the sad thing," said Henry. "I don't believe that Murray was a blackmailer. He had Robert Meakin's contact lenses in his possession, but I don't think there was anything very sinister about that. He'd picked them up in the dressing room after the accident, but that was all. However, after Meakin's death he found himself out of a job and short of money, and it was only natural that he should approach Mrs. Meakin and Mr. Potman to ask for help.

"He rang Mrs. Meakin and she made an appointment to go and meet him on the evening he died. Very sensibly, she came around to see me first, to ask my advice; but unfortunately I was entertaining other people . . ." Henry's glance only just grazed my eyes. "Not only did Mrs. Meakin have no opportunity to speak to me about Murray, but she was kept late for her appointment with him. He got tired of waiting, and went to see Mr. Potman."

Henry sighed. "I wish to God I could have stopped him. Of course, it was only natural that Potman should interpret the old man's quite innocent requests for help and money as an attempt at blackmail, when Murray produced the contact lenses at the same time. By then, Potman had one object only in life—to finish his film. He was becoming more and more unbalanced. Murray seemed to threaten him, so Murray was killed in a fit of blind panic. Then, common sense took over. The fact of a corpse in his house, which would normally be an embarrassment, could be turned to good account.

"Once again, the plans were well laid. The Pardoes, who were necessary to the completion of the film, must have alibis. So must Miss Fettini. I think I am right in saying that Potman telephoned the Pardoes, and, without giving any reason, told them to go to the Belgrave Towers at once and stay for several hours with Miss Fettini and her husband. It that so?"

Henry addressed himself to Biddy, who nodded. "I couldn't think why," she said, "but we dared not refuse. We knew—or guessed—too much already . . ."

"Exactly," said Henry. "So the four of you were provided with a let out, and Potman proceeded to drag Mr. Croombe-Peters into the affair to the point where he was hopelessly incriminated."

"How do you know all this?" I demanded.

"When you left my house that evening," said Henry, "you tried to telephone Mr. Potman and found his number engaged. He explained that by saying that he was trying to contact you. This was patently untrue, because your manservant, who let him in later on, was in your apartment and received no phone call. Shortly afterward, the Pardoes turned up at the Belgrave Towers to call on Miss Fettini. They were unannounced and very unexpected, because film people with early morning calls don't as a rule go out at night. It didn't need a great deal of intelligence to reconstruct what actually happened."

"Then why didn't you arrest Potman?" I began.

"My dear Pudge," said Henry, "all this was simply my—what I thought. I had no proof. I deliberately came down to the studios and spoke to Potman about the roll of film showing Meakin's death. I put a guard on the incinerator, hoping to catch Potman in the act of destroying evidence. But he was too clever for me. All I caught was poor old Pudge.

"As I have explained to him, I was probably the only man in London who didn't think Croombe-Peters was guilty; and after the episode of trying to burn the film, my case in Pudge's defense looked very meager indeed. The only good thing about his sojourn at headquarters was that it made Potman feel quite safe and secure, and that helped me. Having previously tried to poison Pudge's mind against Mr. Pardoe, Potman now denounced Pudge to the rest of the unit, I understand."

Keith had gone whiter than ever. "Yes, he did, the devil," Keith said. "Tried to pretend he'd been covering up for you as long as he could. And I believed him. I'm sorry, Pudge."

"Never mind," I said. I tried not to sound smug.

"Today," Henry went on, "I decided that I must try to smoke him out. It was now or never. I asked Mrs. Meakin to come down here, with Croombe-Peters and myself, and I asked her to bring along a pair of glasses made up to her late husband's prescription. Through the kind offices of Mr. Mountjoy, I arranged for these to fall into Miss Fettini's hands. As I thought, she had been feeling somewhat unkindly toward Mr. Pardoe of late. Unfortunately for her, Mr. Pardoe is very much in love with his wife. So Miss Fettini decided to play the same trick on him—in reverse—as she played on Mr. Meakin. She substituted the spectacles, and Mr. Pardoe had a nasty fall. I'm extremely sorry about it," he added, to Keith, "but I could think of no other way of demonstrating beyond all doubt what had happened to Meakin, and who was responsible. None of you would have admitted it, without this rather dramatic incident. So I was at least able to clear Pudge of the first charge—that he had engineered Meakin's death.

"I did realize, of course, that by asking Mrs. Meakin to bring the spectacles here, I was exposing her to the possible risk of Potman's revenge. But there seemed no possibility of them being alone together. You can imagine my horror when I found that he had so maneuvered matters as to get her up onto that terrible gallery. Thank goodness Pudge and I were there.

"Well." Henry looked around the office. "That's about all. Mr. Potman lost his footing and fell to his death. Some of you have behaved stupidly and some reprehensibly, but a rough sort of justice has been done, and I don't think we can hope for anything better. As far as I am concerned, the various cases are closed."

It was some time later, when the others had gone, that I had the chance of a word alone with Henry. There were a few points I still wanted to clear up.

"About the insurance, Henry," I said, tentatively.

He grinned. "I shall have to ask you to make a complete report to the company, of course," he said, "but there's one point in your favor that you may have overlooked. The spectacles were switched by Miss Fettini, and she is not a member of the Northburn Film unit. Just bear that in mind."

"You should have been a lawyer, not a policeman," I said. There was a pause. Then I added, on impulse, "Henry, up there on the gallery—what actually happened?"

Henry looked at me sadly. "He jumped, of course," he said. "As soon as he saw me, he realized . . ." There was a pause, and then he added, "He was a great man, in his own way. I admired him deeply. I'm glad he was able to finish the film after all."

"All except the last shot," I said. "There's still the retake to be done."

"No, there isn't," said Henry. "I'm afraid I persuaded Mountjoy to deliver a false message about the earlier takes being spoiled. No, the film is safely in the can." He looked at me steadily for a moment, and then he said, "I believe it is a great film, Pudge. I just wish . . ."

"What?"

"I wish," said Henry, "that I had even a rudimentary understanding of what makes people what they are."

Epilogue

There's very little to add. I made a clean breast of Fiametta's prank to our insurance company, but the lawyers plugged the point about La Fettini not being a member of the unit, and the claim was allowed to stand. I need hardly remind you of the fantastic success of *Street Scene*. I sent Henry seats for the première, for which he seemed suitably grateful.

Without Sam, there seemed little point in continuing Northburn Films, but of course Keith has gone from strength to strength, and Biddy's new book came out a few weeks ago. I haven't read it yet, but I suppose I must. Sonia tells me it is remarkable.

Fiametta is currently in Hollywood, and currently involved in a tempestuous love affair with her new leading man. I presume that Palladio and Peppi are with her. I can't say I care.

As for myself, I have decided that it is really more in my line to settle down quietly and manage the family estates, rather than to get involved with the highly colored personalities of the film world. And Sonia agrees with me.

Which reminds me. In case you missed it, there was a small, discreet announcement in the *Times* last week in the "Marriages" column:

> Croombe-Peters: Meakin. On
> Saturday, November 30th,
> very quietly, in London. An-
> thony, only son of Baron
> Northburn of Hocking and
> the late Lady Northburn, to
> Mrs. Sonia Meakin (nee
> Marchmont).